I0795800

THE ESCAPE *Game*

Also by Marissa Meyer

The Lunar Chronicles

Cinder
Scarlet
Cress
Winter

The Renegades Trilogy

Renegades
Archenemies
Supernova

The Gilded Duology

Gilded
Cursed

Heartless

Also by Tamara Moss

The Lintang Series

Lintang and the Pirate Queen
Lintang and the Forbidden Island
Lintang and the Brightest Star

THE ESCAPE *Game*

MARISSA MEYER
AND
TAMARA MOSS

putnam
G. P. Putnam's Sons

G. P. PUTNAM'S SONS
An imprint of Penguin Random House LLC
1745 Broadway, New York, NY 10019
penguinrandomhouse.com

Edited by Gretchen Durning and Rūta Rimas
Design by Alex Campbell | Text set in Arno Pro

Library of Congress Cataloging-in-Publication Data
Names: Meyer, Marissa author | Moss, Tamara author
Title: The escape game / Marissa Meyer and Tamara Moss.
Description: New York, NY : G.P. Putnam's Sons, [2026] |
Audience: Ages 14 years and up |
Summary: After her sister is murdered during season four, Sierra Angelos joins season five of a televised escape-room competition, where contestants solve high-stakes puzzles to win, as she searches for the truth before history repeats itself.
Identifiers: LCCN 2025027587 (print) | LCCN 2025027588 (ebook) |
ISBN 9798217006120 hardcover | ISBN 9798217006137 epub
Subjects: CYAC: Television game shows—Fiction | Contests—Fiction |
Escape room games—Fiction | Murder—Fiction | Mystery and detective stories |
LCGFT: Detective and mystery fiction | Thrillers (Fiction) | Novels
Classification: LCC PZ7.M571737 Es 2026 (print) | LCC PZ7.M571737 (ebook)
| DDC [Fic]—dc23/eng/20250614
LC record available at https://lccn.loc.gov/2025027587
LC ebook record available at https://lccn.loc.gov/2025027588

Manufactured in China

RRD

ISBN 9798217006120

10 9 8 7 6 5 4 3 2

The authorized representative in the EU for product safety and compliance is Penguin Random House Ireland, Morrison Chambers, 32 Nassau Street, Dublin D02 YH68, Ireland, https://eu-contact.penguin.ie.

For all the friends and family who have tolerated having total strangers lock us in a room together and demand that we solve random puzzles in order to escape. It is a peculiar passion, and I appreciate you humoring me.

—**Marissa**

To Chris, for being my partner in crime. To Marguerite, for hiring a limo to take me to an escape room. And to Scout, because you had to share me with this manuscript for so long.

—**Tamara**

THE ESCAPE GAME

SEASON FOUR FINALE

A Bloody Good Time Was Had by All

Sierra paced the greenroom, fidgeting with her lip ring as her skirts dragged across the carpet. It had taken several members of the costuming department to wrestle her into this monstrosity of a Victorian-era dress. The corset was suffocating, the ruffles enormous, the lace itchy as hell. The outfits were supposed to be a clue to the finale's theme, but there were too many options. A parlor mystery? A hot-air balloon race? The *Titanic*?

Sprawled out on the sofa, his tailcoat on his knees, Cruz moaned. "That breakfast sandwich is not sitting well with me. Why did they get us changed so early?"

"More mind games," drawled Elijah, their team captain, sitting at the table. He looked half asleep. No wonder, considering he was up swimming at an ungodly hour that morning.

Not that Sierra could talk—she hadn't exactly slept last night, either.

She continued to pace. She had to keep moving or anxiety would eat her alive. *Two hours.* Two more hours and this nightmare of a game show would be over. They could win. That prize money could be hers.

"You feeling okay?" Missy said. At first Sierra thought the question was for Cruz, still groaning on the couch. But no. Missy was watching *her*.

"Yeah, sure. Just want to get this over with."

"We need to stay focused." Elijah opened his eyes. "Now more than ever."

"No shit, Sherlock."

"I'm serious, Sierra. Maybe there's something you want to tell us? We've got the time."

"Now that you mention it, I have been meaning to point out what a pretentious asshat you are."

Cruz snorted. "I'm going to miss you all."

"I mean about you and Alicia," said Elijah. "There was a lot of shouting last night."

Sierra's mouth went dry. The villa walls weren't exactly soundproof, and Elijah had a bad habit of following Alicia around like a lost puppy.

"None of your business," she snapped. Alicia had been even more condescending and cagey than usual last night, and Sierra was still pissed off about it.

"I didn't see her this morning," Elijah said. "What did you say to make her so upset?"

"How about you focus on the game rather than my goddamn sister?"

A knock drew their attention to the door. Vera stalked in, wearing her usual sparkly outfit and scowl. "Team Hourglass, there's been a change. You're going to run the game first."

Elijah frowned. "Why?"

"Because Ranielle said so. She wants you on set. Now."

Cruz climbed to his feet. "Sure thing. Right after I make a quick pit stop."

He ran to the restroom while Sierra followed the others out of the greenroom. They'd never changed the filming schedule before, but she didn't mind. She could practically smell the cash prize. She didn't need Alicia, or her charity, or her judgments.

The crew hurried to set them up with earpieces and lapel mics. Cruz returned looking a little better, a makeup assistant touched up Sierra's black lipstick, and before Sierra could catch her breath, the contestants were ushered onto the set, where the show's icons—Fitzy and Louis—were waiting. Missy cheered and gave them high fives.

"Team Hourglass!" yelled James "Fitzy" Fitzgerald. "You've made it to the finale!"

Sierra hated Fitzy. Maybe it was his Australian surfer persona—

that sun-bleached hair, his easy grin, his terrible jokes. Or maybe it was that he was a clueless teenage sidekick next to—

"Welcome," said Louis Augustus Russell. The Game Master was nearly twenty years older, tall and barrel-chested, with a light brown goatee and his signature newsboy cap. He looked more like a WWE fighter than the genius who designed some of the nation's most beloved escape rooms. He hooked his thumbs into his suspenders. "You're about to be tested as never before."

"I bet Sierra's ready to flaunt that cash in her sister's face," Fitzy said, waggling his eyebrows.

Sierra clenched her jaw. The producers had been milking the built-in family dynamics since the beginning. Fans had compared the sisters in every possible way, from their skills (Alicia was "gifted and clever"; Sierra was "scrappy and cunning") to their looks (Alicia's straight nose and olive skin tone were reminiscent of a Grecian goddess, while Sierra looked like "Hades's sickly goth stepchild"—thanks for that, anonymous commenter).

Alicia was the fan favorite, and Sierra was the villain.

In Sierra's earpiece, the director ordered, "Give us something good."

"I'm ready to slaughter her," Sierra said, deadpan.

Fitzy choked out a surprised laugh. "We can't wait."

Sierra noticed with vindictive pleasure that the makeup team had failed to completely cover the dark shadows under his eyes. He'd been up late livestreaming the show's time-honored season recap for his Australian fans, and it showed. Perfect Fitzy didn't look so perfect today.

"This has been one cutthroat season. These teams have fought tooth and nail to be here, and we're expecting one epic finale." Fitzy addressed the Game Master. "Here we go, Louis. Any advice for Team Hourglass?"

"Yes," Louis said, "and I hope they'll take it to heart." He paused for dramatic effect. "In order to be victorious, you have to be willing to get your hands a little . . . *bloody.*"

"Blood, huh?" Cruz cackled and elbowed Sierra in the ribs. "Right up your alley."

They were given blindfolds, then guided toward the next set. Sierra had gotten used to the chaos of the studio. The constant movement of cameras and lights and set pieces. Interns running back and forth with clipboards and cups of coffee. The makeup team, powder brushes primed and ready, because heaven forbid the general public noticed that Fitzy had *pores.*

But then a door closed, and the sounds dulled until it was just their own heavy breathing. Sierra's heartbeat ratcheted. They were inside the escape room.

"Team Hourglass in position," someone said through their earpieces. "Finale is a go."

"Team Hourglass," boomed Fitzy. "When I say 'escape,' you may remove your blindfolds and begin. In three . . . two . . . one . . . *Escape!*"

Sierra threw her blindfold to the floor. Dim, flickering light came from ensconced torches. A coffin sat in the center of the room. Three plastic skeletons hung on the walls with strings of garlic bulbs around their necks.

"Vampires," she whispered, thinking of the Game Master's clue. In order to escape, they would have to get their hands bloody. They would have to slay the vampire.

Cruz had already charged for the coffin and was examining the lid. "Locked. Three-digit code." He punctuated the statement with a muffled groan, pressing a hand to his side.

Sierra swore, hoping he wasn't about to spew all over the room's carefully orchestrated clues. That would be the icing on the cake of this season's absolute shit show.

The team searched the skeletons and found a crucifix and a velvet pouch, padlocked. The third skeleton had a parchment that turned out to be a map.

"We need to find a key," Missy said, tugging on the padlock.

"Does this mean anything?" Sierra indicated a row of dark splotches on the concrete floor and what seemed to be tracks in the dust that led to the coffin. The splotches looked like water droplets but could have been paint, or even fake blood.

"Dunno," said Elijah. "Let's focus on this three-digit code for now."

Three numbers. Three skeletons. Three—

"Strings of garlic!" Sierra cried. With that realization, the code worked itself out easily—just a matter of counting the bulbs. Elijah entered the digits and the coffin's lid clicked open.

On top of a lumpy bed of black velvet sat a long wooden stake, pointed sharply on one end. Sierra inspected it. "No markings that I can see."

"Maybe it's for killing Dracula at the end," Missy said.

"There are words here." Cruz pointed at sharply scrawled letters on the underside of the coffin's lid. Sierra had to squint to see them in the torchlight and could picture one of the hidden cameras zooming in at the same time.

WE GET WHAT WE DESERVE

That had to be an anagram. Her mind was already whirling with possibilities as she took a handful of the velvet, which felt cool and strangely damp, and yanked it out of the coffin.

The world stilled. Her blood ran frigid. She blinked several times, sure she was seeing things.

"Oh god," said Cruz, before turning and vomiting onto the floor.

The director's voice screamed through their earpieces, bringing the game to a halt. "What the *hell*?"

The team gaped—first at the coffin, and then at Sierra, standing with the velvet clutched in one hand and the wooden stake in the other.

Staring down at the unnaturally still, unnaturally pale body of her older sister.

SIX MONTHS LATER . . .

Audition Video: Carter Kelly

THE ESCAPE GAME

SEASON FIVE

The girl sits as still as a mannequin, her hands clutched in her lap. To her right: an old-school chalkboard covered in mathematical equations and pi written out to far too many digits. To her left: bookshelves displaying pyramids of textbooks; a pastel-colored Rubik's Cube; a large stuffed snail; and a gallery of framed prints showing the center of a sunflower, a nautilus seashell, a pineapple. Everything is illuminated by fairy lights.

The girl herself has brown skin, tight curly black hair, and a constellation of freckles across her full cheeks.

"Hello, producers, casting directors, and anyone else watching. In case you don't recognize me . . ." Her hands tremble as she holds up a pair of glasses with large round frames. "Maybe this helps? If not—then I bet this will." She snaps her fingers, and her image dissolves in a waterfall of neon-green numerals.

The girl has disappeared. In her place is a cartoon version of herself. The cartoon is poised, in a plaid minidress and thigh-high boots—a far cry from the girl's *Scooby Doo* T-shirt. Her curls are now fire-engine red, and the thick round glasses are perched on the end of her nose.

"I'm Kick It Carter," says the avatar. "The highest-ranking Solve Specialist on the Domain."

She holds a palm flat, and a graphic is superimposed above it, showing a scrolling social media feed with videos of Carter's avatar exuberantly explaining various puzzles and codes, opening complicated locks, interviewing past contestants. The effects look professional.

"I joined the Clue Masters as an intern in the third season and have built a platform with hundreds of thousands of followers. I'm super excited to give them a sneak peek behind the scenes of *The Escape Game*. But that's not why you should pick me as a season five contestant. You should pick me because I live for puzzles and logic and problem-solving. I'm captain of the chess club, I took my school to our state's math competition last year, and in my spare time I am also an amateur photographer. My passion?" The cartoon gestures, and photos appear around her. Sunflowers. Seashells. Pineapples. "The Fibonacci sequence! Isn't it beautiful?"

She winks. "Millions of likes and comments don't lie. Together, we're going to make *Escape Game* history. Ciao!"

The cartoon pretends to pull down a blind, and her image is replaced with the real Carter Kelly again, still anxious. "So that's my audition video. Um. Thanks for watching!"

Producer notes:

Too bad we can't get the cartoon instead of the girl

Overachiever, goody-two-shoes vibe . . . pair with a rule breaker for drama?

Math whiz. Check with V—how much math involved this season?

Built-in fan base doesn't hurt

Alert costuming department—makeover needed

01

Carter

"Which makes this one a three . . . and seven here, and eight . . . five . . . two, and done!" Carter hit the stop button on her phone's timer. Her momentary elation fizzled. "Three minutes and fifty-four seconds? Pathetic." She ripped out the page from her sudoku book, crumpled it up, and tossed it at the trash can in the corner of the classroom. It bounced off the edge, skittering across the carpet.

The bell rang as Mrs. Melnyk walked in. She'd had no qualms letting Carter eat lunch in her classroom this semester, and if she suspected that the request had more to do with Carter's dismal social life than her need for peace and quiet while she studied for the next math competition, she didn't let on.

Carter checked her emails again. Still nothing.

As her classmates took their seats, she wondered for the millionth time which of them were *Escape Game* fans. Which of them had accounts on the Domain, the most comprehensive fan-run website about the show. Which of them followed *her*.

Kick It Carter. Highest-Ranking Solve Specialist. It was an honor that filled her with giddy pride. It was also an honor that meant absolutely nothing in real life. No one here knew who she was.

But if she got chosen for the show . . .

She knew it was an enormous risk, announcing her identity publicly. Her parents had looked at her like she'd lost her Fibonacci-loving mind when she'd told them about the audition. Her father's bewildered words had plagued her ever since. *You don't even like getting your school photos taken.*

Which was true.

But they couldn't understand how much she wanted this. No—

needed this. It wasn't about fame or money. It was about finding her people. Not faceless usernames, but real friends.

Kick It Carter was popular and self-assured. Beautiful and confident, thanks to the cartoon avatar her app-developer father and fashionista mother had helped her build. A hero to awkward, math-loving girls everywhere. But there would be no hiding behind her alter ego on set. It would be Carter and the cameras and the Game Master's puzzles . . . and her team. People who were as obsessed with puzzles and escape rooms as she was. People who admired her for her brain, not her clever online quips. People who *got it.*

The idea was as foreign as it was tantalizing. She'd brainstormed more than a hundred potential team names. She had plans to order team T-shirts as soon as she knew their sizes. She would finally be included in one of those group chats that evidently every teen in the world was in except for her.

Once she got on the show, Carter would never have to hide her true self again.

Before class could start, she dared to check her emails. One last time.

Her heart launched into her throat.

> Re: Carter Kelly Audition
>
> Dear Miss Kelly,
> We are thrilled to extend an invitation for you to be a contestant in season five of *The Escape Game* . . .

Audition Video: Beck Matheson

THE ESCAPE GAME

SEASON FIVE

The boy has a swoop of thick brown hair beneath a cowboy hat, lips so red he might have been sucking on a cherry lollipop, and an angelic smile. He also appears to be standing in a Wild West saloon.

"Howdy. The name's Beck, and I'd like to welcome you to the Sweetbrier Saloon. Also known as . . . my parents' gardening shed." He bats at a kerosene lamp hanging from the ceiling. Shadows dance across the wood walls. "Last year, I converted this place into my sixth escape room. And yes, the theme is *heavily* inspired by the Sweetbrier Treasure. I'm obsessed with that stuff. The moment I heard about this season's prize—!" He mimes his head exploding. "But I can't be the only one who feels that way, so what makes me stand out from the crowd? One word: lasers. As in, laser focus."

He picks up a deck of playing cards and starts to shuffle. "This room took me five weeks to create. I scoured flea markets and craft stores for the props. The stag antlers over there came from an estate sale. The whiskey kegs and liquor bottles are mostly from thrift stores." He starts doing tricks—fanning the cards in a line down his arm, then flipping them over in a mesmerizing wave. "This old cash register is a kid's toy, painted to look authentic. Even these cards are handmade." He fans the cards out and flips them toward the camera, revealing aces and spades, hearts and clubs. "Hint: there's a clue hidden in the face cards, but you'll have to play the game to find out what it is."

He slings himself onto a barstool. "I've had a lot of hobbies. Coding. Mechanics. Pinball competitions. Alpacas . . . Long story. But escape rooms have been my passion for years. Playing them *and* creating them. It's one thing to solve puzzles, it's another to mastermind them yourself. Now, I'm not saying I'm gunning for the Game Master's job, but I like to think that I'll be able to hold my own in this competition. So, Louis Augustus Russell?" He hops off the stool and pulls a pistol from a holster at his side, aiming it at the camera. "I challenge you to a duel!"

The gun *clicks* anticlimactically. Beck grins. "It's also possible that I have way too much time on my hands. So . . . call me? Though I also accept communications via telegraph and pony express."

He laughs at his own joke, and the video ends.

Producer notes:

Inside knowledge of escape rooms, good for media interviews

Did he say alpacas??

Obsession with Sweetbrier—he'll be motivated

Loving the doe-eyed look, the optimism. We're going to eat this kid alive.

02
Beck

There was an ongoing debate in the world of forensic science over how much information could be gleaned from the patterns in blood spatter. But in the case of the medieval-torture-chamber-themed escape room Beck had recently started creating in his parents' garage, the blood spatter was going to be a *literal* message. If the "prisoners" were paying attention, they would see that the splotches of crimson blood on the concrete floor matched the alphabet code that would be written beneath the wall shackles.

Designing escape rooms was the rare hobby that held Beck's attention because it was actually a hundred hobbies mixed into one. Here, he was an engineer, an archaeologist, a scholar, a mathematician, an artist, an electrician, a cryptographer, a historian, and a storyteller all in one.

Here, he was a Game Master.

And like the great Game Masters before him—Louis Augustus Russell, Victor Cunningham, Jasper Barrett—he knew the importance of getting the details just so. It was painstaking work. Mixing the paint to be the right shade of red, the right consistency, the right sheen when it dried. Styling it in a way that would appear random at first . . . but not after careful examination.

His laptop was set up on the bench, playing through old *Escape Game* episodes while he worked. He'd been watching the series on repeat ever since he got chosen as an upcoming contestant. He was back to season four, episode two—the speakeasy room, one of his favorites.

He paused his painting to look up as Sierra Angelos fumed about

Elijah's incompetence. It was hard to tell who she hated more, Elijah or her sister. As Sierra ranted, Beck's mouth fizzed with a distinctive mixture of blue Kool-Aid and sherbet. All noises had this effect on him—a form of synesthesia that Beck liked to think of as his secret superpower. The flavors were mostly random. Sirens tasted of ash mixed with chili pepper. Barking dogs were like chewing on sticks, unless they were small yappy dogs—then it was more like a mouthful of splinters. Pinball machines translated into sour candy and pennies on the tongue, and musical instruments ranged from pretzels to marshmallows to asphalt.

"He never should have been chosen as team leader," Sierra continued. She had a punk look—one of those keep-a-knife-in-her-combat-boots types. Her straight, jet-black hair and black lipstick contrasted with her pasty skin. "Everyone knows that I'm—"

"*—the smartest person on this team,*" Beck mimicked. "Yeah, Sierra, we know."

She never tired of saying it. And maybe it was true. Beck figured you had to be pretty smart to get away with murder. Though everyone knew she'd done it, there hadn't been enough evidence for the police to make the arrest.

"I swear to god," she went on, "if Elijah ruins my chance of reaching the finale, he'll have hell to pay."

Every single word she spoke was sour and sweet and effervescent. Even when she was being cantankerous, he loved the taste of her voice.

He had just gone back to painting when his mom cried out, "Beck! They're here!"

Heart leaping, he threw his paintbrush into a tub of murky red water and peeked out the garage's window. An unmarked van was out front. The sort that belonged to either a kidnapper or a reality TV crew.

A Black woman in a pristine white suit stood in the middle of the driveway surveying the front of Beck's house, while a frizzy-haired white guy in jeans and sandals opened the back of the van and pulled out a massive camera. Beck scrubbed the fake blood from his hands in the utility sink before heading into the house.

His parents were at the front door, welcoming the newcomers.

"Hi," Beck said. "Thanks for coming."

The woman's sharp gaze traveled from Beck's bare feet to his paint-smeared T-shirt. Her black hair was shiny and straight, bobbed at her shoulders, and her lips were crimson. "I'm Ranielle Russell, executive producer of *The Escape Game*."

Her voice was expensive perfume on Beck's tongue. He tried not to cough.

"Ranielle Russell," he mused. "Any relation to the Game Master?"

Her lips thinned into a tight smile. "Louis is my husband." She then gestured at the frizzy-haired guy behind her. "We'll be filming today. Pretend he's not here."

Ranielle shook Beck's parents' hands, then took stock of the living room. The secondhand furniture. The framed Thomas Kinkade print. The embroidered pillow of wild horses his mom had bought at a yard sale. "Mind if we do some rearranging?"

The camera guy didn't wait for approval before he started moving the coffee table.

"Uh . . . sure?" said Beck's dad, casting Beck a *who are these people?* look that Beck could only respond to with a shrug that he hoped was interpreted as, *Hollywood*.

"Today we'll be filming what we call greenlights," said Ranielle. "We'll use these shots to give viewers a glimpse of your home life. No one cares how many puzzles a teenager can solve if their personality is as flat as a pancake. Our viewers want contestants they can cheer for. You want to be likable, yes, but it's even more important that we can tell a story. We need to know why anyone should care about you."

She stared at Beck, and it was a moment before he realized she expected an answer.

He was tempted to point out that, generally speaking, people did care about him. He didn't necessarily try to be likable, he just . . . was. It was almost as if a fairy godmother had waved her magic wand over Beck's cradle, back when his blankets were pink and his first name was three syllables instead of one. *This kid shall be adored by all!*

Homeschooled from the start, he'd spent his formative years running around his grandpa's ranch in Montana. After the ranch was sold—a decision that was still a sore spot among his relatives—Beck and his parents had become seminomadic, always bouncing from town to town, state to state.

People were always saying that homeschooled kids were socially awkward, but in his opinion, his unconventional childhood meant that he'd encountered all sorts of different people growing up, and had gotten really good at winning them over.

Winning over the show's viewers would be no different. He wasn't worried about that.

His other purpose for going on *The Escape Game*?

Now *that* was going to be a challenge. And Beck freaking loved a challenge.

But he couldn't exactly share his biggest secret with the executive producer.

"Why should anyone care about me?" he repeated, buying himself time. "Well. I'm trans. Happy. Accepted by my family."

"That's your angle?" Ranielle said, in a way that suggested perhaps Beck wasn't the only trans contestant they'd considered for the show. She gave him the once-over. "Are you on any medication we should be aware of?"

"Just the binder for now." Beck gave a winning smile. "But no, that's not my angle." He glanced at his parents, then back again. "How do you feel about intergenerational family dramas that revolve around deception, betrayal, and millions of dollars lost to gambling debts?"

Beck's mom inhaled sharply. His dad crossed his arms. But neither of them spoke.

"I'm intrigued," Ranielle said.

"Then let me tell you why I'm going to win."

Audition Video: Aditya Parvesh

THE ESCAPE GAME

SEASON FIVE

The woman has waist-length black hair, perfect posture, and flawless brown skin. Her lips are full and glossy, but her eyes are hidden behind a pair of enormous Dolce & Gabbana sunglasses. She is supermodel stunning, and it's clear that she knows it.

She is also decidedly *not* a teenager.

"Ranielle, darling," she purrs before fluttering pink manicured fingernails in a careless wave. "And . . . other casting directors. Symphony here. You probably recognize me as the star of multiple box office hits and current spokeswoman for Best Life Nutrition. Remember—a healthy life is your *best* life." Behind her there are glimpses of an infinity pool and teak sun umbrellas, but then she steps through gauzy curtains into a sleek living area. Mid-century modern furniture. Abstract art.

"This is the official audition video for my son, Aditya Parvesh. As you'll see, he's made for the screen—just like his mama. He's smart. Charming." She smirks knowingly at the camera. "Ridiculously handsome. He obviously gets those genes from me." She titters, but then her voice lowers as she adds, "Heaven knows they didn't come from his father."

She pushes open a swinging door and enters a bright kitchen. A metal bowl filled with papayas and dragon fruit sits beside a box of Froot Loops on the granite counter. A boy hunches over a bowl, spoon in one hand and an enormous tome of a book in the other. He doesn't move when his mother enters, just shoots his gaze suspiciously in her direction.

"Aditya! Say hello to the producers of *The Escape Game*."

The boy swallows and lowers the spoon into the bowl. He *is* ridiculously handsome, with thick black hair that falls over broody eyebrows, and a strong jawline touched with stubble.

"What's going on?" he says, shifting the book a few inches closer, like it could be a shield between him and the camera. Or possibly him and his mother.

"You're going to be on *The Escape Game*."

"Ugh, Mom. Not this again. We agreed no more auditions."

"My Aditya is *very* good at puzzle-solving." Symphony bends close to the boy, angling the phone to put them both in the frame. "Especially those word ones. What do you call them? Where you mix up the letters to spell something new? An analogy?"

"Anagram."

"Right! Here, watch this. What's a word that can be formed from some of the letters in . . . *Symphony*?" She lifts her sunglasses to wink at the camera.

Adi stares at her for a beat, then deadpans, "'Phony.'"

His mother beams. "Isn't he clever? He's especially excited at the prospect of winning tickets to that new little puzzle resort."

"Wait, what?"

Despite her son finally showing some interest, Symphony pulls away, keeping the camera on herself. "Of course, this is just a formality. We look forward to hearing from you, Ranielle. Au revoir!"

Producer notes:

Having regrets.

Although the kid seemed witty—loved the phony comment.

And he **is** *gorgeous. The next Alicia?*

03

Adi

"Why did you audition for *The Escape Game*, Mr. Parvesh?"

Adi spun around in the desk chair—the one his mother had reupholstered in ostrich leather—stopping to face the woman on the video call. She looked fresh out of grad school, her self-importance bolstered by her shiny new psychology degree.

"I didn't," he said.

"You didn't?"

"Nope." He said the word slowly, popping the *p*. His fingers trailed along a lampshade made of hundreds of Swarovski crystals. "The audition was my mother's doing. She made some deal with the executive producer, and . . . here we are." Adi wasn't privy to the details of this deal, but knowing his mother, there was something in it for her. Typical Symphony. Clamber over everyone on her way to the top, giving them a swift kick in the face as she went.

"So you don't want to be on the show?" the therapist asked.

"I didn't say that."

The therapist waited.

Adi considered his words carefully. "Let's just say . . . puzzle-solving's in my blood."

"Care to elaborate?"

"No."

She had to know about his dad. Someone would've sent her an email at least.

"All right," she said, picking up a pen. "But you enjoy escape rooms?"

"Hell yeah. I've been obsessed ever since I went to one for a sixth-grade field trip. I've done every online room available."

"Online?" the therapist said, scribbling diligently. "Not with friends?"

Adi grimaced.

The therapist's pen paused. "Would you say you're a team player, Aditya?"

A crystal snapped off in his fingers. With a wince, he tucked it into his jeans pocket. "Of course I'm a team player. I love people."

"I see." She resumed tapping. "No family members interested in joining you? Siblings? Cousins?"

No, in fact, he did not have a community to fall back on. When his mother ran away from her parents in her teens, she ensured his existence was wiped from the family tree, just like she ensured he grew up as American as her favorite television shows.

As if he were going down that rabbit hole with a one-off therapist. "Look, Doc, let's not waste any more time. I'm already guaranteed a spot." He didn't admit it, but that had been the biggest shock—when Ranielle Russell had called and confirmed it to him directly. Up until that moment, he'd assumed this was one of Symphony's delusions, like that time some review had praised her character's death as an Oscar-worthy performance and his mother thought she'd *actually* been nominated for an Oscar.

The shrink tapped her pen on her notepad. "Reality television attracts a wide range of applicants. I'm here to make sure—"

"There's not a repeat of last season?"

She didn't miss a beat. "How do you feel about the murder of Alicia Angelos?"

He remembered reading the announcement—Symphony had been in another hellish mood, and he'd thought that yeah, his life was bad, but it wasn't found-murdered-on-a-reality-game-show bad. Perspective, etc.

He shrugged. "Sad that she died."

"Alicia didn't just die."

"No. She was killed by her wacko sister."

"Sierra Angelos was never charged."

"Everyone knows she did it. What does this have to do with me?"

"Maybe nothing," said the therapist. "But I have to write something in this report." She held up her notes. "So if you don't want to talk about Alicia Angelos, what should we talk about?"

Adi thought about the countless auditions growing up, where he'd been paraded around like a show pony before being ultimately declared too difficult to work with.

He thought about the long nights immersed in online escape rooms, the highs of success, the joy of completion, the temporary absence of loneliness.

He thought about his mother, practically in raptures when she announced his guaranteed spot on some gaudy Hollywood version of his beloved game, her rage when he told her he wasn't interested, and her lavish gifts when he changed his mind.

He thought about the reason he'd changed his mind in the first place. The chance to escape, so close, so unbearably close . . .

What should they talk about?

He leaned back in his chair, steepling his fingers. "Read any good books lately?"

Audition Video: YOU OWE ME

THE ESCAPE GAME

SEASON FIVE

A girl sits on her unmade bed, white foundation caked on, eyes rimmed with smoky smudges, lipstick as black as her hair. A painting hangs on the wall behind her of an angel kneeling in front of a tombstone, crying tears of blood.

Her expression is all hatred. She doesn't try to smile. Doesn't try to charm the viewer like the others.

She stares into the camera long enough that it becomes uncomfortable. Almost threatening.

Sierra Angelos says one thing before the footage ends.

"I want my prize money."

Producer notes:

Over my dead body.

04
Adi

Adi dropped his duffel bag onto the marble floor of the foyer. It landed with a heavy thud, thanks to the library's worth of books inside—and one change of clothes. He checked the time.

"Symphony!" he shouted.

No response.

Groaning, he jogged up the spiral staircase. His mother was in her silk robe at the vanity in her huge dressing room.

"Mom, we need to leave. We're going to be late."

Symphony leaned closer to the mirror. "What's the hurry?" she said, swiping shimmery powder on her cheekbones. She never set foot outside without first applying sixty-two different types of skin care, makeup, and hair products. "You're the star of the show. They can't exactly start without you."

"I'm *not* the star of the show. I'm one of twenty contestants, and if I'm late, they'll call a backup and start without me."

She snorted, closed the powder, and picked up an eyebrow pencil.

He pressed his palms together in supplication. "You look fine. Let's go."

"You can't hurry perfection," she sang, then waved him off with the pencil. "Make yourself useful and grab my driving gloves from the closet. Second drawer from the left."

"Driving gloves," he muttered. "This isn't the thirties."

"UV rays are as real now as they were then, and I refuse to get age spots like those . . ."—she visibly cringed—". . . elderly women. Oh, grab a pair of sunglasses while you're in there. The Prada—no, let's go with Versace."

"Yes, Your Majesty."

"Aditya. It's one minor request. Considering I spent twenty-three hours in labor and the past seventeen years providing you with food and clothing and shelter, not to mention securing you a spot on a famous television show—"

Her ramblings faded as Adi stepped into the walk-in closet.

"Gross, gross, gross," he whispered, feeling as if he were being suffocated by overpriced perfume, plastic dry cleaning bags, and consumerism. Half the clothes still had tags.

He found the drawer and opened it, revealing an array of accessories. One of the many phone cases was covered in faux zebra fur. Another, with pink and gold rhinestones in the shape of a dolphin, had an actual phone inside. "Seriously?" he muttered, tossing it back in with the others.

He grabbed a pair of gloves and a sunglasses case and slammed the drawer shut, heading back into the dressing room.

But Symphony was no longer there. He frowned, listening, and . . . *yep*. A blender. The soundtrack to his life.

Adi jogged down the stairs and into the kitchen, dropping the accessories onto the counter. Now, his mom was in tight jeans, high heels, and a glitzy off-the-shoulder top. Quite the outfit for a car ride.

She shot him an appraising look. "Is that what you're wearing?"

He glanced down at his T-shirt and old jeans. "Yep."

"Hmm." Her disapproval was clear over the noise. "You're still a bit scrawny." She switched off the blender. "I put some Best Life packets in your bag. That'll help you build some muscle."

He stopped himself tugging self-consciously on his shirt. No matter how bad she made him feel, he was not going to drink the fake-food protein shakes his mom hawked on those informercials.

She poured the blender contents into a to-go cup while Adi tapped his fingers against his scrawny forearms. "Can we leave?"

"Ha! I had to beg you to go on this show, and now who's desperate to get there?"

"When I make a commitment, I follow through." Adi's implication hung in the air.

Sure, when Adi was growing up, if Symphony was in a good mood she might take him to the zoo like she'd promised. Or it might end up being another audition, or an afternoon shopping at her favorite boutiques, or a coffee with some has-been celebrity. Adi had learned from a young age to never leave the house without a book in hand.

Symphony was too distracted to notice his comment as she reached for her sunglasses. "I said *Versace*. Honestly. You are so useless."

"Who cares? Let's go." He grabbed the car key as Symphony's phone rang.

She gasped. "Oh! I have to take this."

"You're kidding."

"It's Sandra Fabinyi. That agent I was telling you about? She's calling to chat about *future prospects*." With a beatific smile, she strolled toward the pool deck, lifting the phone to her ear. "Symphony here."

It was so painfully on-brand, Adi was surprised he hadn't expected it.

He looked down at the key in his hand.

He technically didn't have a driver's license, and his mother refused to let him take the test using her *baby*—the pink BMW she loved far more than her actual kid. If he borrowed it, she would be apoplectic.

What a shame.

Returning to the foyer, he pulled out the protein shake packets she'd stuffed in his duffel bag and dumped them on the floor.

Then, swinging the key ring on his finger, he sauntered out the door.

05

Carter

Carter, who got nervous taking a selfie, was now being dogged by camerapeople. She hadn't been allowed to stop smiling since seven a.m., and her cheeks were killing her. First there was the shoot for the show's opening credits, then publicity shots in which they had her wear some ridiculous white pleather miniskirt and a beaded top that itched like hell, then social media reels filmed by this morose-looking girl who looked like she'd rather be doing literally anything else. Every time Carter thought they were going to break for food, she was accosted by another team of hair and makeup professionals, sat down in front of another camera, and ordered around by some crabby director.

"Sit up taller!"

"Smile more!"

"Stop fidgeting!"

"No, a real smile—honestly, who picked this girl?"

Finally, she'd been stuck alone in a room plastered in posters and told to wait until someone came to get her.

Judging from the itinerary she'd received that morning, her team was supposed to start the snag room in—what, an hour? She should have met them by now.

Carter twined a finger around one of her curls. A stylist from the show had come to her house yesterday and spent more than twelve hours bleaching and fashioning her hair.

Which meant it was red.

Fire-engine red.

Combined with the uncomfortable yet inarguably fashionable clothes they'd put her in, she looked more like her avatar than ever before.

She wanted to feel transformed, like a modern-day Cinderella.

Instead, she felt like a fraud.

She collapsed onto the sofa. All seven trillion nerves vibrated through her body. Coming on this show was a mistake. The constant snapping from the crew had made it quite clear she wasn't cut out for this. Her smile was too nervous. Her mannerisms too awkward. Her voice too quiet.

She covered her face and let out a frazzled groan—then yanked her hands away when she remembered her makeup.

She was an impostor.

She would be the laughingstock of the fandom.

It was one thing watching the games from the comfort of her bedroom, having the advantage of cameras zooming in on certain clues and seeing the rooms from multiple angles. Anyone could solve a puzzle that way, pausing and going back when necessary.

But to be in the actual game, in real time, with real consequences, was totally different. What if the pressure got to her and she couldn't decipher an obvious clue? What if her teammates were brilliant and wonderful and she ruined everything for them?

They would hate her.

She stood and paced from one end of the cramped room to the other. She needed a distraction before this downward spiral of doubt had her running for the first flight home.

Maybe she should call her parents. They always knew what to say to calm her anxiety, and at that moment, she would have given anything to hear her dad's warm Trinidadian accent or her mom's robust laugh as she fought to push back her wayward ginger curls. Carter got so far as to pull out her phone and find them at the top of her contacts, where a small bubble next to her dad's cell number showed their goofy grins, cheeks squashed happily together.

No. She couldn't call them. The homesickness would be too much.

Gripping her phone, she stared around at the promotional *Escape*

Game posters. There was a signed photo in a silver frame of Fitzy and Louis from their YouTube days, in season one. Fitzy looked so young then, even younger than Carter was now.

Carter leaned closer to read the message scrawled in cursive beneath the photo. She recognized the handwriting as the Game Master's—she'd received a postcard from him during season three after she'd sent him a fan letter with a homemade puzzle. She instinctively lifted her phone to take a picture of the message.

This is just the beginning. —Louis

She smiled as she took the shot. Louis Augustus Russell had believed even back then that the show was something special.

There was a knock. At the door was the morose interviewer from before—a short, plump girl in her early twenties, sporting blond pigtails, garish blue eye shadow, and one long silver earring in her left lobe. A tattoo of a reptilian tail snaked beneath her sparkly halterneck top. Carter was about to ask what it was—a dragon, maybe?—but the girl cut her off.

"What are you doing?"

Carter jumped at her angry tone. "Um . . . taking pictures?"

"Why?"

"For . . . my fans?"

The girl stared at her for a second, then grinned. "Oh my god, it really is you!"

Carter blinked, trying to remember the girl's name. Vera? Yes, Vera. She was pretty sure. "Yeah. Um, hi."

The girl stepped closer, beaming enthusiastically. "*The* Kick It Carter! Solve Specialist! O-M-G, I am, like, such a big fan!"

Her voice had taken on an odd Valley-girl tinge that made Carter extra nervous.

"Really?"

Vera's smile vanished. "No. You influencers are so full of yourselves." She lifted the iPad she was holding. "Say cheese."

Carter barely had time to twist her lips into a semblance of a smile as Vera snapped a photo. She was on *The Escape Game*. She was supposed to be with her people. She hadn't come here to trade in the relative strangers at school for a set of jerks. Jerks with cameras.

If only she had the guts to say as much.

Vera checked the screen and frowned. "Where are your glasses?"

"Glasses?"

"The big round ones?"

"O-oh. My avatar wears those, but I don't actually need them."

Vera's scowl deepened. "I'll bring it up with costuming."

"You're the social media manager, right?" said Carter. "I think you're the one who shared my memorial video for Alicia Angelos. That got me a lot of new followers, so . . . thanks."

"Just keeping the show trending." Vera tucked her iPad beneath her arm. "If it were up to me, I'd be happy to drag that bitch's name through the mud."

"You—what?"

But Vera was already walking away.

06
Beck

Beck looked down at the ocean-blue lab coat, then up at the mirror. He liked the effect. The color matched his eyes. The stylists hadn't done much—a bit of powder, a pencil to his eyebrows, a slick of mousse. He still looked like himself, just turned up a notch.

Plus, the lab coat. Beck liked the lab coat.

He mimed fidgeting with invisible glasses. "The specimen has taken on properties that we could not have accounted for," he said in his best serious-scientist voice. "It will soon infect us with a flesh-eating virus that will spread across the planet, devouring everything it comes into contact with . . . and there is simply nothing we can do." He clicked his tongue. "Terrible shame." The TV on the wall flickered in the reflection. Beck spun around as the blue screen switched to an internal channel to reveal Fitzy, the show's host, in a linen shirt and faded jeans, beaming at the camera. He might not have been the brains of the show, but his offbeat charm and utter lack of pretension were part of what made it work.

"Welcome to season five of *The Escape Game*!" he said, his Australian accent tasting like salty oysters. "The show where we lock teenagers in rooms full of puzzles, clues, and codes to see who can escape the fastest. I'm your host, Fitzy, and this season, our teams will be competing for the biggest cash prize ever offered on *The Escape Game*. The winning team will be awarded . . . wait for it . . . one million dollars!"

The screen changed to B-roll footage of hundred-dollar bills dropping from the sky onto an enormous pile of cash. A gaudy reminder. If Beck's team won, he'd have a whopping two hundred and fifty grand to call his own . . . for at least five minutes, before he paid off his parents' bills and told the debt collectors to suck it.

"But that's not all," Fitzy continued, and Beck took an eager step closer to the screen. "Because this season, we're offering an exclusive early-access invitation to Sweetbrier Resort!" Drone footage played across the screen: a glamorous hotel, a lake with an anchored pirate ship at its center, a flag with the logo for Victory Escapades, Inc.™ fluttering over a castle drawbridge. "The team who comes out on top this season will be the first members of the public to explore Victor Cunningham's highly anticipated playground for puzzle lovers. But we've got a lot of escape room shenanigans coming up before we declare our winners, so let's go over the rules."

The screen switched to fancy graphics of clocks and flashlights. "Today's room is what we call our snag round. It's a chance to see what these teams can do, and it's the only round during this competition in which no team will be eliminated. However, there's plenty of incentive for them to do well, as the fastest team to solve each puzzle will earn the Game Master's highly coveted 'snags,' which is our clever word for"—he lowered his voice to a sinister stage whisper—"'sabotage.' Unlock a bonus today, and our teams will be able to royally screw over their competitors in future rounds. And you know they're gonna want those snags, because after today, the team that takes the longest to escape each room will be going home. Now, let's give it up for the man who's been working hard to bring you the most brain-twisting escape rooms around . . . the Game Master himself, Louis Augustus Russell!"

The Game Master strode onto the set, thumbs hooked behind his suspenders. "Thanks, Fitzy. It's great to be back."

While Beck's synesthesia made Fitzy's voice taste like shellfish, the Game Master's deep baritone was like the first glass of eggnog on Christmas Eve—smooth and rich and overly decadent.

Fitzy draped an elbow over Louis's shoulder. "Word is, you've mixed things up this season . . ."

"Beck Matheson?"

Beck spun to see a man from the set crew holding a headset. "Time to get mic'd up."

Beck's heart galloped. "Cool," he said breathlessly. "Uh . . . where's my team?"

"Put this in your right ear," the man said, attaching a tiny microphone to the lab coat's lapel.

"This way," said yet another crew member, a woman with a clipboard and walkie-talkie. Beck followed her out through a dingy mustard-yellow hallway.

"Say cheese," barked a voice. Beck turned to see a girl with blond pigtails and a lot of makeup. Her iPad camera flashed in his face. Beck jolted back, but the girl was already walking past him.

He shook his head, trying to clear the sparkles in his eyes, then a door was opening and there it was—the main soundstage, where Fitzy greeted contestants. Where he and Louis joked about what devious puzzles the Game Master had planned. Where, once a week, a team would have their hopes crushed as they were eliminated from the competition.

Not Beck's team, though. He was here for the long haul.

Come hell or high water. Even in his head, his grandfather's raspy drawl tasted like pipe smoke and cedar trees.

The set looked smaller in real life. Where the cameras cut off the edges of the backgrounds, Beck could see the scaffolding made of two-by-fours and plywood, the leftover paint splatter on the floor. As someone who prided himself on his attention to detail, especially when he was constructing one of his own escape rooms, he found messy craftsmanship disappointing.

But he didn't let himself dwell on it. This was reality, this was Hollywood, and *that* was—

Louis Augustus Russell.

"Holy crap," Beck said.

Fitzy and Louis stood in the middle of the set, but rather than chatting like they'd been on the television screen, Fitzy was looking at his phone while Louis had powder dabbed onto his chin by someone from makeup. Maybe the footage they'd been showing backstage had been recorded in advance.

Beck's earpiece crackled. "Next contestant, Beck Matheson, in place."

The makeup person disappeared. The lights brightened. Fitzy's phone vanished into a pocket and his smile returned full-wattage. Louis folded his arms stoically over his barrel chest.

"Action!"

A script scrolled across a blue screen beside the cameras. "Let's welcome another contestant," read Fitzy. "Don't be fooled by his sunny disposition and those baby-blue eyes. This one makes his own escape rooms in his spare time and has a particular taste for Wild West saloons and medieval torture chambers." Fitzy raised an eyebrow at Louis. "Fancy he might be gunning for your job, Game Master?"

"I don't mind some healthy competition."

"You heard it here, folks. Let's welcome: Beck Matheson!"

Beck was shoved between the shoulder blades. He stumbled forward. Glaring lights surrounded him. The temperature seemed to spike ten degrees.

That same voice rasped in his ear, with the texture and taste of gravel. "Smile, kid. You look like a deer staring down a hunter's rifle."

That was about how he felt. But he plastered on a smile, and as he crossed the set, his fear began to fade, replaced with a sense of euphoria. Hell's kittens, he was on *The Escape Game*!

He danced the rest of the way across the stage to the music thrumming through overhead speakers.

"Yeah!" said Fitzy, breaking into some sort of hip-hop move himself. "He's got style!"

Beck grooved to a stop and couldn't help laughing, more exhilarated than embarrassed. "Fitzy! Game Master! Hi!"

Louis gave a stoic nod while Fitzy wrapped an arm around Beck's shoulders. "Beck! Are you excited? Are you ready?"

"Yes! I can't wait to get started!"

Fitzy turned to the Game Master. "So, Louis, what can you tell Beck about this first room?"

"Wait," said Beck, and made a show of looking around. "Where's the rest of my team?"

Louis's lips curled into a secretive smile. "Don't worry about them. Now, listen closely. You and your teammates are laboratory assistants working for the genius chemist Dr. Adam Theery. You have been tasked with creating a serum that will enhance the power of the human brain to astronomical levels, unleashing our true potential for ultimate intelligence. However, a spy has sneaked into your laboratory, locked you and your team in the supply closets, and kidnapped your boss. You must follow the clues left by Dr. Theery in order to finish the final serum . . . before your opponents can obtain all the doctor's secrets."

Beck whispered, "*Cool.*"

Fitzy chuckled. "I wonder if our Game Master might have a hint to help you complete this task?"

Beck stood straighter. The Game Master's clue had been known to make or break a round.

"As you know," said Louis, "winning teams aren't always those with the smartest players or the most experience. Sometimes the winning team is the one that has the best . . . *chemistry.*"

Chemistry. Laboratory. Got it.

Except that didn't seem like much of a clue.

Beck had no time to ponder it because Fitzy was handing him a blindfold. "Ready?"

"Heck yeah." Beck slid the mask over his eyes, blacking out the world. Everything but the sounds and the tastes. "Wherever you are, Dr. Theery, I won't let you down."

"Nice one," mumbled the director's voice in his earpiece.

Beck preened.

He was led off the stage. They didn't walk far.

"Through here," said his guide. "One more step. And . . . stop."

Beck listened to his own breath and refrained from rubbing his sweating palms on his lab coat. "But my team—?"

"I'm going to activate the door," the guide said. "It's self-locking, but we'll be on the other side if there's trouble."

Something rumbled. The doors, closing Beck in.

Fitzy's voice came through his earpiece. "When I say the magic word, you may remove your blindfolds and begin. Three . . . two . . . one . . . *Escape!*"

Beck yanked off the blindfold.

He was alone in a room not much bigger than a storage closet, the walls painted slate gray and the floor speckled linoleum. Everything had a pink glow about it. No indication of his entry point—it had merged seamlessly into the wall. A light bulb hung overhead. Before him was a metal door with a three-digit padlock on the handle. A piece of torn paper was tacked to the center of the door. The scrawled message read *no one nor*.

He turned around. A shelf at eye level held a collection of glass jars with a strange assortment of items in them. The pink glow, he saw now, was coming from a neon sign that said, simply, ESCAPE.

In case he forgot what he was here for.

Already, his nerves were dissipating. Codes. Logic. Patterns. This was his happy place. No matter his reasons for being here—the tarnish of resentment that had plagued his relatives for the last decade, his plans to finally set things right—here, he was in control. Beck versus the puzzle room. Beck versus the Game Master.

He was reaching for the first jar when a new voice crackled in his ear.

"Roll call. Who's here with me?"

Beck froze. The voice was familiar. The texture. The taste. It was so unexpected and so . . . *impossible* that Beck swiveled around in a full circle, sure this was a practical joke.

"Hello?" said another feminine voice, warm and comforting, like chamomile tea. "I'm Carter. Where are you?"

"A very, very small room," said the final team member, a guy, this one with a husky drawl like aged leather and currants.

"Name?" came the first voice again. Beck shut his eyes. He had to be wrong.

"Adi," the boy grunted.

"That it? Should be four of us. Come on, clock's ticking."

Every word made Beck's mouth water with the distinctive mixture of blue Kool-Aid and sherbet fizzing along his tongue.

If he wasn't mistaken, he was locked in an escape room with Sierra freaking Angelos.

THE ESCAPE GAME

SEASON FIVE

Snag Round: It's All About the Chemistry

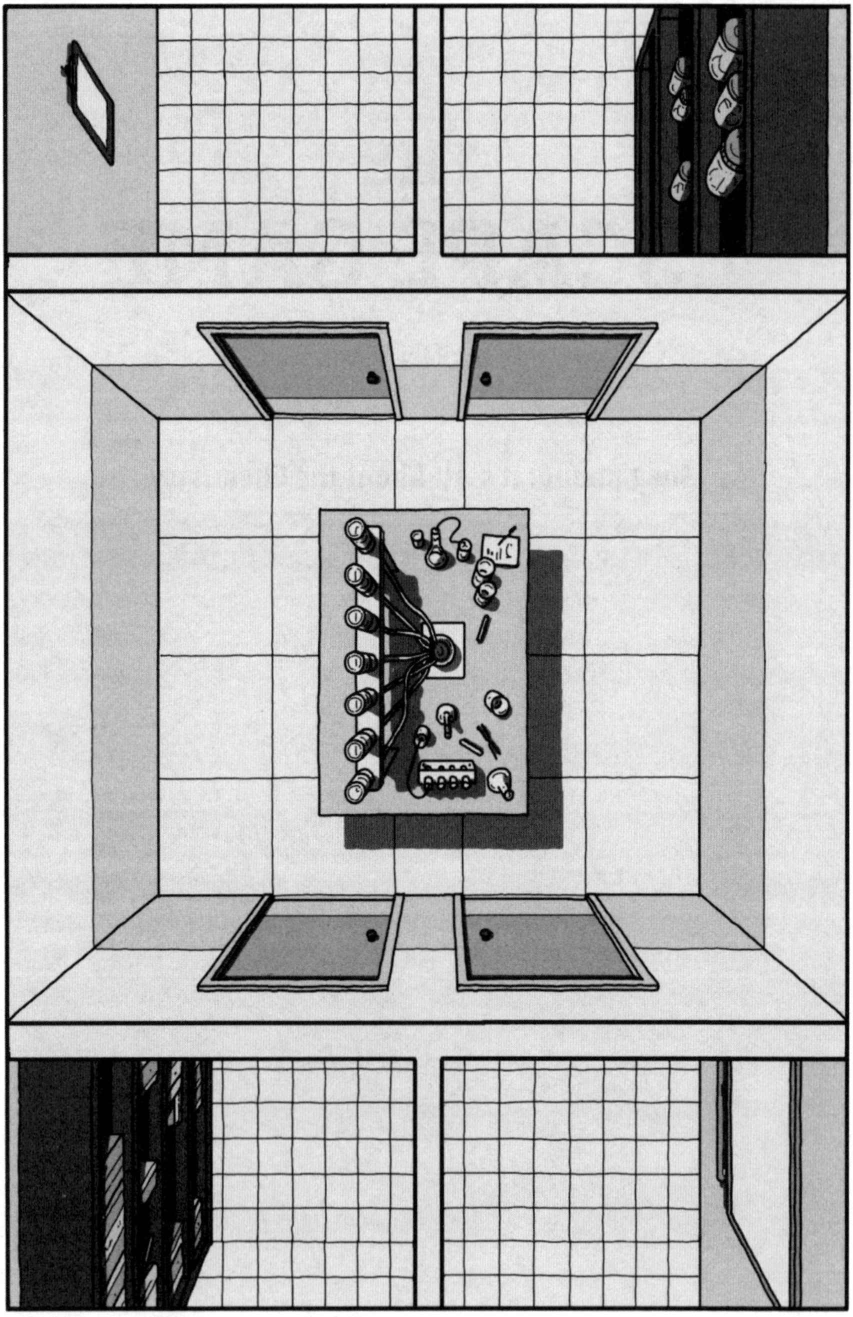

07

Sierra

"Beck," said the fourth member of Sierra's team. Finally. "My name is Beck."

Hopefully he was better at decoding than he was at speaking.

"Let's take a tally of our clues," Sierra said, sweeping her attention over the room she'd been studying from the moment the blindfold came off. She didn't have much. A sign on the door that read *silence me* and a clipboard on a peg.

"Wait," said the girl, Carter, "you didn't tell us your name." She sounded suspicious.

Rather than answer, Sierra read through a series of lab notes that detailed various experiments.

Experiment 1: 2 parts solution A + 1 part solution J
Result: forest green, mostly opaque

Experiment 2: 3 parts solution A + 1 parts solution K
Result: violet purple, gummy texture

And so on, for seven experiments total. She flipped the page up, but there was nothing else. "I've got a clipboard with a list of lab experiments talking about different solutions, coded alphabetically, and some colorful results. Beck, what do you have?"

"Uh—okay, right." Beck cleared his throat. "I've got a three-digit padlock on the door, plus a bunch of jars with random things in them. A battery, a glove, a bone, a . . . I think this is a ball of crumpled foil? A silver earring and . . ." Slight pause. "Huh. The last one's empty. Oh, and there's a neon sign that says 'escape.'"

Sierra grunted. "In case we forget why we're here?"

Beck gave a nervous chuckle. "That's what I thought."

"I've got a bunch of books," said Carter. "Textbooks. Physics, astronomy, chemistry, biology."

"Look closely," said Sierra. "There could be something hidden in the pages, or writing that could be useful."

"This is supposed to be a chemistry lab," Beck added. "Maybe start with that one?"

"Good point," Sierra said. So he *did* have a brain, thank god. "Let me read these lab notes to you. Maybe it connects with something in those books."

She read off the experiments, from beginning to end. Even as she did so, she thought of how this would be edited out during production. Reading arbitrary lab notes did not make for great television.

"I'm not seeing anything, but I'll keep looking," said Carter. "What happened to our other teammate?"

"I'm busy," said Adi testily.

Sierra scowled. She had a reputation on this show. She wasn't about to be out-sulked by an amateur. "Play the misunderstood loner later. Right now we need to know what you've got."

"I'm trying to decipher a code," he said. "Got a fake name that's an anagram, and a whiteboard to work it out. 'Deleted.' 'Timeline.' 'Middle.' 'Meddle.' 'Divide'—there are heaps of options."

"Okay . . ." said Sierra. "But we need numbers to open our padlocks."

"I get that. I can make 'ten' or 'eleven,' but that's it."

"Will each door unlock with the same three-digit combination, or will they be different?" said Carter. "Anyone got a twelve-digit number? Person with the whiteboard—Adi, right? How long is the fake name? Maybe you can replace the numbers with letters, like A is 1, B is 2, you know."

"Nah, it's fifteen letters long."

"Try it anyway," Sierra said, and she hated that she heard Elijah's voice in her head, telling his team that every idea was worth exploring. He'd been wrong. Most ideas were worthless. But time was ticking.

Adi rattled off the numbers faster than she'd expected, which was a promising sign. But the numbers didn't amount to anything.

"Does anyone else have a piece of torn paper stuck to their door?" asked Beck. "I've got 'no one nor.'"

"Right!" said Carter. "I was so busy looking at these books, I forgot about it. Mine says 'anything can.'"

"'Silence me,'" added Sierra.

"Oh, the torn paper is where I got the name," said Adi. "Dmitri Mendeleev."

"Dmitri who?" said Beck.

"Exactly. I'm working on it. Give me a sec to—"

"Mendeleev-comma-Dmitri," said Carter. "Found him!"

"Found . . . who?" said Adi.

"Dmitri Mendeleev." Then, more hesitantly, "That's what you said, isn't it?"

"Hold on," said Adi. "He's a real person?"

"Says here he was the creator of the periodic table of elements."

"Oh," said Adi. He sounded disappointed.

"The words are a quote," said Carter. "*No one nor anything can silence me,* credited to Dmitri Mendeleev."

"What does that mean?" Adi said.

"Elements!" Beck sounded like a sugared-up preteen. "All these things in the jars. They're elements. Like the battery. Lithium, right? The glove is a dishwashing glove. So maybe latex or . . ."

"Silicon?" said Sierra. "Hey, Carter. Do you have a periodic table in that book?"

Flipping pages, then—"Yes, but . . . I don't see anything unusual. Nothing handwritten on the page. Oh, maybe we use the page number? I'm gonna try it on my lock."

"Wait," said Sierra. "Beck, you tell us the elements. Carter, look them up. Adi, write them down."

"I'm not your secretary," Adi said.

Sweet Jesus.

"You're the only one with a way to record anything," she said. "Let's start with lithium."

"Um, yeah, lithium," said Carter. "Li. Number 3."

"Silicon for the glove," said Beck.

"Silicon. Si, 14," said Carter.

"The bone. Calcium?"

"Ca, 20."

They quickly worked out the rest.

Earring—Silver—Ag—47

Foil—Aluminum—Al—13

The empty jar—

"Oxygen," Carter and Adi said simultaneously, followed by a giggle from Carter and an annoyed huff from Adi.

"Oxygen is O—8," said Carter.

"That gives us ten digits," said Adi. "We need two more."

"Maybe it's the jars themselves?" said Carter. "They're glass, right? Glass is made of sand. Um . . . that doesn't seem right."

Carter continued to ramble nervously as Sierra ran her finger down the lab notes on the clipboard, which had yet to be used. She was missing a clue.

"The sign!" said Beck. "Neon is an element, isn't it?"

"Wait . . . yes," said Carter. "Neon—Ne—10!"

"Ne," Adi said thoughtfully. "It feels like these letters are supposed to mean something."

"Don't worry about the letters," Sierra said. "We have our twelve digits. That's our code."

"But how do we know what order to put them in?" said Beck.

A silence followed.

"Twelve digits," said Carter. "That's over four thousand combinations. We already took out some of the guesswork, given the multiple double-digit combos, but even if you consider there are only seven numbers to put in order, there are still hundreds of possible answers—"

"What about the lab notes?" said Beck.

Sierra studied her notes. "Was there a *J* in any of those element abbreviations? Or a *K*?"

"Nope," said Adi.

Sierra tapped her clipboard. The solutions, the experiment numbers, the results . . .

"Colors," she whispered. "Carter, the elements on the periodic table. Are they all different colors?"

"Not all of them," she said. "But the elements are grouped into various colors. It explains in this sidebar that the elements are often color-coded by specific properties, such as the metalloids and nonmetals, or something about electronegativity—"

"Yes, fine," Sierra interrupted. "But are the elements we have all different colors? Like—forest green or violet purple?"

"Yeah. Silicon is in the dark green section, and calcium is purple."

Sierra's lips curled upward. "That's the order. It's tied to the experiments on this list. Adi, write this down." She read through the list of colors in the experiment results. Carter found each one on the chart, and Adi put the numbers into their new order.

14-20-8-3-47-13-10

"But if those twelve digits correspond to our locks," said Beck, "how do we know which one to start with?"

"Guess and check," said Adi. "I'll go first. 142 . . ."

"No, the quote," said Sierra. "We put them in order of the quote. "Who had 'no one nor'?"

"Me!" said Beck.

"And I had 'anything can,'" said Carter.

Adi read off the numbers so everyone could input them. One by one, the locks clicked.

Sierra pulled off the padlock. She hesitated, knowing that as soon as her teammates laid eyes on her, everything would change. They'd be distracted. Confused. Curious. And she didn't have time for any of that. They needed to win those snags.

She pushed open the door, entering a large central room that was severe in its cleanliness. A metal table held an assortment of chemistry equipment—Bunsen burners and test tubes—like something from the lab of a mad scientist. Seven large beakers were suspended over a series of twisty tubes that fed into one central glass pot. Each beaker was filled with a liquid, making up the colors of the rainbow. They were stoppered with individual wheels that would let the liquids flow down to the pot.

A gasp drew her attention to her left, where a Black girl with bright red curls, round glasses, and a green lab coat was staring at Sierra, a hand to her mouth. This must be Carter.

"It *is* you," the girl whispered.

Beyond her was a boy—Adi?—in a yellow lab coat that stood out against his brown skin. He was obnoxiously good-looking, though his astonished expression marred the effect.

A door clicked and Sierra turned to their fourth teammate. Beck. Their gazes met. He had a swoop of brown hair, moussed into perfection. His blue lab coat highlighted his bright blue eyes, but the most striking thing about him was that he didn't act surprised to see Sierra. In fact, he seemed grimly resigned.

It was Beck, not her, who said, "Process later. We're almost through this."

Well. Proof he had his head in the game, at least.

He approached the table full of lab equipment. "Let's assume we need to turn some of these wheels and combine certain chemicals. Sierra, think there could be a clue in those lab notes?"

It took her a moment to recalibrate. Adi and Carter were still gawking at her, so she studied the suspended beakers and said, "The colors don't match up with the ones on the clipboard. And I don't see anything to indicate which experiment we'd want to replicate. But if we get it wrong, then . . . that's it. We can't take it back. We'd fail."

She paced in front of the table. There had never been an automatic fail option on the show before.

"Well then," said Beck, "let's get it right."

He started turning one of the wheels.

Sierra's pulse jumped. "What are you doing?" she shouted as blue liquid coursed through the tubes.

Beck turned the next wheel. Red flowed into the pot, mixing with the blue.

"Stop!" said Sierra. "You can't do this without consulting me! Us. Without consulting *us*."

"It's okay. I have a theory," he said.

Another wheel. Green combined with the liquids.

"Beck! You've—ugh!" Sierra threaded her fingers into her hair, nails digging into her scalp, as Beck tuned a fourth wheel, adding yellow to the mix. "If you ruin this for me, I will murder you in your sleep!"

Beck spun to her, and *now* she had his attention, but from his horrified expression she realized it wasn't the sort of attention she wanted.

She had to stop saying stuff like that.

Carter gasped again, even louder than when she'd recognized Sierra.

The pot of liquid was glowing.

A bell chimed.

"Congratulations!" rang out Fitzy's familiar voice. "You've escaped!"

A door hidden in the wall swung open, revealing Fitzy and Louis Augustus Russell.

Sierra's mouth fell open. Beck had actually done it.

"Crikey, Beck, what a ballsy move!" said Fitzy. "How did you solve that final puzzle so fast?"

Beck shrugged, his gaze fixed on Sierra. "I thought of what the Game Master said before we started. The best teams have the best chemistry, right? And when we met up, I noticed our different lab coats matched some of the liquids. So . . . I figured those had to be the colors we were supposed to pick."

Sierra looked down at her own red lab coat.

The best teams have the best chemistry.

She knew the Game Master's clues were important. And yet, with the adrenaline rushing through her veins—and her distraction at wondering what her teammates would think when they saw her—she'd forgotten all about it.

"Sierra," said Fitzy, sidling up, microphone in hand. "What do you think about being back on *The Escape Game*?"

Everyone waited for her answer, including the Game Master, who had a carefully neutral expression. She grabbed the mic out of Fitzy's hand, ignoring his "Oi!" of surprise.

"You want to know how it feels to be back?" she said, staring straight down the barrel of the robotic camera. "It feels fantastic. Not only is there a bigger prize, but this time, I'm in charge. And I'm not going to let anyone get in my way."

Interview Room: Alicia Angelos

SEASON FOUR

END OF SNAG ROUND: DEM BONES

Alicia Angelos sits in the interview room, still in the Indiana Jones–style outfit she'd been wearing for the round. While her leather jacket is draped over the back of her seat, the pink fedora remains on her head. There's a smudge of dust on her cheek.

"All righty, Alicia, before we get started on the play-by-play, what did you think of the snag theme?" Fitzy's on the other side of the table.

"Got to admit, the catacombs creeped me out. In the gloom, making the skeletal jigsaw . . ." Alicia shivers and wags her finger teasingly at the camera. "Louis Augustus Russell, you have a sick mind, buddy."

Fitzy chuckles. With his wavy, sun-bleached hair, breezy linen shirt, and a shark tooth pendant around his neck, he looks ready to hit the beach. "Do you think your team was good enough to *snag* a few snags?"

After a giggle and a finger-twirl of one of her twin blond braids, she says, "Yeah. I think we did great. But you probably know better than I do." She leans forward conspiratorially. "How do *you* think we did?"

"You know I can't share trade secrets."

She shrugs and leans back. "It was worth a shot."

"What do you think of your teammates?"

Her hazel eyes dart to the camera. "They're lovely. And clever. Our achievements in the snag round proved we could work together. I'm optimistic we can go all the way."

"You're up against some tough competition, though." Fitzy presses a finger to his earpiece. "Word is, one of your opponents has dropped by to say hello."

There's a brief wrinkle in Alicia's charm.

A door behind her opens. A pale, raven-haired girl stomps in.

"Hey, sis."

Savvy viewers might notice, if they pause at precisely the right point, that Alicia's eyes widen when she hears the voice, her shoulders lifting with a sharp inhalation. But she whips around so quickly, it's almost impossible to spot.

Her words, however, are crystal clear.

"What the actual *[redacted]*?"

08
Adi

Backstage, Adi watched Sierra wrench off her lab coat and shove it into an intern's arms. The intern stammered that they were supposed to keep the coats on but was answered with a lewd gesture.

Adi couldn't process it. *Sierra Angelos* was on his team.

She was in her signature dark clothes, tattoos wending up her pale arms and under the sleeves of her tight tee, hair cinched in a high ponytail. Same old vengeful, villainous Sierra from season four.

She spotted Adi staring at her. "What're you slack-jawing at?"

Adi couldn't help himself. He laughed.

Sierra stomped forward. In her boots, she was almost his height. "You think this is funny?"

Adi tried to suppress his grin. There was seriously something wrong with him. It was bad enough to make a hobby of riling up his mother, but at least she wouldn't leave him dead in a prop coffin. Hollywood didn't look kindly on people who murdered family members.

Usually.

"Kudos to the producers," he said. "Bringing you back was a genius move."

Sierra gave Adi the once-over. "Let's not give them too much credit. Just do as I say, and maybe this time everyone will make it through the season alive."

The air between them frosted over, but Adi held her gaze. "I want to win as much as you."

When Sierra lifted her eyebrow, her barbell piercing glinted in the light. "Then we won't have a problem, will we?"

"Right, contestants, this way," said one of the older crew members, pushing Adi's backpack into his arms. The tension snapped.

They were herded into the corridor. Adi was certain he couldn't be the only one harboring a morbid curiosity at being in the presence of a real-life killer. That must've been why the therapist asked how he felt about Alicia's death—she'd wanted to know if he'd be put off his game with Sierra Angelos as a teammate.

Well. *He* wasn't going to let this distract him. Now that the initial shock had worn off, he was going to treat her like anyone else. Whatever beef Sierra had with her sister had nothing to do with him, and the shrink would've had to clear her before she came on the show. Besides, she was a damn good puzzle solver. Maybe she'd even be an asset.

As for the others . . .

Beck had kept his cool through the round and been the first one to figure out the Game Master's clue. But Carter had been anxious from the start. Adi eyed her now. Unlike the rest of them, who had been given black pants and sneakers, she was wearing shiny white boots and a skirt so short it barely peeked out beneath the green lab coat. As Adi watched, she removed her thick-framed eyeglasses and tucked them into a pocket.

He rolled his eyes. They were on a puzzle-solving show, and still he was surrounded by frauds.

They were led into a greenroom, which looked like it had been decorated by a middle-aged hack trying to imitate a teenager's natural habitat. There was a dusty foosball table and a TV hooked up to a bunch of video game consoles. Beanbag chairs in primary colors were scattered around a geometric carpet, and a huge mirror hung on the wall, framed by Edison lightbulbs.

A buffet table held coffee and tea, a dispenser filled with ice water, trays of sad-looking sandwiches, and bags of generic potato chips.

The other contestants were eating and mingling, but a hush fell when Adi's team entered.

"Shiiiiit," said a bulky guy with a sports jacket and spiky brown hair. He—along with everyone else—was staring at Sierra Angelos.

Sierra's cool gaze swept over the room, meeting the stares. After a painfully awkward silence, she dipped into an elaborate, flourishing bow that culminated in a raised middle finger before walking out again.

The jock barked a laugh. "Class act there. And do my eyes deceive me?" He strutted over and took Carter's shoulders in his meaty hands, eyeing her up and down. Her body stiffened. "You are a spitting image of that sexy cartoon character on the Domain. Don't tell me. Kick It Carter?"

"Uh—yeah," said Carter, laughing uncomfortably. "That's me."

He released her in exchange for a fist bump. "Jarius Baisley-Selkirk. Massive fan. Has this been a wild day or what?"

"Wild," Carter agreed, though her voice barely reached normal decibels. "Are we the last ones to run the room?"

"Looks like. Guess they wanted to save the big reveal until the end."

Adi examined Carter more closely, and suddenly it clicked. He didn't do social media. Being online, publicly posing and peacocking, was as superficial as Hollywood. But he'd watched every episode of *The Escape Game* to study for this, as well as some videos on a fan website. He'd seen Kick It Carter's stuff, but he'd never seen the girl behind the videos before, only her avatar, who was as sharply polished as his mom's lacquered fingernails.

Yuck.

Jarius clicked his tongue sympathetically. "Man, were the producers *trying* to screw you over? You know why they did it, too. The ads write themselves. 'Come for the puzzles, stay for the psychopath.'" He slapped Carter on the back. "Let's chat."

The rest of the contestants returned to their conversations. Adi and Beck hung back. Adi knew what he was supposed to do. Play nice. Shake hands. Make small talk.

Instead, he headed to a table, digging a book from his backpack. He was only a few pages in before he realized he wasn't retaining anything. There was too much buzzing in his brain. Killers with tattoos on their arms. Shrinks asking about murders. The abbreviations from the periodic table of elements.

Now, *there* was something that would keep him up at night.

Li Si O Ca Ne Ag Al

Alliances. Gallons. Calling. Closing. Lasagna.

"What are you reading?" said an attractive apple-shaped girl with a maroon hijab as she sat beside him.

"*Playboy*," said Adi, because he was clearly holding a thriller.

"Funny. I'm Nadia."

Adi let his book thud to the table. Not like he was concentrating, anyway. "Adi."

"How'd you do in the snag round?" Nadia held out an open packet of salt-and-vinegar chips as an offering, which almost made up for the interruption.

"It was fine," he said between crunches. "A cinch."

"I didn't like not knowing my team beforehand. What did you think when you saw Sierra Angelos?"

Adi shrugged. "That it was a practical joke."

"I heard the producers mess with contestants, but this is next level. And to be with Carter Kelly, too! You're on the team everyone's going to be watching."

Adi made a noncommittal noise. He only cared if one specific person watched.

Nadia jerked her chin toward Jarius. "And then we've got Jock Face over there. I'm pretty sure the producers cast him for entertainment value, because he couldn't even figure out how to get hot water out of the dispenser."

Adi helped himself to more of Nadia's chips. "What'd you make of the element anagram?"

"The what?"

"In the room. The element numbers corresponded to our combination locks, but I never figured out what their abbreviations were supposed to spell."

It was murder to admit, but he'd rather find out the answer from someone else than never know.

"They weren't supposed to spell anything," Nadia said. "We just needed the numbers."

"You don't think it was a snag we missed?"

"Naw. I thought the same thing at first." She held up her phone. "I even checked an anagram solver when I got out. I know what you mean—it *feels* like they're supposed to spell something. But I guess they were a red herring."

The chair on the other side of Adi pulled out and Carter swooped into it. Her mouth was locked into a painful-looking grin as she whispered through her teeth, "Save. Me."

Half a second later, four more people descended on their table—Jarius Paisley-Whatever, a ghost-pale girl with a bubblegum-pink pixie cut and dark sunglasses, another white kid who looked like a poster boy for Old Navy, and a Latina girl with enormous turquoise earrings who could have been a supermodel. Jarius's team, Adi guessed, judging from how they shared the same predatory grins.

"Kick It Carter," said Jarius, "meet Delphi, Neil, and Gabriela. We're still figuring out our team name, but we're leaning toward Team Dread. You know, like we strike *dread* into the hearts of our competitors."

Carter giggled uncomfortably and scooted her chair an inch closer to Adi's. He wasn't sure why. He'd assumed an influencer would be excited to be recognized.

"Yeah," said Carter. "That's a good name. I like it. We, um, haven't had a chance to decide ours yet. In fact, Adi, maybe we should—"

"So, hey," Neil interrupted. "Jarius said you're some sort of math whiz?"

Adi could feel Carter tense beside him. "I . . . like math . . ."

"Me too," said Neil. "So if a rectangle is altered by increasing its length by twenty-two percent and decreasing its width by sixteen percent, by what percentage has the total area of the rectangle been altered?"

Carter gaped at him. "What?"

"Dude," said Adi, "you're literally just throwing out random numbers."

Jarius swooped across the table to grab Adi's book. "What have we here? A nerd?"

"Are you kidding me? Have you seen where we are?" Adi said.

He was used to this—the macho guys, the high school taunts, the hatred of literacy. He just hadn't expected it *here*.

He stood. "Keep the book. Maybe you'll learn something. Thanks for the chat, Nadia. Carter, come on. Let's go decide . . . team stuff."

Carter bounded up beside him. "Yeah, um, nice to meet you all!"

"What a pack of hyenas," Adi muttered as they passed the other tables of teams.

Beck intercepted them halfway to the door, a Pop-Tart in hand. "Great, I was coming to get you. Do you think we could talk? Somewhere less crowded?"

"Yes. *Please*," said Carter.

"Sure," said Adi. "Think we should track down our resident social outcast?"

"That's actually what I want to talk to you about," said Beck as they stepped into the hall. "This way." Not far down the corridor, he pushed open another door, revealing a concrete stairwell. The door shut behind them with a heavy *clunk*.

"Are we supposed to be here?" Carter asked. "What if the producers come looking for us?"

"This won't take long. I hope," said Beck.

Adi sat down on one of the steps, long legs sprawled in front of him. The stairwell had an unusual scent—stale air and old concrete mixed with something . . . sweet? "What is it?"

"Sierra," said Beck. "We can't have her on our team. The episode won't drop for a few more days, so maybe there's still time for the producers to find someone else and—"

Adi held up a hand. "The producers aren't going to find someone else. Do you know how many people will tune in to see Sierra again? Ranielle Russell knows exactly what she's doing."

"But she *murdered* her *sister,*" said Beck. "Right here. Not *here,* here, in the stairwell. But on the set."

"She was never arrested," Carter said, wrapping her arms around herself. "Although, isn't the investigation ongoing? She's still a suspect."

"Innocent until proven guilty," said Adi. "They don't have the evidence to pin it on her."

"You don't think she'd hurt us, do you?" Carter said.

"Not unless we lose a round," Adi said with a grin, but Carter looked so terrified he added, "I'm kidding. She knows she's not going to get away with it again."

Beck clawed his hands into his hair. "Look, I'm all for giving people second chances, but she's a loose cannon. What if she ruins our chances at getting to the finale?"

"Her team made it to the finale last season," Adi pointed out.

"A miracle, given how she was at Elijah's throat the whole time," said Beck. Then he waved his arms through the air, as if to clear away the distraction. "Here's the thing. Jarius called Sierra a psychopath, and he might be right. I know people like to throw that word around, assuming all psychopaths are serial killers, but they're a lot more common than we think. I researched them when I was designing my torture chamber, and it's fascinating"—Beck caught himself and added quickly—"I mean, my torture chamber *escape room.* In case that wasn't clear." He pointed at himself with his thumb. "I swear I am not a psychopath. My brain is ninety-five percent empathy and five percent confetti."

"I hope there's a point somewhere in that confetti," Adi said.

"What I'm saying is, Sierra came back after everything that happened. Wouldn't there be, like, trauma or something? She found her sister dead in a coffin. Only a psychopath wouldn't care. They can mimic social behavior, but they don't feel empathy."

"Sounds like my mother," Adi drawled.

"This isn't a joke," Carter cried. "I'm going to be sharing a room with her!"

They were interrupted by a slow clap echoing through the stairwell. Bootsteps clomped down from the next floor. Adi stood as Sierra appeared on the landing. Her dark makeup made her look like a vengeful demon beneath the harsh fluorescent lights—at odds with the half-eaten cookie she held up as if to toast them. That sweetness Adi had smelled. She'd been there this whole time.

"Great talk," she said. "Sounds like you've got this puzzled out." She finished off the cookie. "You know, while you were chatting, I was thinking about our team name. What do you think of . . . the Psychopaths?"

When no one responded, she grinned cruelly, licking butter and crumbs from her fingertips. "Or the Killers? Oh—I know. The *Sister Slayers*. Gotta give the people what they want, right?"

"S-Sierra . . ." started Carter.

"Oh, don't worry," Sierra interrupted. "As long as you don't get in my way of winning that prize money, I won't kill you in your sleep." She came down the stairs and paused in front of Beck, who shivered, although whether in fear or thrill, it was hard for Adi to tell. After all, this was a guy who apparently built torture rooms for fun. He appeared almost hypnotized as he stared into Sierra's eyes.

"Thanks for the diagnosis, doctor," she said to him. "You really cleared some things up."

Beck's swallow was comically loud in the silent stairwell. Beside them, the door swung open, hitting the wall so hard Adi jumped.

That god-awful social media girl, Vera, stood at the threshold, white-knuckling her iPad. "There you are! Come on, Fitzy is ready for your post-round interviews." Turning away, she threw one arm into the air. "Everything I do around here, and now I have to play babysitter, too?"

09

Carter

"Kick It Carter." Fitzy said her name with a hint of awe, making her want to crawl beneath the metal lab table that stood between them.

You've got the wrong girl, she was tempted to say. *I'm the impostor. Can I go home now?*

Instead, she tried to smile as the stage lights glared down on her. "Hi, Fitzy."

A gruff voice burst through her earpiece. "Where are the glasses?"

"Oh! Right. Sorry." She dug the round glasses from her lab coat pocket and put them on, even though they pinched her nose.

"A lot of our viewers are squealing right now," said Fitzy, gesturing at the camera. "To be honest, when I heard that Kick It Carter, the Domain's highest-ranking Solve Specialist, was going to be on this season, I might have squealed a bit myself."

Heat rushed to her cheeks. "You did not."

"I did! I'm a fan. Your analysis videos . . ." He chef-kissed. "I don't usually have any idea what you're talking about, but man, do you make me feel like I could!"

Carter's shoulders started to relax. She supposed this was Fitzy's magic, and what made him such a good host, despite his utter cluelessness when it came to ciphers and math equations and basically all the things that made the show incredible.

It didn't hurt that he was so flipping attractive, especially with that dreamy accent. Not Carter's type, of course. She was more likely to swoon over cerebral than hot. But still. She could see the appeal.

"Thanks, Fitzy. That's kind of you."

"Speak up!" yelled the director.

She flinched. "I'm going to try my hardest not to disappoint."

"Not even possible," he said.

It was a blatant lie, no matter how genuine he sounded. Her viewers were going to think she'd been abducted and replaced by some Carter-clone. Who could blame them? When she should have been taking charge and getting her team organized, she'd instead been distracted by trying to place why her teammate's voice was so familiar, when surely, surely it couldn't be *Sierra*.

Robotic cameras swooped and zoomed. Carter didn't know what to do with her hands. She wished the producers could use her bespoke Kick It Carter avatar for the final edit. She never spoke meekly when she knew she'd be behind her cartoon. Why was it so hard to pretend to be that girl now?

"But you're not a Solve Specialist anymore," said Fitzy. "How was being in the game in real time?"

Something in his demeanor changed, and it took Carter a moment to realize he'd started reading off the script running across a blue screen—canned dialogue for a typical post-round interview.

"It was . . . horrifying, frankly. I felt like I'd never solved a puzzle in my life."

"Then your team entered the laboratory and you met your teammates face-to-face. What was going through your head in that moment?"

Carter thought back. "*Sierra Angelos,*" she said simply. "Over and over. *That's Sierra Angelos.*"

"Something tells me your fans might be crying foul," said Fitzy. "I mean, none of the other teams have quite so much"—he shot a mischievous look at the camera—"baggage."

Carter hadn't thought of that before, but he was right. It was sort of unfair.

"What about your other teammates? Beck and Adi?"

"We've hardly had a chance to talk. But Beck seems great. He solved that last puzzle so fast."

"True, though some might call that overly impulsive. Shouldn't he have communicated with his team?"

Carter bit the inside of her cheek. "Maybe," she said slowly, "but Adi and I were pretty shell-shocked. I appreciate that Beck listened to his instincts. It paid off."

"It certainly did. What about Adi?"

If this was a video for her channel, her avatar would be staring straight into the camera, unimpressed. Adi had been uncommunicative, irritable, and wasted way too much time on that Dmitri Mendeleev thing. And in the stairwell, he'd been downright dismissive of Beck's concerns.

But Carter wasn't going to say any of that, no matter how much the producers wanted her to spill the tea. Instead, she shrugged. "I'm looking forward to getting to know him better."

"How diplomatic." Fitzy's voice dropped conspiratorially, like they weren't mic'd up and being filmed from three different angles. "Believe me, not everyone would be so generous. But if anyone can handle this unlikely group of teammates, I think it's you, Carter."

She blushed to the red roots of her hair. "Please. I was anything but impressive today."

"Something tells me you're just getting warmed up."

"And cut!" yelled the director.

Carter slumped. She wasn't sure she'd breathed at all during that interview.

"Whew," said Fitzy, taking off his mic. "How are you holding up? Really?"

It was the *really* that caught her attention. Carter looked at him, then the cameras. The little recording lights were off.

"Honestly?" she said, ripping off the faux glasses. "This has been the most stressful day of my life."

"They sure dumped you in the middle of it, hey? I felt like a snake talking to you before the round, knowing what Ranielle had planned."

She gave a wry smile. "I figured you relished the drama."

"Me? Nah, mate. I jumped at the chance to be on this show because it was supposed to be different. Getting to see Louis create masterpieces, watching people barely my age unpick the clues . . . It's the best fun. Even if I don't understand half of it."

Someone behind the lights gave them the go-ahead to leave. Fitzy lifted a hand in acknowledgment and gestured for Carter to follow him off the stage.

"I'll take her back," he said to the intern hurrying toward them.

Carter was flattered, but— "You don't have to. Surely you have better things to do."

"Than talk to my favorite Solve Specialist?" Fitzy said. "Hard disagree."

She ducked her head. "You're much nicer than everyone else here."

"There are a few grizzlies, I'll admit." He shot her a grin as he held open the soundstage door for her. "Can't blame most of them. The team's under a lot of pressure, you know?"

"I can imagine."

"But Louis's a teddy bear. You'll see."

"Oh god. The Game Master. I wanted to impress him today, and I totally blew it."

"I feel like you might be slightly overreacting."

"I stood there like a gaping fish!"

"At the end with Sierra, sure, but that was done to you on purpose. Before that, you were great. Looking through the textbooks, working out Demeter Mev-Meevmember?"

"Dmitri Mendeleev."

"That's what I said." Fitzy laughed self-consciously. It was a different experience talking to him offstage. When he was in front of the camera, he held his shoulders straight, spoke with flair, threw in clichés and puns. But in real life, he seemed unsure of himself . . . sort of like how she felt without her avatar. It was mind-boggling to think she could have anything in common with James Fitzgerald.

"Louis understands how much pressure there is on the contestants," Fitzy went on. "He won't judge you. Trust me." His eyes brightened. "I have the best idea. Come on."

He turned down a corridor, away from the greenroom.

Carter slowed. "Where are we going?"

"To see the Game Master!"

Carter stopped completely, nearly twisting her ankle in the knee-high boots. *"Now?"*

"Yep. You'll see there's nothing to be scared of, *and* you can give your followers an exclusive interview at the same time. How's that for entertainment?"

Carter's breath hiccuped. "I don't think that's a good idea."

"C'mon." Fitzy was getting farther away. "I'm sure he's keen to talk to you, too. He's seen some of your videos."

That had Carter hurrying to catch up. "He has not."

"He has!" They veered around a crew member pushing a trolley full of rattling glass beakers. "I made him watch the one where you broke down our on-screen chemistry and why we're such a stellar hosting duo. I've never been so flattered."

"Oh my god." Carter was mortified. "If I'd known *you* would watch those . . ."

His dimples flashed. "I meant it before. I'm a fan. And you hear things, right? *Oh, the Game Master is irreplaceable, but Fitzy? Anyone can do his job.*" He grimaced. "That video . . . the things you said. It meant something to me. Made me feel like I was more than the goofy sidekick."

"You are more than the goofy sidekick. Everyone loves you."

"Thanks," said Fitzy, "but sometimes I wonder if the fans think the show would be better with someone else in the role. Someone smart—like you."

"No way. You're the heart and spirit of this show."

Fitzy slapped a hand over his chest. "Lucky we're here, so you can stop embarrassing me. My head will get too big to fit on the screen." He gestured at a door with the name LOUIS AUGUSTUS RUSSELL on a plaque. "Ready to meet the Game Master?"

He didn't wait for an answer before pushing open the door. Beyond it was a gray-and-black dressing room lined with brimming bookshelves and lit by brass lamps. The Game Master lounged in a leather computer chair, one ankle kicked over his knee, halfway through a crossword book. He glanced up. A hint of irritation shot through his eyes when he spotted Fitzy but faded the moment he noticed Carter. "Well, well," he said in his deep voice, tucking the pen behind his ear. "If it isn't our resident influencer."

He stood, swiftly and gracefully despite his size. Carter found herself inching closer to Fitzy.

"You got a minute?" Fitzy asked. "I thought you could do a one-on-one with Carter. Drum up some early buzz for the season?"

"Oh, um, thanks Fitzy," she said. "But I don't want to be a bother, and I should probably check with the producer before—"

"No, that's a fantastic idea," said Louis. "My wife won't mind. What's good for the show is good for her."

Carter flushed. She knew that Louis and Ranielle were married, but it was easy to forget. He seemed so easygoing, so cheerful, so warm, and she . . . didn't. But maybe there was some truth to that whole *opposites attract* thing.

"I mean . . . if you're sure she won't mind . . ." She reached for the phone in her pocket, hands shaking. Kick It Carter would never waste such an opportunity. An exclusive with the Game Master himself. She pictured her avatar jumping gleefully.

Fitzy's phone vibrated. He checked it, his face falling. "Vera needs me to film some reels."

"What?" said Carter. "Now?"

"I'd prefer to stay. But rule number one around here is—don't piss off Ranielle. Rule number two is don't piss off Vera." His expression softened. "You've got this, Kick It Carter." He slipped out the door, throwing her an encouraging thumbs-up on the way.

Carter turned back to Louis. He leaned against the desk, smiling patiently.

Suddenly, every question she'd ever had vanished.

"How did you like the room?" he said after the silence stretched on too long.

She opened her mouth. Nothing came out.

"The escape room," he prompted.

"It was great," she said, too quickly. She'd literally forgotten everything that had happened in the round.

Louis seemed to notice her panic. "I'm sure today's been a lot, and I know I can be intimidating when people first meet me, but I swear I'm just a guy who loves puzzles." He chuckled and adjusted his newsboy cap, then gestured at the mini fridge in the corner. "Can I get you something to drink?"

Something to do with her hands, something to concentrate on. A moment to gather her thoughts. "Yes. Sure. Thank you."

But then the dressing room door opened and a woman in a blood-red suit walked in. Her expression was as severe as her slick black hair.

Ranielle Russell, executive producer. And Louis's wife.

"What the hell are you doing in here?" she snapped to Carter.

"Um—"

"Relax, love, she was just going to interview me for the Domain."

Ranielle's glare toward Carter hardened. "All interviews with the crew and cast need to be preapproved. Or did you not read the contract?"

"N-No, I did. I'm sorry. I forgot. I was—"

"The bus for the villas is leaving, so I suggest you get moving, unless you want to sleep on set tonight." Ranielle stepped sharply aside, gesturing toward the door. Carter couldn't lift her burning face to look back at Louis.

"Sorry," she whispered again as she slunk past the executive producer.

"Bye," Louis called out behind her. "Maybe next time?"

Ranielle snapped the door shut and led Carter down the corridor, stilettos loud even on the carpet. "The Game Master is exceptionally busy. He doesn't have time to chat with contestants."

"Okay." Carter would've liked nothing more than to take the first flight home and disappear under her comforter forever.

"We also maintain a strict media policy. If news outlets thought any teenager with a phone could interview the Game Master, they wouldn't exactly be tripping over themselves to book him, would they?"

"I didn't think about that. I'm sorry, I didn't mean—"

"I highly doubt you were thinking at all," said Ranielle. "I don't want to see you talking to him again. Do you understand?"

When Ranielle glanced back, Carter swallowed the lump in her throat. "Of course. It won't happen again."

10

Beck

Beck felt uncharacteristically adrift as he waited to board the shuttle bus. Around him, other teams gleefully rehashed the snag round. Forming bonds. Making friends. Exactly how he'd imagined his evening would go. But Sierra was leaning against the studio wall, arms crossed and scowling. Carter was scrolling through social media feeds—she'd been quiet since her post-round interview with Fitzy. She looked different, too, having changed out of her fancy clothes into a faded Mathletes sweatshirt. Adi was staring into the distance.

Or—not into the distance, Beck realized. His attention was on a vivid pink BMW parked on the side of the street. A slip of paper flapped beneath a windshield wiper.

"Sweet car," said Beck, as the shuttle door opened, welcoming the contestants aboard. "Think it belongs to the executive producer? Or maybe Fitzy?"

Adi pulled his gaze away. "No clue," he said, hiking his backpack onto a shoulder and climbing onto the bus. "But it's already got a parking ticket. If they don't fill the meter, it's gonna get towed."

Beck and Carter followed. Carter slumped onto a seat and let her forehead fall against one of the windows. Adi sat behind her.

When Sierra boarded, she didn't even look at them as she walked past and claimed the entire back row.

As the bus pulled away from the studio, Beck could hear Adi muttering things like, "Ceiling. Collagen. Analgesic. Angel. Analogies." Beck wanted to ask what he was doing, but each of his teammates was giving off *don't talk to me* vibes, so he held his tongue, enormously disappointed with how this whole day was going.

Sierra was his biggest concern. *The winning team is the one that has the best chemistry.* More than a clue, it was the truth, and she should've learned that last season. Yet there she sat. Meeting every curious gaze with a challenging stare as the shuttle wound its way through LA's crowded streets.

The right thing to do would be to move and sit next to her. Try to make peace. If he was stuck with her, it was in his best interest to reach a truce.

Except, Beck was sort of terrified. What was Sierra's game plan? *Was* there a game plan? Surely she had one. She couldn't expect to win if they didn't work together.

Beck had almost convinced himself to talk to her when the shuttle bus pulled into a small complex. A paved roundabout led to six sandstone units that surrounded a courtyard with a bright blue pool in the middle, shaded by palm trees.

An overly chipper pair in their twenties climbed aboard. They were in polo shirts and cargo pants, looking like volunteer tour guides at a zoo. The guy was southeast Asian, with a mop of unruly brown hair.

Elijah, Sierra's team leader from last season.

"Oh, fuck *off*."

Everyone fell silent, twisting their heads to stare at Sierra, whose toxic glare was on the guy. "What are you doing here?"

Elijah's serene smile remained fixed in place. A little too rehearsed. "Afternoon," he said to the group. "Yes, I'm another former contestant returning this season. Ranielle Russell suggested I stay on to support the new recruits."

Sierra guffawed.

Elijah continued as if he hadn't heard. "This is Lisa." He gestured to the pretty girl next to him. Her olive-green glasses were a contrast against her black skin, her curls short enough to frame her face.

"Heya. We're your resident advisors, or RAs," she said in a Southern drawl. "If you have a problem, come to one of us. Our unit is closest to the dining hall. You've signed an agreement to follow the rules—any drugs, alcohol, or other illegal contraband will mean automatic disqualification from the show and a ticket home. No visitors unless it's parents or guardians. No leaving the grounds without signing in and out."

Elijah referred to the tablet in his hand. "When we call your names, come and get the keys to your unit. Your luggage is already inside. Dinner is served from five to seven in the dining hall; after that, you're on your own."

He read out the names, one team at a time.

Beck's team was called last. He took the keys and stepped off the bus, noticing Elijah move as far back as possible as Sierra passed him. She bared her teeth like a wild animal before jumping down the steps to the ground.

"Okay," Beck said, spinning the key ring on his finger. "Let's go, team!"

"Urk," Sierra said under her breath.

Beck led the way to the villa on the other side of the pool.

As promised, their luggage was waiting inside the door—Beck's zippy weekender; Sierra's battered red suitcase; Carter's matching carry-on, tote, and garment bags, all purple, all neatly clipped together. Adi's duffel was squashed beneath them. He yanked it out—it looked unusually heavy, like it was filled with bricks or something—and went straight to the front bedroom, slamming the door behind him.

Sierra stood at the lounge window. Her attention was on Elijah, who was leaning against the pool gate, conversing with some of the other contestants. Beck thought things might've changed between them after finding her sister's body.

Obviously not.

"Those are new," she grumbled.

"What are?" Beck said, startled she was speaking to him. Though she might have been talking to herself.

"Security cameras." She gave a sardonic chuckle. "What a novel idea."

"Oh. Yeah. It's nice to have . . . security?"

She cast him an irritated look.

His cheeks flamed. "I'm gonna make tea. Anyone want some?"

Carter paused in her effort to drag her luggage to the second bedroom. "Sure! That'd be great."

Relieved to have an excuse to escape Sierra's hostile glare, he walked around the island that separated the kitchen from the sitting room and pulled out a tray of assorted teas and Keurig cups. "We've got Earl Grey, chamomile, peppermint . . . Wait, let me check if there's mil—"

The word shriveled in his throat as he yanked open the fridge door. The thick, metallic stench of blood hit his nose.

A heart—a real heart—sat on the fridge's middle shelf. A kitchen knife was sticking out of it, a piece of paper skewered higher on the blade.

Without a plate to sit on, the blood made a puddle across the shelf that oozed into the crisper drawer beneath.

A body pressed up beside Beck, so close he yelped.

Sierra gave him an amused smirk and grabbed the knife. It pulled free from the organ with a squelch.

"That's a new low," she said, sliding off the note and showing it to Beck.

WE GET WHAT WE DESERVE

It was written in fat red marker.

"Isn't—" Beck gulped and tried again. "Isn't that what was written—"

"On my sister's coffin?" Sierra's tone was mild. "Yeah. All chicken-scratch caps like that, too."

"And that's . . ." He looked at the mess in the fridge.

"Cow heart. Easy to get at any butcher." She added lightly, "High in zinc."

Why wasn't she more freaked out by this?

Psychopath.

Sierra tossed the knife into the sink and tore the note into pieces. "Welcome to reality television."

"Sorry . . . what? But—but they don't film in the villas."

"Doesn't stop them from playing with you like a wild cat toying with its prey." Sierra let the note pieces flutter into the trash. "That's what they do here. Prepare yourself for an absolute mindfuck."

Beck furrowed his brow. "Don't they want us on top of our game?"

"Aren't you adorably naive." Turning away, she pulled a satchel out of her suitcase and walked toward the front door. "You might want to clean that up. Some contestants got food poisoning last season. It would be a shame for it to happen again."

Then she was gone.

Beck went in search of disinfectant. He wasn't a squeamish person. His family had raised cattle for generations before the ranch was sold, and he was no stranger to butcher floors and meat cellars. It didn't bother him to pick up the organ and throw it in the trash, or to mop up the juices with paper towels. If anything, he was irritated more by the wastefulness.

An animal had lost its life for this insipid prank. The thought made his teeth grind.

Was it to throw Sierra off her game? Or had the threat been meant for all of them?

He couldn't fathom who would do such a thing, or why.

His mind kept circling back to Elijah, who despised Sierra. He had keys to the villa and plenty of opportunity to sneak inside. Plus, he'd seen the message in Alicia's coffin up close.

But there was no obvious motive. He wasn't a contestant this season. He didn't have stakes in this game.

Laser focus.

That irked Beck more than anything as he scrubbed.

He couldn't afford to lose focus. And if he was stuck with Sierra Angelos, then he'd have to find a way to make it work.

"I wish she'd chosen a bed before she left."

Beck stood next to Carter in the doorway of the second bedroom. The room was minimally decorated, with white comforters on twin beds, a vase of yellow roses on a desk, and a framed reproduction of one of Monet's water lily paintings on the wall. The only thing that looked out of place were the prisonlike bars on the window, disrupting the view of the pinkening sky. It was an unnerving reminder of what had happened last season.

Carter looked at Beck, her voice strained as she added, "What if I accidentally choose the one she wants?"

"She doesn't strike me as the type to care," Beck assured her. "Why don't you just pick one, and then we can see what's in those?"

He gestured to the large black tote bags at the foot of each bed. He would've loved to dive into one himself, but he didn't want to disturb Adi, who'd already fallen asleep in the other room.

Carter moved toward the bed near the window, then hesitated. "Do you think she'd want a view? Or maybe there's a draft there, and she'd be too cold?"

"Carter," Beck said, "if she's cold, she can add a blanket. Really."

"Easy for you to say," Carter grumbled. "Your roommate isn't likely to kill you in your sleep."

"To be fair, that's yet to be established."

Carter gave him a look of despair as she picked up the tote bag on her chosen bed. But her misery transformed as she peeked inside.

"Oooh!" She withdrew a mug branded with the *Escape Game* logo.

Beck joined her, digging out a magnifying glass. He held it to his eye. *"It is the little gray cells on which one must rely."*

"Check it out!" squealed Carter.

She was holding a glossy magazine with a man on the cover. Beck didn't have to read the headline to recognize Victor Cunningham, founder and owner of Victory Escapades, Inc.™ Beloved by escape room fanatics everywhere, he was considered the master of mazes. The prince of puzzles. The king of codes. Not only had he built a worldwide franchise of escape rooms, but his brand carried everything from at-home puzzle boxes to murder mystery party kits. He was the genius behind Sweetbrier Resort, and the reason Beck was going to do whatever it took—including put up with an alleged killer as a teammate—to win an invitation to that Clue Master mecca.

Apparently not able to maintain attention on a single piece of swag, Carter tossed the magazine aside, whooping as she withdrew a small book of sudoku puzzles. "Sweet! I don't have this one."

They continued inspecting the gifts. A fancy gold Cryptex lock, a branded USB drive, a small box of hand-carved wooden brain teasers courtesy of Victory Escapades, Inc.™ Carter gave Beck the Rubik's Cube, claiming she already owned several, and then fangirled as she held up a T-shirt signed by Fitzy and Louis.

Beck pulled out the final item—a tiny flashlight with various settings. "Cool. You never know when you're going to need a black light."

"To . . . search for blood spatter?"

"I was thinking more, like, an impromptu rave."

Carter laughed. "Right. Sorry. This whole thing with Sierra has me on edge."

And Beck hadn't even told her about the beef heart and creepy note. Her anxious expression confirmed that it had been a good decision.

"I think she's got us all on edge."

"I don't know. Adi doesn't seem too put off by her."

"He might be one of those people that doesn't emote a whole lot. I have no idea what that would be like. I'm, like, the ultimate *emoter*."

"You should coin that word."

"I think I just did." He picked up the Rubik's Cube and tossed it from hand to hand. "You're not quite what I expected."

She flinched. "I know."

"You know?"

"That I'm nowhere near as cool as Kick It Carter? I'm *very* aware."

"But you *are* Kick It Carter."

"No, I'm not." Carter sounded exasperated. "Not the Kick It Carter that everyone expects, anyway. The filter I use is this cute, fashionable cartoon. And I'm . . ." She gestured helplessly at her Mathletes shirt.

Beck tossed the Rubik's Cube higher, working it into a nice spin in the air. "In our circles, math makes you cool."

"Not the point. But it's probably easy for you." Carter dropped onto the mattress. "You seem like you have no problem talking to people. I wish I could walk into a room and know what to say to strangers. But without a preplanned script and a video editing feature, I turn into this awkward, bumbling mess." She watched the Rubik's Cube rocket up and down. "I thought it would be different inside the room. Like I'd hear Fitzy's voice telling me to escape, and boom! I'd become a whole new person who's confident and smart and all the things I pretend to be online. But I was useless in the snag round."

"You weren't useless." Beck stopped tossing the Rubik's Cube.

It was like breaking a spell. Carter wrapped her arms around her chest and curled into herself. "When people see the real me, they're going to be so disappointed. I shouldn't have come here."

Beck tried to empathize, but he'd never wanted to hide who he was. He refused to wear dresses after age three, started going by Beck at age five, and no one in his family had been surprised when he'd officially declared that he was a boy. A couple of aunts and uncles admitted that they didn't quite "get it," but they were still supportive in their own way.

And sure, some people thought his personality was a bit *much*, but boo to the haters. He was a born optimist, and if the pessimists wanted to criticize that, let them. Given half a chance—and an endless supply of cat videos and Skittles—he was pretty sure he could win them over to his side in the long run.

It baffled him how so many people could walk around pretending to be anyone other than their awesome selves. And this was *Carter Kelly* he was talking to. One of the coolest people—well, avatars—he followed online.

"My cousin has a Domain channel, too. KaPowPow?"

"Oh, I've seen her stuff. She's the one that talks about all the tech in the show, right? She's really good."

"Yeah, she is. But she's told me that her influencer persona sometimes feels like wearing a costume. It gives her confidence, but it's not really her. Sort of like you and your avatar. Have you tried pretending that you're behind a filter when the cameras are on?"

"It's not that easy. Today it was like I had these two voices screaming inside my head. One was telling me to focus on the puzzles and not worry about anything else. The other was criticizing everything I did. Reminding me that I was on camera. The Clue Masters are going to see this. They'll be watching—judging. And now I'm worried that everyone will expect me to step up as leader, but I can't compete with Sierra!"

Beck began twisting the colored blocks. "Do you even want to compete with Sierra?"

"And have her treat me the same way she treated Elijah? No thank you."

"Okay. But if it wasn't for Sierra, would you want to be leader?"

"Everyone expects—"

"Forget what everyone expects. What do *you* want?"

Carter let out a dramatic sigh. "To have never auditioned for this show in the first place."

Beck managed to turn a whole side of the Rubik's Cube red, but there was no way to complete the other sides without ruining his progress. "How about we start with something we can actually achieve, then work our way up to time travel?"

"Great idea. I vote we start with me not getting murdered in my sleep." Carter sat up. Her perfect curls had started to frizz. "Also, not getting yelled at by executive producers."

"Those should be easy enough to avoid."

Carter smiled wryly. "You'd think so, wouldn't you? Here." She plucked the Rubik's Cube from his hand. "There are tricks to this." A few twists of the wrist later, and the cube was solved.

"Whaaaat!" Beck took the cube back from her, inspecting all six sides. "That was incredible. And you think you're not cool?"

Carter smiled slightly. That was encouraging. Beck was nervous enough about having Sierra on his team. He couldn't have Carter falling apart on him, too.

"Any other mad skills I should know about?" he asked.

Carter considered the question more seriously than Beck had expected. "I know pi up to a hundred places?"

"Again. *Cool.* See, Carter? You have to stay. You're the best chance we have of winning this thing. Forget about Sierra. You're here because you're ridiculously smart."

"I guess so . . ."

"That's the spirit," Beck said. "Now you just need to show the fans what you're really capable of."

11
Sierra

Sierra woke before six. She slipped from the bedroom with her toiletry bag and bundle of clothes, Carter's soft snores remaining undisturbed. Sierra had returned to the complex late last night to find her roommate asleep and a tote full of *Escape Game* merch on her bed, which she'd promptly dumped into the trash. All the same crap they'd gotten last year.

She brushed her teeth and took a quick shower, giving herself plenty of time to apply her armor. There was a soothing quality to the ritual, layering the pale foundation, the eye makeup so thick it made her eyelids heavy, the black lipstick sticky from an outer coat of gloss. In the mirror, she watched herself become a girl who didn't care. Who could take every hit without a flinch.

While her hands went through the morning ritual, her mind replayed the snag round. She didn't know what to make of her new team. She needed people who were hungry to win. Desperate, even. Carter might feel the pressure of the fan base, but Beck's and Adi's stakes were harder to gauge. What were they really here for? Ranielle had a reason for bringing them on. Plenty of teens could do escape rooms. It was the ones with the crunchy backgrounds that made for good TV.

Sierra cinched her ponytail so high on her head that the tips of her coarse inky hair hung above her shoulder line. The effect was marred by the fluffy white towel she was wrapped in. Soon she'd be decked in her costume, clomping around in her boots, but for now her skinny shoulders and knobbly knees made her look like a kid who'd been playing with her mother's makeup.

Her phone dinged on the counter. Not a text message—she

couldn't remember the last time she'd gotten one of those—but a sale alert. She swiped it open. Sales of her artwork weren't exactly lucrative, but they made enough to keep her afloat from month to month. Every order helped, and someone had just bought a print of *Dance Macabre*, one of her older paintings.

"Thank you for your patronage," she muttered, approving the order and submitting it to the third-party printer that fulfilled the sales. "And that is deserving of a celebration."

She dug into the ziplock bag hidden in her clothes and pulled out her last chocolate chip cookie. Breakfast of champions. She savored it as she got changed, careful not to leave behind any crumbs.

Fueled, armored, and ready for battle.

As expected, Elijah was swimming laps in the pool when Sierra slipped out her villa's door. He had done the same thing every morning last season. Overachieving prick.

Lucky for her, it made him oblivious to the world. Now that she thought about it, he was awfully vulnerable, paddling his way up and down the length of the pool. Goggles on and earplugs in. How easy it would be to sneak up on someone like that. A knife to the back. A rope around his throat.

We get what we deserve.

Sierra circled the pool deck, staying close to the fringes, until she came to Villa 4. It was Elijah and Lisa's villa now, but last season, it had belonged to her sister's team. The last place Alicia had ever slept. Sierra's steps led her past where she and Alicia had had their final argument.

The memories from that night were engraved on her mind. A million questions. A million doubts.

She rounded the villa, standing on tiptoes to see over the privacy wall. No sign of the other RA.

Annoyingly, the gate handle didn't budge. One little murder and suddenly everyone was paranoid enough to lock up.

Sierra backed up and surveyed the wall. It was too high to climb without drawing attention to herself.

The rhythmic splashing stopped.

With a kick at the wall, Sierra skulked back toward the pool. Elijah was drying his hair with a towel, his back to her.

He really was an easy target, wasn't he?

She was mere steps away when he finally turned. He yelped, stumbled—and fell into the water.

Sierra crouched at the edge while he came up.

"Sierra," he spluttered. "What are you doing here?"

"Scaring the crap out of you."

His eyes narrowed. "I don't remember you being a morning person."

"People change. What are *you* doing here?"

Elijah looked pointedly around the pool.

"I mean, what are you doing *here*?"

Elijah hauled himself out of the water and grabbed a fresh towel off one of the lounge chairs. "I had so much fun last season, I couldn't imagine leaving."

"Right. Especially that part where we found my sister's body in a coffin. That was a real blast." Sierra crossed her arms. "You know, they say killers like to return to the scene of the crime."

"I'm familiar. So what are *you* doing here?"

"Collecting my prize money."

He scoffed, toweling his hair. "It was always about the money to you."

"Are you trying to pretend you're above it all?"

He cast his gaze toward his villa, like he was wondering how best to escape this conversation. He seemed resigned when he turned back to her. "You know I wanted to win, but the odds were stacked against us from the start. We were the villains of the season. Ranielle never intended for us to walk away with that prize."

"And now you're here, getting paid to hang out where my sister was last seen alive. You gotta admit, Elijah. It's kind of creepy."

"You always assume the worst of everyone."

There was a slight flush on his cheeks—from the swim . . . or something else? "What were you doing in the pool that morning?"

He squinted at her. "Excuse me?"

"The day Alicia died. I came back to the complex at four thirty a.m. Too early for a swim, even by your standards."

"What were you doing out all night?" he shot back.

"Not killing my sister, if that's what you're implying."

"You can't even say her name, can you?"

"Nice dodge."

He wrapped the towel around his swim trunks with a sniff. "I heard a car and thought it was Alicia coming back. So I went outside to see if she'd join me in the pool."

Sierra's arms slowly unfolded. "You heard a car?"

"Yeah."

"Did you tell the cops?" Sierra's voice had raised in pitch.

"Of course I did," he said with a scowl. "Right after I told them how I heard you two fighting."

She dismissed that—ever since they'd found Alicia's body, he seemed to think sibling rivalry was grounds for murder. "Did you see the car? Recognize the make or model? Was it electric?"

"No idea. I was half asleep. The only things I heard was a door slam and the car drive away. The cops don't think it had anything to do with Alicia, though. The car was out front—it might've been anyone. And it was well after she'd been . . ." He faltered, finally finding some grace to look uncomfortable.

He was probably right, though. The GPS data from Alicia's phone showed she was a mile south of the complex at 10:28 p.m., when she had either switched off her cell or the battery died. A few hours later, she was dead. Sierra didn't know where her sister had gone that night, but she hadn't stayed here.

She scanned the sandstone buildings. "Someone was in our villa before we arrived yesterday. Any idea who it was?"

Elijah stalked past her, opening the pool gate. "No idea. This place was pandemonium last week. Camera crews, publicists—"

"Camera crews? Why?"

He shrugged. "They did some photoshoot here with Fitzy and Louis to promote the new season. Ranielle, too. But as far as I know, the only people who went into your villa were the cleaning crew."

"Something tells me the cleaning crew didn't leave behind a bloody cow heart."

"A *what*?"

"It had a note stuck in it." She paused, because Ranielle wasn't the only one who could do drama. "It said: *We get what we deserve.*"

Elijah's eyes widened. "You're kidding."

"I thought maybe it was another competitor." Sierra eyed the security cameras. "Did someone get in early? Trying to put me off my game?"

"No one even knew you were going to be here. You're the season's big shock factor. Maybe the producers were messing with you."

"Or maybe it was *you*. Are you worried that if I stick around, I might stumble onto some secrets you'd rather keep hidden?"

A muscle jumped in Elijah's jaw. "Nice deflection, Sierra. We all know you did it."

"I was never the only suspect. Vera hated her."

"Vera hates everyone."

Elijah finally walked out of the gate, slamming it shut on her. She wrenched up the latch and hurried after him.

"Alicia was seeing someone," she said to his back.

His reaction did not disappoint. The shoulders bunching toward his ears. The hands curling into fists.

He liked to pretend he was so calm, so grounded, so balanced.

Sierra knew better.

"That's a lie," he said quietly.

She matched his pace. "No, it's not, and I think you know it. All those times she disappeared, or came in late to the studio, smelling like high-end perfume, and practically *glowing* . . ."

"She wasn't," he said, more intensely now. "She wasn't that kind of girl."

Sierra lifted an eyebrow. "What kind of girl, exactly? The kind who flirts? The kind who dates people who aren't you?" She lowered her voice to a whisper. "The kind of girl who *gets what she deserves*?"

For a moment, she thought his anger might overcome him. She could see it simmering, simmering . . .

But then he stopped walking and took a long, slow breath. When he looked at Sierra again, his composure had returned. "I could never have hurt Alicia."

"Do you know who she was seeing?"

His jaw remained firmly shut.

"Right," she said. "Well. Thanks for nothing, I guess."

She turned on her heel and strode away. She'd lied—he hadn't given her *nothing*. Elijah had been in possession of her villa's keys the entire time. If he was telling the truth and he hadn't let any of the crew inside, either there was another set of keys somewhere, or he'd written the threatening note himself.

Sierra had managed to steer clear of her team all morning, but she had no chance avoiding them on the shuttle bus to the studio. Beck marched down the aisle and sat beside her on the back bench.

"Oh goody," she said.

There was a determined shine to his eyes. "We haven't had a chance to talk."

"That was on purpose."

"I saw your welcome bag in the garbage, so I'm assuming it's okay if I keep the coffee mug? Thought I'd give the matching set to my parents for their anniversary."

She glared at him.

"Excellent," he said. "Thanks. Also, the rest of us decided to let you be team captain."

"That wasn't open for discussion."

"But a team captain has to lead, so at some point you're going to have to, you know, talk to us."

Carter was stealing glances at them from the middle row. When she saw Sierra looking, she spun away again. Adi, in the seat across from her, was pretending to read a book, but Sierra could tell he was paying more attention than it appeared.

"I'll talk to you during the round," Sierra said to Beck.

"We'd work better as a team if we got to know each other."

Sierra ground her teeth. He had a point, but she didn't want to concede.

"As for the team name," he went on, opening the Notes app on his phone, "Carter and I were brainstorming, and we have a few ideas—"

"Team Helsing."

Beck looked up from his screen. "What?"

"Or Van Helsing. I'll let you decide." There. Some generosity for the group.

"Hel—" Beck's eyes cleared. "Like the vampire hunter?"

"You *are* a smart one."

"But isn't . . . ?" Beck closed his phone, glancing around to make sure none of the nearby contestants were listening. "Isn't that . . . ?"

"A reference to the room my sister was found dead in? Yeah." Sierra bared her teeth in a smile. "The producers will eat it up."

"I don't think—"

"Listen. I know how this works. They want drama. Outrage. That's why they brought me back. So let's give them what they want."

"You don't seem like the type to give people what they want."

"Are you kidding? You think I'm *accidentally* creating scandal?" She lowered her voice so Beck had to crane closer to hear. "And if we provide it, what might the producers do to keep us playing?"

Beck's expression slowly shifted. From confusion to comprehension to stubborn disbelief. "They wouldn't rig the game."

"It's a reality show, not reality. We're their puppets. So dance, little Pinocchio, and maybe they'll keep us on the strings long enough to get that cash. That's what you want, isn't it?"

A beat.

"Yeah. Obviously."

The hesitation was interesting.

What did Beck want besides the cash?

His expression changed again, into one of curiosity. "So then . . ." He gestured to her. "How much of this is an act?"

"Fuck off, Pinocchio."

"Okay, for the record, I'm clearly Geppetto. But, like, way younger and hotter."

She bit her tongue, hard, to keep her lips from twitching. "Go. Away."

"Right-o, leader of Team Helsing." He began to swing off his seat, then paused and leaned back, adding, "It flows better without the 'Van.'"

Sierra watched him trot down the aisle before turning her gaze toward the window. Everyone was going to lose their minds when they heard the team name. *How appalling! Distasteful! Disrespectful to her sister's memory!*

There'd be such an outcry, perhaps no one would pick up on the fact that Van Helsing was more than a callback to last season's finale.

It was the name of the one who'd slain the monster.

12
Adi

Adi's phone buzzed multiple times in his jeans pocket while his team waited backstage for filming. He checked the messages.

Symphony: Talked to the tow company. Evidently my entitled, ungrateful son thought he could leave my baby illegally parked.

Symphony: What the hell is wrong with you?

Symphony: You're lucky the tow truck driver was a fan.

Symphony: But you're paying me back for the parking ticket.

Symphony: Are you getting these? Don't ignore me, Aditya Parvesh. I made you and I can unmake you!

Whoa. It had been a long time since she pulled out that particular threat. Adi switched his phone to Do Not Disturb as the teams were called on stage.

On television, the studio backdrop where the eliminations were filmed had a moody, steampunk-inspired vibe. Drapes of burgundy fabric, enormous brass gears like the inner workings of a clock, intricate keys and padlocks hanging like chandeliers from rustic metal pipes.

But in real life, the effect was underwhelming. As an intern set the teams up on a series of two-step risers, Adi saw the dust gathered in the folds of the curtains, the bits of glue and scaffolding barely holding everything together.

His team had been put on the final riser, stage left, farthest from where Fitzy was getting accosted with powder brushes and hair spray. Adi and Sierra—with her enormous boots—stood on the second riser, towering over Carter and Beck in the front.

"Oh my god," Carter whispered as they waited for filming to begin. "I'm so nervous."

She was in a white off-the-shoulder knitted top and black leather pants, totally different from the Mathletes sweatshirt she'd been wearing around the villas. The nerdy glasses were back on, too. The swing in her personality was dizzying and, honestly, a bit annoying. No one else was trying so hard in front of the cameras.

"They're just handing out the snags," Adi said. "No one's getting eliminated."

"I know that." She peeked at him over her bare shoulder. "It's still terrifying. What if I get turned into a meme?"

Adi lifted an eyebrow. "*That's* what you're afraid of?" He'd assumed she'd be desperate for attention.

"Being immortalized on the internet for one embarrassing facial expression or ridiculous comment? Yeah, of course I am. Aren't you?"

Ah. So she couldn't handle criticism.

"That's funny," said Beck. "Being turned into a meme is pretty much my life's ambition."

"Been there, done that," said Sierra.

They looked at her, and it took Adi a moment to remember the memes he'd seen on the Domain's forums when he'd been researching the show. Jokes about Wednesday Addams. Jokes about goth girlfriends. Jokes about murder.

Adi studied her expression as she stared straight ahead, but it was hard to tell under the thick makeup whether she was sorry, embarrassed, proud, or something else.

The answer would depend on whether she regretted killing her sister. And that, of course, depended on why she did it in the first place.

Adi had read enough books to know the most common motives for murder: jealousy, love, revenge, fear.

Money.

Sierra seemed pretty hell-bent on that cash prize. But surely it was easier to win a round of the show than murder someone.

Fitzy hopped onto the stage, composed, as the director called for action. His sleeves were rolled up, the top buttons of his shirt undone, playing to the fans who cared more about his charisma than any of the Game Master's puzzles. "It's time to get to know this season's roster of brainiacs!"

Fitzy approached Jarius's team first. They chatted about the snag round—the elements in the jars, the Dmitri Mendeleev quote, the padlock numbers coming from the periodic table of elements.

That damn periodic table. Adi still couldn't shake the feeling he was missing something.

Jarius claimed the role of team leader, and they'd indeed gone with Dread as their team name. Predictable.

Fitzy moved to the next team. Nadia was chosen as the leader. Their name: Mind Hack.

After that, a team full of people Adi hadn't bothered to meet yet called themselves the Crown Jewels. Then there was Team Illuminati.

Finally, Fitzy approached Adi's riser. "Our last team consists of Aditya Parvesh, Beck Matheson, the lovely Carter Kelly"—he turned to the camera—"though that's *Kick It Carter* to you. And for the first time in *Escape Game* history, the return of a past contestant . . . the one, the only . . . Alicia Ange—oh!" Fitzy's eyes widened. There was a second in which he stared, speechless, into the camera lens. "I mean, Sierra—"

"Cut!" yelled the director in their earpieces.

"I'm sorry," Fitzy said. "It just came out. I didn't mean . . ." He turned to Sierra with a wince. "I'm so sorry."

"Speak her name two more times, Fitzy," Sierra said, deadpan. "They say it'll bring her back from beyond the grave." She wiggled her fingers like a witch over a cauldron.

Beck edged away.

The director ordered Fitzy to start at the top with their introductions.

Sending one more uncomfortable glance at Sierra, Fitzy tried to regain his composure as the cameras started filming again. But this time, Adi didn't hear their introductions. He stared into midair, the gears in his brain turning faster than the giant fake ones behind him.

Alicia Angelos.

Alicia Angelos.

He pictured the letters from the periodic table that had been swirling in his brain for twenty-four hours.

Li Si O Ca Ne Ag Al.

He watched the invisible letters rearrange themselves.

ALICIA ANGELOS.

"It wasn't a word," he whispered. "It was a name."

Carter glanced back at him.

"So, Sierra," said Fitzy, rocking back on his heels, "is this season about redemption for you?"

"Redemption can bite me," said Sierra, and the vitriol in her tone shook Adi from his daze. "This season is about winning."

"I've missed your spirit," said Fitzy, seemingly genuine. "If you're in it to win it this time, who's the leader that's going to take your team to the finale?"

"I am, obviously," said Sierra.

Carter tensed, almost imperceptibly. Her mouth puckered as if she tasted something sour and, a moment later, smoothed out. So fast even the editors weren't likely to pick up on it.

But Adi did.

She was a big-time Solve Specialist. He hadn't even thought to ask if she wanted to be leader—just agreed when Beck suggested Sierra. No pissing off the psychopath. It was a smart play.

But Carter must've been irked to be shoved out of the limelight.

"So let's hear it," said Fitzy. "What's your team name?"

Sierra leaned closer to the microphone and said in an ominous voice, "Helsing."

"Helsing? Sounds . . . familiar. Where do I know that from?"

Adi scoffed quietly as Sierra drawled, "People who have the slightest knowledge of classic literature will recognize the name from Bram Stoker's *Dracula*. But *Escape Game* fans will appreciate that we drew inspiration from a certain vampire-themed room. Season four. The finale."

Fitzy's eyebrows shot upward.

"Roll with it," said the director's voice in their earpieces.

Fitzy made a sound that was part cough, part laugh. "All right, Team . . . *Helsing*. Great. So now that we've met our teams, let's see how they did in the snag round."

Footage played on a large screen, a montage of the five teams in their colorful lab coats and significant moments from the round interspersed with "getting to know you" snippets they'd filmed in their greenlights. Adi watched the teams solve the puzzle for their combination locks, kicking himself for not realizing sooner that the abbreviations spelled out Alicia's name.

The footage ended and the lights came back up. It was impossible to tell how the teams had fared. The editors were good at their jobs.

"Wow," said Fitzy. "That snag round was a real sizzler, wasn't it?" He beamed. "Sizzler? Get it? Because 'snags' is an Aussie word for 'sausages'?" When a few of the contestants groaned, he waved his arm at them. "That joke gets funnier every season." Then he faced the cameras. "Let's find out who'll be entering into round one with some coveted snags, and who's about to be at a severe disadvantage."

A scoreboard appeared on the giant screen, listing the new team names, each with a zeroed-out clock to their right.

"The first snag of season five," continued Fitzy, "will be awarded to the team who was fastest in figuring out the quote."

The words "No one nor anything can silence me. —Dmitri Mendeleev" appeared on the screen, and the clocks began to tick upward—numbers blinking and flashing, until . . .

"Team Mind Hack!" shouted Fitzy.

Nadia whooped, pulling her teammates in for a hug.

"Having worked out the quote a full thirty-seven seconds faster than the second-fastest team," continued Fitzy, "you will receive the chance to add thirty-seven seconds to an opponent's final time during a round of your choice."

Adi kept his gaze on the board, ignoring the looks burning into him from his teammates. Yeah, he *knew* he had held them up for that puzzle. There was nothing he could do about it now.

"Next, let's see which team first put together the element numbers from the periodic table."

The clocks on the board ticked again, this time landing on—

"Team Dread!"

Adi could hear Carter take in a long, slow breath in front of him.

"For this victory, you can add an error penalty to any opponent's escape room. If they make a mistake during the round, they'll gain one whole minute on their final time."

Team Dread shoved each other on the shoulders. Gabriela flashed a peace sign at the other teams, while Delphi raised her middle finger—to which the director barked into their earpieces to knock it off; this was a family show.

"Our third snag," Fitzy went on, "will go to the team who made it out of their storage closets the fastest. Who was it?"

Adi had a bad feeling about this . . . which was confirmed when Fitzy shouted, "Team Dread again! Your second snag can be used to plunge an opposing team into pitch blackness for one full minute during a round."

"It's okay," Beck whispered. "We're still good."

Sierra gave a bitter laugh. "We sucked."

Adi kept his gaze on the scoreboard. Come on. *Come on.*

"Our fourth snag," said Fitzy, "is for the team that solved the room's final puzzle and correctly completed Dr. Adam Theery's colorful formula in the shortest amount of time. That team is . . . Helsing!"

Adi's spine straightened.

Beck cheered. "I knew that kid's chemistry set I had would be worth more than making slime someday."

"You didn't actually do any chemistry," Adi pointed out.

"Okay, that watercolor set then."

"Your snag," said Fitzy, "will grant you the power to force two members of an opposing team to start their round wearing . . . handcuffs! Although, our Game Master might hide a couple of keys for them to find."

"Oh, that's a good one," said Carter. "They've been doing the handcuff snag since the first season. Probably the best thing to come out of that season, actually. The puzzles themselves were pretty meh back then, but this can make or break a team."

Adi didn't want to admit it, but in that moment, he was grateful for Beck and his watercolor set, too.

"And now," said Fitzy, "it's time for our final snag—this one to be awarded to the team with the fastest overall time."

The clocks began to tick again. The team names shifted up and down.

It felt like hours passed before the ticking slowed, the team names stopped, and the results were revealed.

1.	Dread	19:46
2.	Mind Hack	21:02
3.	The Illuminati	22:17
4.	The Crown Jewels	22:58
5.	Helsing	24:09

Adi's chest tightened. After the elation of winning a snag, it was like being struck in the gut all over again.

Last place. A screwup that almost cost his team everything.

He couldn't impress his father if they failed.

"But wait," said Fitzy. "We need to make one correction." He turned toward the teams, his face tight with sympathy. "Crown Jewels, you failed to guess Dr. Theery's formula correctly, which means that while your time was faster than Team Helsing, you technically . . . did not escape."

The scoreboard changed, crossing out the Crown Jewels' time and replacing it with the words, bolded, **DID NOT ESCAPE.**

The scores rearranged, putting Helsing in fourth. The Crown Jewels looked disappointed but stoic. "Not a problem," said their leader, Emma. "We're warmed up now and ready for the next round. As long as it doesn't involve chemistry."

Fitzy chuckled. "I've got no idea what the Game Master's going to throw at you next, but one thing I do know—it's going to be a blast watching you puzzle your way through it." He turned to the main camera. "That makes Team Dread our big winner for the snag round. For being the fastest team to escape the laboratory, you can choose which member of a competing team must complete the semifinal's infamous dexterity challenge!"

"Damn," muttered Sierra. "That'd be a good one to have."

"They'd all be good to have," said Adi.

"One is better than nothing," said Beck. "And we didn't come in last place."

"On a technicality," said both Carter and Adi in unison. They glanced at each other in surprise.

"It doesn't matter," said Sierra. "We don't need the snags. We just need to be better."

Adi smirked. "And here I was starting to think you didn't know how to give a decent pep talk."

13

Carter

"But I don't *want* to go to a party," said Carter, unable to fully eliminate the whine from her voice. "Can't we go back to the villa?"

"Hear, hear," said Sierra, leaning against the dressing room wall. "Let's blow this joint and go get wasted."

Carter shot her a bewildered look. "That's not what I said."

"I improved upon your suggestion."

An intern knocked at the door. "Limo's waiting."

"A limo!" said Beck, hopping off the counter.

Carter groaned. No one, in all the Domain posts, had ever mentioned there being a season kickoff party for the cast and crew.

She did not like parties. Parties came with expectations. You had to mingle. You had to be pleasant and interesting and make scintillating conversation.

Essentially, you had to be . . . not Carter.

Plus, she hadn't been given a chance to change back into her normal clothes, and she could barely breathe in the leather pants they'd put her in.

But no one seemed interested in her discomfort—physical or emotional—and soon they were out in front of the studio, filing into a stretch limousine. She climbed into the back seat and her heart sank.

Team Dread grinned at them from the other side of the limo.

"Sweet, sharing a ride with Kick It Carter," said Jarius, crossing his legs at the ankles. "Or should I say, Totally-Choked-in-the-First-Round Carter?" He guffawed, but even his teammates seemed annoyed by his terrible humor.

Carter smiled wanly, avoiding the stare of Neil—the jerk who had quizzed her on inane math equations.

"You cleaned up in the snag round," Carter said, because being nice was her default when she felt like prey. Be nice enough, and maybe they wouldn't want to eat her alive. "Congratulations."

Pink-haired Delphi smacked her bubble gum. She was still wearing sunglasses, even in the dim glow of the car's blue LED lights. "The Game Master was going easy on us. Hope he tries harder for the next round, or this competition is going to be a breeze."

"Don't tease, Delphi," said Gabriela, with her supermodel smirk as she let her gaze travel slowly over Beck, Carter, and Adi. "It seems that some of our competitors actually found the room to be a little . . . challenging." She pouted dramatically and turned her focus to Sierra. "Best stick to plotting murders, goth girl."

Sierra threw her arms over the back of the seat. "Don't worry. I am."

Gabriela muttered something in Delphi's ear. The two giggled cruelly, and just like that Carter was back in school, enthusiastically raising her hand to answer the teachers' questions while the girls in the back row laughed together.

"Is that your natural hair color?" asked Jarius. It took Carter a moment to realize he was talking to her. "I've heard red hair is good luck. Don't suppose you'd let me pet you for a while?"

Gross wink.

Carter stared at him, disgusted, even as she could feel her cheeks flaming.

"Go ahead," Sierra answered for her. "I've been looking for an excuse to put a ballpoint pen through someone's eyeball."

Adi gave a soft snort.

"Feisty," said Jarius. "It's nice to see that wasn't just for the cameras."

Another wink.

Beck leaned forward. "Is there something in your eye? You keep doing this creepy winking thing."

"I'm just making small talk," said Jarius, clearly enjoying how easily he could annoy them. "Might as well get to know each other."

"Don't waste your time, Jarius," said Gabriela. "They'll be the first to be sent home."

Delphi snapped her gum. "It's obvious who does and doesn't belong here."

"Gotta agree," said Jarius. "Carter, you're such a badass online! But in person, I dunno . . . you strike me as . . ." He shrugged. "A little soft. No offense."

"Yeah, bet you know all about going soft," said Adi, raising his eyebrows. "No offense."

Carter's heart drummed. She wanted to defend herself, but how could she? They were right. Watching the clips from the snag round had proven how inadequate she was. All her supposed Solve Specialist skills had evaporated the moment she was locked in that room.

"What do you think it takes to stay in the show?" said Beck. "You know, if we're so lacking."

"An IQ somewhere above the average dalmatian?" suggested Gabriela.

Beck frowned. "Actually, dalmatians are really—"

"Don't," said Sierra. "Don't say smart."

Beck's mouth twisted.

"Naw, you know what it is?" said Jarius. "More than problem-solving, or teamwork, or any of that crap? You gotta want it. You gotta want it so bad you'd do anything to win. Whatever it takes to get your hands on that prize money. One. Million. Bones."

"I mean," said Carter, "I'm pretty sure it also has something to do with teamwork and problem-solving."

Jarius grinned. "Guess we'll find out, won't we?"

The producers had booked an entire restaurant to host the season kickoff party—one of those hip places that charged twenty dollars for a ginseng-infused mocktail and cared more about Instagram-mable decor than good food. Servers in sequined suspenders passed by with trays of tiny hors d'oeuvres, though most of the guests were crowded around a marble bar at the back of the room, everything backlit in red neon.

The party was hopping when they arrived. The crew members who'd left the set early were clumped together in small groups throughout the restaurant. Carter spotted Elijah and Lisa, their RAs from the villas. She hadn't had a chance to talk to Elijah yet, but at some point she should probably ask him for a one-on-one interview for her channel.

She glanced back, tempted to ask Sierra about last season's party and if the contestants were expected to do anything, but Sierra had already disappeared. Carter frowned. Was leaving an option?

Vera, the social media manager with the lurid eye shadow, approached the group. "What am I supposed to do, post pictures of our teams cowering in the doorway?" She gestured toward the room. "Spread out. *Mingle.*" She said it like it was a bad word.

Carter stepped farther into the room, glad when Beck hovered close to her side. Adi wasted no time in heading for a booth in the corner and pulling out a book from his backpack. *Darn it.* Why hadn't she thought to bring a book?

"What are we supposed to do, exactly?" said Beck. "Schmooze?"

"I'm not very good at schmoozing," Carter admitted.

"Then stick with me."

Carter made a suction-cup noise as she grabbed his arm. "Okay. I'm stuck to you now."

Beck laughed. "First rule of schmoozing: always have a beverage. That way, you're ready to do a spit-take whenever you hear something scandalous."

"How many scandalous things are you expecting to hear?"

"In Hollywood? Tons."

They headed to the bar. But the moment the bartender put up their drinks—root beer for Beck, pineapple juice for Carter—Vera popped back into view, a little too close for comfort. "You. I need an interview about that thing you did with the colored beakers."

"I already did the post-round with Fitzy."

"That's for the show. This is for socials. Come with me." She stalked off.

Beck waved regretfully at Carter before following Vera to what looked like a legit old phone booth in the corner, covered in long strands of tinsel and enormous faux flowers.

Trying not to feel abandoned, Carter took a long drink while digging her phone out of her handbag. She might not know anyone here, but her hundreds of thousands of followers would love to be at this party.

Her thumb hovered over the record button. On the screen, her own uncertain eyes stared back at her. It was a moment of truth. The avatar version of herself would've jumped right in, knowing exactly what to say and how to say it. She would be fun. Smart. Vivacious.

"Be Kick It Carter," she whispered. "You can do this."

She didn't know if she believed that, but she forced herself to tap the button anyway.

"Hey, Clue Masters!" Her voice squeaked. She coughed and almost stopped the video to start over, but she worried that if she did that, she wouldn't have the guts to hit record again. She gripped her smile and kept going. "Kick It Carter here, and you're going to flip when you see where I am right now." She turned the phone around to scan the swanky restaurant before turning it back on herself. "*The Escape Game*'s season five kickoff party! Everyone, and I do mean everyone, is here."

So far, so good. She began to feel like she was channeling her online persona as she zoomed in on various members of the cast. "All twenty contestants from this season are hanging out and celebrating how we did in the snag round. Oh, you want to know how *my* team did?" She paused, tempted to spill the truth here and now. *My greatest contribution was proving I know how to look things up in an index. Go me!* It would be like ripping off the Band-Aid. If she hadn't signed that NDA, she might have done it, too. Instead, she shrugged at the camera. "You're going to have to wait for the episode to land this Sunday night. Oh, look! It's the Game Master!"

Louis Augustus Russell was at the bar, talking to Gabriela from Team Dread and Emma from Crown Jewels. As Carter framed them in the shot, Gabriela tossed her hair off her shoulder and let out a laugh, while Louis pulled his newsboy cap down over his face as if to hide his own laughter.

A pang of envy hit Carter in the stomach. What she wouldn't give to be sitting there, laughing at whatever brilliant thing Louis had said. Some people made it look so easy, like they weren't agonizing over every word.

She blew out a breath and refocused the camera on Adi ordering a drink at the bar. "There's my teammate, Adi Parvesh. He's"—she hesitated, searching for the right word to describe him to her followers, but all that came to her was *aloof*—"even more gorgeous in person. Just wait, Clue Masters. I guarantee there's going to be a lot of swooning this season."

She lifted her drink in a mock toast, then cringed at how cheesy that was. She would definitely be editing that part out.

An arm dropped around her shoulders, startling her so much that some of the drink sloshed onto her hand.

"Hey, Carter! Whatcha doin'?"

She looked at her phone screen, wide-eyed. Her avatar would have squealed like an anime schoolgirl, but Carter couldn't bring herself to do it.

"Fitzy! Hi! Um. You know, recording a little behind-the-scenes footage for our favorite fandom. Do you want to say hello?"

"Heck yeah, I want to say hello!" To Carter's surprise, he took the phone away from her so he could speak directly into the camera. Doubly to her surprise, he didn't take his arm off her shoulders. "What's happening, Clue Masters? You're hearing it here first—the other teams need to bring their A game if they have any hope of beating this genius right here." He tipped his head closer to Carter's, framing them both in the video. "I'm contractually obligated not to show bias toward our contestants, but . . ." He made a humorously pained face. "I am *so biased*. All right, I better not say any more, or I'm going to be in breach of, like, a really scary contract. Point is, I can't wait to watch this superstar do her thing in the next round."

Warmth flooded Carter from her curly red hair all the way to the tips of her fingers.

"Th-thanks, Fitzy. I guess we'll see."

"This girl is way too humble," he said into the camera, clicking his tongue. "Now, if your doting fans don't mind . . . could I borrow you for a minute? Off the record?"

Gloriously relieved to have a reason to stop filming, Carter attempted to look apologetic. "I can't say no to that. This is Kick It Carter, and I'll be bringing you more behind-the-scenes looks throughout the season. As long as I don't get eliminated." With one last half-panicked smile that she hoped came off as more silly than legitimately terrified, she stopped the recording and put her phone away.

"Thanks," she said. "I guarantee that's going to be my most-viewed video of all time." She started to lick her spilled drink from the back of her hand before realizing that it was probably a weird thing to do in public.

If Fitzy was judging her lack of swanky-bar etiquette, it didn't show. "Happy to be of service. Sorry for startling you earlier. Can I get you another drink? What are you having—screwdriver?"

She flushed, not entirely sure what that was, but it definitely sounded alcoholic. And strangely euphemistic. "It's pineapple juice. I'm underage."

His dimples appeared, and she realized with a grimace—

"Right. We all are. Obviously."

"Yeah, I was joking. Ranielle's pretty strict with the no-drinking policy."

She smiled, more than a little distracted by the warmth of his hand on her upper arm, the clean scent of his shirt, like laundry detergent but . . . sexier?

Oh *god.*

Nope. No way was she going to be one of those girls crushing on the dopey surfer-boy host. Carter was into the intellectual aspects of *The Escape Game*. The clues, the puzzles, the red herrings. She was a Solve Specialist, not some groupie.

"So . . . one pineapple juice? Coming up?" Fitzy prompted, and Carter realized she'd been staring awkwardly.

"Oh! Yeah. Sure. That'd be great. Thanks."

She lingered behind while he took her empty glass to the bar and placed a new order. He reappeared minutes later, holding Carter's drink and an orange soda for himself. "Look, I wanted to apologize," he said, handing her the drink. "I heard what happened in Louis's office the other day."

At the reminder, Carter shrank back and took another gulp.

"I really didn't think Ranielle would flip out like that," he continued. "I thought she'd see it as a good thing. Why did she pick you as a contestant if she didn't want fan videos, right? But—whatever. The point is, I messed up, and as soon as I heard, I went straight to Ranielle's office and told her it was my idea." He hesitated. "I really am sorry. I didn't mean to get you in trouble."

"It's okay. I signed the NDA. I knew I wasn't supposed to interview the Game Master without permission."

"So . . . am I forgiven?"

"There's nothing to forgive."

Fitzy let out a relieved breath, then clinked their glasses together. "Here's to Team Helsing."

"You really *are* biased."

She meant it as a joke, but Fitzy appeared troubled by the comment. "Unfortunately, I wasn't joking about that scary contract." He hastily pulled his arm off Carter's shoulder. "We're not supposed to canoodle with the contestants, either."

Canoodle. Funny choice of word. Carter would've teased him for it if he hadn't looked so uneasy.

"You're just being nice. Surely the producers can't fault you for that."

He met her gaze. It took him a long time to respond. But when he finally opened his mouth—

"Carter! There you are."

Sierra appeared, black-coated lips twisted into a scowl as she grabbed Carter's arm and pulled her away so quickly that some of Carter's drink sloshed onto her wrist—again.

"I need you," Sierra said, throwing a half-hearted wave over her shoulder at Fitzy. "Go pester another contestant."

"Great seeing you, too, Sierra!" he shouted after them.

"What's going on?" said Carter.

"A friendly PSA." Sierra wheeled on Carter. "Fitzy's trouble. As your team leader, I'm ordering you to stay away from him."

Carter blinked. "Excuse me?"

"You heard me. If I catch you flirting with him again, so help me—getting murdered in your sleep is going to be the least of your worries."

14

Beck

"What do you think of your team?" asked Vera. She had her smartphone propped up on a tripod and was looking into the screen, not at Beck, and he wasn't entirely sure how she could make such an innocuous question sound like a threat.

"Oh—they're great," he said instinctively. But then, after pausing to consider it for a moment, he felt it was close enough to the truth. "Carter's a dynamo in the fandom, and incredible at math. Adi's obviously the cool one, and he seems to be into anagrams and word puzzles. And Sierra . . ." He glanced past Vera's shoulder to where he could see Carter and Sierra together. "She's the only contestant who's been here before. She knows what to expect from the game. Anyone who watched last season knows how brilliant she is."

He figured this wasn't the time or place to point out that Sierra was still under investigation for murder. It also wasn't the time or place to point out that being in a room with Sierra was like trying to decode one of the Game Master's clues. He could tell she was hiding something. But was that *something* a soft, squishy interior that longed to be loved and understood? Or was that *something* the fact that she was a psychopath who could at any minute start stabbing people with tiny olive forks, like the one she was holding now?

Wait—where had she gotten an olive fork?

Vera cleared her throat.

Beck jumped. It was hard to concentrate in here. There were too many sounds and, consequently, a horrendous buffet going on in his mouth. The cocktail shakers tasted like Coca-Cola and shaved ice. The buzz of conversations was like chewing on grass. Vera's voice was tart, like cranberries.

He struggled to remember her question. "Er . . . yeah. We're getting along great."

Vera made an exaggerated show of falling asleep. "Are you always such a Gary Stu, or are you playing nice for the cameras?"

"What does that mean?"

"Never mind. Helsing was an interesting choice for your team name."

"It was Sierra's idea."

"How do you think it would feel, finding your sister dead in a coffin?"

His mouth opened and closed a couple of times. "I . . . don't have a sister."

Vera stared at him.

"I've got a cousin I'm pretty close to. Does that count?"

Still no response.

"Are we even allowed to talk about this?"

"It's a free country," said Vera. "Freedom of speech or whatever."

"Yeah, but—"

"Someone got away with murder last year. The police still aren't sure how they did it. It would have taken a criminal mastermind to pull it off, and here we are, surrounded by"—she took the phone off the tripod and swiveled it to show the crowded restaurant—"actual masterminds." She turned the camera back to Beck. "What do you think?"

"I—I don't know," Beck stammered, his hands getting clammy beneath Vera's intense stare.

"Do you think Sierra could have pulled off something like that?"

"Um."

Vera's left eye began to twitch, the movement more noticeable with the fluorescent blue eyeliner. "She has a reputation for running her mouth at every opportunity. Has she let something slip?"

"I really don't . . ." He looked at Sierra again as she stole a cherry out of Carter's glass and popped it into her mouth. "She's my teammate. I'm trying to give her the benefit of the doubt."

"So you think she's innocent?"

"I don't know what I think. Look, are you okay? You seem stressed."

This only made her angrier. "You referred to Adi as *the cool one.* Do you think the producers are setting him up to be this season's dreamboat?"

"Dreamboat? This isn't the type of show for that."

"Isn't it?" She flicked at her single dangly earring. "It must be tough. Adi's hot. Carter's got the followers. Sierra's already infamous. And you are . . . no one." She clicked her tongue. "I bet you wish you could knock the popular ones down a peg or two."

"Not . . . really," said Beck.

"Oh, come on," said Vera. "A little cosmic justice would be nice now and then."

It would. Beck could think of a few people who deserved cosmic justice. But he refused to take the bait, and instead grinned into the camera. "I'll leave cosmic justice to the universe. I'm just here to solve some puzzles."

"Vera terrifies me," Beck said, sidling up to Sierra and Carter. Carter looked relieved to see him.

"Tell me about it," she said. "She's so . . ."

"Morose? Surly? Churlish?" Beck supplied.

Carter laughed. "All of the above."

"You say these things like they're insults," Sierra muttered.

"Is she new?" Carter asked.

Sierra shook her head. "She's been around for a while. Since, like, the second season, when the show was still on YouTube. I think she was in high school at the time. Pretty sure she's related to one of the higher-ups. Nepotism is big in Hollywood."

"Why make her the social media manager?" asked Carter. "She doesn't seem happy doing it, and there are loads of people on the Domain who would love to have that job."

"Like you?" said Sierra.

"That's not what I meant." Carter hesitated. "But, I mean . . . I think I could do it better than her."

Sierra made an unconvinced noise in her throat. "The show has a huge following on their socials, so she must be doing something right."

"I'm thirsty," said Beck, his root beer long gone. "Anyone want to head to the bar with me?"

Carter frowned and looked around. "Actually, I had a . . . Oh, there." She grabbed a glass half-full of juice that was sitting on a nearby table and quickly sucked the rest up through the straw, before shaking what was left of the ice. The sound made Beck's teeth go cold. "I'd love another."

Beck expected Sierra to disappear again and was surprised when she followed them to the line. Her spine was taut, her attention roving the room, scoping out the cast, the crew, the other contestants.

Beck followed her gaze. The entirety of Team Dread were at the bar, posing for a photo with Fitzy and Louis, while Vera kept barking at Jarius to stop making lewd hand gestures every time he was on camera.

Classy.

Adi appeared seconds later, clutching a fizzy yellowish drink and sliding his way into the group like he'd been there all along.

"What are you drinking?" said Beck. "You know if we're caught with alcohol—"

"Relax, it's Mountain Dew. Listen. We need to talk about the periodic table in the snag round."

Sierra rolled her eyes. "Move on, Adi. There was no anagr—"

"Alicia Angelos."

The name sent a shock wave down Beck's spine.

Sierra inhaled sharply. "What?"

"It *was* an anagram, and it spelled your sister's name." Adi lifted an eyebrow. "Any thoughts on why that might be?"

For a brief moment, a crack appeared in Sierra's guarded expression. A hint of vulnerability. But as soon as Beck saw it, she covered it up again, growing even thornier than usual. "Why the hell would I know anything about that?"

"I thought maybe you told someone to plant it in the episode."

"Like who? The Game Master?" Sierra scoffed. "News flash, nobody liked me last season, and this season, they *really* hate me. If you're right about this, I guarantee it was intended as some sick joke to throw me off my game during the round."

"Maybe not," Beck mused, while Carter ordered another round of drinks. "Maybe it was intended as, like, a memorial. It pays homage to her as a contestant, not just a"—he cut off suddenly, but then gulped and finished—"a victim."

Sierra's eyes blazed. "No one here gives a shit about my sister or her memory."

"All right, fine," said Adi. "That couldn't have been an easy puzzle to orchestrate, with the numbers, the colors, the elements . . . It's an awful lot of work to mess with one contestant."

Sierra grunted. "All these people ever want to do is mess with us."

"You sound very cynical," said Carter, stumbling into Elijah as she reached past him to grab her juice. "Oops. Sorry."

Sierra glared at the back of Elijah's head. Then she glared at Carter. "Four weeks from now, you will be, too. If we last that long."

Carter opened her mouth to retort, but then her gaze slid past Adi and Sierra.

Beck followed the look.

Fitzy and the Game Master were talking with Delphi and Gabriela.

Gabriela had a martini glass in her hand—a mocktail? She tried to offer Fitzy a sip, but Louis scooped it up instead. He looked like he was giving Fitzy a hard time, although Fitzy took it in stride.

"I'm tired," Carter said, loudly and unprompted. She chugged her drink and left the glass on a nearby table. "When can we go?"

"Agreed," said Sierra. "We've paid our dues. Let's get out of here."

"Should we let someone know we're leaving?" asked Beck.

Sierra waved the question away. "They aren't our parents."

"Yeah," said Carter, taking a step toward the door. "Besides. We're responsible teenagers, and—" She lurched sideways, her shoulder colliding with Adi's chest.

Adi steadied her. "You okay?"

"Yep! Just fine!" Carter pulled away from him for a second, but then reached for his supporting arm. "Why is the room spinning?"

Beck traded looks with his other teammates, then glanced at Carter's abandoned glass. "How many of those have you had?"

Carter frowned at him, confused, then counted on her fingers. "Three? I think? But it's just pineapple juice." Her words were starting to slur. Her brow glistened.

Adi picked up her empty glass and gave it a sniff. "I think she may have grabbed the wrong drink. Have you had anything to eat tonight?"

"Not really. I don't eat much when I'm nervous . . . and I've been nervous, like, *all* day. Actually, if you must know, I pretty much exist as a big ball of tension. Better learn that now." She laughed.

"Would alcohol really hit her that fast?" said Beck.

"If it's strong enough," said Sierra, "and she doesn't have anything else in her system, and . . . I'm going to guess you haven't built up much of a tolerance?"

Carter giggled. "I had champagne at a wedding when I was eleven. Shhhhh. Don't tell anyone."

"We need to get her out of here."

"Yes, please," said Carter, an almost-whine in her voice. "Am I drunk? Is this what drunk feels like? Oh god, Ranielle Russell will *kill me*."

Adi took hold of Carter's arm to guide her through the crowd. Sierra led, clearing a path for them.

They were intercepted halfway across the restaurant by broad shoulders, a square jaw, and a cruel smirk. Jarius.

"Whoa," he said, eyeing Carter. "What's happening here? Is it my imagination, or is Kick It Carter inebriated?"

Carter glared. "That's *Kiss* It Carter to you, buddy. As in, you can kiss my—"

"Okay!" Adi shouted, and tried to shove past Jarius. "Fun times. Keep moving, Carter."

Jarius laughed and refused to budge. "Nice. I bet Hitflix will love to hear how one of their underage contestants got smashed at the kickoff party."

"I am not *smashed*." Carter yanked her arm away from Adi so she could jut a finger under Jarius's nose. "You know what? I have a finely tuned radar for bullies, and you are a bully! Which makes you . . ." She swallowed hard while she searched for the right word, finally landing on: "Not. Nice."

"Aw," said Jarius, "and here I thought we were getting along."

"Okay, Carter," said Beck, as they started to draw curious stares. He tried to coax her away. "Let's—"

"Where's my phone?" said Carter, fumbling to extract it from her handbag. "I need to take a video. The world needs to know he is . . . that Team Dread is . . ."

She didn't finish. Instead, she hiccuped, then pressed a hand to her mouth. A look of panic flashed across her eyes.

"Carter?" said Adi.

"Oh god," she moaned. Then she bent forward and spewed bright yellow pineapple juice all over Jarius.

15

Sierra

Sierra cracked a fourth egg into the pan and watched the goo turn white with a satisfying sizzle. On the other pan, strips of bacon cracked and snapped happily in oil.

"What is happening right now?" Beck said, stumbling out of his room bleary-eyed.

Sierra pointed her spatula at the popped toast. "Butter those."

He sleepily pulled a knife from the cutlery drawer and dug butter out of the fridge as Sierra flipped the bacon.

"Why are you making breakfast?"

"Because it's breakfast time. Sort of." The clock showed eleven.

"There's a dining hall full of food across the courtyard."

"Are you complaining?" Sierra snapped.

"No. Nope. Definitely not."

Sierra was in a bad mood, and she had no qualms taking it out on her teammates. They'd only scored one snag, while Team Dread had swept up three. That gave them far too many advantages. Seeing Carter puke all over Jarius might have helped Sierra feel better if she wasn't sure that something was off about the way that drink had hit Carter last night. It had happened too fast, and Carter had been completely out of it when the car brought them back to the villas. Something wasn't right.

Worst of all, Sierra hadn't had any opportunities to check out Elijah and Lisa's terrace. There was always someone around, and Elijah's window was right off the patio, so no hope of searching when he was asleep. The only time she'd managed to get out there while he and Lisa were at dinner, the gate had been locked.

She *needed* to get to that terrace.

"What's going on?" Adi appeared, hair freshly damp from the shower.

"Evidently Sierra is making us breakfast?" Beck said, with an exaggerated shrug.

Adi looked equally suspicious as he took in the scene. "Why are we not eating in the dining hall?"

"What? A leader can't make breakfast for her team?"

Adi stage-whispered to Beck, "Is she trying to poison us?"

But Beck, who had taken a bite of bacon, moaned giddily. "I dunno, but O-M-G, why does this taste so good?"

"I soaked it in maple syrup." Sierra smiled sweetly. "It covers the taste of the arsenic."

Beck stopped chewing. Then he shrugged and swallowed. "Worth it."

"Real talk," she said. "I don't trust the executive producers not to mess with the food. Like I told Beck before, some people got food poisoning right before last season's finale. I'd bet anything it was done on purpose. You know. For the *drama*." She danced her fingers along with the word.

"You sound paranoid," said Adi.

"My sister was left dead in a coffin, and you think I'm paranoid?"

"Fair point."

The boys took their plates to the dining table as Sierra headed down the corridor. She knocked on the bedroom door. "Carter?"

No answer.

Sierra opened up. Carter had been breathing through the night and continued to do so now. Sierra used her foot to nudge the trash can away from the bed—she'd put it there in case Carter needed to vomit again.

A croaky voice said from under the blanket, "I don't feel so good."

"I'm not surprised."

"What happened?"

Sierra pulled off the blanket. "We got a car back from the party. Hopefully before any executive producers caught wind of the incident."

Carter flung an arm over her eyes. Her hair was beginning to frizz out of the bonnet that Sierra had clumsily put on her last night. "What incident?"

"You threw up on Jarius."

"I—*what?*" Carter's arm flung away again. Her eyes were wide and slightly red.

"You remember Fitzy buying you a drink, right?" Sierra said darkly.

"Yes, but . . . not much after that. And it wasn't alcohol!" Carter rolled out of bed, staggering slightly, then pulled off her bonnet. "I swear."

"Come on." Sierra ushered her out the door, to the dining table where Beck and Adi were halfway through their eggs. "Sit. Eat."

"Ish sho good," Beck said through his bulging cheeks.

Carter sank unsteadily onto a seat. Sierra served her a plate and a cup of coffee.

"I don't understand," Carter said.

"Fitzy spiked your drink."

Adi and Beck stopped eating.

"It's obvious," she said, pouring herself the rest of the coffee. "He got you a drink and threw a pill in it."

"In a room full of people?" Adi said. "Someone would've seen him."

"Do you have any other ideas how her drink was spiked?"

"She had more than one drink last night," Beck said.

"I was with her the rest of the time."

"Yeah, but—"

"Fitzy wouldn't spike my drink," Carter said quietly. "He's not like that."

Sierra scoffed, leaning back on the kitchen counter as she sipped her coffee.

Carter frowned. "Why are you so against him?"

"Someone here killed Alicia."

"Yeah, *you*!" shouted Carter. But then she flinched and pressed a hand to her temple. "At least, we think so. Is that what we still think?" She looked to Beck and Adi for confirmation. Adi shrugged, and Beck ducked his head to shovel more food into his mouth. Carter groaned. "My head hurts."

"Eat," Sierra ordered, as there was a sharp knock on the front door. She glanced out the window, swore under her breath, and went to unlock it. "Hello, Ranielle."

Ranielle Russell, in a forest-green power suit, burst past her, a long, manicured fingernail pointing at Carter. *"You."*

Carter looked like a rabbit caught in a snare.

"Out," Ranielle said. "Pack your bags. You're gone."

"Hang on—" Adi started, half getting out of his chair.

"Sit down, or you're gone, too." Ranielle's knife-sharp glare returned to Carter. "We have rules on this show for a reason, and you think because you're a filthy little influencer you can break them?"

"I—I—didn't—" Carter's eyes were wet.

"Save it. You're done. Delete your account. Stay off social media." Ranielle's lips curved into a cruel smile. "You're going to want to, anyway, after the videos that have been posted."

Carter let out a horrified sob.

"Oh, come off the power trip," Sierra said, slamming the door shut. "She didn't touch any alcohol. Her drink was spiked. By *your* host."

At this, Ranielle's expression flickered. It was incredibly brief, but Sierra was watching for it. The uncertainty. The . . . panic?

Sierra added with a snarl, "If you take Carter out of the game, you can be sure it'll come out how dodgy your precious James Fitzgerald is."

"Fitzy?" Of all things, Ranielle laughed. Her tense posture relaxed. "Nice try, Sierra."

"He was the one who ordered her drink."

"Fitzy's under a stricter contract than you, and has way more to lose. Besides, the bar staff was told to watch everyone like a hawk. The last thing we need is more bad publicity." At this, Ranielle scoffed. "So much for that."

"Well, *someone* spiked Carter's drink," Beck said. "We were with her, and she definitely didn't have any alcohol."

Ranielle's fury wavered. She stared at Beck, but it was more with contemplation than fury. Sierra recognized that expression. Ranielle Russell was about to turn things in her favor.

"Are you saying," Ranielle said slowly, "that one of the other competitors tried to sabotage you?"

Beck looked alarmed. "I— No, I didn't mean—"

"A vicious attack on an opposing team." Ranielle practically breathed it. "A jealous rival desperate to win the cash—desperate enough to poison the fandom's beloved Kick It Carter."

"Beloved?" Adi said. "A second ago, you were calling her a filthy little influencer."

"That's show business," Ranielle said without a hint of remorse. "Carter, clean yourself up and shoot a video explaining what happened. No—better yet, stay a mess. Do it now, while those big brown eyes are still filled with tears. Really sell how violated you feel, and make sure you finish with a statement that you're going to win this season no matter what. Send it to me for review before you post."

Carter looked horrified. "If my parents find out, they'll freak."

"As will our viewers," said Ranielle, smirking. "What are you waiting for? Go!"

Carter pulled herself from the table and trudged back into the bedroom. Satisfied, Ranielle turned back toward the door, where Sierra was still standing.

"And you," she said. "Keep my crew out of it."

"I don't take orders from you, Ranielle."

"You do now, if you want that prize money. I can boot you from the show as quickly as I rubber-stamped your return." Ranielle Russell stalked to the door, leaning close before whispering, "And believe me, if I'd had my way, you wouldn't have been rubber-stamped at all."

"Please. I'm the best thing that could have happened to you this season. Watch the viewer numbers soar when the first episode drops this weekend."

"You are a liability and a huge pain in my neck. But Hitflix thought you'd make for great entertainment. 'The Sister Slayer, back for redemption, or back for revenge?'" She rolled her eyes, like such clickbait was beneath her, even though Sierra knew she lived for precisely that sort of manufactured drama. "But I'm warning you, Sierra. You want to be in the finale? Then you'd better play the game."

16

Adi

Adi fumbled with the combination lock. The symbols didn't make sense. They weren't numbers or letters, just squiggles. How was he supposed to escape the room if he couldn't read them?

"Come on!" Beck cried on his left. "Work it out, Adi!"

"What's taking so long?" barked Sierra. "We'd be better off without you."

Carter, in a short dress and knee-high boots, took off her glasses and wailed.

"It would be nice if you helped," he said through his teeth. He spun the combination lock, only to find the door was a coffin. The lid opened, and inside was a girl with golden, kinky hair and dark roots, her eyes milky white, a trickle of blood running down her nose—

BEEP BEEP BEEP

Red lights flashed. Time was up, he'd failed to escape—

BEEP BEEP BEEP

Adi's eyes snapped open. He wasn't in an escape room. He was in the villa.

Beck sat up in the bed across from Adi's. "Oh god. Ash," he muttered. *"Yuck."*

"Ash?" asked Adi.

"Nothing. What time is it?"

Adi's phone said four a.m.

"Shit." He flopped back onto the mattress. Monday. The first episode had dropped last night, and they'd stayed up late discussing how the editors had made them look. The final cut had amped up specific aspects of their personalities. Unsurprisingly, they'd framed Sierra as a ruthless antagonist, with Beck's chipper, can-do attitude as her foil. Carter, who'd been hyped as the season's puzzle-solving savant, came across lackluster. It probably helped sell her victim story better.

But it was how they portrayed Adi that confused him the most. Despite his fears, they hadn't made him the bumbling fool. Instead, one of the higher-ups had decided to omit the entire scene with him attempting to make an anagram. The way they zoomed in on his smile and overlaid his post-round comments during crucial aspects of the room made Adi think they were setting him up to be a main player in the show.

His relief at being portrayed in a good light wasn't enough to keep his brain from conjuring that terrible anxiety dream, but still, it was something to know the producers weren't already against for him. He needed his father to see him at his best.

Outside, beyond the incessant beeping, he heard other villa doors opening, contestants calling to one another.

"We should get up," said Beck, but neither of them moved until Carter pounded at their door.

Adi groaned and dragged himself out of bed. "It's probably a prank," he said, stepping into the hall to find Carter wrapping a cardigan around herself and slipping into a pair of flip-flops.

"Maybe," she said. "But we're still supposed to vacate the buildings."

"Says who?"

"Everyone. That's the entire point of fire alarms."

Ugh. Rule followers. She and Beck walked out. He sighed, trailing after them. "Where's Sierra?"

"She refused to come," said Carter. "She also thinks it's a prank. Or the producers messing with us."

Shaking his head, Adi turned around. "I'm going back to bed."

Carter grabbed him. "Ranielle Russell has already yelled at me twice. I'm not going to give her any more reasons to be mad at us."

He rolled his eyes but didn't argue.

Elijah and Lisa were doing a head count as the crowd gathered by the pool. All the contestants were in pajamas and bathrobes except Jarius, who strutted around in a pair of plaid boxer briefs, crushing an empty energy drink with one hand.

Maybe the fire alarm wasn't caused by the producers at all, but by *that* jackass.

No sooner had Adi thought it than that jackass started walking their way.

"Yo, Carter Kelly."

When she saw him, Carter threw her hands over her eyes. "Oh my god, Jarius, put on some clothes!"

"Can't," he said, jutting a thumb toward his villa. "Not allowed to go back in yet."

Adi grabbed a towel on a lounge chair and tossed it at him. Jarius caught it with a laugh. "Thanks, dude. I might need this after I go for a dip." He sidled closer to Carter. "Saw your video. That was a nice story you told, grabbing the wrong drink before you—" He pretended to vomit, making Henri from Team Mind Hack take a disgusted step away. When he smirked at Carter, his voice took on an edge that made Adi bristle. "But I'm still waiting for my in-person apology."

He expected Carter to stammer out some weak excuse. Instead, she lowered her hands and turned to face Jarius with squared shoulders. "You're right," she said through her teeth. "I'm really sorry for throwing up all over your nice clothes, Jarius." Turning away, she muttered under her breath, "Next time I'll aim for your face."

Adi guffawed. Maybe Carter did have some bite after all. Jarius started to ask what she'd said when Elijah appeared, clipboard in hand. "Where's Sierra? She's the only one I don't have eyes on."

Beck said, "She's not here. She likes to go for early morning walks sometimes."

"She was already gone when the alarm went off," Carter added.

"It's barely four o'clock," said Elijah, "and you're filming a round today."

Beck shrugged.

Elijah looked like he wanted to argue, but he made a note on the clipboard and walked away as flashing lights signaled the fire department's arrival.

It was ages before they were allowed back into the complex, and the day didn't get better after that. Something was wrong with the water system, which meant no one could take a shower and their only option for coffee was the sugar-packed "lattes" in the vending machines. With no water to wash dishes, the dining hall put out some energy bars and prepackaged pastries and called it good. It would've been fine if Sierra could've cooked for them, but there was no time.

The air-conditioning on their shuttle bus was broken, and the day was already hot. When the bus driver announced there'd been a delay and they had to drive around for an extra hour, Adi no longer doubted Sierra's claim.

Ranielle Russell was screwing with them.

On the second hour of being stuck on the sweltering bus, Sierra stealthily handed each of her teammates a water bottle.

Beck unscrewed the cap of his. "I might be a little bit in love with you," he whispered.

"Gross," Sierra muttered.

They finally arrived at the studio and filed into the air-conditioned greenroom, but their relief was short-lived.

"There was a mix-up with the caterer today," said one of the interns. "Your lunch wasn't delivered."

Jarius laughed bitterly. "Is this show being run by amateurs?"

The intern shrugged. "Helsing, you're up first. Hand over your phones and bags, then head straight to costumes and makeup. Illuminati, you're next, so be ready when you're called. We've already lost a lot of time today."

"Not through any fault of ours," Adi grumbled as they followed the intern into the hall.

This day needed to get in the freaking trash, and they hadn't even run the room yet.

"Is this a pirate-themed room?" Beck said the moment the director called for action. "Because I *love* pirates."

It was a worthwhile guess—they were in identical emerald-green, puffy-sleeved blouses—but Adi wished Beck would tone down the zeal. Surely no one could be that happy *all* the time.

Fitzy's mouth hung open in surprise, not used to contestants talking before he did.

Louis Augustus Russell, however, smirked and held a finger to his lips. "All is soon to be revealed."

Fitzy looked from Beck to Sierra to Adi and finally to Carter. His words seemed to carry a double meaning as he asked, "Everyone feeling good?"

Adi frowned, trying to decipher if he was asking Carter out of honest concern, or if there was more behind it. Could he really have tried to drug her at the party last week? And if so, what for? Ranielle Russell had insinuated a potential sabotage, but Fitzy shouldn't care which teams did well and which didn't.

Right?

"We're doing great," Carter said—a blatant lie.

Adi raised an eyebrow behind her back. It had been impossible not to overhear bits of the hour-long phone calls she had with her parents every night, including when she tried to explain what had happened at the party. He might have felt worse for her if he hadn't been the tiniest bit jealous at the thought of having parents who actually cared. Symphony would've found it hilarious if Adi had gotten wasted and puked on the competition. He could hear her now. *Welcome to showbiz, sweetie!*

"How about you, team leader?" said Fitzy. "Are you ready?"

Sierra eyed him coldly. "Yeah, Fitzy. We're ready. To slay the competition."

"Ha! Slay! Like your namesake, Van Helsing, am I right?" He winked. "I've been studying."

Carter laughed, and Fitzy's smile widened briefly before he turned to Louis. "Game Master, why don't you reveal what's in store for our first elimination round?"

"With pleasure." Louis's voice dropped dramatically. "The four of you have been invited to have your fortunes told by the great Madame Clara Voyance. But when you arrive, you discover that a curse has befallen the diviner!"

"How un*fortunate,*" said Fitzy. "Fortune teller? Fortunate? Get it?"

Adi wanted to smack him over the head.

Louis continued as if he hadn't been interrupted. "Her spirit has been sealed inside her crystal ball. You must solve the mysteries of the fortune teller's tent to free her . . . and yourselves."

Fitzy made an eerie *oooh* noise. "With that spine-tingling introduction, Game Master, do you have any wisdom to offer our intrepid team?"

"Indeed. To control your fate . . . let intuition be your guide."

They were given blindfolds, but before they were led off the stage, a loud buzzer sounded through the set.

"Yikes," said Fitzy, grimacing. "I forgot to mention the snag."

"You're kidding," Sierra said.

"Team Dread has chosen to target you with our very first snag of the season. Because they were the fastest to figure out the element numbers in the last round, they're allowed to give a rival team an error penalty. Be forewarned: the Game Master has slipped in one nasty punishment if you get a particular part of the room wrong. Best of luck!"

"Great," Adi muttered, putting on his blindfold.

As they were guided toward the escape room, he tried to shake off their terrible morning and get into the puzzle-solving mindset. It wouldn't be easy. He was hungry. And thirsty. And so tired.

A door closed behind them. Adi picked up the scents of earthy incense, wood recently sawn and stained, the lingering aroma of paint.

Fitzy's voice came through his earpiece. "Team Helsing, you may take off your blindfolds and begin in three . . . two . . . one . . . *Escape!*"

THE ESCAPE GAME

SEASON FIVE

Round One: Fortune Favors the Brave

FIVE TEAMS REMAINING

17
Adi

The room was roughly the size of his bedroom and decorated with old-fashioned maroon wallpaper, jewel-toned silky drapes tied back with golden tassels, and eclectic rugs underfoot. They had entered through a wooden door that was now shut tight, its surface intricately carved into an image of an old man in long robes holding a walking stick and a lantern. There was a large keyhole beneath the lantern.

Adi approached a table and rapped the top of a crystal ball, which felt like plastic. The moment he did, the fogginess cleared inside the ball, revealing a projection of a cliché fortune teller with enormous hoop earrings and a shawl around her shoulders.

"Greetings," she said in a dramatic voice. "If your freedom should await, choose three cards to learn your fate. I am trapped deep inside, so let intuition be your guide . . ."

Let intuition be your guide. The same clue the Game Master had given.

But Adi was more annoyed than intrigued. "Romani stereotyping. Classic Hollywood."

Carter snickered.

Adi glanced at her, lips twitching in an almost-smile. "There are spaces here for three cards," he said, trailing his finger along rectangular outlines on the tablecloth.

"Tarot," said Beck, gesturing at the door. "That carving looks like the Hermit from the classic Rider–Waite deck. A card that represents a period of solitude and being guided by our own internal wisdom."

They looked at him.

He shrugged. "I went through a phase."

"All right," said Sierra. "Enough goofing off. Let's find these cards."

They began scouring the room, calling out their findings.

Above the door was a red clock—the room's official timer. They'd been here only forty-two seconds, but it felt like it was ticking way too fast.

A lantern hung directly over the center table, unlit and identical to the lantern held by the Hermit on the door.

Twelve small paintings were spaced around the room, based on the Western astrology signs—the ram, the scorpion, the twins . . .

A trunk in one corner was locked with a four-letter code.

A sideboard had three tiny holes in its top, and beside each was a symbol carved into the wood: a rose, an apple, and a feather.

Beck and Carter hunted through the drawers in the sideboard. One was locked, but in the others they found a booklet about tarot cards and their meanings, a chart explaining various chakra colors, and a map of constellations.

Adi scoured the tarot book for clues while Carter compared the star chart to the astrology paintings.

"Wait," she said, stopping in front of the Gemini illustration. "There are hidden letters in these paintings."

Sure enough, once Adi was looking for them, the letters were obvious. An *E* made out of the crab's claws. A *T* in the minotaur's bow and arrow.

"Adi, can you unscramble them to spell something?" said Sierra.

"No need. They're already in order, starting here." He pointed to the *F* in one of Pisces's fish scales. "It spells FIND THE TRUTH."

"Helpful," Beck muttered.

Adi inspected the lantern hanging above the table. There was a space for a candle, but the candle was missing.

Crouching, he lifted the edge of the tablecloth and spied a wooden box. "Found something." He pulled it into the dim light. The box was divided into nine equal squares, each holding a short white candle. "Candles labeled with numbers. One through nine."

"Put one on the lantern and see what happens," suggested Sierra.

Adi put the first candle into the lantern. Immediately, the room went black. Carter squeaked. The crystal ball glowed again—green this time, and the same fortune teller appeared. But now she looked pissed.

"You claim to seek the truth, but you are only wasting my time!" she cried. "For your error, I will add one minute to the clock."

"What? No!" Carter shouted as an ominous bell tolled and the red clock above the door clicked forward a full minute.

"The snag penalty," said Beck with a groan.

The lights came back on.

"Shit," said Sierra. "I shouldn't have asked you to do that."

"No, it was a good idea," said Adi. "I thought we were supposed to be trying to free the fortune teller's spirit. What's all this about seeking the truth?"

"We have to find the truth of who trapped her?" Carter suggested.

Suddenly, Beck gasped. "Try number nine." But then he hesitated. "I'm just guessing, though."

"Why nine?" asked Sierra.

He gestured at the carved door. "The Hermit is the ninth card in the Major Arcana, and the lantern looks exactly like the one in the carving."

"Confirmed," said Adi, holding up the tarot booklet to the Hermit page.

"I say we try it," said Carter, "or we're going to waste another full minute spinning our metaphorical wheels."

Adi smirked, amused at her need to specify "metaphorical."

Sierra nodded. "Try it."

Picking the ninth candle from the box, Adi set it into the lantern.

Again they were plunged into darkness, and Sierra cursed loud enough that Adi could imagine the editing team cursing *her* later.

But then the lantern started to glow, and a collection of tiny lights appeared on the ceiling, illuminating a series of constellations that had been invisible before.

"Yes!" said Carter. "Good work, Beck. MVP all the way."

"Look," said Sierra. "There are hooks on the walls. Let's arrange the paintings to match up with their constellations."

They scrambled about, grabbing the paintings and hanging them according to the star chart. Once the last painting was up, they stood back, expecting more flickering lights or some message from the fortune teller . . . but nothing happened.

"Did we get one wrong?" asked Beck, peeking over Carter's shoulder to study the star chart.

"It spells something new now," said Adi, pointing to each painting in turn. "TENTH. THIRD . . . *F U*."

Carter giggled abruptly, then clapped her hand over mouth. "Wait, really?"

"Hold on," said Sierra. "Tenth, third? As in . . . October third?"

"Maybe . . ." said Adi, sounding unconvinced.

"What are we supposed to do with that?" asked Beck.

"No, I don't think it's a date," said Carter, approaching the locked trunk with the four-letter code. "Adi, what are the tenth and third letters of the alphabet?"

"*J* and *C*."

She spun the dials. *J. C. F. U.*

The lid popped open.

"You're kidding me," said Adi. "The last two letters didn't fit the pattern. That's . . . I don't know. Cheating."

"Actually," said Sierra, her voice with a newly sharpened edge, "it seems like someone is sending a message."

Adi raised an eyebrow.

Sierra glanced at the clock. "Carter, what do we have?"

"A box with a six-digit numeral code," said Carter, pulling their new props from the trunk, "a bunch of scarves, a ribbon with a code or something on it, and . . . incense sticks."

Adi grabbed the ribbon from her hand to check the code.

Oaelnibtskati klcilcectiphc ailedthoileee yvuBihiufltfw teeydanliehii
eSstftdderinl aeshiwAndwsal mapenanoBotlb srocdsatuniee
lctoAlrbttmjm ohtfrereteeui othfefejhsAsn kheiltsuectte

"Okay . . ." He tried to pick out a pattern.

"Oh!" said Carter. "There were those holes in the sideboard! I bet the scents of the incense match up with the symbols."

"Yes, good call," said Sierra. "Who's got a strong sense of smell?"

"On it," said Beck, taking the incense sticks to the sideboard. "But you'll have to stop talking because it messes with my olfactory senses."

He started to sniff through the incense sticks.

Adi went back to studying the code on the ribbon, but he hadn't made any progress before Beck shouted victoriously—something about "it's a pine branch, not a feather!"—then popped in the final stick. The locked drawer in the sideboard popped open, and the clock on the wall froze at twenty-three minutes, nine seconds. They were in the homestretch.

"Tarot cards!" Beck yelled, flaunting some fancy shuffling trick before spreading them on the table.

"There has to be a mistake. There's no purple here!" Sierra and Carter were poring over the chakra scroll, the colorful scarves scattered around them. Sierra looked peevish.

"Maybe it's not the scarves?" Carter suggested.

"It has to be the scarves!" Sierra bit back, making Carter recoil.

"What's going on?" asked Adi.

Sierra huffed. "Right here, the chakra chart says that readings are most effective when the atmosphere matches a person's aura. Red is for passion, orange for creativity, etc. And purple is for *intuition*. The fortune teller mentioned intuition, and so did Louis. So we've got to be looking for purple, but there's no purple scarf!"

"Maybe it's not about the scarves at all," said Carter. "Maybe there's . . . I don't know . . . something purple in one of the paintings, or—"

"No, it's the scarves," said Sierra. "Look! There are these hooks up here." She pointed to hooks Adi hadn't noticed, spaced evenly around the lantern that hung over the table. "And each scarf has a ring sewn into the corners, exactly the right size, but there's no purple!"

"You have red and blue," said Beck. "Am I the only one who remembers the color wheel? What do they teach you in real school?"

"*Real* school?" said Carter. "As opposed to what? Muppet school?"

"Wait, he's right!" said Sierra. "I can't believe I missed that. I'm a literal artist. What is wrong with me?"

"You're hungry," Beck said.

Sierra hung the blue and red scarves so the light from the lantern passed through the fabric and shaded the room in deep violet.

As soon as she finished, clouds swirled inside the crystal ball and it began to glow.

The fortune teller appeared again, but she looked less furious this time, more thoughtful. Her eyes were cast down, as if staring at invisible cards on the table before her. "Your first card speaks of upcoming change, a swift and brutal transformation. Your second card shows ruin and betrayal brought on not by an act of God but one's own transgressions. Your third card shows that past grievances will be addressed and order finally restored." The video flickered out for a second, then started up again from the top. "Your first card speaks of upcoming change . . ."

"Adi, she's telling us the three cards we need to find," said Carter. "Check the book!"

"I'm working on it," said Adi, flipping through the pages. "But there are like a hundred cards in here!"

"Seventy-eight, actually," said Beck.

"Fine, we get it!" barked Adi. "You know this woo-woo stuff and the rest of us are useless."

"Adi!" said Carter, aghast.

He sucked in a breath and rubbed a palm against his eyes. Sierra had warned them about this.

"I know. Okay. I'm pretty sure the last one is referring to Justice. Order restored, and all that. But the first two . . ." His shoulders slumped and he looked at Beck, borderline apologetic. "Any insights?"

"I'm thinking," said Beck, listening to the fortune teller. "The first one could be the Tower. Or the Ten of Swords. Wait—which one was about an act of God?"

"*Not* an act of God," Adi corrected. "Ruin and betrayal, but not an act of God. That's the second one."

"Most likely the Ten of Swords for that one," said Beck. "Okay, try: Death, Ten of Swords, Justice."

Adi picked out the three cards and set them into the spaces on the tablecloth. The Roman numerals at the top of each card lit up. *XIII—X—XI.*

"Whoa, *cool,*" said Beck. "How are they doing that?" He peered beneath the table. "There's got to be a sensor . . ."

"Thirteen, ten, eleven!" cried Carter. "Six digits!"

Sierra already had the small box in her hands, her fingers dialing through the digits. *131011 . . .*

The lid sprang open, revealing a giant skeleton key. Carter cheered as Sierra strode to the door, inserted the key into the keyhole, and turned it.

The door swung open. That bell dinged.

They had escaped.

Hold on.

They had *escaped*?

But.

They hadn't used all the clues.

Adi looked down at the ribbon in his palm. The long string of letters in an unsolved code.

As Fitzy's voice blasted across his earpiece, congratulating Team Helsing on their escape, Adi frowned and tucked the ribbon into his pocket.

Interview Room: Alicia Angelos

SEASON FOUR

END OF ROUND ONE: ALL THAT JAZZ

"How do you reckon your team went?" asks Fitzy.

Alicia laughs—a boisterous, heartfelt sound. "That room was *amazing*. The liquor bottles, the piano, the costumes!" She jumps up from her wooden chair and sashays, the fringe of her silver flapper-style dress swishing hypnotically around her hips. "I loved it."

"Your team seems to have figured out some things the others haven't."

"You mean cooperation?" Alicia sits down. "You don't have to play coy with me. Everyone knows Team Hourglass is struggling. You should hear them bickering in the greenroom."

"Why do you think that is?"

"Why do I think my team is killing it?" She jokingly flips her hair back. "Because I'm such a fantastic leader, obviously."

"And Hourglass? You think Elijah is killing it?"

She gives a one-shouldered shrug. "He's nice enough. But every time I talk to him, he gets all tangled and tongue-tied."

"Gee, I wonder why."

"It's probably Sierra getting in his head. She doesn't make for an easy teammate."

"Right. That must be why." Fitzy grins as he sucks on the straw of his iced lemonade. "You really think your sister is to blame for their . . . issues?"

"I saw the writing on the wall as soon as I heard she hadn't been chosen as team leader. Sierra hates anyone telling her what to do."

"Hey, now. She has some good ideas. She was the fastest contestant to realize the piano music had to be played backward."

"She has her moments," acknowledges Alicia. "But her delivery leaves something to be desired."

"I still can't believe you're sisters. I've never met such complete opposites. You're a ray of sunshine and she's—"

"A storm cloud," Alicia finishes.

"Exactly. So . . . any chance you've reconsidered sharing your prize money with her if you win?"

Alicia picks up her virgin pink gin fizz. "Not a chance. This show was *my* thing. She was never interested until she found out I was doing it. If she thinks she can waltz in and steal my prize, she's got another thing coming."

"Crikey. No love lost between you two, is there?"

Alicia sips her drink. "It's such a shame, isn't it?"

18

Carter

Carter crunched on a chip and transferred another video from her phone to her laptop's editing program. She'd been sifting through footage for hours, trying to strike the right balance of *exclusive, VIP, behind-the-scenes!* stuff her followers craved while also keeping everything hush-hush enough that Ranielle Russell wouldn't yell at her.

It didn't help that she'd also spent an hour editing content of herself only to decide that, nope, her own footage couldn't compete with her avatar. She redid everything, inserting the filter over herself.

That's what her followers really wanted, anyway.

Her phone dinged with a notification from the Clue Master forums.

It was late enough that the overseas crowd was starting to wake up. Fitzy had garnered attention from his home audience, and also from the Brits, who loved him from his Australian soap opera days. Now that it was easily accessible to everyone on a streaming service, *The Escape Game* was officially an international success.

Being a contestant hadn't hurt Carter's brand. There'd been a huge uptick in followers when she first announced she was going to be on the show, along with an outpouring of encouragement from her longtime fans.

After the snag round had aired, things had been . . . more subdued. Some fans had defended her, but the online trolls had claimed that surely the highest-ranking Solve Specialist should've done better. Clearly, Kick It Carter was all talk.

Their words nagged at her. She'd been so eager to be on the show, to surround herself with other Clue Masters, people she could actually relate to. It hadn't occurred to her when she'd sent in her audition video that not only might she remain alone . . . she might lose the online support she relied on to get through each day.

What would people say when the next episode ran? The fortune teller room hadn't been as terrible as the chemistry lab, but she wished she could have contributed more. She was letting her followers down. She was letting her team down.

And maybe, a little, she was letting herself down.

Another ding from the Domain.

Then another. And another. Seven more in fast succession.

Carter finally stopped organizing the video files to check her phone. A new episode wouldn't drop until next Sunday; there wasn't anything to be excited about.

She pulled up the forums, and there, at the top—a headline that hadn't been there when she'd checked an hour ago.

RIP ALICIA

She clicked the link.

Someone calling themselves the Real Game Master had posted a bunch of screen grabs from the snag round episode showing the different elements from the periodic table, and ultimately the anagram that Adi had figured out. *Alicia Angelos.*

The comments were lighting up. A whole lot of *WTF*s and talk of Easter eggs and in memoriams. But no one knew why the Game Master would have hidden Alicia's name inside a clue. Carter certainly didn't.

She clicked on the profile of this 'Real Game Master,' but it was blank.

As she was reading the rush of new comments, another post popped up, this one a photo of a ribbon covered in code. Carter zoomed in on the image. She could have sworn she'd seen—

She gasped.

She definitely *had* seen it before.

Clambering from her bed, she rushed into the villa's living room, where Beck was sitting on one side of the couch reading a magazine and Sierra was on the other doing a crossword puzzle.

"Where's Adi?" Carter said.

They both jumped and looked at her.

"What happened?" Sierra asked as Beck pointed to his and Adi's shared bedroom.

Carter spun around and knocked on the door. "Adi? Are you awake?"

She was about to knock again when the door opened. "What?" said Adi. He was wearing gray flannel pajama pants and nothing else.

Carter screamed, pressing her hands over her eyes. "Oh my god, why do you boys never have shirts on? You're as bad as Jarius!"

"I was getting ready for bed," said Adi, grabbing a T-shirt off the dresser. "And I am definitely *not* as bad as Jarius."

Carter peeked through her fingers as he yanked the shirt over his head, and even she had to admit that, yeah, okay, he wasn't as bad as Jarius. In fact—

Oh god, Carter, no. You're here to win.

She spun away, forcing herself to picture anything else, but for some reason now she was thinking of *Fitzy* shirtless and *where were all these hormones coming from?*

"What did you want?" asked Adi.

She took a deep breath. "The ribbon. From the fortune teller room. It's been uploaded onto the Domain. Did you ever figure it out?"

He frowned.

"There was a ribbon, with a code? It came out of that box with the scarves."

Adi's eyes widened. "I forgot about that." He disappeared into his room and emerged a moment later with the ribbon in his hand.

"Hold on—what ribbon?" asked Sierra.

Carter showed them the post on the Domain.

"It's definitely the same one," said Adi, perching on the edge of the couch cushion and spreading the ribbon out on the coffee table.

Oaelnibtskati klcilcectiphc ailedthoileee yvuBihiufltfw teeydanliehii
eSstftdderinl aeshiwAndwsal mapenanoBotlb srocdsatuniee
lctoAlrbttmjm ohtfrereteeui othfefejhsAsn kheiltsuectte

"Another anagram?" Beck asked. "Though that would be one heck of an anagram . . ."

"I'll plug it into a decoder," said Carter, opening her phone.

Adi shook his head. "It's not an anagram."

"Oh, come on," said Carter, nudging him. "You think everything's an anagram."

He scowled half-heartedly. "This one's not. I can tell by the feel of it."

"It wasn't necessary to complete the room," Beck said with a frown. "Do they normally put extra clues in there? Big red herrings like this?"

"No," Adi said. "Did you say it was on the Domain? The episode hasn't even dropped yet."

"The person who uploaded this picture figured out the *Alicia Angelos* anagram, too," said Carter.

"It's someone involved with the show, if they have access to the ribbon," Beck said.

"It has to be Louis," Carter said.

Adi snapped his fingers at Beck. "I need a pen and paper."

"Am I your maid?"

Before Adi could respond, a ballpoint pen smacked him in the forehead. It rebounded onto the table as he reeled back, pressing a hand to his forehead and gaping at Sierra.

"Oops," she said unapologetically.

Carter passed him a notepad. They gathered closer as he copied down the first line of the note, squished together on the sofa, shoulder to shoulder, knee to knee.

"A one-letter Caesar cipher gets us . . . *P-B-F-M* . . . That's not it. Two letters . . . *Q-C* . . . obviously not. Three letters . . ."

"Could be a keyword cipher?" said Carter.

"Was just thinking that." Adi doodled a question mark on the page. "Does anyone remember some sort of keyword planted in the room?"

"Try 'Alicia,'" said Sierra.

"It's not 'Alicia.' The two *A*s throw it off, and keyword ciphers work best if they include at least one letter from the end of the alphabet."

"'Voyance'? As in, Clara Voyance?" Beck suggested, but that didn't get them anywhere, either.

They fell silent, thinking. Adi tried redoing the cipher using "Angelos" and "escape" and "tarot" and "hermit" and "tower" before he finally snapped at everyone to stop throwing out ideas because they weren't helping.

"There must have been something else in the room," he said, tapping the pen rapidly against his knee. "A keyword no one picked up on, or a cipher wheel or something."

"You'd think we would have noticed a cipher wheel lying around," muttered Sierra.

Adi tried "Louis" as the keyword for the cipher. Nothing.

"There are eight capital letters," said Carter, running a finger along the message. *"O-I-B-S-A-B-A-A."*

"You're right," said Adi, circling the capital letters.

"Is *that* an anagram?" asked Beck. "Sob . . . Bib . . . Abba?"

"I don't think so. Could indicate names or initials or . . ." Adi's breath caught. "Or . . . poetry."

"Poetry?" Carter said with an abrupt laugh. "Now you're going romantic on us?"

Adi lifted his focus from the paper and peered at her. *"She walks in beauty, like the night of cloudless climes and starry skies; and all that's best of dark and bright meet in her aspect and her eyes; thus mellowed to that tender light which heaven to gaudy day denies."*

Beck whistled lowly, while Carter blushed.

Sierra rolled her eyes. "Exactly how many books did you bring with you on this trip?"

"His entire duffel bag is full of them," Beck said in slight awe. "He has one change of clothes and one bag of toiletries, and the rest is books."

"How do you not stink all the time?" Sierra demanded.

"I send my laundry bag out like everyone else," Adi said, putting on exaggerated affronted airs, but his focus was already lost in the ribbon again. "I think we're looking at a poem . . . or seven sentences. Maybe less, given that the *I* could be a pronoun, and some of these could be proper names. What's interesting is that the very first letter is one of our capitals, suggesting it might actually be the start of the note. It could be . . ." He paused. "That's it."

He flipped to a clean sheet of paper and started writing again—copying down the letters from the note, but instead of writing them left to write, he wrote the first line in a column, top to bottom.

O
a
e
l
n
i
b
t
s
k
a
t
i

"What are you doing?" asked Carter.

"There are thirteen lines, and each one is exactly thirteen letters," he said, starting in on a second column.

Ok
al
ec
li
nI
ic
be
tc
st
ki
ap
th
ic

"That's awfully symmetrical," he went on, "which means we could be looking at a simplified columnar transposition cipher."

"Yeah, sure," Beck said. "I totally know what that is."

Adi ignored him, adding a third line, then a fourth, continuing the painstaking process of writing down each letter, each line, each column, until they were staring at a block of text.

Okayteamslook
aliveSearchth
ecluesspotthe
lieBythecoffi
nIdidfindArel
icthatwasleft
behindAnarres

tcouldnotbeju
stifiedButthe
killerwontesc
apethistimeAt
thefinalejust
icewillbemine

"*Okay teams look alive . . .*" Carter read, as Adi rewrote the message at the bottom of the page, adding breaks and punctuation, revealing the clue that, even solved, struck Carter as unnecessarily cryptic.

Okay, teams, look alive.
Search the clues, spot the lie.
By the coffin, I did find
A relic that was left behind.
An arrest could not be justified,
But the killer won't escape this time.
At the finale, justice will be mine.

Carter looked at Sierra, trying to judge her reaction, but Sierra was expressionless.

After a long silence, Sierra said, "Put the solution on the Domain."

Carter blinked. "What?"

"Whoever posted that wanted it to be solved, and we solved it. So put it up now before someone else figures it out."

"But . . . why?"

Sierra shot her a disgruntled look. "Are you effing Kick It Carter, or not?"

Carter grabbed her phone. "Yeah. Okay. Fine." She transcribed the message into a comment below the picture of the ribbon code. When she was finished, she took an uncertain breath, hoping this wasn't something Ranielle Russell would be mad about, and hit post.

"But what does it mean?" asked Beck. "What clues? What relic?"

"*By the coffin I did find . . .*" read Adi. "Maybe the killer dropped something that night?"

"Okay," said Carter, "but then why didn't this so-called Real Game Master tell the police?"

"It sounds like they did," said Beck. "Or at least, they tried to, but either the police didn't believe them, or it wasn't enough to make an arrest. It would be easy for the killer to say they'd dropped something the day before."

"Maybe the Real Game Master is one of their suspects," Sierra mused. "Maybe the police thought the story was fake, as a deflection. They never believed me, either."

"Was Louis a suspect?" said Carter, setting down the phone.

"Everyone's a suspect," said Sierra. "But he may not be the one planting these clues."

"It *has* to be him. Who else has control of the rooms?"

Sierra shrugged. "It would be easy enough to slip a ribbon into the room."

"What about the Alicia anagram?" Adi said. "That was linked to the padlock code. A puzzle within a puzzle. It has the Game Master written all over it."

"Possibly a publicity stunt," said Sierra offhandedly. "The producers trying to drum up ratings."

Beck frowned. "You are the most cynical person I've ever met."

"Thank you," said Sierra.

Carter's phone dinged with a new notification. "They responded! The Real Game Master, whoever that is."

The four of them gathered around Carter's phone to read.

CLUE MASTERS DOMAIN

HOME	MERCH	ROOM ANALYSIS	CLUE ROOMS
NEWS	PUZZLECON	ONLINE ESCAPE GAMES	SEARCH

RIP ALICIA

New Post from @TheRealGameMaster

Nice work, @KickItCarter. Now, are you ready for a REAL puzzle?

As promised, here are your clues:

WHO KILLED ALICIA ANGELOS? A TIMELINE

Prior to 8 p.m.: Alicia's whereabouts unestablished. (Contestant statements concur that she often left the complex for unknown reasons throughout the season's run.)

Approx. 9 p.m.: Last known sighting of Alicia in contestants' living complex. Witnesses overheard her arguing with Sierra Angelos, sister.

10:28 p.m.: Alicia's phone either turned off or died. Last traceable location: the intersection of Riverside and Mariposa, approx. 1 mile south of the complex and 1.5 miles southeast of the studio. (Phone NEVER RECOVERED.)

1 .a.m.–2 a.m.: approximate time of death, according to coroner report; location of death never determined.

Approx. 9 a.m.: Alicia's teammates notice her missing but SAY NOTHING.

12:25 p.m.: Alicia is LATE for filming; producers rearrange schedule but DO NOT alert police.

1:13 p.m.: Body discovered in studio prop (a coffin, no less, how convenient) during filming. Words on coffin lid: WE GET WHAT WE DESERVE.

Other Important (???) Details:

Bruising indicates she was suffocated, patterns on skin suggest gloved hands over mouth. Clothing fibers on body and in lungs could not be traced to any known suspects.

Body was wet—police believe killer hosed it down to clean off DNA evidence. Successfully, it would seem.

Rolling blackout across area means NO security footage at studio.

Bed comforter MISSING from room, never found.

SO WHO DID IT?

Two of the show's set designers had fingerprints matching those on the coffin, but their whereabouts the night before were verified by apartment security cameras.

These are the other suspects whose fingerprints were on the coffin, along with their alibis for the time of death:

Sierra Angelos (sister, Team Hourglass): claimed to be taking a walk around town—UNVERIFIED

Missy Mizuno (Team Hourglass): in bed—also UNVERIFIED b/c again, where the hell was her roomie, Sierra?

Elijah Kua (Team Hourglass): in bed at villas (verified by Cruz, but what, was he watching him the whole night? Let's assume not.)

Cruz Fernandes (Team Hourglass): in bed at villas ("verified" by Elijah, see above)

Ranielle Russell (executive producer) and Louis Augustus Russell (Game Master): at home, verified by each other (but, like, they're married, so what are they going to say?)

James "Fitzy" Fitzgerald (host): At home, livestreaming his usual pre-finale Q&A for Australian fans (Sydney time: 6–8 p.m.)

Vera Jolly (social media manager): at home—specific location UNVERIFIED but was actively answering comments on the show's social media and livestream chat at time of death

I KNOW WHO KILLED ALICIA, and their name is IN THIS POST.

I HAVE EVIDENCE.

But the police won't listen to me, so now it's your turn, Solve Specialists.

FIGURE OUT WHO'S LYING.

FIGURE OUT HOW THEY GOT AWAY WITH IT.

If you can help me with the missing information, I'll plant the evidence in the finale room, which, if you've been paying attention, will REVEAL THE KILLER.

The countdown's begun, Clue Masters. Tick tick.

19

Beck

After silently reading the post on the Domain multiple times, Beck couldn't stand it any longer. "So . . ." he started, burying a nervous hand in his hair. "Sierra, we appreciate you not killing us in our sleep, but it feels like it's time to address the elephant in the room. Did you kill your sister?"

Sierra blinked, as if emerging from a dream. Her gaze shifted to him for a long moment. Then she pushed off from the couch and headed to the kitchen. "I need to bake."

Her movements were robotic as she pulled bowls and baking sheets from the cabinets, then flour, sugar, baking soda, oranges, measuring cups and spoons. She didn't look at a recipe as she started adding ingredients to a mixing bowl.

"That wasn't an answer," Beck said, glancing at Carter and Adi. "Was it?"

"Not an answer," Carter confirmed, reading the post again. "But this can't be Louis Augustus Russell. He doesn't speak like that."

"No, I think we can agree that whoever's calling themselves the *Real* Game Master isn't our current Game Master," Adi said. "What I want to know is, how did they get all this information?"

Sierra slammed an egg down so hard the shell shattered, spilling its guts across the counter. She growled and threw the remnants into the sink before trying again.

"I remember the police releasing reports from the case, hoping it would bring in new evidence," Carter said, frowning. "It was all over the Domain at the time. This information could be from that."

Beck stood. "Sierra—"

Sierra cursed loudly, glaring into the open fridge. "Which of you asshats finished off the milk?"

Beck slowly raised a hand. "Guilty."

"You should've told me we were out. I went shopping after the round."

"*That's* where you go when you leave the complex?" Carter said. "Grocery shopping?"

"You think this food miraculously appears overnight?" Sierra yelled. "Now we don't have any milk to go with the cookies, and you can't have cookies without milk, can you?" She reached for the bowl of cookie dough. Beck got there first. She tried to grab it back, but Beck didn't let go.

"Here's the thing," he said. "I don't care if you killed your sister. I mean—no, not true. I definitely care if you killed your sister. But as far as I'm concerned, that's between you and the police department. What I need to know is how we are going to stay in this competition."

A muscle twitched in Sierra's jaw. For a second, her fingers pressed into his, squeezing the ceramic bowl between them.

Finally, she looked away. "This was my mom's cookie recipe. She died when I was ten. Alicia and I used to bake when we were missing her the most." She grabbed a spoon, scooped a hearty bite of cookie dough out of the bowl, and stuffed it into her mouth.

Carter squeaked and whispered, "There were raw eggs in there."

If Sierra cared, it didn't show.

Screw it.

Beck grabbed a spoon and took a bite, too.

God, that was good. The orange zest stole the show.

"I didn't kill my sister," Sierra said. "But someone here did, and I'm going to find out who."

Beck examined her hunched shoulders. Her black eyeliner, dry and cracked in the corners.

She could have been lying. But in that moment, Beck believed her. Sierra Angelos hadn't killed her sister.

But if she hadn't . . . who had?

"Someone already knows," said Adi, nodding toward Carter's phone, still displaying the RIP ALICIA post. "If we make it to the finale, we can find out, too."

"Only if someone figures out the lie in the clues," Carter said. "The poster said they'd only leave the evidence *if* we solve the mystery." She tugged idly on one of her curls. "It must be one heck of a lie for the police to have completely dismissed this person's claims. The poster seems really sure they know who did it."

"Maybe they'll reveal more clues in the next rooms," Beck said.

Adi grabbed a spoon from the cutlery drawer and tried a bite of the raw cookie dough. He chewed thoughtfully before nodding in approval. "How about this," he said to Sierra. "You tell us what your deal is, and I'll get you some milk."

20

Sierra

Sierra had worried her teammates weren't cutthroat enough to reach the finale. But somehow, they kept surprising her. Carter with her math. Beck's broad proficiencies. Adi recognizing the columnar transposition cipher before any Solve Specialist.

Now Adi knelt by the dining hall door with a small metal tube containing lock-picking tools. When there was a click, Sierra had to admit she was impressed.

Adi held the door open into the darkness. "Shall we?"

"You have to teach me how to do that," Beck said, using the welcome pack flashlight to guide his way.

"What's that?" Carter whispered.

Sierra followed her stare toward the driveway. "What?"

"I thought I saw something . . ." Carter trailed off, eyes darting around the shadows. Then she shook her head. "The wind, probably."

Sierra couldn't see anything but swaying palm trees. It was a blustery night, a welcome reprieve from the day's heat.

She and Carter stepped inside. Adi led them beyond the swinging door at the back of the hall into the kitchen.

"Ice creeeam," Beck sang, grabbing the key from the hook and unlocking the padlock to the walk-in freezer.

"I thought we were getting milk," Carter said.

"It's a two-for-one sale. I hope they have caramel swirl. It tastes like my favorite song."

"You keep saying stuff like that," Carter said. "What are you talking about?"

"I taste sounds," Beck said, like it was a totally normal thing to say.

He had to drag out boxes of meat that were stacked on the freezer floor to get in.

"The FDA's dream," Adi drawled, nudging a box of raw chicken away with his shoe.

When Beck was done, he gave a dramatic gasp. "Ice cream mother lode! Look—they've got Ben & Jerry's Chunky Monkey, and Cherry Garcia, and oh my giddy aunt—is that Phish Food?"

"I'll be a part of this," Adi said, lunging inside.

"I'm sorry," said Sierra. "You *taste sounds*?"

Beck looked up from the two pints of ice cream in his hands. "It's a type of synesthesia. Different sounds make me taste different flavors, and sometimes textures." He pointed an ice cream carton at Sierra. "Your voice is like blue Kool-Aid and sherbet. That's how I knew it was you in the snag round before we saw you."

The three of them stared at him for a long moment. Finally, Carter whispered, "That's really cool. So, um, do you see any strawberry?"

"There might be some in the back?" Beck started searching again.

"Shove over." Sierra jostled past to get to the chocolate mint she'd spied. It was a tight squeeze, with shelves on either side of them and Beck at the end.

"Oh, there!" Beck said cheerfully. "I think I can reach it—"

Sierra glanced toward the door. Her heart nearly shot out of her throat.

A figure dressed in black stood there, face covered by a balaclava. Sierra sucked in a breath to cry out when the figure shoved Carter in the back.

Carter stumbled into Adi and Sierra, who fell into Beck, who crashed against the rear shelving. The freezer door slammed shut, plunging them into darkness.

Sierra gaped at the heavy door, that breath still trapped in her throat.

"What the hell!" Adi roared, breaking Sierra from her shock.

She lurched to shove the door open. It was stuck. "Hey. *Hey!* Shit, I think they've padlocked it."

Light flooded the room as Beck clicked the flashlight back on. His breath steamed before his face. "Is everyone okay? Carter?"

"I think so." Carter's voice was shaky. "Who pushed me?"

"I didn't see," Sierra said. "They were wearing a balaclava."

"They were *what*?" Adi said as Beck hissed out a breath.

"What's a balaclava?" asked Carter.

"A mask that covers everything but your eyes."

"I told you I saw something," Carter said. "In the bushes outside. I told you!"

"Maybe it was Jarius being an asshole?" Adi sounded like he didn't believe himself.

"Jarius didn't know we'd be out here," Sierra said.

"*We* didn't know we'd be out here," Beck pointed out.

"So . . . someone was roaming around the complex in that mask for the fun of it?" Carter whispered.

Beck dug out his phone. "I'm calling Elijah."

The line rang. And rang.

"He's asleep," Sierra said.

"Or lurking around the place in a balaclava," Adi muttered.

"Could this be another attempt at sabotaging us?" Carter hugged herself as Beck tried calling Lisa's number. "Like whoever spiked my drink? Maybe they were hanging around our villas, saw us heading in here, and decided to use the opportunity to their advantage."

Beck gasped. "Maybe it's the same person who put the cow heart in our fridge!"

Carter's jaw dropped as Adi asked, "What cow heart?"

"Whoops. Sorry. We didn't tell you because Sierra thought someone was trying to put us off our game." Beck explained about finding the heart and the knife with the creepy note, finishing the story with a full-body shiver. "Jeez, it's freezing in here."

"Yeah," Adi said. "It's a freezer."

But Sierra could see the worry behind his facade. Her own face was going numb from the cold.

"This is probably a silly question," Carter said, "but do people die in freezers?"

No one answered.

Beck cleared his throat and said, "I'll try Lisa again."

Lisa's number rang through as well.

"Does anyone have another contestant's phone number?" asked Beck.

They didn't.

"We need someone who'll wake up when their phone is ringing," Adi growled.

"Or someone who's already awake." Carter sighed a steamy breath and pulled out her phone, showing them the notifications of new posts on *The Escape Game*'s social media accounts.

"Oh no," Adi said.

"Yep." Carter opened her Instagram messages and sent the account moderator—Vera—a short explanation.

A short time later, a reply buzzed through. This better not be a prank.

I wish, Carter responded.

Seconds passed, feeling like minutes, before Vera replied, Fine, I'm coming.

Carter shoved her phone in her pocket, along with her hands. "I'm sure she'll get here as fast as she can. Right?"

"If she's not here in twenty minutes, we'll call the fire department," Adi said.

"Did anyone else notice from the Real Game Master's post that her last name is 'Jolly'?" Beck said with a blue-lipped grin.

Adi snorted, steam billowing from his nose. "I always appreciate a good dose of irony." He was tapping away at his phone, occasionally pausing to rub warmth into his fingers. "Everyone online says it's impossible to get locked in an industrial freezer. There's an unlock mechanism inside."

"Yeah," Sierra drawled, "except when someone *padlocks the outside*."

"Psychopath," Beck whispered. When Sierra shot him a glare, he added hastily, "Not you. Whoever locked us in. This isn't some harmless prank . . . unless they're planning on letting us out again soon."

Sierra strained to hear any sound outside, but it was impossible through the door.

"I've decided you're not a psychopath," Beck added. "You've got some of the traits. Vindictive. Smart. You like to collect information."

Sierra raised her eyebrows. "Isn't that most people on the show? Including you?"

Beck pointed at his temple. "Empathy. Confetti."

"So I've heard," Sierra said.

"But you don't seem like a narcissist," Beck said. "You react to upsetting situations automatically. There's no delay, like a psychopath would need. And you don't suck up to your superiors."

"You've noticed that, huh?"

"There's literally a website that tells you what to do if you accidentally end up in a walk-in freezer," said Adi, still on his phone. "Is there a safety bell in here?"

"Who's going to hear it?" Carter said.

"Good point." He skimmed the article. "Okay, we have to worry about hypothermia, frostbite, and air supply. We could break the air-conditioning fan."

"Vera will be here soon," said Carter, though she sounded uncertain.

"Should we do a group cuddle?" Beck suggested.

"Absolutely not," Adi said.

Beck jiggled on the spot. "Ranielle's going to be so mad. Anyone got a good reason for why we're in the freezer besides breaking in to steal ice cream?"

"Forget that. We have something more important to talk about." Adi looked at Sierra. "How about you tell us what happened the night Alicia was murdered?"

21
Adi

Adi stood apart from the others, waiting for an answer. Beck and Carter huddled together for warmth. Even Sierra inched closer to them.

"Okay," she said. "You wanna know? The last time I talked to Alicia was by the pool around nine o'clock. I asked where the hell she'd been sneaking off to. She was hardly ever in the complex. Always disappearing, sometimes for hours at a time. She wouldn't even take the shuttle to the studio most of the time, just show up later in an Uber. She never told anyone where she was going or who she was meeting, and I suspected she was cheating. I wanted to confront her before the finale."

"What does disappearing have to do with cheating?" Beck said.

"She wasn't as clever as the show made her out to be. I thought maybe she was meeting with someone and they were feeding her answers."

"Really?" Carter said, voice lifting in surprise.

"She was charming and beautiful, a great foil for her villainous sister. Remember when they revealed I was one of her opponents and she flipped out? She thought I was there to steal her limelight. But the truth was, I never auditioned the first time. I was offered a spot to create sibling rivalry. They wanted her, but they'd done their research. My job was to create drama, while she was there to win over the audience."

"Typical show business," Adi muttered.

"So I played the villain and Alicia played the hero. But she *knew* stuff in the game. Math, ciphers, literature references—there's no way she was solving them on her own."

"A week ago, I wouldn't have believed it," Beck said. "Now I know how Ranielle Russell works, I'm not surprised."

"They wanted the sisters to be in the finale, head-to-head," Adi said.

"Exactly," Sierra said. "And it wasn't hard to figure out who the audience was rooting for—which meant the producers wanted her to win, too."

"What happened when you confronted her?" Carter asked.

"I asked to talk outside. You can imagine how it went down when I accused her of cheating."

Adi laughed dryly.

"But Elijah heard us fighting," Sierra continued, "which obviously looked pretty bad for me after the fact."

"And was she?" asked Carter. "Cheating, I mean."

"Nothing she admitted to. She claimed I didn't give her enough credit. But then she said something *bizarre*." Sierra's brow furrowed as Carter's teeth chattered loudly. "Put your hood over your head. It'll keep the heat from escaping too quickly."

Carter followed her advice.

"What did Alicia say?" Adi asked.

Sierra huddled deeper into her jacket. "She offered to give me her share of the prize money if her team won."

"No way," Carter said. "Sh-she said in all the interviews that you two wouldn't share."

"Exactly. And it pissed me off. I was sure it was another mind game, but she kept insisting it was real. She said the prize money was small pickings compared to what was coming."

"Alicia had other money coming in?" Beck said. "Shhhhivers, it's cold. Join our huddle, Sierra. We need more body warmth."

Adi was sure Sierra wouldn't budge, but she shuffled over, next to Carter and Beck.

"You too," Beck said, reaching out to Adi.

"Not a chance," Adi said.

"Alicia worked retail before the show," Sierra said. "Minimum wage. It wasn't coming from there. It must've been from someone in Hollywood."

"A boyfriend?" Beck said. "Or girlfriend? Maybe the same person who was giving her the answers?"

"Maybe, yeah." Sierra paused. "Okay. Here's the thing. There's something only a very small number of people know. But you have to understand what it was like for us, growing up."

She fell silent.

Adi was beginning to wonder whether Sierra's brain had frozen over or something when Beck squeezed her shoulder gently and said, "It's okay. Whenever you're ready," and Sierra released a shuddering breath.

"I told you our parents had died. Well . . . our first foster home . . . it wasn't . . . it wasn't safe."

Her lashes, flecked with small icicles, blinked rapidly.

She drew another breath and said, much steadier, "I won't bore you with the details, but basically, by the time social services found out what was going on, Alicia and I were already broken."

The raw cookie dough churned in Adi's stomach.

"Oh, Sierra," Carter whispered.

"After that, Alicia survived by doing whatever it took to be liked. She gave away any piece of herself others wanted, manipulating everyone to get her way. My theory is she was seeing someone at the studio, whoever was helping her cheat, and they filled her head with some Hollywood nonsense about making her a star."

Carter tried to draw Sierra into a proper hug, but Sierra gently pushed her away.

"None of that means she deserved what happened to her," Sierra said. "I still remember her as the little girl who put stuffed toys to bed every night, and who held me tight when social services told us Mom and Dad had—"

The sentence ended as an exhalation of steam, Sierra's face ghost-white in the glow of Beck's flashlight.

"You didn't stay close, though?" Beck asked. "You and Alicia?"

Sierra snapped back from wherever she'd gone. "We'd been through too much. She left as soon as she aged out of the system, abandoning me with foster family number thirteen. They weren't all bad, but the later ones didn't like my attitude."

Adi sank against the shelves, then jumped up again, since they were metal and icy. The huddle in the corner was starting to look inviting.

Sierra's fingers curled in her inner elbows. "I don't—I don't have anything. I wake up in my shitty room in my shitty rental, sell my art, eat my food, then lie awake most of the night wondering what the hell happened. Finding out who killed my sister is the only thing that matters to me." A bitter laugh escaped her. "I shouldn't have left the complex that night. I was so angry with her. As soon as she mentioned some other money, I knew she was going to get into trouble. That's why we fought. She wouldn't tell me who she was seeing. Just kept saying things were going to get better."

"You're sure she was getting the cheats from a secret lover?" Adi said.

"I can't be sure of anything. But she was so smug that night. Like she had a foolproof plan. I remember . . . She had her comforter with her. You know, the one from her room they never found? She wore it like a cape, like she was queen of the villas. Like everything was finally going her way. I *wish* I knew what she'd been hiding."

"You didn't see anyone hanging around the complex?" Beck said.

"No. We fought. I left. Elijah was already swimming laps when I got back at four thirty. That was early, even for him. I figured it was nerves before the finale." She shrugged. "There were no security cameras back then, so they couldn't track what time she left. They just know her phone wasn't at the villas when the signal went dead."

"And cameras didn't catch the killer at the studio?" asked Beck.

"No, because of the power outage. The power company had been doing rolling blackouts for weeks, trying to lessen the load on the power grid. It didn't affect us here, but the power was down around the studio. No lights. No cameras. No security gates." She rattled the facts off like they were just that—simple, basic facts. Not the convenient details that had kept her sister's killer from ever being found. Adi couldn't imagine how much she'd had to compartmentalize.

"So that's it. That's all I know. I'd wandered the streets for a few hours, slept at a park, and headed back. I have no idea where Alicia went that night, who she saw, or how she ended up in that coffin. I didn't even know she was missing until . . . until we found her."

A contemplative silence fell over the group, punctured only by their shivery breaths and chattering teeth.

"You th-think it was Fitzy," Carter said.

Sierra fixed her with a look. "He's the obvious choice."

"Young, hot, flirtatious," Adi muttered.

"Access to producers and agents," Beck added. "Not to mention the Game Master. Probably wouldn't be hard to get info on upcoming rooms."

"There are so many people in the studio, all the time," Carter argued. "It could have been anyone. A sound tech, a set designer, someone in costuming, an assistant."

"I know," said Sierra. "But whoever it was must have had money. And Fitzy—"

"Was doing a livestream," Carter reminded her. "You know how it feels to be accused of something without any proof. You c-can't just—"

"I know," Sierra said again. "I just . . . have a feeling."

"You mean like how millions of viewers had a feeling about *you*?"

Sierra's dark lips thinned in irritation. "Until we know for sure, you need to be careful. We all have to be c-careful."

"I think we need to sit," Beck said.

"Don't sit," Adi said. "The floor is way too cold."

But Carter was already sinking down. Beck joined her. Adi regarded them, wondering how much warmer it was against other people.

"You're wrong, Sierra," Beck murmured. "You said you were broken. But you're always trying to look after us. With the cooking and wanting to protect Carter. After everything that's happened to you, after that first foster family, after losing your sister, after the world accused you of murdering her—you still have the capacity to care about other people. That's not broken. That's . . . that's incredible."

It looked like Sierra couldn't speak, even if she wanted to.

Carter reached for her. "Come down here. It's warmer with three of us."

Hesitantly, Sierra lowered herself to the floor. Beck and Carter hugged either side of her.

"You just haven't found your people yet," Beck said, putting his chin on her shoulder. "But it's okay. We'll be your people."

"Y-y-y-yep," Carter said. "Come d-down here, A-Adi."

"The floor is a terrible idea," Adi said. "We'll definitely freeze to death."

"Come down here and be Sierra's people!"

"Jee-*sus*," Adi snapped, but he was grateful as he dropped down to find it a touch warmer in the huddle.

Carter squeezed his side. "Hey," she whispered. "D-don't think I haven't noticed."

"Noticed what?"

"That you haven't gotten any phone calls or messages since we got here."

Adi's jaw tensed. "That's not true. My mom's texted." He tried to laugh, but his mouth was too cold to do the sound justice. "To ch-chew me out for getting her c-c-car towed."

"Then we'll be your people, t-too," Carter said.

He grimaced.

"My s-sister left a clue," Sierra said. "She told me if anything happened to her, I had to look under the terrace in her villa. At the time, I assumed she was being melodramatic, but now I think she might have left me a note."

"W-wait," said Beck. "She knew something was going to happen to her?"

"Yeah. At least, that's what she said a week before she died. And then something changed. I guess she thought she had everything under control."

"Did you tell the police?" Beck said. "They could have searched—"

"They did. They thought I was lying to save my ass. If I could have a look at the terrace myself, maybe I'll find what they missed."

Adi tried to process this, but his brain was no longer cooperating.

"So?" Carter asked. "Have you searched the terrace?"

"I've been t-trying. Alicia's old villa is the one Elijah and Lisa are in now. I can't get close without them seeing or hearing me."

"Sounds like you need a team," Beck said.

"How long has it been?" Carter whispered. "Maybe Vera's not coming."

"Let's call the police," Adi said, though his sludgy brain could barely comprehend the words.

But as his numb fingers fumbled for his phone, light flooded his vision. He blinked up at a furious Vera in a long floral nightdress, holding the padlock's key in her hand.

"I got accepted to *four* Ivy League universities," she said. "I could be halfway through a degree on mechanical engineering. Instead, here I am, dealing with you." She grunted and spun away. "Big regrets."

22

Carter

Carter woke to an email from Ranielle granting permission to film an exclusive studio tour. At least Ranielle recognized that Carter had some influence over the fandom. Or maybe it was to smooth over any unpleasantness from the freezer fiasco.

It would have been a major honor when Carter had first proposed the tour a week ago, but now she was in no hurry to set foot inside the place where Alicia Angelos had been stuffed into a prop. It had been horrifying enough when she thought the killer was Sierra, but at least then she could play nice and try to stay on her good side. If Sierra was innocent, that meant the killer could be anyone.

Even Fitzy—Sierra's top suspect.

Carter couldn't picture it. He was too . . . *Fitzy.*

While they were recovering from the freezer incident yesterday, she had made the team watch a recording of the livestream Fitzy had filmed the night Alicia disappeared—the whole two hours of it. She'd seen it before, but back then she hadn't fully appreciated how good he looked in that pale blue shirt, buttons open to reveal some surfer-boy shark tooth pendant, hair tousled to give a windswept look. He was patiently answering fans' questions for the entirety of the time-of-death window and then some. He'd only gotten up from his sofa once, to make popcorn in his kitchen microwave as he continued to read comments and make jokes. His alibi was solid. Even Sierra reluctantly admitted it.

But there were hundreds of people working on this show, and they didn't have anywhere near as airtight an alibi.

Carter's thoughts spiraled, always coming back to the masked assailant who had locked them inside a freezer. She wanted to believe it was an act of sabotage—someone trying to throw them off their game.

Now she wasn't so sure.

It turned out they should've contacted emergency services in the first place. After Vera arrived, paramedics had been called. Parents had been notified. Carter had needed a heated intravenous saltwater solution to warm her body. They could have died.

Maybe that had been the point.

Carter's parents had asked her to quit the show, a suggestion that would have tempted her that first day on set. But no way was she leaving now. Sierra needed her. The *team* needed her.

But their time might be limited. After the studio tour, Carter would head straight to the elimination round. There was a good chance they would be packing their bags and heading home. Well . . . not home, exactly. Eliminated teams were checked in to a hotel to wait until Sunday—a way for the producers to ensure no spoilers were leaked.

When the studio came into view, her insides clenched and she almost asked the driver to take her back to the villas.

But no. She was Kick It Carter, the Domain's highest-ranking Solve Specialist. She had been granted exclusive access to the studio—a privilege never offered to any other Clue Master. She could do this. She had to do this.

She climbed out of the car, trying to convince herself that she was in no danger. The studio would have cameras, other people around. She was safe here.

The receptionist finished signing her in as Vera stalked into the lobby. Carter tensed. She had promised herself that the first chance she got, she would tell Vera how grateful she was—they all were—that she had come to their aid.

But Vera spoke first. "Why did they ask you to do this instead of me?"

"Um. I . . . I don't know." Carter scrunched her shoulders by her ears. "Listen, I wanted to say—"

Vera held up a hand. "Not interested in how four teens who are supposedly geniuses got themselves locked in a freezer. I want to know why Ranielle thinks it's okay for an overrated influencer to film a studio tour when I've been suggesting it for the last two years."

Overrated?

Every ounce of gratitude evaporated.

"I guess she thought I'd do a good job with it," Carter said coolly.

Vera stepped closer. Carter couldn't help backing away, even though Vera was a couple of inches shorter than her. "Do not mess with me, Carter Kelly. You have no idea what I'm capable of."

Carter's brain was scrambling for some sort of response when a voice called out in an Australian accent, "Vee, there you are! I've been looking all over for you."

Vera growled—literally growled—as she spun to face Fitzy. "What?"

"Whoa, down, girl," said Fitzy, raising his hands. "I was talking with Ranielle. She wants you to make a series of countdown reels for the fortune teller room. You know, bonus content, maybe reaching out to the actress in the crystal ball video and stuff. And . . . there was something else." He thought for a moment, then snapped his fingers. "Right! She wants tarot-themed posts, where viewers get randomly selected cards with fortunes tied to them."

Vera gaped at him for a long moment before exploding. "You can't be serious! I already have this week's posts scheduled. I don't have time for any of that!"

"You could talk to Ranielle, but she stepped out for a coffee date with one of the Hitflix execs, and then she'll be up to her ears getting ready for the elimination. Probably best not to procrastinate too long, yeah?"

With a guttural scream, Vera marched away.

"Wow," breathed Carter. "I didn't realize her job was so intense."

Fitzy grinned. "Please. I made all that up. It'll keep her out of your hair while you film your studio tour. And honestly, she shouldn't be talking to you that way."

A giddy laugh climbed out of Carter's throat. "Thanks."

"Anytime." He offered an arm. "Shall we get started?"

Carter looked from the creased linen of his sleeve to his dimples. "Are you . . . ?"

"Joining you? Of course I am. Wouldn't be much of a tour without a professional host, would it?"

"Wow. My subscribers are going to flip."

"Well, my agent's always telling me I need to step up my social media game." He shrugged self-consciously. "He's got much bigger celebrities to worry about than me, so when he gives advice, I try to listen. Are you ready?"

Carter found herself smiling. Five minutes ago she wouldn't have been able to answer that question with anything positive.

Now?

"Yeah. I am." She held up her phone. Fitzy squeezed in close. She summoned her brightest smile and hit record. "Hey, gang, I'm Kick It Carter, and I have a surprise for you. Today, I've been given exclusive access behind the scenes of the *Escape Game* studio, and as you can see, I'm joined by a very special guest."

"'Ello, 'ello," said Fitzy. "Welcome to my little home away from home. Can't wait to show you what it's really like on set. You ready, Carter?"

Her insides fluttered. Her name, that accent . . . "Lead the way."

With Fitzy taking control, the video was infinitely better than anything she could have recorded on her own. He took her through the greenrooms, the costume closet, even the editing suites, where Carter overheard someone ranting about "those horoscope letters—what was Louis thinking? We can't air that!"

On Soundstage A, Fitzy walked her through the chemistry lab and talked about how they'd consulted with chemists to concoct a formula that would glow once the four correct liquids were combined.

On Soundstage B, Carter got to properly take in the details of the fortune teller's tent. With the lights on full power, the set was less mystical than before—the curtains and tablecloth were cheap fabric, and the crystal ball was just plastic with a projector inside. Funny how real it had felt at the time.

"What do you think about taking a peek at the *finale* room?" Fitzy said, waggling his eyebrows as they exited through the carved Hermit door.

Carter's pulse jumped. She stared across the corridor at the large closed doors of Soundstage E. She could hear the thumps of nail guns, the grind of table saws. Her thoughts skipped back to the post on the Domain.

1:13 p. m.: Body discovered in studio prop . . .

"Is that where she was found?" she whispered. For a moment, she forgot that she was filming. But then Fitzy's smile slipped and his gaze darted to the phone, which was now aimed at some random utility cart. Carter quickly realigned it. "Sorry. I was . . . There's been a lot of talk lately. On the Domain . . ."

"No, it's good. The producers want to pretend nothing happened, but . . . it *did*." Distress crept into his tone, reminding Carter it wasn't just Sierra and her team on the set that day. Fitzy had seen the body, too. It must've been awful.

"A lot of people think the post on the Domain is a hoax," Carter murmured. "A publicity stunt."

Fitzy grimaced. "Ranielle was *not* happy about it. She's ordered the webmaster to take it down, but every time they try, it keeps getting put back up."

"So it's not a publicity stunt?"

"If it is, I'm not in on the joke." A heady silence hung between them.

Carter looked apologetically at the screen. "Whew, that got a lot darker than I'd intended." She shrugged, trying to lighten the mood. "I won't be looking in the finale room today. Hopefully, my team will last long enough to tackle it together in a few weeks."

"You will," said Fitzy. "I believe in you."

Carter wished she had his confidence. With the elimination mere hours away, fear was beginning to gnaw at her that they wouldn't be continuing. "I bet you say that to all the contestants."

"No," Fitzy said. "I definitely don't." They made eye contact, and Carter's pulse fluttered. "Hey, let me ask you a question. What's your favorite thing about being on the show?"

It took a moment to register his question. Not that long ago, she would've said that her favorite thing was getting into the rhythm of the room, absorbed in solving the puzzles. But now?

"The people," she said. "It's so nice being around others who are as obsessed with escape rooms as I am. I feel like I've really started to click with my team."

Fitzy made a buzzer sound, so loud it made her jump.

"Wrong!" he declared. "The correct answer was *me*. I'm your favorite part of the show!" He mimed stabbing a knife into his heart. "You destroy me, Carter Kelly."

Carter laughed, feeling electric. "You're a close runner-up."

"Aww. I'll have to take it. How about your least favorite thing?"

The pressure. The doubts. The constant anxiety over whether or not she was meeting everyone's expectations.

But Kick It Carter would never admit to any of that.

"I'm paranoid about having to do something physical. Mind puzzles, no problem. Shooting hoops to open a door? Not happening."

"I guess you won't be putting your hand up for the dexterity challenge."

"No way."

Alicia had crushed the dexterity challenge. Sierra might have believed her sister was cheating, but the maze, the obstacles, had been pure skill.

And Sierra's other suspicions . . .

Alicia was seeing someone.

Maybe Carter could take advantage of this behind-the-scenes tour for more than just her followers.

Tucking a curl behind her ear, Carter turned back to Fitzy with a look she hoped was a lot more nonchalant than she felt. "Here's one thing everyone wants to know. What's the tea when it comes to off-screen romances?"

She heard the words come out of her mouth and regretted them instantly. She sounded like some sleazy gossip-rag reporter.

But Fitzy took it in stride, even as he literally strode down a hall full of construction workers and building supplies. "Well . . . obviously the contestants are teenagers. It'd be very inappropriate for the crew to—"

"You're a teenager."

He gave a laugh that sounded almost nervous. "Yes. Um. But remember my contract? There's a clause." He swallowed hard. "Like a . . . *I could get fired* sort of clause."

"Oh," said Carter, surprised at how her stomach lurched. "That sounds intense."

His smile turned wry. "It's never been an issue. Lots of fish in the sea, and all that." He didn't look at Carter as he said it.

Motive, her mind whispered. If Fitzy had been dating Alicia, he didn't want anyone to find out because he'd lose his job.

But—he'd been filming a livestream! There was no way it was Fitzy.

Right?

"Fitzy, Fitzy, Fitzy."

Louis Augustus Russell sauntered down the hall, his gold suspenders shimmering. "Are you keeping Miss Kelly to yourself?"

Panic spiked through Carter as Ranielle's missive to leave the

Game Master alone echoed in her brain. Hastily turning her attention back to the camera lens, she stammered, "And that puts a wrap on the tour! Drop me a comment about what behind-the-scenes *Escape Game* content you want to see next!" She stopped the recording. "Oh, hey, Game Master."

She tried to sound casual.

She failed.

"Carter," he said. "You're here early today."

"Filming some content for the fans." She waved the phone at him. "Don't worry. Ranielle approved it. I promise."

"She's giving a studio tour," said Fitzy. "I thought I'd show her around."

"How generous of you," said Louis, but his gaze stayed fixed on Carter. "Ranielle told me about what happened the other night. It's a relief you're all right."

Carter forced a smile. "Thanks. We're fine. Just . . . shook up a bit."

Fitzy cast his attention between the two of them. "What happened the other night?"

Louis opened his mouth, but Carter jumped in first, "One of the other contestants thought it would be funny to lock my team in the cafeteria's industrial freezer." She laughed, trying to play it off like no big deal. "A prank."

"*What?* Is everyone okay?"

She waved away his worries. The last thing she wanted was for Fitzy to think she was a whiner. "We weren't in there for long."

Fitzy's face was still creased with concern. "Do they know who it was?"

"Not yet. But we have our suspicions."

Understanding darkened Fitzy's eyes. "I can make a few guesses myself."

"The security company is looking into it," said Louis. "But we're relieved no one was seriously hurt. And now, I do believe it's time to get into wardrobe." He sent a lopsided smile toward Carter. "You don't mind if I steal our host away, do you?"

"No, of course not. My team should be here soon. I think I need to start getting ready, too."

"Wait, wait," said Fitzy, snapping his fingers. "Carter, you never got that exclusive Game Master interview."

She tensed. "That's okay. I shouldn't have tried to—"

"No, Fitzy's right," said Louis. "You're a great asset this season. I don't know what my wife's problem is. Let me see your phone."

She handed it to him uncertainly. Louis created a new contact for himself. Under the Company tab, he added, Game Master.

Then he entered his number.

Carter gaped. "Is this . . . your direct line?"

He chuckled as he handed it back. "Whenever you want that interview, send me a message. It's the least I can do."

"Um. Sure. Okay. Thanks?" She couldn't help being a little thrilled, but also confused. Wouldn't an email have been better?

Sierra's dire warnings echoed in her head, but she dismissed them. Of all the people on this show, Louis was least likely to be the murderer. The love and attention to detail he put into his escape rooms proved how deeply he cared for the game, and the contestants.

Which reminded her—

"Actually . . . Game Master," she said, as he started to turn away. "Can I ask a question now? Off the record."

"That depends on your question," said Louis, though he'd noticeably preened when she called him Game Master.

"I was wondering about something in the fortune teller room. The, um . . . the horoscope pictures. We were surprised by *Tenth-Third-F-U.* Was there a meaning behind that? A message you were trying to send to somebody?"

Louis's broad smile faded at the same time Fitzy gave a low whistle and said, "See? I told you you'd have to watch for this one."

"Yes, our Solve Specialist," said Louis, his assured expression returning. "You know me, Carter. I like to mix things up. Keep contestants on their toes. I never want anyone saying that our clues have gotten . . . predictable. Why don't you—"

He was interrupted by a high-pitched, saccharine voice. "Oh, Mr. Game Master?"

A woman strode toward them in clacking heels. She looked vaguely familiar, but Carter couldn't place her.

"Holy hell," Fitzy muttered under his breath. "What's *she* doing here?"

Louis didn't smile as he stepped forward. "Symphony. Can I help you?"

"Oh yes," she said. "I'm here to talk to your wife."

"Is she expecting you?"

"Am I supposed to make an appointment now? After everything I've done for this show?"

A muscle flexed in Louis's jaw. "Of course not. But Ranielle is very busy."

"Never too busy for me, I'm sure." Her gaze slid past Louis to Carter. She scanned her from head to foot and gave a slight scoff.

Carter immediately felt as small as a snail. But then an arm was around her. Fitzy squeezed her to his side while reaching his other hand toward the woman. "Don't believe we've met. I'm Fitzy."

Symphony didn't take the outstretched hand. "Enchanted," she said, before turning to Louis. "Shall we?"

As Louis led the way toward the producer's office, Fitzy let his hand drop with a bemused chuckle. "What a piece of work."

"Who is she?" asked Carter, noting that Fitzy's arm was still around her.

"Symphony Parvesh. Used to be an A-lister. Now she's the face of some fitness lifestyle brand."

"Right," said Carter. "That's where I've seen her. Hawking those god-awful shakes."

"That's the one. Course, she's also Adi's mum."

Her eyes bugged. "*My* Adi? Er—my team's Adi?"

"He hasn't mentioned his famous parentage?" His dimples flashed, though his smile was rueful. "Can't say I blame him."

"Wow. I'm beginning to feel guilty for having normal, boring parents."

Fitzy gave a pained look that made Carter feel like she'd said something wrong.

Crap. She hadn't even thought about what *his* childhood might have been like.

"Except Beck!" she said quickly, in an effort to cover up whatever faux pas she'd just made.

"Beck?" said Fitzy, apparently grateful for the subject change.

"Yeah. We haven't discussed it at length, but he seems relatively well-adjusted. No way he has any secret family drama." She laughed nervously. "No way at all."

23

Beck

As soon as they'd all been herded into the greenroom, Team Dread challenged the other teams to a foosball tournament, leading to a lot of cheers and colorful swearing. Beck supposed it made for a fine distraction from the upcoming elimination round, but despite the raucousness, his thoughts were elsewhere.

Solve the murder. Win the grand prize.

No biggie.

He looked at Adi on the opposite side of the couch, wondering how he could act so casual. For once, Adi wasn't nose-deep in a book but rather on his phone, where Beck could make out the Domain's forums.

Beck's attention traveled to Sierra, who was sitting on a beanbag in the corner, her face obscured by the same magazine that had been in their welcome bags. Victor Cunningham's gaze pierced into Beck.

The headline promised a glimpse behind the scenes of Cunningham's state-of-the-art Sweetbrier Resort. Beck had already read the article four times, practically drooling over the scant details the writer had given about the labyrinthine, puzzle-filled complex.

"That place sounds like paradise, doesn't it?" Beck said, loud enough to get Sierra's attention but not so much as to draw the other teams' notice. "I'm obsessed."

Sierra glanced at him in confusion, then turned the magazine over to see the cover. "Ugh. You're one of those. I should have known."

"What? You aren't curious?"

"About some pompous nerd Disneyland? Nope."

It seemed incomprehensible that any contestant on *The Escape Game* wouldn't be clamoring over themself to get to Sweetbrier. "But there are over two dozen escape rooms in one complex. Even the hotel rooms have built-in puzzles. I heard you need to solve a code to access your minibar!"

"Why would anyone want that?"

"So you can feel like you earned your M&M's?"

"Uh-huh." Sierra turned a page of the magazine. "I'm not wasting my time or money on some cheesy, overhyped resort that was built with stolen treasure. Victor Cunningham can bite me."

Stolen treasure.

Adi's head swung toward them so fast he dropped his phone on the floor. "What are you talking about?"

"Sweetbrier," Beck said, not taking his attention from Sierra. "Why did you say the treasure was stolen?"

"He totally lowballed some family out of their property when he bought it. He had Jasper Barrett's map. He knew the treasure was there. All he had to do was wait for a drought year and buy the land for dirt cheap. It may be legal, but it's a dog act."

"I'm sure he compensated the family when he found the treasure," Adi muttered, picking up his phone.

Sierra snorted. "Yeah. Because multimillionaires love giving handouts to the people they've screwed over."

Victor Cunningham's confident grin crinkled as Sierra folded the magazine in half. Though only in his forties, Victor was practically a folklore hero.

More than a century ago, a pioneer named Jasper Barrett had struck it rich in the California Gold Rush, only to become so paranoid that he was driven to bury his wealth in the foothills of the Rocky Mountains before he vanished completely, leaving behind a letter and a cryptic map to indicate the location of the gold. Though countless treasure seekers had searched, it was Victor Cunningham—already a self-made entrepreneur by that point—who ultimately cracked the code and unearthed millions of dollars' worth of gold bars less than a mile from Sweetbrier Creek.

A few years after making headlines, Victor Cunningham broke ground on that same land, naming his resort after the treasure that had changed his reputation from nerdy puzzle maker to legendary treasure hunter.

Beck might have loathed the guy . . . if he wasn't so effing *cool*.

The greenroom door swung open and Carter walked in.

"Where have you been?" Beck asked as she trudged to the sofa and sat down between him and Adi.

"The studio tour for the Domain ran long," she said. "I just got out of hair and makeup."

A series of deafening *bangs* and *cracks* came from the foosball table, followed by Gabriela throwing victorious arms into the air.

Carter swiveled to face Adi. "Did you know your mom's here?"

Adi's body jolted like he'd been given an electric shock. "Now?"

"Yeah, I ran into her when I was in the hall."

"Why is she here?" asked Beck. "Is she freaked out about the freezer incident? She's not taking you home, is she?"

"She's not here because of the freezer," said Adi, shutting off his phone screen. "She doesn't care about that."

Beck frowned. *His* parents had certainly cared when he'd called to tell them. It was a borderline hysteria level of caring. In the end, he had spent much more time comforting them than they did comforting him.

"She said she wanted to talk to Ranielle," said Carter. Her tone lightened. "You could have told us your mom is a celebrity."

Adi scoffed. "*Was* a celebrity."

"Who is she?" Beck asked.

When it was clear Adi didn't intend to answer, Carter said, "Symphony Parvesh."

Beck clutched at his heart. "The archaeologist from the Cursed Tomb franchise?"

Carter shrugged.

"What? Don't tell me you haven't seen them!" said Beck. "They were what first got me into puzzles. Well, that and the Jasper Barrett treasure."

"I don't know about the movies, but lately she's been doing these infomercials—"

Adi groaned loudly and slumped down until his head rested on the back of the couch.

Carter grimaced. "That's probably not important. Why do you think she's here, if not because of the freezer?"

"To continue her crusade of making my life hell?" Adi said, staring dolefully at the ceiling. "Actually, strike that. By this point I'm sure she's much more focused on torturing the producers instead. That'll teach Ranielle to get in bed with the devil."

"She did mention something about how she helped the show . . ."

"Uh-huh. I'm sure Ranielle regrets getting her involved."

They waited for an explanation. When one wasn't immediately forthcoming, Carter poked him on the shoulder.

He sat up again. "She's trying to claw her way back into Hollywood, either through me or through *that* guy." He tipped his head toward Sierra.

Beck looked disbelievingly at the crumpled magazine cover. His attention whipped back to Adi, whose frown had turned into a scowl. "Victor Cunningham?"

"That's the one."

"That makes so much sense!" said Carter. "The fans *love* him."

"I've been thinking maybe my mom cajoled him into helping out the show in return for getting her own fingers in the pie."

Beck tilted his head to one side. "Your mom knows Victor Cunningham?"

"They had a fling when he was a consultant on the first Cursed Tomb movie. That's why they killed off her character in the second movie. Because she was pregnant."

"Harsh," Carter said.

"Hollywood," Adi reminded her.

"But that movie came out, like . . . seventeen? Eighteen years ago?" said Beck. "Wouldn't that mean . . ."

There was a long, silent moment. Carter gasped. Beck's eyes rounded in disbelief. "Victor Cunningham is your *dad*?"

Adi's lips tightened.

"No freaking way," Beck said. "What's he like?"

"No idea. Never met him. Symphony didn't tell him I existed, and I can't contact him without sounding deranged. *Hey, Victor, remember that woman you slept with eighteen years ago . . . ?* He'd think it was some scam to get his money."

"Great mom," Sierra said, deadpan.

"Except," Adi said, "if she got him to agree to sponsor this show, she *must* have told him about me. Maybe even got a paternity test. He wouldn't be going along with her shenanigans otherwise."

"Then why hasn't he contacted you?" Beck said.

"Because . . . I'm Symphony Parvesh's son? I figure he's waiting to see whether I take after her."

"I don't think—" Sierra started, but the room erupted in a chorus of groans and boos, cutting her off.

"That's cheating!" yelled Ollie from Team Illuminati.

Delphi cackled. "That's winning."

Ollie reached out and gave one of the handles an angry spin. "I'm done."

"Sore loser," Neil muttered. But the other teams were clearly finished with the tournament, and no amount of Jarius calling them scared little wimps was going to change it.

When things had settled down, Nadia, the leader of Team Mind Hack, asked loudly, "So are we going to talk about it or not?"

"What?" said Neil. "That four of you losers are going home today?"

Delphi smacked her bubble gum, her glance cutting toward Carter. "Or the fact that Team Hell-Suck got themselves stuck in a freezer?"

Beck felt his teammates tense. By now everyone had heard that someone had locked them in with a padlock and that the masked assailant wasn't identifiable on the new security cameras. Only Team Dread had mocked them for it.

"Or maybe we should talk about how Ginger spewed all over me?" Jarius added.

"None of that is what I meant," Nadia said, raising her voice. "I was talking about the coded ribbon." She paused, waiting. "From the last room? Asking us to solve a murder?"

Emma from Crown Jewels piped up, "We figured it was the producers messing with us. Same as the Alicia Angelos anagram in the snag round. A publicity stunt."

"We thought it could be some sort of memorial to Alicia," said Beck, "but that note was . . ."

"Real," said Carter.

"But what's the lie in the clues?" Nadia demanded. "And why has this person asked *us* to figure it out?"

"Um, because we're supposed to be the smartest people in the studio?" Jarius said. "Though that's obviously not the case for all of us."

"*F-U*," said Sierra.

Everyone's heads swiveled toward her.

"Excuse me?" Jarius demanded.

Sierra lowered her magazine. "*J-C-F-U*. The code from the fortune teller's room. *F-U* sounds like a message to the killer. The producers wouldn't put something like that in." She sank deeper into her beanbag. "And October third was Alicia's birthday."

Her words were met with silence. Even Jarius frowned thoughtfully. Beck remembered how Sierra had asked in the room whether the numbers meant a date.

She had known what this was about, even then.

"But how can someone be slipping these clues into the game without Louis knowing?" Nadia said finally.

"Maybe he *does* know," Sierra said. "Maybe he's letting them do it so he can find the killer, too."

"Or maybe it's him," said Emma. "Calling himself the *Real* Game Master on the forums to throw people off."

"The Game Master doesn't speak like that," Adi said, waving his phone, which was open to the ribbon clue post.

"Right, and no one can fake a voice online," Emma shot back.

Delphi curled her lip. "No matter who's doing it, Ranielle will put a stop to it. Her precious *family* show."

A throat cleared in the doorway. An intern with a headset and clipboard was waiting. "They're ready for you on set." He turned away, then paused and looked back at the crowded room again. "A word of advice. Don't let Ranielle Russell catch you talking about Alicia, or those messages that have been cropping up in the rooms. She's ready to murder the next person who brings it up."

24
Sierra

Sierra and the others followed the intern through the studio to the show's main set, with its steampunk vibe and five risers, one for each team.

After today, there would be only four.

Sierra gazed around, wondering who here had the guts to slip coded messages under Ranielle's nose. The nerve to lock her team in a freezer. The stomach to kill her sister.

There was Fitzy in a tall director's chair, an assistant holding a bottled water for him to drink through a straw while a makeup artist dabbed powder onto his brow.

Ranielle Russell and Vera, having a muttered conversation over a notebook. Ranielle looked as displeased as usual.

The Game Master, strutting across the front of the stage, high-fiving members of the Crown Jewels as he passed.

The intern scurrying through with a coffee. The woman with muscles to rival Jarius's, adjusting massive lights on the side of the stage. How strong did a person have to be to suffocate someone? Alicia wasn't muscular, but Sierra knew she would have fought with everything she had.

It was hot beneath the lights. Sweat dripped down the backs of her knees.

After the final mic check, Ranielle stood before them on the stage. She surveyed each contestant, then turned in a slow circle, her gaze carrying over the rest of the crew, until every person in the room was staring back at her, silent.

"As many of you know," she said, "this show very nearly got canceled after the tragic events of last season. They say no publicity is bad publicity, but they're full of shit. Our reputation is everything. We are a feel-good family show, featuring some of the most brilliant minds of the next generation. A little puzzle-solving, a little wholesome conversation . . . a little *teamwork*. And yet." Her gaze sharpened. "And yet, here we are. The show where a teenage contestant was brutally murdered. The killer never found. The media throwing around words like 'corruption' and 'cheating.'" Her voice took on a new edge. "I have clawed our way back onto the air. I have fought to win over Hitflix, our sponsors, the media, the fans. And I will not have my efforts ruined by some smart-ass who thinks it's funny to put these *messages*"—she punctuated the word with air quotes—"inside our escape rooms."

Sierra glanced at Louis. He was standing to the side of the stage, nodding along with a serious—almost angry—expression. Sierra wished she could tell if it was an act.

"This nonsense ends today," Ranielle continued. "My legal team is standing by, ready to destroy any one of you who even *thinks* about commenting on that perverse message. Remember: Family show. Puzzles and games. A million dollars at stake." She finished this speech with a predatory smile. "And don't forget to have fun."

She stalked off the stage, flicking a hand to the cameras. "Carry on."

"You heard the boss," came the director's voice. "Action!"

Sierra put on her game face as the cameras started rolling. The *Escape Game* theme music played through the studio as the crane camera swooped toward the hosts.

"Wow, Game Master," said Fitzy. "You really outdid yourself with that fortune teller room."

"Thanks, Fitzy. I wanted our contestants to feel like the fortune teller's spirit was right there in the room with them."

"I'd say you succeeded." Fitzy looked fearfully over his shoulder. "In fact—I think I feel her presence now!"

Sierra didn't bother to hide an exaggerated eye roll, knowing it would make it onto the aired footage.

"If Madame Clara Voyance were here," Fitzy continued, growing serious, "she'd be telling us that the fate of one of these teams is about to be changed forever. Tonight, one team will be eliminated."

"A real shame. I've been genuinely impressed by the skills and strategies put forward by our teams this season. I would love to see them all go through to the next round."

"Me too. But that's not how the show works." Fitzy turned toward the teams, poised on their risers. "Leaders, come forward, please."

Sierra sauntered between Beck and Carter, moving to the front of the stage with the four other leaders of her rival teams.

"How are we feeling?" Fitzy asked them.

Jarius crossed his arms. "Ready to seal our victory. Let's get on with it!"

"The swagger!" said Fitzy.

"I said we were here to win, and that hasn't changed. We're taking this all the way to the finale."

Sierra barely registered his peacock posing. There was so much riding on this moment. She'd known it would be intense—she recalled this feeling well—but the weight of possible failure was like a sword dangling over her head. She couldn't leave. She hadn't managed to get to the terrace yet. She had to find whatever her sister had left for her.

But she kept her expression neutral—callous, even, hiding the storm of emotions inside.

The music swelled to a crescendo, then stopped. The screen on the wall flashed the name of the fastest team.

"Well, Jarius," said Fitzy, "it's no surprise you're confident, because Team Dread came in first, at twenty-four minutes and thirty-seven seconds!"

Jarius pumped a fist in the air as his team whooped from their riser.

Sierra wanted to hit something. She wished the rest of her team was up here, standing by her side.

Which was unexpected. Nothing like nearly dying of hypothermia to bring people closer together.

Fitzy turned to the remaining four leaders. "In second place, finishing at twenty-five minutes and eleven seconds, is . . ."

An agonizing pause.

"Team Mind Hack!"

Nadia gave a satisfied sigh and beamed at her teammates.

"Third place, at twenty-six minutes, fourteen seconds, is . . ."

Another brutal pause.

"Team Crown Jewels!"

Emma squealed and jumped up and down.

Sierra's teeth ground. *Crap, crap, crap.*

"Which means," Fitzy continued, "Ollie, Sierra—one of you is going to have to lead your team right on home." His gaze darted past Sierra, and she scowled, certain he was looking at Carter. He needed to find someone else to feed his ego. "Team Helsing, you completed the escape room in twenty-eight minutes, two seconds."

Louis whistled. Almost two full minutes behind third place. That did not bode well. This couldn't be happening.

"While the Illuminati," Fitzy said, turning his attention to Ollie, "came in at . . ."

Pause.

"Twenty-eight minutes, thirty seconds." His voice lifted triumphantly. "Which means Team Helsing still has their name on the board!"

Ollie's head dropped as Sierra processed the words. She could hear Carter shriek distantly.

They had done it. They were still in.

But barely.

She needed to get to that terrace. *Soon.*

25
Adi

Adi's legs trembled as he stepped off the stage. Carter and Beck looked elated but kept their celebrations subdued for Ollie and his team. Sierra said nothing as she rejoined the group. Her expression was tight, mirroring how Adi felt. That had been close—too close.

Three more rounds to pass. Three more rounds to show his dad what he could do.

Adi had spent every night for months lying awake, imagining Victor Cunningham watching his son on the show. Analyzing his moves. Waiting to see if he was as clever as his old man . . . and nothing like his mother.

Adi had been determined to prove his worth. And maybe, just maybe, Victor would be so impressed that he'd ask Adi to live with him. They could catch up on lost time. Adi would never have to deal with Symphony again. The dream was almost too much to bear.

The thought of returning to his regular life, of being ignored or forgotten or treated like nothing more than Symphony's ticket back to Hollywood, made Adi feel physically ill.

He knew Symphony had used the freezer incident as an excuse to show up today, citing concern for her son. He also knew Ranielle had told her not to come, but predictably, she didn't listen. The fact that she hadn't even said hi to him—

Equally predictable.

"Aditya."

Ranielle beckoned him with a clawed finger. "With me."

Carter, Beck, and Sierra shot him questioning looks. He shrugged and split from the group.

Ranielle led Adi out of the set in the direction of her office. When they got there, Vera was sitting at the desk. She jumped up when they entered.

"What now?" Ranielle said.

"We have an appointment. Don't tell me you forgot again."

Ranielle gestured to the door. "I don't need to sign off on every damn detail. Just do your job, Vera."

Vera stormed away, casting a livid glare at Adi as she passed.

"So, what am I in trouble for, exactly?" said Adi, when she'd slammed the door behind her. "If this is about picking the lock on the dining hall . . ."

"It's not." Ranielle leaned back against the desk and folded her arms, as if she were trying to be intimidating but cool. "Take a seat."

Adi ignored the visitor's chair and wandered to the gray couch. He sat dead center, slinging both arms over the back.

He expected irritation, but Ranielle only smiled. "You have a noticeable presence on camera."

Adi opened his mouth to make a smart-ass comment and found he had nothing. Of all the things he'd expected from the executive producer, that wasn't one of them.

"I like you, Aditya," she continued. "The audience does, too. You've got a vibe. A look. An attitude. Vera tells me your name has been all over the Clue Master forums . . . but you probably know that already."

He'd had no idea. It was strange Carter hadn't told him. Maybe she was jealous of his popularity. Although . . . from everything he'd seen, she seemed like the type who would cheer a teammate on rather than compete against them.

"Okay?" he said when he realized Ranielle was waiting for an answer.

"There are people who have suggested you'd make an exceptional show host." She paused, letting this sink in. "I'm wondering if you might be interested in the position, starting next season."

Adi dropped his arms to his sides. "Sorry, what? Why? Is Fitzy quitting?"

"It's time for Fitzy's career to take a new direction."

"Is this from him, or you?"

"From Hitflix. They don't think he's the right fit for the role. They want"—she gestured vaguely in Adi's direction—"a fresh perspective."

"Right," Adi drawled.

"I'm serious. You're good-looking. Charming. Smart enough to hold your own with Louis. You could help elevate the show to a whole new level."

He tried to imagine reading cheesy cue cards and sipping water through a straw while people dabbed at his face. *No thank you.*

"I can see your hesitation," Ranielle said, "and I'd like to add that we're planning to make significant changes next season."

"What kind of changes?"

"I'm not legally allowed to disclose that information, but I can promise new destinations. First-class flights. The most elaborate puzzles in the world."

Sweetbrier Resort.

It couldn't be.

But maybe it could. Maybe the invitations were only the beginning, and Victor Cunningham was extending his offer to a fresh slew of puzzle-loving teens. In that case, Adi would be receiving more than a one-off chance to visit the resort. He'd have a whole season to get to know his dad.

He felt like a fish staring at an obvious bait on a hook. But he'd be out of his mind to turn down an opportunity like that.

"Did my mother put you up to this?"

Ranielle bristled. "Don't insult me. I'm still the executive producer here."

Maybe. But Symphony had a way of twisting things in her favor, and the fact that she happened to be skulking around the studio only made Adi more suspicious. It was too much of a coincidence.

No wonder the editing team had made him look better than he was. This whole thing was preplanned.

Being the host of a reality show wouldn't swing Victor's vote in his favor, especially not if Symphony had anything to do with it.

On the other hand, if Adi could spend some time with his dad, prove he wasn't some shallow Hollywood type—

"I'm not making this proposal lightly," Ranielle said. "Give it some thought, and let's discuss again after the next round. I trust you can keep this between us until then? Fitzy doesn't know, and I don't see the point in enlightening him until after this season is wrapped."

Rough break for Fitzy.

"Oh—and there is one small stipulation."

Adi sighed. There was always a catch. "What?"

"I like winners, Aditya."

His eyelid twitched. "So . . . your offer only stands if my team wins the season?"

"I knew you were a smart kid. I'm thinking it might be . . . prudent . . . to have a strategy in place in the event your team continues to struggle. You might require, let's say, *extra assistance* for some of the clues."

"You want me to cheat?"

"I want you to see the big picture. This is show business. You can't be naive enough to think we don't tweak and edit to our advantage."

"Of course I know that," Adi snapped. "Reality shows are never actual reality."

She laughed. "Oh, they are. They're the producer's reality. And my reality is seeing you as a winner, and host of next season."

Adi got up. As if he needed help solving a few puzzles.

"I'll think about your host offer," he said, "but I don't need the 'extra assistance.' I'm perfectly capable of solving a couple of escape rooms on my own."

"Except you're not on your own, are you? You have an entire team. One that hasn't proven to be completely reliable."

Adi hesitated. She had an annoying point. And he *really* wanted a way to talk to his dad.

But then—Victor would be mortified if he discovered his son was a cheat.

"No," Adi said. "I can do it, even if they can't. I don't need help."

"If you say so. Just know, Aditya, the offer is only good as long as you stay in the game."

"What was that about?" Beck said as Adi rejoined his team on their way to the shuttle.

"I'll tell you later," Adi muttered, aware that Jarius was watching them. He sat by the window for the trip back to the complex, considering his options. Despite what Ranielle thought she saw in him, he was no showman. He didn't have Fitzy's pizzazz. And he had no desire to do the job.

But maybe it would be worth it, if he got to see his dad . . .

When they were back in their unit, he dumped his backpack by the wall and sat in the center of the sofa, fingers steepled like he was a villainous mastermind hatching a plan. The others hovered nearby.

"Well?" said Sierra.

"Ranielle wants me to do promo for Sweetbrier Resort," Adi said. There was *some* truth in it, at least. "After Victor announces that I'm his son."

They were quiet as they digested this.

"So he knows?" Beck said. "He's going to contact you?"

"Sure. After the season's finished." A guy could dream.

Sierra wrinkled her nose. "I'm hardly the poster girl for a happy childhood, but even I can see something's up with that. Why do you have to prove yourself to your own father?"

A tiny part of Adi argued that Sierra might be right, but he banished it. "He didn't even know I existed until a few months ago. And he's one of the busiest guys on the planet. Of course he's not going to drop everything for a forced family reunion—involving my mother, I might add. That's enough to put anyone off." He swung his gaze to Beck. "Ranielle hinted that they might be filming the next season at Victor's resort."

Beck's eyes widened. "Seriously?"

"That's so cool," Carter whispered.

But Beck let out a disappointed groan. "You mean if I'd waited to audition for the next season . . . ? Aw, man."

"You'll still get the invitation if we win," Sierra reminded him. "Our team would be the first ones to try his rooms. Of course, they'll probably make us do a bunch of gross publicity for it, too. So—hard pass from me."

"Wait," said Beck. Then, more forcefully. "Wait! They're *filming* the next season at the resort?"

"Sounds like," said Adi. "Why?"

A change came over Beck. He sank onto the coffee table, rubbing his bottom lip, staring at nothing.

"Beck?" said Carter. "You okay?"

"Yeah. Awesome," he said distantly. "Do you know what this means?"

"That Victor Cunningham's bank account will grow along with his humongous ego?" said Sierra. Then she looked at Adi, borderline sheepish. "Er. I'm sure he's a totally upstanding dude when you get to know him."

"You're very convincing," said Adi.

"No, listen." Beck waved his arms at them. "If the show is filming there, they'll need information about the place. Photos from a location scout. Maybe even maps or blueprints?" His gaze flickered to Adi. "Any chance Ranielle will be calling you into her office again?"

"Uh . . . yeah, probably. She wants to talk after the next round. Why?"

Beck got up, pacing in a way that was reminiscent of Sierra when she was strategizing. "This is going to sound sus, but stick with me. I need to know everything you can find out about that place. And I mean *everything*."

"Oh god," said Sierra. "You're not just a fanboy. You're a stalker."

"No," said Beck. "I mean—sort of. But not the way you're thinking." His eyes were almost feverish. "Do you remember when we were talking about how Victor lowballed that family out of their land?"

"Sure," said Sierra.

He took in a deep breath before blurting, "That was my family."

"What?" Adi straightened.

"Sweetbrier Ranch. It was ours since the early 1900s. I practically grew up there. But my grandpa got into some trouble—horse races, mostly—and he ended up selling the ranch for a fraction of what it was worth. My whole family was outraged. He didn't talk to any of them before he did it, and then . . ." He paused, his expression tightening. "Well. Gambling's an addiction, and . . . it didn't exactly get better. He passed away last year. No one realized until after he was gone that there was nothing left. No inheritance. No college funds. Just a bunch of debt piling up because everyone thought the profit from the ranch would cover them, and it was like they were waiting for him to die, and—" He cut himself off.

Adi gaped at him, trying to process what Beck was saying. His family, his ranch . . . and a literal trove of gold bars found buried there after the ranch was sold. To *Adi's dad*. "You've got to be kidding me."

Beck shook his head. "It's true."

Sierra cursed lowly. "How have you kept this from us? Not to mention the producers."

"Ranielle knows. I mean, she knows that my family got scammed by a property developer and we haven't recovered. It was my sob story. For the greenlights. She ate it up."

"But she doesn't know the property developer was Victor Cunningham?" asked Carter.

"Of course not. There's no way she would have brought me onto the show if she knew what I really wanted."

"Revenge," Sierra said solemnly, nodding in understanding.

But Beck looked startled. "No! Jasper Barrett buried his gold on my family's ranch almost a hundred and fifty years ago. It was right there, all along. His codes. His puzzles. If I'd had the map, I would have found it first. But here's the thing . . . I have reason to believe there's more out there. If I could just get to the resort, I really think I have a chance of finding it. *All* of it." He laughed. "I don't care about *revenge*. I want that treasure."

26

Carter

"Team Helsing, back for more! How are we feeling today?"

"Fan-freaking-tastic," deadpanned Sierra.

"A delight to talk to you, as usual." Fitzy grinned past Sierra to Carter, making her heart skip. His attention jotted to Beck and Adi. "Are you nervous?"

"Not at all," said Sierra. "We're prepared to win."

Carter wished she could channel Sierra's devil-may-care attitude, but she couldn't stop fidgeting with the cuff of her metallic jumpsuit costume. Finding Alicia's note—maybe even uncovering her killer—started with not getting eliminated in this round.

Their lack of progress this past week had left them frustrated and discouraged. Five whole days had passed since the elimination. Five days of waiting around in the villas while the show's editors put together the second episode of the season, which had gone up the night before. Plotting how Adi might be able to get more information about Sweetbrier Resort and speculating over why Alicia had been acting so cryptic the night she was murdered. Five. Whole. Days. And they hadn't found whatever Alicia had wanted Sierra to find.

Not for lack of trying. They'd taken turns distracting Elijah and Lisa so Sierra could sneak into their villa's back gate, on those rare occasions when they found it unlocked, and search around the terrace. But without more specific instructions, it was like searching for a solution to the Collatz conjecture. They didn't even know what they were looking for. They assumed it was a note of some sort, but maybe Alicia had carved a word into a tree trunk or buried a bag of evidence. Beck had suggested they bring in a metal detector, but how were they supposed to do *that* without drawing attention?

"Don't tell the other teams this," said Fitzy, leaning forward conspiratorially, "but I'm rooting for you, Helsings."

"I'm sure you are," muttered Adi.

Carter elbowed him in the side. Even though she was *positive* Fitzy wasn't a murderer, Adi had taken Sierra's side on the matter, certain that Fitzy couldn't be trusted. "He's too polished," Adi had said. "He's hiding something."

Yeah, Carter had thought. *He's hiding the fact that he's not actually that polished.*

She could relate.

"Game Master, don't keep us in suspense! We're dying to know what you have up your sleeve." Fitzy turned to Louis, who had been patiently waiting his turn to take center stage.

Louis rubbed his hands together. "How's your geography?"

Carter winced. *Terrible.*

Luckily, Beck spoke up. "For the US, fantastic! For everywhere else . . ." He waved his hand, so-so.

"Mine's not bad," Adi said.

"Let's hope it's enough," said Louis, "because I have devastating news." His expression grew serious. "Aliens are invading the planet."

Beck whispered, "I love aliens."

"Shocker," said Sierra.

Louis continued. "A globally united resistance put together a team and found the extraterrestrials' hidden base, wiping out the alien soldiers stationed there. They're now sending in you, the intelligence team, to stop—and even reverse—the attacks. The longer you take, the more cities will be wiped off the face of the planet, and the more human lives will be lost."

"So, the fate of the entire planet rests on your shoulders," Fitzy said. "No pressure."

"None at all," Carter said with a nervous giggle.

"Try not to get abducted." Fitzy winked at her, sending Carter's stomach into an inexplicable free fall. "Game Master, what clue can you offer to help our operatives?"

"Your clue today is: The enemy of your enemy is your friend."

Carter tried to commit the clue to memory as they were handed their blindfolds.

And then—the buzzer. That *obnoxious* buzzer.

"Are you messing with me?" Sierra demanded.

"Afraid not," Fitzy said. "Team Dread has once again chosen to target you with a snag. Seems a bit like a grudge, eh? Because they were the fastest team to get through the first lot of doors in the snag round, they won the ability to give a rival team a blackout period. You'll enjoy full darkness sometime during this round for *one whole minute*."

The team groaned.

Fitzy winced sympathetically. "Good luck?"

As they were led blindfolded toward the escape room, the naysayers' comments that had been posted on the Domain that morning echoed in Carter's head.

What a hack. She should've stuck with making videos.

Solve Specialist? More like Suck *Specialist.*

Guess Carter can't kick it after all.

At first, the comments had made her want to crawl beneath her bedspread. But between Fitzy's encouraging grin and the presence of her teammates, she felt resolve harden inside her chest. Her desire to do well crystallized into something else entirely.

A refusal to fail.

She was Kick It Carter. She would show them what she could do.

The heavy door slammed shut, followed by the auto-lock and Fitzy's voice in her earpiece.

"Three . . . two . . . one . . . *Escape!*"

THE ESCAPE GAME

SEASON FIVE

Round Two: The Truth Is Out There

FOUR TEAMS REMAINING

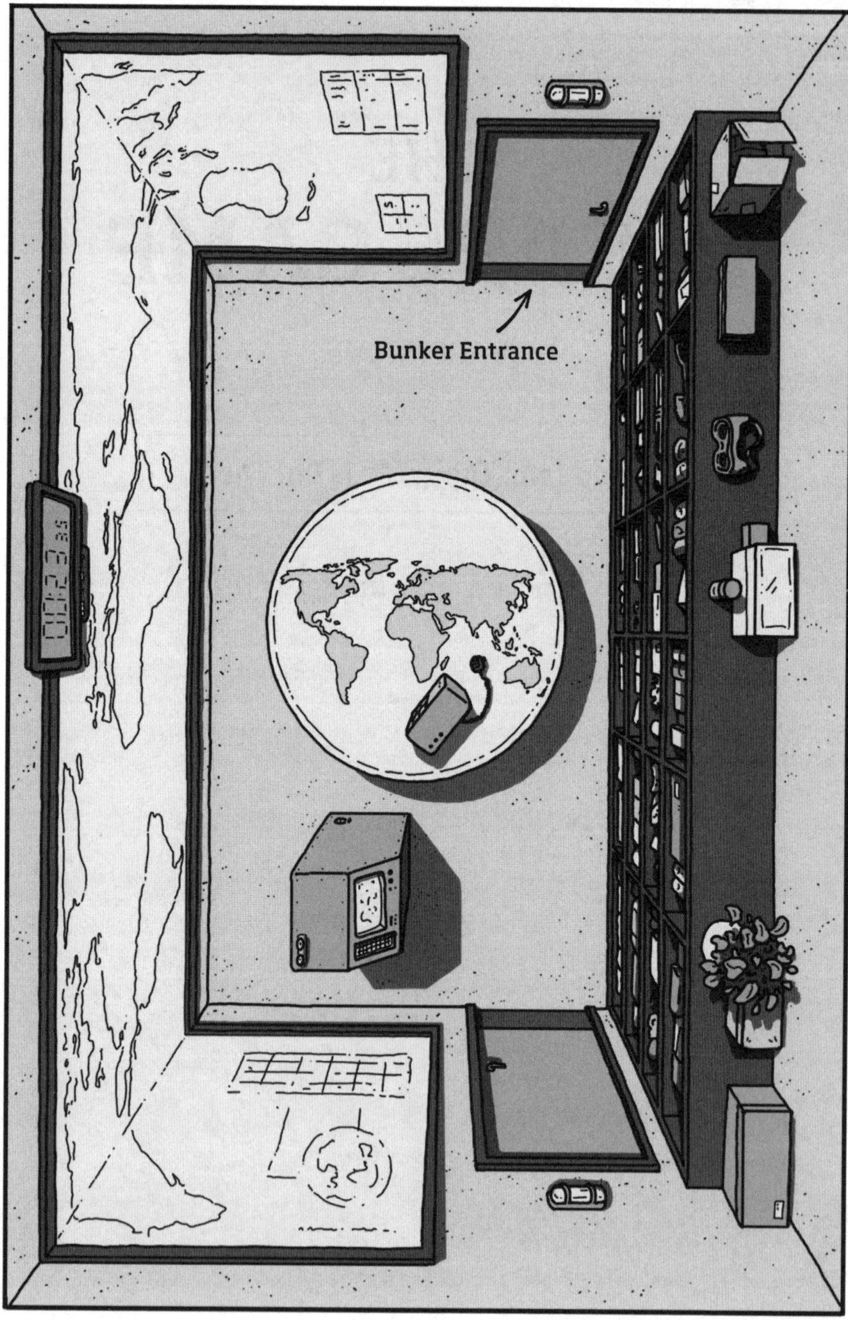
Bunker Entrance

27

Carter

Carter pulled off the blindfold. They were in a small concrete bunker with a single desk and a locked door with hazard tape around the edges. Above, a light bulb flickered in a protective cage. A digital clock displayed 00:02, the seconds steadily ticking upward.

Adi moved to the opposite door. "Four-letter combination on the lock."

Carter went to the desk and picked up a notebook, flipping the pages. "This has symbols, maybe an alien language? But I don't see a key."

Beck took a closer look under the desk while Sierra paced around the room, examining the walls.

Carter handed the notebook to Adi and inspected the black and yellow stripes on the caution tape.

Beck ducked out from under the desk with a strip of paper. "Found a note. It says: *To keep civilians from getting into the bunker, we've locked the door. Find the code, get in, stop the attacks. And remember: they may be from outer space, but they're using our resources.*"

"Any letters marked in the note?" asked Sierra, still pacing.

Beck held the strip of paper up to the flickering light. "Doesn't look like it."

"Wait. Here," said Carter, one finger jabbing the hazard tape. "There are markings and—oh, it's the key for Morse code. Is there any Morse code in the room? That could be the lock combination."

They continued searching. Beck examined the message on the strip of paper more carefully. The minutes ticked steadily up.

"This is nuts," said Carter. "It's only the first part of the room. What was the clue again?"

"*The enemy of your enemy is your friend*," said Adi, tugging on the lock. "Our enemy is this damn thing."

"The clues are always for a big part of the room," Beck said. "I don't think it's for the lock combination."

He, Adi, and Sierra began to talk at once. Carter squeezed her eyes shut, trying to concentrate. The flickering light bulb was giving her a headache. The eyeglasses were hurting her face.

A four-letter code. She tried to imagine she was sitting cross-legged on top of her duvet cover, her laptop propped on a stack of pillows, watching this episode play out on her screen. She would pause it right here. Consider what they'd found so far. A notebook. A message in strange symbols. A four-letter padlock. A note about civilians and resources. A key for Morse code.

Come on, Solve Specialist. The puzzle pieces are there. You just have to put them together.

"I can't think," she muttered, ripping off the glasses and slamming them onto the desk. "Someone should fix that darn light—" Her eyes flew open. "Everyone! Everyone, stop talking!"

The room fell silent. She pointed upward. The light would flutter, then stay on for a second or two, then flutter, flutter, flutter, stay . . .

It only took a few seconds for the others to get it.

Sierra cursed. "How did I not notice that?"

Beck joined Carter at the hazard tape, but Adi raised his hand. "I've got Morse code memorized," he said. "Give me a second."

Carter followed along with the key in the hazard tape.

Flutter, flick, flick, flutter—the equivalent of a dot, two dashes, and another dot—was the letter *P*.

Pause.

Four flutters—*H*.

Pause.

One flutter—*E*.

Pause.

Flutter, flick, flutter, flutter—*L*.

"*P-H-E-L*?" Beck said, grabbing the lock.

"*H-E-L-P*," Adi said.

"Help, right." Beck input the letters. When he pulled the lock, it opened.

Carter followed the others through the door and—

They were plunged into darkness.

"Dammit," said Sierra.

Their blackout minute had begun.

"Bet this is exciting for the viewers at home," Beck joked.

"They'll use night vision cameras," said Carter, cautiously moving forward until she bumped into something. "Oof!"

"Are you okay?" Beck asked.

"Yeah . . . I think I ran into a table."

Her teammates shuffled around in the dark, occasionally with grunts and *ows*. She edged her way along the large round table, feeling for anything that might be a clue, but it was useless. Nothing but a wide, smooth surface, and a clock ticking, ticking, ticking . . .

Finally, light erupted across the room. Carter blinked in the brightness. Her gaze instinctively went to the digital clock high on the wall, frozen at the time they'd come into the room. Thirteen minutes, eleven seconds. Way too long.

"Epic," Beck murmured as they took it in.

Three walls of the room displayed a giant world map, covered with tiny blinking lights of various colors. Though the outlines of each continent and island were obvious, everything was labeled in the alien language.

In the middle of the room was the huge circular table Carter had run into. Stuck across the entire surface was another world map. More than a dozen countries had been marked with yellow *X*s.

The wall not covered with a map was lined with shelves, each one scattered with military gear and MREs, plus a bunch of random objects. A pitcher of water, a rainbow bath bomb, a makeup palette, some sort of springy contraption, a houseplant, a steel pointer, an old radio, a glass bottle, bug spray, a bag of sand, and dozens of other knickknacks that didn't have anything in common.

"Jesus," said Beck.

Carter spun around. "What now?"

"No—literally, Jesus." He pointed at a dashboard where a screen showed an enormous statue of Jesus Christ with outstretched arms, overlooking a coastal city. Carter only caught a glimpse of it before the screen switched to the Pyramids of Giza, then the Eiffel Tower. Each landmark was being attacked in some way, by lightning, fire, earthquakes, and other disasters. Very apocalyptic.

"We're trying to stop an invasion," Sierra reminded them. "With as few cities destroyed as possible."

Adi held up the book of alien language. "The script on the map is the same as this."

Sierra marched over to him. "Let me take a look."

"Have at it," he said, handing it over, then joining Beck at the screen.

Carter grabbed the radio on one of the shelves and switched it on. Through the speaker came the sound of crackling voices—some crying for help, some giving coordinates, some issuing military orders.

"We're picking up radio frequencies," she said.

Then a voice came through loud and clear. "Oslo is down! I repeat, Oslo has been eradicated!"

"What? No!" Carter yelled, looking first at Adi, then at the wall. "Where's Oslo?"

He pointed at Norway and, as they watched, a tiny blue light turned purple.

"Hold on," Adi said, snapping his fingers between Sierra's face and the notebook. She made a disgusted face and snapped her fingers back at him, but he ignored it. "The city names, in the alien language. Look, four characters for Oslo, and the first and last ones are the same. They correspond to our alphabet."

"Right," said Sierra, grabbing a pencil from among the knick-knacks on the shelves. She started scribbling, making her own key from the cities listed on the wall. "This is going to take a minute. Carter, you inspect the objects, see if anything has writing on it. Adi, you work out what's going on with the landmarks and call them out as you see them."

"A purple light must mean a city has been wiped out," said Adi. Even as he said it, more blue lights flashed to purple.

"Wait—didn't the Game Master say we were supposed to stop the attacks, but that some could also be reversed?" said Beck. "How are we supposed to do that?"

Carter gestured to the objects on the shelves. "Something to do with these? Here, help me look through them."

As they worked, more transmissions came across the radio as cities continued to fall. It became background noise, punctuated by Adi's recitation of the rotating pictures. "The Eiffel Tower is being hit by lightning. The Sydney Opera House is getting washed away by a tsunami. That's, er—where is that? Oh, the Kremlin in Moscow. That's on fire. Taj Mahal looks like it's cracking from an earthquake. Don't know where the fifth one is, but it's being hit by acid rain, I think. Pyramids of Giza, locusts. Of course. *Christ the Redeemer*—a landslide?"

"Wait, locusts?" Beck turned to the shelf opposite Adi. "There's bug spray over there."

"*The enemy of your enemy is your friend!*" Carter said excitedly. "The enemy of locusts is bug spray. Quick, grab it!"

Beck snatched it from the shelf.

"Okay," said Adi. "We're back to the Eiffel Tower and electricity."

"Lightning rod!" Beck said, picking up the steel pointer.

Carter found a sponge for the Opera House tsunami and grabbed the pitcher of water for the burning Kremlin.

"An earthquake," Adi said, staring at the Taj Mahal. "What's the enemy of an earthquake?"

Beck laughed, holding up the springy contraption. "Shock absorbers!"

"Huh," said Carter, "and here I thought they were fancy bed-springs."

"The plant could be for the landslide," said Adi. "Roots help with soil erosion. Does anyone know what the enemy of acid rain is?"

"Try a neutralizing solution," Sierra said without looking up from her decoding work.

Carter hurried over to the glass bottle. "This says it's sodium hydroxide."

Beck flashed her a thumbs-up.

"Okay, the bug spray goes on Egypt," Adi said, directing them where to place all the objects on the huge map spread across the table. "The plant on Brazil. The sponge on Australia . . ."

"Got it!" Sierra shouted, slapping the pencil down. "The first page says: *Do not let our rainbow dissolve, lest our forces be weakened.*"

"So . . . the aliens control rainbows?" said Beck, grinning. "Cool superpower."

Carter shouted gleefully and grabbed the rainbow bath bomb. "It has to mean this!"

"A side quest?" Adi said as Carter dropped the bath bomb in the pitcher of water. They watched it fizz away.

Adi scanned the room. "Nothing's happening."

"Maybe we have to wait until the bath bomb dissolves completely," Beck said. "Sometimes they have little toys inside." He paused before adding, "Dibs."

"I'll decode the next page," Sierra said, returning to the book.

"So . . . where does the sodium hydroxide go?" asked Carter.

Adi glanced back at the rotating pictures, then pointed at one that showed a temple with a Buddha statue. "I think that might be in Thailand. Or . . . Indonesia?"

Beck looked at the map. "There are *Xs* on both of those. Choose one."

"Thailand?"

"Thailand it is." Carter put the sodium hydroxide on the map.

They waited, hoping for a flashing light or the click of mechanics.

Nothing.

"Um," Carter said.

"Maybe it's Indonesia then," Beck said.

"Or something is wrong," murmured Adi.

"Are we sure this one is in Brazil?" asked Carter, pointing. "There are *Xs* on Mexico and Peru, too."

"I'm sure."

Four more blue lights turned purple. Four more cities down. How many had the other teams lost? Carter liked to think they were solving this part of the game quickly thanks to Adi's geographical knowledge, but the time wasted in the front room could be their downfall.

Suddenly, the screen showing the disasters flickered. Carter held her breath, hoping it wasn't about to turn off. If they had to rely on memory to place these objects—

But the screen didn't turn off. Instead it changed from a picture of the pyramids to a picture of . . .

"Sierra?"

"What?" said Sierra, looking up from the notebook. Her attention landed on the screen, and her expression froze. "What the hell?"

There was Sierra's face, a screenshot taken from a post-round interview in season four. Then the screen glitched again and changed to an image of . . . Cruz Fernandes, one of Sierra's teammates last season. But he was replaced by a photo of Fitzy's playful grin. Then

Louis Augustus Russell. Followed by another of Sierra's old teammates, Missy Mizuno. Then Ranielle Russell. Alicia's teammates. Elijah Kua. Vera. Then it started from the top again. Sierra. Cruz. Fitzy. Louis—all suspects in Alicia's murder, their photos flashing by faster and faster.

Until the images stopped—and they were staring at the beautiful smile of Alicia Angelos. A voice, distorted by auto-tune, rasped, "*I know the truth. Have you figured it out yet?*"

Then it was gone, and the slideshow of landmarks was back.

"What. The. Actual," whispered Adi.

Beck smacked his lips, frowning thoughtfully. "That voice—"

"Don't," said Sierra, a tight line between her eyebrows. "Not here. Stay focused. We're almost done, I can feel it."

But with that creepy video turning in her thoughts, Carter felt like they were suddenly playing an entirely different game.

"Got it," Sierra said, grabbing the pitcher of now-murky water and pulling out a dripping crystal. "Adi," she said, tossing the crystal across the table to him. "The book says to replace the radio batteries with this."

Adi grabbed the radio and wrenched open the cover to the battery compartment. There was a divot where the crystal fit precisely. The voices from the speaker fell silent. Around the room, the tiny lights on the map stopped blinking and turned their solid colors.

"What happened?" Carter said.

"We blocked their radio communication," Sierra said smugly. "They won't be destroying any more cities."

"Yes!" Beck offered her a fist bump, which she begrudgingly accepted.

"But we still haven't managed to reverse the disasters," said Adi.

They went through the list of places again, double-checking the landmarks, disasters, and solutions. Beck wandered around, looking at the items on the shelves in more detail.

"It all makes sense," Carter said, moving the sodium hydroxide back and forth between Thailand and Indonesia. "I don't know what else it could be." She glanced up at the frozen digital clock. How much more time had passed? Ten minutes? Fifteen?

She scanned the shelves again. Her attention landed on a small red sandbag, the type used for playing cornhole at the county fair. The pictures rotated back to the Sydney Opera House, half covered in water.

Carter gasped. "It's not a tsunami, it's a flood! Quick, Beck!"

She grabbed the sandbag and tossed it at Beck, who caught it one-handed. He yanked off the sponge and slapped down the bag of sand.

All the lights in the room turned green, and Carter heard the most beautiful words in the world.

"Team Helsing, you have escaped!"

Interview Room: Alicia Angelos

SEASON FOUR

END OF ROUND TWO: TREASURES OF THE DEEP

Though Alicia is usually cheerful during her interviews, now her smile is tight, her spine stiff as she sits on a high-backed throne. The wetsuit from the round has been unzipped to her waist, revealing a white bikini top. She rolls a red gemstone between her palms.

"Alicia," says Fitzy, dismayed. "What happened?"

"It was a rough one," she admits. "We were hungry. And thirsty."

"And snarky."

She cocks an eyebrow. "But we still finished in good time."

"That you did."

"Better than Sierra's team."

"I can't comment on that."

"One day I'll catch you out, Fitzy."

"I sure hope not," he says, making himself comfortable on his own high-backed throne.

"It's lucky I solved Louis's clue."

"*Look for the Verne.* Honestly, I still don't get it."

"You should try picking up a book some time. *Twenty Thousand Leagues*?"

"No idea, mate. I'm nothing but a pretty face."

"It's a classic." She holds the red gemstone up to the light and smiles dreamily. "One of the Game Master's favorites."

"No kidding. Although, interestingly, another contestant figured it out even quicker than you."

"What?" Alicia snaps out of her reverie. "Who?"

"I'm sure you can guess."

Alicia smiles, but her fist tightens around the gemstone. "Yes. I'm sure I can."

28

Beck

Beck sat on one of the pool lounge chairs, pretending to be engrossed in some serious social media scrolling. After five minutes of "acting normal," it had become clear to him that he was not cut out for surveillance. His foot wouldn't stop bouncing. His fingers were leaving sweaty prints on the phone's screen.

He glanced at Sierra, who was laid out on the next lounge chair with one arm tossed over her eyes. Without her boots, her torn-up stockings made her legs look infinite.

In front of her, Adi sat on the edge of the pool, feet in the water, book on his lap. Neither of them struggled with *acting normal*.

Beck returned his focus to the phone, pausing on a pop-up ad teasing exclusive reveals about Victor Cunningham and his puzzle resort. Like the advertising algorithm knew him or something.

To think that Victor Cunningham was Adi's *dad* was beyond mind-blowing. If their team won those Sweetbrier passes, that was going to be one heck of a family reunion.

"So," he said, feeling like he had to say *something* before he exploded from nerves, "that video in the alien room was nuts, wasn't it? I wish we had a recording of it."

"Why?" asked Sierra. "It didn't tell us anything we didn't already know."

"Think the murderer is getting anxious?" asked Adi. "If they really are on that list, they've got to be thinking their days are numbered."

"The Real Game Master better be watching their back," said Sierra. "If the killer figures out who's leaving the clues . . ."

Beck recrossed his ankles so his other foot could take its turn jiggling uncontrollably. "I think I recognized the voice in that video.

It was distorted because of the auto-tuner, but there was something familiar about it." His mouth watered as he tried to recall the flavor he'd tasted while the video played. Rhubarb pie? No—not quite. If he could hear it again . . .

"He's leaving," Adi said suddenly.

It took Beck's brain a moment to shift directions. But there was Elijah Kua, traipsing casually out his front door, right on time for his prescheduled interview for Carter's channel. He waved at the three of them as he headed toward the dining hall.

Beck waved back. Sierra and Adi did not.

The moment Elijah had rounded the corner, Adi climbed to his feet and tossed his book onto an empty table. "This shouldn't take long," he said, before strolling to the RAs' door. He knocked.

"Stop staring," said Sierra.

Beck lifted his phone in front of his face again.

Lisa answered the door. She and Adi talked a moment, then she beamed and stepped outside, shutting the door behind her. Seconds later, the two of them were on their way to the dining hall, too.

"Adi's got game," Beck murmured, impressed.

Sierra pulled on her boots. "Let's do this."

They hurried toward the villa, down the pathway that ran along the side of the building. Sierra strode with purpose, like she had every right to be there, but Beck glanced around every few seconds to make sure no one was watching. With the back gate visible from the pool, it wasn't exactly the most private place to try breaking and entering.

Sierra pulled on the gate, then cursed. "It's locked again." She gave it a frustrated shake.

"I've got this." Beck eyed the wall on either side of the wrought iron gate. It was a foot or so taller than him and covered in stucco like the villas. Mostly smooth, but with a few minuscule imperfections scattered across the surface.

Nothing to it.

He grasped the top ledge and hauled himself upward. His toes found placement on some of the tiny ledges. Pressing with his legs, he brought one elbow onto the top, then planted his palm and used it to leverage his body weight up and over. He doubted it took more than five seconds before he was dropping quietly down to the other side.

Sierra had her hands on her hips and a skeptical frown when he unlocked the gate and let her in. "You know, if you'd told me you could do that a week ago, we could have finished this a lot sooner."

"I didn't realize it was the gate holding you up. I thought you were more concerned with getting Elijah and Lisa out of the way."

"That too," she said, shutting the gate behind them. "For the record, I choose you as our dexterity competitor in the semifinals."

"Really? Cool!"

"Let's get started."

Beck surveyed the swath of patio that stretched before him. It was a pretty design, the pavers spiraling outward from the center. A flower bed along one edge sported palm trees and ornamental grasses. A café table with two chairs sat off to one side. "Where do we start?"

"I checked around the flower bed last time, and along the walls," said Sierra. "I also checked the light fixtures. But all my sister told me to do was to look under the terrace, so . . . I've sort of been avoiding the obvious."

They both stared down at the spiraling pavers. There must have been a thousand of them—easily three hundred square feet of outdoor living space to explore. And they didn't even know what they were looking for. An incriminating photo? A murder weapon?

"And the police didn't find anything?" Beck asked.

"That's what they told me, but I'm pretty sure they half-assed it. They made it clear they thought I was making it up to waste their time."

Beck frowned. He didn't want to believe that any detective worth their salt would botch such a clear lead. But then, he hadn't wanted to believe that the show's producers would manipulate the contestants to fabricate more drama, and he'd clearly been proven wrong on that front.

A loud screech made him jump. But it was just a bird in one of the palm trees—not the creak of a gate, not the trill of an alarm, not Elijah or Lisa coming to ask what on earth Beck and Sierra were doing.

Every second they stood there was wasting time. Adi and Carter had thought they could distract Lisa and Elijah for at least an hour, but that hour would go fast.

"I'll start at the center and work my way out," said Sierra. "You start on the outside and work your way in. I figure, if I was going to hide something under this terrace, I'd either put it beneath one of the exterior edges or right smack in the middle."

Beck picked a spot in the shade of the villa's overhanging roof and dug his fingers beneath the first paver—a reddish square block about the size of his hand. It took some wiggling before he was able to pry it up from the sandy layer underneath. He looked at the sand. He looked at the bottom of the paver.

It was . . . just a paver.

He set it back into place.

One down. Countless more to go.

"So, do you think Jarius was the one who locked us in the freezer?" he said, shuffling on his knees to the next group of pavers. "Maybe he wanted to get back at Carter for throwing up on him."

"It tracks," said Sierra. "For whatever reason, they're targeting us with their snags. They must see us as a threat."

"Well . . . we are, aren't we? I mean, you have experience on the show, and Carter's a Solve Specialist, and Adi's so good at anagrams and word puzzles, and I've built my own rooms, so I like to think I have some idea of how the Game Master's mind works."

"And yet, we bombed the first two rounds."

Fair point, although Beck had faith in his team. He knew they could beat Jarius and his cronies. He knew they could make it to the finale. He knew—

Familiar-flavored voices caught his attention. Carter and Elijah were heading their way, arguing.

Beck froze, a paver in his grip. His eyes met Sierra's.

"I'm sorry!" Carter was saying. "Elijah, wait. Come back. Please!"

"This conversation is over," said Elijah. "You want to rehash season four, fine. But I'm not going to be strong-armed into talking about Alicia's private business. I've already given my statement to the police."

"Okay, okay!" As they came closer, Carter's voice became increasingly desperate. "No talk of Alicia! Totally fine. I had no idea it was such a sore spot. Let's finish the interview."

"Maybe later. I'm not in the mood anymore."

Beck held his breath, hoping Elijah would go around to the front and give him and Sierra a chance to slip out the gate.

But no—he turned down the path. He was heading toward the terrace.

Beck nestled his paver back into place and bounded to his feet. "I'll distract him," he whispered. "You go out through the front."

Sierra started to disagree, but Beck bolted forward and grabbed the gate, yanking it open just as Elijah was reaching forward, key in hand.

Elijah yelped and jumped back.

"Elijah!" Beck cried, slipping out the gate and closing it behind him with a loud *clank*. "I've been waiting for you. I hope you don't mind if I made myself at home. It's really peaceful back there, and it's been hard to find any solitude lately."

"How . . . ? Wasn't the gate locked?"

Beck made a confused face. "Nope. Opened right up. Do you have a minute? I could use some advice."

"I . . . uh. Okay. Carter, we're done here."

Beck feigned surprise. "Oh. Hey, Carter! Didn't see you there."

"Hi?" squeaked Carter, eyes wide.

"I'm sorry," said Beck. "I didn't mean to interrupt. But I needed someone to talk to."

Carter's gaze slipped toward the gate, probably searching for signs of Sierra.

Elijah looked like he wanted to tell Beck to get lost, but then he twisted his face into something like understanding. "Of course. I'm here. I'm glad you waited." He reached for the gate, then hesitated. "Carter, a little privacy?"

"Oh! Yeah! Right. Um . . . if you need me, Beck, you know where to find me." Carter slowly backed down the path.

"Come have a seat," said Elijah.

Beck held his breath as he opened the gate and they stepped onto the terrace, but Sierra had disappeared into the house. If a paver was crooked here or there, Elijah didn't seem to notice.

Beck perched on the edge of one of the metal café chairs and immediately started rambling. The clues in the game. The message on the cow's heart. Being locked in a freezer, the culprit still unknown. Saboteurs and mind games and—

Elijah raised a hand, stopping Beck's tirade.

Beck took a breath. Actually, it felt pretty good to get all that out.

"I know it's been a lot," said Elijah, "but most of what's happened is probably the producers trying to stir up drama. They do that."

"Yeah, I've noticed," Beck said dryly. "It must have been hard for you to come back here, after everything. I know what happened in that finale was really traumatic for all of you."

Elijah's voice became rough. "It was awful. When Ranielle offered me this job, I almost said no. But ultimately . . . I couldn't imagine staying away."

"Why?"

"It's complicated. And I honestly don't expect anyone to understand."

"Try me."

A muscle ticked in Elijah's jaw. He seemed to be considering something, but then he shook his head.

"Come on." The legs of Beck's chair scraped against pavers as he scooted closer. "Everyone is so secretive around here. It helps to open up, you know? And I'm a really good listener. Ask anyone."

Elijah peered at Beck through the mop of curls that fell over his brow. Cautious and suspicious.

Beck cupped his face in his hands, the picture of sincerity.

Elijah took in a long breath. When he finally spoke, his voice was almost inaudible. "I came back because . . . because this is the last place I ever saw her."

"Alicia?" Beck whispered, reverent.

"Who else?" Elijah shuddered and looked toward the pool. "I watched her leave the villas that night. I could tell she was upset. I thought about going after her, but . . . I didn't." He shut his eyes. "I have many regrets, but that will always be the worst one."

"She was your competition," said Beck.

"In the game, sure. But outside the game? No." He gave a wistful sigh. "Coming back . . . I thought I could still be close to her. Like I didn't have to say goodbye."

Beck could hardly believe what he was hearing. "Was it *you*?"

Elijah's dreamy expression clouded. "That killed her? Aren't you listening to what I—"

"No, not that," Beck interrupted. "There are rumors that she was seeing somebody on the set. Was it you?"

Elijah's nostrils flared, his quiet melancholy immediately overshadowed with irritation. "Did Sierra tell you that? You should know she's a compulsive liar, and she's been trying to convince people of her innocence since day one. It would be convenient for her if there was some *secret beau*, but I've seen no proof of it."

"Okay," said Beck. "But if she was dating someone, that would be important. That person would be a suspect."

"She wasn't seeing anyone!" Elijah stood. "I shouldn't have said anything. It was unprofessional."

"Don't you want to know what happened to her?" Beck said.

"I do know what happened to her." Elijah swung the gate open and stood next to it, tension radiating off him. "Sierra and Alicia were fighting hours before Alicia wound up dead. Sierra has anger management issues and paints disturbing images of people suffering and dying. Of all the suspects, she's the one whose whereabouts weren't accounted for that night." His eyes burned into Beck. "It isn't hard to figure out."

Beck knew it wasn't Sierra. He believed her, body and soul. There was grief in her, and kindness. He'd seen past the crack in her facade.

Sierra had not killed her sister.

But Beck was almost certain that Elijah was hiding something.

29

Sierra

Sierra let the villa's back door close softly. She could hear Beck outside the gate, distracting Elijah.

It was a bold move, she'd give him that.

Alicia's old villa was a mirror-image layout to the one Sierra's team shared on the other side of the pool: a central living area with an open kitchen and two bedroom suites on opposite sides of a short hallway. This villa smelled better though, like someone burned a lot of scented candles.

She hurried past the bedrooms into the living area. There was a reproduction Van Gogh on the wall—not as famous as *Starry Night* but one of Sierra's favorites, with its vibrant Parisian setting, the warm yellows and oranges beneath a star-dusted sky.

She'd always admired Van Gogh. Not just because he was a visionary in a world of critics, but because she found something appealing about a person being dedicated enough to cut off their own ear.

A MacBook was sitting open on the kitchen island, along with a mess of papers and a spiral-bound notebook. Sierra scanned the windows, making sure no one could see her as she slipped past.

But then she froze.

Tiptoed back.

The computer screen was open to the Domain, showing the forum started by the Real Game Master.

Scribbles filled the notebook. Elijah's penmanship was normally neat, but the first page was a mess, most of the letters scratched out. Sierra realized he'd been trying to solve the ribbon clue—the one Adi had figured out.

Sierra shuffled some papers to the side, seeing lists of names, times, notes about Elijah's memories from the night, interspersed with question marks and exclamation points.

A handwritten note in red ink caught Sierra's eye. She bent closer.

4a.m.—door slamming. Car pulling out of driveway.
Why no headlights?

Wait. Elijah hadn't said anything about the mystery car having no headlights.

She puzzled through the timing. The argument around nine. Alicia's phone turning off around ten thirty, a mile away from the complex. Alicia murdered after one in the morning. A mysterious car pulling out of the driveway hours later.

Growling in frustration, she turned the page and her breath left her. She was staring at a photo of her sister. It was a little grainy, like it had been taken from far away and blown up. Alicia was caught mid-laugh, her eyes squinting in delight. She was wearing a yellow swimsuit, a hint of the pool visible in the background.

Beneath the picture, Elijah had written a haiku in his same tidy, precise letters:

She walked out the gate
With a blanket and my heart.
Should I have followed?

"Yuck," Sierra muttered. "Don't quit your day job."

But then . . . *a blanket.* The image of Alicia wearing that comforter over her shoulders was forever burned into Sierra's memory.

She had always assumed that she was the last person, other than the killer, to see her sister alive. But evidently Elijah had watched her walk out the gate that night.

She flipped back through his notes, and yes, there—

Approx. 9:10—Sierra left through front gate.
Approx. 9:15—Alicia left w/ comforter. Followed Sierra?

She turned back to the poem, rereading its final line, her thoughts flipping it back and forth between two possible meanings.

"Should I have followed?" *I didn't follow.*

"Should I have followed?" *Following was a mistake.*

He was obsessed with her sister. He could have been jealous. He could have gone after her. He could have killed her, returning at four in the morning to go for a swim. Washing off the blood? Did the pool have something to do with Alicia being wet?

And the car with no headlights . . . Had someone followed *him* back to the villas?

Sierra rubbed her brow. What was she missing?

Out on the patio, the grating of metal café chairs on the pavers pulled her back to the moment. Right—she was supposed to be leaving.

Turning away from Elijah's notes, she ducked past the coffee table with a burnt candle and the same edition of the *Hollywood Herald* they had in their villa. Past the sofa table with the decorative glass bowl holding three random twine balls. Past the Van Gogh painting—

Sierra jerked to a stop. Pivoted in one swift movement.

She stared at the framed picture on the wall. A café at night. Patrons enjoying a quiet repose.

She knew this painting. *Café Terrace at Night.*

Sierra's whole body shook with adrenaline as she glanced over her shoulder, wondering how much time she had.

She lifted the picture frame away from the wall and set it against the back of the sofa. Seeing nothing out of the ordinary on the wall, she felt around the edges of the picture's frame. Then . . . she spotted it. The small incision cut into the brown paper that covered the back.

She used a black fingernail to pry, just a little . . .

A piece of paper fell into her hand. It was neatly folded into a small, tight square.

Alicia's last note.

Sierra jumped to her feet as the gate's hinges creaked outside.

She pocketed the paper and grabbed the painting. By the time she'd hooked the wire hanger onto its screw, she could hear the back door opening. The scuff of Elijah's sneakers.

She scurried to the entryway, shutting the front door as quietly as she could, then dashed around the bushes—and crashed right into Beck.

"Sierra!" he said, as breathless as she was. "What are you . . . I didn't think you'd still be in there!"

"I found it." She grabbed Beck's arm and pulled him away from Elijah's villa. "Alicia's letter." They rounded the edge of the pool. Elijah wasn't following them. Nobody was paying them any attention. "She didn't mean the terrace as in the patio. She was referring to Van Gogh's *Café Terrace at Night* hanging in their living room. Look." She pulled the note from her pocket.

"Oh my god. You did it!"

The two shared a quick grin, then broke into a sprint.

Carter was waiting impatiently in their living room, chewing a fingernail. "Finally!" she said when they burst through the door. "What took you so long? Did he catch you?"

"No," said Sierra, holding up the note. "And we found it."

Carter eagerly snatched it from her hands. She was halfway through opening it when she froze and gave Sierra an apologetic look and slowly handed it back. "I guess you should have the honors."

"You think?" said Sierra, but she wasn't too upset. Carter had been acting more confident ever since the alien room. Between the Morse code, the sandbag, and figuring out the importance of Louis's clue, it seemed her Solve Specialist instincts had finally kicked in. Sierra felt oddly proud of her.

"Should we wait for Adi?" Beck asked as Sierra started to unfold the note.

Sierra stilled. Her jaw tensed, her curiosity to know what her sister had wanted to tell her at war with her conscience, until Beck sing-songed, "We are a team . . ."

Letting out a long groan, Sierra set the unopened note on the counter and picked up her phone. "I'm giving him five minutes. If he's not back by then, we're reading it without him."

Adi was back in one minute and forty-nine seconds.

"*Thank you,*" he said earnestly as he burst into their villa. "I've never been so grateful to escape a conversation. Word of advice: do *not* ask Lisa what kind of movies she likes unless you want an in-depth analysis of every plot hole in the *Back to the Future* franchise." He shook his arms, as if trying to clear the conversation from the air. Then— "Where is it? What does it say?"

Carter pointed at the note in Sierra's hand. "We haven't opened it yet."

"We thought we'd wait for you," said Beck.

Adi looked momentarily surprised. "Oh. Thanks. I'm here now. Let's see it."

Sierra was already unfolding it, revealing a typed message in huge font, spanning the width of a piece of printer paper.

Well.. shit. This letter=a last dangerous plot, a last futil hope.
Maybe I'me now dead and buried. Or maybe just_missing?
R u ready? Ive been w/ Louis. (Louis Augustus R!)
Was only flirting first, that turnd into **more**

I abso!!lutely don'twant the cops to know the _rest
It's complex, baby sis. i'd really love if u avenged me - good luck
Remember ~~a~~ the inane clue in the ...
2nd episode?If u first cn find ~~a~~ the light from the #4 villa
it should guide u.Will reveal every thing. My secret, my error.

If I've already lost, I hav 1 big request:Lay waste to Rani+Louis.

Do not trust the Russells.
-Alicia

"Holy . . ." Carter muttered, which was about as far as Sierra's mind was able to process, too. "Does this mean . . . Is she saying what I think she's saying?"

"Do you think she's saying that she was sleeping with Louis?" said Beck. "Because yes. And yuck."

Sierra read through the note again. And again.

Her sister. And the *Game Master*?

Adi snatched the note away to examine it closer. "Maybe, maybe not. This is clearly a code."

"But what if she was?" Beck said quietly. "How old was she? Was that . . . I mean, was it . . . illegal?"

"She was eighteen," said Sierra, and with those words, her dismay hardened into something else. Revulsion. As if Alicia hadn't already been through enough for one lifetime.

Sierra turned away, pacing back and forth across the rug. "What a predator. It may not have been statutory rape, but it was still fucked. For one, he's married. Two, he's almost twenty years older than her. And three—that is such a disgusting power imbalance! She had no money. She was desperate to win the show and score the final prize. He was . . . How *could* he? To my sister!" She was practically shouting now, and when she picked up a throw pillow and whacked it repeatedly against the back of the sofa, no one tried to stop her. "Gross! Disgusting! Manipulative! Men!"

She paused to catch her breath, some of the anger fading as she looked over at Beck and Adi. "Not you. But . . . *ugh*."

"We get it," said Adi.

"Yeah," agreed Beck. "Totally fair."

Sierra hurled herself onto the couch and screamed into the pillow.

"So . . ." Carter started. "Does this mean . . . What do we think this means, exactly?" She sounded distressed. Sierra lifted her face to look at her. She knew enough about Kick It Carter, who idolized the Game Master, to know this was a huge blow for her, too.

"It's usually the boyfriend or the husband," said Beck. "At least, according to every true crime show ever. So . . ." He trailed off, like he couldn't quite find the words to say what they were thinking.

But Sierra could.

Her sister had been afraid that something would happen to her, and then . . . and then . . .

Sierra shut her eyes, seeing what she always saw now. Alicia in the coffin, her body pale, stiff, *wet*. In a way, the drenching of her corpse was a violation all on its own.

She sat up, squeezing the life from the throw pillow. "It was the Game Master," she said. "That bastard killed my sister."

30
Adi

"We shouldn't jump to conclusions," said Adi. He was still studying the note, trying to figure out the patterns, but so far was at a loss. The stilted language, the odd punctuation, the typos . . . Clearly there was more to it, something Alicia had wanted only Sierra to figure out. "We need to decode the rest of this message."

Carter peered over his shoulder. "What do you think all the strikethroughs mean?"

"Not sure. Give me a minute."

"She wasn't *that* smart," Sierra said. "How did she write a code that's too complicated for you?"

"I've had it for like twenty seconds!"

"Also, this," said Beck, peering over Adi's other shoulder and pointing to the bottom of the page. " '*Do not trust the Russells.*' Russells, plural."

"Louis is smart enough to pull off a murder," said Adi. "He had access to Alicia *and* the finale room where she was found . . ."

"And Ranielle was his alibi," said Beck. "What if she was lying for him?"

Carter shook her head. "Why would Ranielle lie for her husband if he was having an affair? This letter only raises more questions."

Adi narrowed his eyes. "You just don't want to believe your precious Game Master could be a murderer."

"Hey!" said Carter, looking truly appalled. "We just learned that my *precious* Game Master is a lying, cheating scumbag, and yeah, I'm not thrilled about it, but I'd say I'm handling the news pretty well." She waved at the letter in his hand. "Just because Alicia had some personal drama with the Russells doesn't mean Louis killed her."

Beck's eyes widened. "Maybe they killed her *together*!" He slapped his hands to his cheeks. "That's where Alicia was disappearing to all the time! She was meeting with Louis!"

"No," Sierra said. "Well . . . I mean, maybe sometimes. But there was also a time she vanished right before filming an elimination round. Louis and Fitzy were both on set. I remember it specifically because it ruled out Fitzy as my top suspect for who she was cheating with—in both senses of the word. But then I figured maybe that time she was just going somewhere else."

"Like where?" Beck said.

Sierra shrugged.

"We need to step back and really think this through," Carter said. "Would you read the letter out loud again?"

Adi did so.

As soon as he finished, Sierra got up from the couch and started her signature pace. "What is she talking about, the light from the number-four villa?"

"I was wondering that, too," said Beck. He took the note from Adi. "There are three digits here: two, four, and one. Could that mean something?"

"She gave us a hint," said Carter. "What was the clue in episode two that everyone was hung up on? And did it have anything to do with a light?"

Sierra fidgeted with her lip ring. "Not that I can remember, but honestly, most of last season is a blur."

"I'll look it up." Carter grabbed her laptop while Beck raised the note to the ceiling light.

"Nothing here. Do we have a black light?" He gasped, answering his own question. "Yes! That flashlight from the welcome bag!" After fetching it, he played around with the settings, running the light back and forth beneath both sides of the paper . . . but there was no invisible ink, no hidden message.

Adi wasn't surprised. No, there was something buried in the actual text. It was written too strangely to be anything else.

Carter skimmed through the footage from season four on her laptop. "Episode two was the speakeasy."

"Oh yeah," said Beck. "I love that episode."

But Sierra groaned. "That's right. The piano."

Adi peeled his gaze from the note to watch the footage. The room had been themed after a Prohibition-era speakeasy, with messages in bottles of moonshine, on old-fashioned cocktail menus, and in the sheet music onstage for a four-piece jazz band. There had been a particularly difficult puzzle where the contestants had to play a piece of music on a grand piano backward.

"Alicia's team didn't struggle too much," said Carter, "but you got really frustrated."

Sierra bristled. "Because Elijah wouldn't listen to me!"

"Okay, okay." Carter held up her hands, pacifying.

Sierra huffed, and muttered, "I was *right,* dammit."

"Music, huh?" said Beck, setting the note down to watch the episode highlights. "Maybe it's something to do with the note scale. A through G, right? Any of us play an instrument?"

"Clarinet in elementary school," said Carter, "but I don't remember much. And what does sheet music have to do with a light guiding us?"

"It doesn't matter!" Sierra snapped. "Alicia told me all I need to know." She jabbed a finger toward the note. "Louis Augustus Russell. Not Fitzy. Not Elijah. Not some random set designer or tech guy. It was the Game Master all along." Her eyes were blazing. "We need to find a way to question him."

Adi exchanged looks with the others. He didn't necessarily disagree with Sierra. If they were going to take this accusation to the police, it might spur new interest in the investigation, but they still wouldn't have any evidence. Real evidence. Like a confession.

Then, in a nervous voice, Carter said, "I might have a way."

She set her phone on the coffee table between the laptop and Alicia's note. "He gave me his phone number. His . . . private phone number."

The statement was met with dismayed silence, before Sierra screamed, "He *what*?"

"Not for anything like that!" Carter said, waving her hands wildly. "He said I could interview him sometime. For my channel. That's all."

Adi bit back a snarky response. Carter looked too horrified to mock.

"Okay," said Sierra, making a considerable effort to calm down. "Let's get you that interview."

Carter gulped, opening her messages.

It took them ten minutes to draft the text . . . but only a moment for Louis to respond. When Carter's phone dinged, they froze like it was a bomb about to explode.

Together, they leaned forward to read.

Great to hear from you, Carter. I feel bad Ranielle cut us off last time. She can be stingy with media interviews, but what she doesn't know won't hurt her. 🤫 My schedule will be packed until after tomorrow night's elimination, but how about we plan on meeting afterward. 8pm? I can send a car to pick you up from the villas.
Looking forward to it. —Louis

THE ESCAPE GAME

SEASON FIVE

ROUND TWO ELIMINATION

"Team Helsing saved Sydney, Australia!" says Fitzy, offering a fist bump to Sierra. She glares at him and he changes direction and fist-bumps Emma instead. "I'd definitely be in mourning if my hometown had been wiped off the map."

"We should be given a medal of honor," Sierra says wryly.

"I don't know about a medal, but maybe you'll be rewarded with one more week on *The Escape Game* and a chance at that one million dollars. Shall we see which team had the best time in our war of the worlds?"

The clocks on the board shuffle.

Tick, tick, tick—

"Team Dread!" bellows Fitzy.

Team Dread erupts into cheers. The camera pans over to Team Mind Hack, who don't try to hide their annoyance, especially after using their one and only snag to add thirty-seven seconds to Dread's final time.

After some back-and-forth with Team Dread and Fitzy, the board blinks, the clocks tick, the team names flash—

"Team Mind Hack!" Fitzy shouts, and Nadia folds over in relief. Sierra's black lips press tight.

Fitzy gestures back to the board. "That leaves two teams. Helsing. Crown Jewels. One of you will be leaving us tonight."

The camera zooms in on Sierra and Emma. Emma's hands are clasped in prayer, but Sierra is stoic, her determined gaze locked on the scoreboard.

Ticking. Blinking. Shuffling.

The dramatic music reaches that thunderous crescendo, and the names on the board finally still, the results flashing.

Emma covers her face, crestfallen, while Sierra tears her attention away from the board. She looks at the Game Master standing on the other side of the stage. Louis Augustus Russell smiles approvingly and claps his hands in congratulations.

Sierra does not smile back.

31

Carter

Carter didn't really believe they'd made it until the four of them were back in their villa, dazed from the emotional roller coaster.

They were still in the game, at least for another week.

And they were meeting Louis Augustus Russell.

Tonight.

"I have to go. Team stuff," she said, faking a smile as she blew a kiss at the phone screen. Her dad jokingly shoved her mom out of the way to "catch" it.

"We love you!" her mom said, pushing her way back into the frame. "Try to get some rest. They're working you too—"

"Okay, I will. I love you too. Bye!" She hung up, guilt gnawing at her. It was getting harder to talk to them. Harder to find safe subjects. The rooms? The elimination rounds? Fine. Literally everything else? No way.

She walked out to the living room and crammed a handful of Beck's Doritos into her mouth. She was stress-eating, she knew, but who could blame her? She gazed around at the rest of her team.

Her . . . friends?

It was what she had hoped for. That she would find her people—puzzle lovers and passionate nerds. People who understood her. People she could be herself around. Not Kick It Carter but the real her.

Team Helsing wasn't *exactly* what she'd had in mind, but now that she thought about it, they were the ones she trusted most to back her up against the Game Master.

Adi was strung across the opposite sofa, staring at the ceiling, his gaze unfocused. He'd been like that since seeing Alicia's cryptic note yesterday. Beck said Adi hadn't touched a book since, not even before bed.

Sierra was in one of the tufted chairs, hunched over her phone. Carter assumed she was studying the clues on the Domain's forum again, but a glimpse of the screen revealed what looked like an online art store.

Beck was practicing a viral dance. Under his breath, he occasionally whispered things like, "Find the light from number four villa. Find the light from hashtag four villa. Find a-strike-through-the light? Strike-through, why the strike-through?"

Carter brushed chip dust from her fingers and leaned over Alicia's note still spread out on the coffee table.

She ignored the part about Louis to focus on the mention of the clue from episode two. Piano, sheet music, sounds.

What are you trying to tell us, Alicia?

"Hey."

It took Carter a moment to realize Sierra was talking to her. She tore her gaze from the note as Sierra put down her phone. "I should probably apologize. You know. For making a big deal about you and Fitzy."

Beck stopped dancing.

"I was wrong," Sierra said. "So . . . yeah. Sorry."

"It's okay," Carter said. "You were trying to protect me."

Beck wriggled his eyebrows. "Does this mean you and Fitzy are a thing?"

Adi shifted to look at Carter, too. She flushed under everyone's expectant stares. "Of course not. It isn't like that." When they seemed unconvinced, Carter added, "He's not my type."

"Oh, sure," said Beck. "No one likes the hot, popular ones. And that accent? Total turnoff."

Carter's flush deepened. "Even if I were . . . a *little* interested . . . he obviously wouldn't be interested in . . ." She gestured at herself.

Adi rolled his eyes and picked up his phone.

"I don't know," said Beck. "We saw the studio tour video. There was tons of chemistry."

"Oh, please. He was just being . . ."

Friendly.

Nice.

Flirty?

She shook her head. "Honestly, it doesn't even matter. There's a strict clause in the contract that says the host isn't allowed to date any contestants."

"Won't be a problem for much longer," Adi muttered.

"What's that supposed to mean?" Sierra said.

"Nothing." Adi rolled onto his back again and continued to stare at the ceiling. "It means nothing."

True to his word, Louis sent a car for Carter just before eight, and if the driver was confused why four teenagers piled in instead of one, he didn't say anything. Louis had sent another text—the number "522"—and Carter had thought maybe it was a puzzle to solve. But when the car pulled up to a hotel, she realized it was actually a room number.

"This doesn't feel like an illicit affair at *all*," Adi drawled.

"Shut up," Carter snapped. Disgust and dread rolled through her as they all slinked through the lobby, which was lush with plants and fountains.

Beck hummed the *Mission Impossible* theme song as they entered the elevator.

This was a terrible idea. They should have gone to the police. Carter said as much out loud, her voice trembling. It wasn't too late. They could still leave—

"Steady, girl," Sierra murmured, squeezing Carter's arm. "The cops have already screwed this case up. And they don't trust anything I say. We need hard evidence, or Louis's never going to be convicted."

"I still don't understand why Ranielle covered for him," Adi said, watching the elevator numbers rise.

"*Do not trust the Russells,*" Beck whispered, quoting Alicia's note.

The elevator dinged and they stepped out, creeping down the empty corridor. When they got to the right door, Carter gestured for the others to leave.

"I'll call for you when his guard is down."

"Are you sure about this?" Adi said.

Carter looked at Sierra. This was for her. And Alicia. And all the other girls Louis had preyed on—or the girls he *would* prey on, if he wasn't put away.

"I'm sure."

Adi must've seen the conviction in her eyes, because he gave a short nod and left. Beck threw up two thumbs, walking backward down the hall.

"Thank you," Sierra whispered. "We won't be far."

When she'd disappeared around the corner with the boys, Carter faced the door and rubbed her sweating palms on her jeans. She was so scared she could hardly breathe.

She knocked, but the door nudged open under her knuckles. She hadn't realized it was already ajar.

There was a moment when she stood there, unsure whether Louis was going to swing it open all the way. When nothing happened, she poked the door with her finger.

"Hello?"

She took a tentative step inside. Ensconced lights illuminated plump white couches, vase-bound peacock feathers, and gilded picture frames. City lights sparkled beyond the windows. The room was so bright. So silent.

And it stank.

She wrinkled her nose. "Louis?" Maybe he was in the bathroom. It sort of smelled like that's where he was.

The television was on, muted, playing an old episode of *The Escape Game*.

"Louis? I'm here for our interview."

She tiptoed farther in to find the bathroom door open. Empty.

An open bottle of wine had been taken out of the minibar. The glass was slick with condensation, forming a wet ring on the counter.

Carter stared at the water slipping down the bottle. A dim thought registered in her mind. Something bothered her about this. A partially empty bottle of wine, covered in condensation . . .

The back of her neck prickled, as if someone was watching her. She spun around to find the room as empty as before. On the television, Elijah was doing a post-round interview, his mouth forming unheard words. He looked out of the screen as if staring right at her.

A sickening doom settled in her stomach. The smell was starting to make her ill.

Her instincts thrummed. She needed to get out of here.

Her path to the door took her back past the lounge suite, with a sofa and a coffee table and . . .

A person. On the floor.

Louis Augustus Russell, mouth foamy, eyes wide and unblinking.

Carter screamed. She ran for him and dropped to her knees, shaking his shoulders.

"Can you hear me? Louis! *Louis!*"

Behind her came a shout and swearing. There was a thunder of footsteps. Hands grabbed her waist.

"Away, away from him. Carter! Get back!"

Sierra pulled her to her feet and spun her from the scene.

Carter tried to get a handle on her racing thoughts. She couldn't breathe. "We—we have to call an ambulance."

"Did you touch him?"

"What?"

"Carter." Sierra's eyes were wide. Frightened. "Did you touch him?"

"I—I—" Her brain barely registered the question. "I shook his shoulders."

"You didn't try giving him CPR?"

"No—I only just found him—"

Sierra wrenched out her phone. "I'm calling 911."

Adi and Beck gaped down at the scene as Sierra dialed with trembling fingers.

"Hi, there's—there's a body. We found a body."

A *body*.

Carter turned to look again at Louis. It was so unnatural, the way he stared at the ceiling.

Louis Augustus Russell was dead.

"Oh my god," she said, no longer able to see through her burning tears. "Oh my god."

She fell forward into Adi. After a brief hesitation, his arms came around her, tight and protective.

In the muddled background, Sierra was giving details of the hotel.

"I'm gonna hurl," Beck said, running to the bathroom.

It was the smell—Louis had soiled himself, and it was visceral and foul and *awful*—

"Get me out," she said into Adi's shoulder. "Get me out of here."

He led her past Sierra, back into the hallway, where the air was clearer. She sucked in fresh breaths, trying to regain herself.

Adi drew away. "I'm going back in."

"No, don't—"

"There's a note. On the coffee table. I want to see what it says."

Adi went into the hotel room. Carter hugged herself, shivering from the sudden cold. The smell was starting to waft out.

She didn't want to be alone. After a hesitant moment, she went back inside, holding her breath.

Sierra was still talking to the emergency services. Adi was on the other side of the coffee table, bent over a piece of hotel paper.

Carter pressed her wrist to her nose and inched closer so she could see what it said, doing her best to keep her gaze away from the body.

Louis's penmanship had been shaky when he wrote it, but Carter recognized the handwriting from countless thank-you notes and autographs posted to the Domain over the years, unmistakable with its elaborate capital letters and flourishing script.

I killed Alicia. Can't live with the guilt anymore. Please apologise to my fans and everyone I've hurt. Tell Rani I love her.

Carter shuddered. Adi took a photo of the letter with his phone. The camera's quiet *click* startled her out of her shock. She scanned the room, needing to look at anything but the body, anything but that horrible confession.

There was a fancy charcuterie board on the coffee table along with two wineglasses—one empty and waiting to be filled, another with the last dregs of wine pooling at the bottom.

A confession. This was a suicide note and a confession and . . . Louis had killed Alicia. The murder was solved.

But she felt no sense of victory.

An entire lifetime passed before she finally heard sirens. The night shredded into disjointed images. Hotel guests peering from their rooms. An investigator placing a sticky note next to the wineglasses. A white sheet draped over the body.

Carter and the others were separated. She sat in some back room behind the hotel's check-in desk, trying her best to answer questions. What had she been doing in Mr. Russell's room? What was the state of the body when she found it? Had she noticed anything unusual about the room when she entered? Had the door been locked when she arrived?

Finally, a detective told her they would reach out tomorrow morning with follow-up questions. But she couldn't leave yet, because one of the investigators was still talking to Sierra. They interviewed her a lot longer than the others.

Carter could now see why Sierra hadn't wanted to take Alicia's note to the police. It was clear that they were deeply mistrustful of her, especially since this was the second suspicious death she'd been connected to.

Finding Louis had been hard, but what had it been like to discover her sister in that coffin? Carter hadn't really comprehended the horror before, not on this level.

It was well past midnight by the time Sierra emerged, and Carter was relieved to see that she hadn't been put into handcuffs.

No one spoke on the ride back to the complex. Louis had confessed to killing Alicia, and now he was dead.

Carter wondered if she should contact Ranielle. She tried to imagine how she'd break it to the executive producer that her husband—and the single most important part of the show—was gone. Somehow, Carter had a feeling Ranielle would be more upset about losing the show than her spouse.

It wasn't until they were back in the villa, after everyone had done their best to shower away the smell of death, after they'd made their way, zombielike, to the living room couches, that Beck finally broke the silence.

"Should we answer that post on the Domain? From the Real Game Master? Tell them we found the lie?"

Carter swallowed, wanting so badly to deny it, to go on believing the brilliant Game Master was still the same man she'd believed him to be.

I killed Alicia. Can't live with the guilt anymore.

"No way," said Sierra. "Why would we?"

Beck shrugged. "They suspected Louis from the start and wanted someone to prove it. They must be dying for an answer. Um. No pun intended."

"They can find out with the rest of the population," Sierra said with a growl.

"The police will be going after Ranielle." Adi frowned. "Lying about Louis's alibi might be a criminal offense."

Carter sank deeper into the couch cushions, bone tired. She pinched the bridge of her nose, listening to the clock tick on the wall.

"Why do you think Louis did it?" Beck whispered. "Killed Alicia, I mean."

"Lover's spat?" suggested Adi. "Maybe she wanted to end it and he got angry. That would explain the words carved inside the coffin lid."

"*We get what we deserve,*" Sierra murmured.

"It could've been revenge for her leaving," Adi said.

Carter drew a steadying breath. "I'm going to have to call my parents. Oh god, they're going to pull me from the show."

Adi smiled bitterly. "What show?"

"What do you mean, what show? *The* show! We're supposed to film the semifinal on Monday!"

Beck, Sierra, and Adi exchanged glances.

"Carter," Beck said gently. "The Game Master is dead. Without him, there is no show."

32

Beck

Beck tossed and turned, unable to fall back asleep. He'd woken entirely too early, images of the Game Master's hotel suite lodged in his mind, and had spent the past hour trying unsuccessfully to switch off his brain.

It was all just so awful. The body on the floor, the note on the table, the condensation dripping down the wine bottle, two glasses set up for a conversation he would never have—

Wait.

Beck sat up suddenly. He ran through the scenario again, the disjointed facts of the evening. The text messages. The wine-glasses. What he knew about Carter and Alicia and, most of all, what he knew about Louis Augustus Russell. He tried to fit the puzzle pieces together in a way that would make sense, but . . . they didn't make sense. And now he knew why.

He threw off his blankets and ran into the hall, nearly crashing into Sierra as she burst out of her own room.

"Why did he invite Carter over?" Sierra cried, stopping Beck in his tracks.

"Holy crap," he said, gesticulating wildly with his arms. "That's what I was going to say!"

Sierra laughed, then clapped a hand over her mouth. It was the first time Beck had ever seen her without dark eyeliner and black lips.

Yet nothing was more surprising than her expression. She looked downright *giddy*.

"Either he wanted to do the interview," Beck said, "or he wanted to seduce her. Which, gross, but there's no reason he would kill himself before she got there!"

"Whassgoinon?" Carter mumbled, staggering out of her room.

"If he was planning to kill himself, why did he invite you over?" Beck said.

Carter stared at him through half-lidded eyes. Then, "I'm making coffee." She shuffled to the kitchen.

Beck's mind whirled. He didn't need coffee. "Louis barely knew Carter. Of all the people in his life, why would he choose her, a contestant, to be the one to find his body? He wouldn't invite her over and then kill himself."

"Maybe because Carter's a Solve Specialist?" suggested Adi, appearing in the doorway. "He wanted her to break the news to the Domain first, before the police did?"

"But that doesn't explain—"

"—the second wineglass," Beck and Sierra said in unison.

He blinked at her in surprise. Okay, now it was getting creepy.

"So . . . what are you saying?" called Carter from the kitchen.

The three of them made their way to the stools around the island.

"Louis didn't kill himself," said Sierra. "And if he didn't kill himself, that means . . ."

"He was murdered," finished Beck.

"But what about the suicide note?" asked Carter. "It was definitely his handwriting."

"Maybe he was under duress?" said Adi. "Forced to write it at gunpoint?"

"Or it was forged," said Sierra. "It's not hard to find samples of his handwriting online."

Beck pinched the bridge of his nose, now trying to remember the details from the hotel room rather than block them out. Louis had been expecting Carter, but his killer had gotten there first.

"Okay," he said slowly, "the killer must be someone he knew well.

Someone who could have put something in his drink without him suspecting them."

Adi's voice hardened. "And who do we think that could be?"

As the smell of strong coffee filled the room, Beck traded grim looks with his teammates.

"Ranielle," said Sierra.

"Ranielle," Adi agreed.

Carter got some creamer out of the fridge and started filling mugs. "So do we still think Louis killed Alicia? Or did Ranielle kill Alicia, and she's trying to frame him for it?"

"Yes, that," Sierra said, without hesitation. "It makes perfect sense. He was having an affair, so she killed Alicia and convinced Louis to provide an alibi. But when he started to feel guilty about lying, he came up with a plan to start putting clues into the game, hoping Ranielle would come clean on her own before he told everyone the truth. We thought Ranielle had given the fake alibi, but it was the other way around. Maybe he was even planning to tell Carter the truth, but Ranielle found out about their meeting, so she went to meet with him first, and . . . well. You know."

"Wow," whispered Beck. "That's . . . That's really good detective work, Sierra."

"Oh, thank god," Carter said, placing a hand over her heart and wilting against the island. "Maybe you're right. It really was an interview he wanted. Not . . . you know . . ."

Adi gave a suspicious grunt. "I wouldn't write off that possibility yet." She shot him a perturbed look as he grimaced. "I was thinking about it last night, and what if Louis was the one who spiked your drink at the party?"

"Shit," Sierra said. "You could be right."

Carter groaned and leaned over the counter, burying her face into her elbows.

"Sorry," Adi muttered. "But he's dead now. So, there's that."

She groaned again, louder this time.

"If we're right," said Beck, "Ranielle might have killed him and left *minutes* before we arrived."

There was a sharp knock at the door. Beck and Sierra looked at each other.

The knock came again.

"All right, all right," Sierra said, slipping off the stool.

She opened the door and cursed.

"Good morning to you, too," said Ranielle Russell, stepping inside. She was impeccably dressed and glossy as always, her yellow suit a blinding beacon.

A stocky Hispanic man followed her, along with a Black woman in a gray power suit.

"Detective Lopez wants to ask the four of you some questions," Ranielle said, gesturing to the man. "My lawyer is here to represent you. I've spoken with your parents, and they've already given their consent to this interview."

All business, Beck noticed, his insides turning at the sight of her. Hardly a grieving widow.

He, Sierra, Carter, and Adi shuffled to one of the sofas, sitting shoulder to shoulder while the detective, Ranielle, and her lawyer stood opposite them.

"Um," said Carter. "Does anyone want coffee?"

"No thank you," said Detective Lopez. He took out his phone. "Mind if I record this?" They murmured their consent, and he continued. "Ms. Angelos, I listened to the 911 call you made. It must've been a horrific experience." He was good at arranging his features into a caring and sympathetic expression.

"Yeah, well, horrific experiences are sort of my thing," said Sierra, arms crossed as she slumped dolefully into the cushions. How easily she could step back into the role of the sullen, hostile villain. Beck hadn't even realized the transformation was underway until it was complete. Though maybe not quite as effective without her usual makeup.

The detective turned to Carter. "Your statement says that you and Louis had scheduled a meeting. Can you elaborate?"

"Uh . . . yeah," Carter said weakly, glancing at Ranielle. "I asked if I could interview him. For my channel."

"We've seen the texts." The detective made a show of flipping through a notebook from his breast pocket. "You'd requested an interview with him previously?"

"Sort of? It was a spontaneous thing, but Ranielle interrupted, so we never got a chance."

Ranielle's gaze was livid.

"What were you planning to ask him about, during this interview last night?" asked Detective Lopez.

Carter fell quiet, and Beck could imagine the fight happening inside her head. A deeply ingrained programming to tell the truth, at odds with, well, the truth.

What was she supposed to say? That Alicia had admitted to having an affair with Louis? That they'd gone to get a confession? That they'd since realized it was his *wife* who'd killed her?

Beck glanced at Ranielle. Actually, it was sort of tempting to spill it all . . .

But it was Sierra who ultimately answered the detective's question. "We wanted to know about the murder clues being planted in the escape rooms. Since he was the Game Master, we figured he knew something."

This seemed to come as a surprise to the detective and the lawyer. Ranielle, on the other hand, tightened her lips into a thin line.

"Clues . . . ?" Detective Lopez said.

"Yeah. *Clues.*" Sierra lifted her pierced eyebrow. "About a lie in the evidence. It's almost like someone didn't trust the police to be able to do their jobs."

Beck nudged her warningly with his elbow.

She nudged him back, way harder than necessary.

"They're on the Domain," Carter said. "The things that have been coming up in the show. Supposedly, someone has been planning to reveal the identity of Alicia's murderer in the finale. But only if the people on the Domain figure out a lie in the clues." She paused, then added in a barely audible whisper, "There were news articles written about it."

Ranielle breathed in through her nose but didn't comment.

Detective Lopez turned to her. "What do you know of this?"

"I know it's been a real pain in the ass," she said. "But Louis assured me he wasn't the one planting them."

Beck gawked at her. How could she sit there acting like she didn't have the blood of two people on her hands? It was despicable.

He couldn't help himself. "You don't seem all that concerned that he's dead."

Ranielle flicked her fingers at the comment. "Please. I was done with him long ago."

"Mrs. Russell," her lawyer said sharply.

"What? The man was a narcissist."

Detective Lopez pulled a stack of photographs out of a folder. Security camera snapshots. "I'd like for each of you to look at these photos," he said, handing the stack to Carter, "and tell me if you recognize anyone."

Beck and Adi peered over Carter's shoulder as she flipped through the pictures, inspecting each one. Beck had the thought that surveillance photos could make an awesome clue in a crime scene–themed escape room. Maybe that could be his next project when he got back home. He'd certainly have plenty of fodder for it.

Carter paused on a photo of a tall woman with platinum-blond hair, an enormous fur coat—in this weather?—and large sunglasses. The hair was almost certainly a wig, and the woman was strutting down the hallway without revealing a scrap of skin—she even had gloves on.

Beck checked Ranielle for her reaction. She was wearing an excellent poker face. It could be her in this photo.

Beck was practically vibrating with the need to tell the police everything they'd figured out, but he couldn't with Ranielle and her fancy lawyer in the room with them.

Detective Lopez seemed like a smart guy. Surely he would figure it out. Surely he saw through Ranielle.

"No," Carter finally said. "I don't recognize anyone."

"Me neither," said Adi. Beck shook his head and passed the pictures over to Sierra, but she just tossed them onto the coffee table.

"The night clerk didn't find it suspicious when someone walked through looking like that?" Beck said, pointing to the photo of the blond woman.

"It's not so out of place at this sort of hotel," said Detective Lopez.

Carter stiffened. "*What* sort of hotel?"

"This hotel caters to a particular type of clientele. Largely celebrities looking for . . . discretion."

Again, Beck glanced at Ranielle. Her expression remained carefully neutral.

"Should we call our parents?" Carter asked.

Ranielle's eyebrows lifted. "What for?"

"To . . . take us home?"

"There's no need for that. We'll provide a counselor for any trauma you may have experienced discovering the body of my husband, blah blah blah—"

Her lawyer coughed.

Ranielle cut short and finished with "You can have as many sessions as you like between shoots."

"Between shoots?" Adi said. "You're going on with the show?"

"Of course we're going on with the show. Hitflix has contracted us for the whole season, the games have already been designed, and the final two rooms are mostly constructed. We'll be down a host, but the editors can do a nice little in memoriam for the semifinal. We're calling a meeting with the cast and crew later today. Until then, I don't want a word of this spoken to anyone. Understand me?" She seemed to take their silence as a yes, and turned to the detective. "Are we finished here?"

"Not quite."

Detective Lopez spent another fifteen minutes asking them the same questions as the ones from the night before, recording notes in his book. Finally, he thanked them for their time and stood to leave. The lawyer walked him to the door of the villa, but Ranielle lingered.

"It is very unfortunate you had to see what you did last night," she said. "But the show must go on, and I need you ready to perform at your best come Monday morning. I recommend staying out of public view and off social media. Nothing has changed. You're still playing for one million dollars, and I expect you to act like it."

33

Sierra

It looked to Sierra, as the studio's lobby sofas were quickly occu-pied, that everyone was at this meeting. Not just the contestants but Fitzy, Vera, Elijah, Lisa, the stylists, the lighting operators, the set crew, the interns, the director, the receptionist, even the shuttle driver.

Everyone except the Game Master.

"Seriously? *Now* what?" said Nadia. "It's supposed to be our day off. I've got passes for the Getty Center this afternoon."

Vera was videoing the crowd when Ranielle marched over and snatched her phone away.

"Hey!"

"No recordings."

Vera took a bewildered step back.

"What's this about, Ranielle?" said Fitzy. He was sitting on the arm of one of the white leather sofas, and it took Sierra a moment to realize what looked different about him today. Without the crisp linen shirt, the carefully tousled hair, or the makeup creating the illusion of flawless skin, he looked . . . normal.

Only once everyone was settled and quiet did Ranielle pace to the front of the crowd, her fingers in front of her red-lacquered lips.

"Before I explain, I want to remind you about the nondisclosure agreements you've signed. What I'm about to tell you is to remain confidential until further notice. Anyone found discussing this information outside of this studio, and with anyone not currently in this room, will be immediately terminated from their position here on *The Escape Game* and facing a very severe lawsuit."

She paused, letting this threat sink in.

Then— "Where's Louis?"

The question came from Gabriela, her brow knitted as she scanned the crowd, and it spurred a flurry of confusion as everyone looked around, confirming that the Game Master was indeed missing.

Sierra ran her tongue against her lip piercing, keeping her eyes on the executive producer. *Yeah, Ranielle,* she wanted to say. *Where's Louis?*

Ranielle briefly met Gabriela's eye, then let her gaze drift over her audience.

"Last night, my husband's body was found in a hotel room." She paused before adding, "He killed himself."

Gasps.

Ranielle went on. "I have not received the coroner's report, but the medical examiner suspects an intentional overdose."

Sierra wondered if Ranielle would mention that it was Carter who had found the body, after being invited to the hotel room for an "interview." She wondered how much Ranielle knew about her husband. She wondered how many contestants he'd preyed on before.

She wondered when Ranielle had started planning his murder.

"But . . . why?" said Fitzy, his voice barely a whisper. "Why would he . . . ?"

"Louis was a talented man," said Ranielle, "but he had his demons to fight, as much as anyone."

She went on to tell them that this show had been her husband's life's work, and he would want them to continue, to have fun, to complete these very last puzzles he had set for his beloved contestants. The show must go on, and all that.

She did not say that Louis's death was a tragedy. She did not say that he would be missed.

She did not even pretend to be sad.

She also did not mention his confession. The suicide note had not been made public, but Sierra assumed it was only a matter of time. The police would probably be glad to get Alicia's cold case permanently off their desks.

They weren't even considering that Louis's death could be a homicide. Ranielle was going to get away with murder. Again.

"I expect a police report to be made public soon," Ranielle added, "at which point you will be free to discuss this with friends and family. Until then, should you feel the need to talk with someone, grief counselors will be provided." She smacked her hands, as if brushing off something dirty. "We'll be back here on Monday to film the semifinals, as scheduled. I'm sure you have many questions, but at this point I am not at liberty to answer most of them."

Fitzy's hand went up anyway, a little hesitant, like a student afraid of getting yelled at by the teacher. He even waited for Ranielle to give him a scowl before he asked, "What about *next* season? Is this . . . I mean. This isn't the end of the show, is it?"

"That is one of the questions we need to work through," she said. "So far, Hitflix is hopeful that we will be able to continue."

Fitzy sank back. He looked shell-shocked, like the rest of them. "This show means too much, Ranielle. To all of us." He swept his arm toward the crowd and received nods of agreement. "I don't know how we'd do it without Louis, but if there's a way . . ."

"He wasn't irreplaceable," said Ranielle—and there, finally. That hint of fury Sierra had been waiting for. "*No one* here is irreplaceable." She let her gaze linger a moment on Fitzy, and hurt flashed across his eyes. Then she turned and said directly to a grim-faced Vera, "Let's try to remember that, shall we?"

THE HOLLYWOOD HERALD

Louis Augustus Russell Found Dead of Cyanide Poisoning, Determined Suicide by Police

TV personality Louis Augustus Russell died after ingesting potassium cyanide, revealed a report by the Los Angeles Chief Medical Examiner early this morning.

According to authorities, Russell, 35, was found dead in a hotel room Wednesday night by a thus-far undisclosed colleague from *The Escape Game*—the popular mystery-themed game show that earned Russell his celebrity status as the puzzle-loving "Game Master."

The Chief Medical Examiner's office confirmed that the police have ruled the death a suicide, citing a letter written to Russell's wife and co-producer, Ranielle Russell.

Russell has been beloved among fans of *The Escape Game* since its inception as a YouTube series nearly three years ago. The show—in which teams of young contestants compete to solve riddles, ciphers, and clues in order to "escape" increasingly complex and highly stylized rooms—grew in popularity largely due to its avid fans, who refer to themselves as Clue Masters. It briefly earned a prime spot on syndicated television before moving to Hitflix after Russell received an Emmy nominee for his role as co-producer in the Outstanding Reality Competition Program category.

Russell's death has come as a shock to his friends and fans alike, with an outpouring of appreciation and emotional tributes taking over social media. A statement on the show's official media page said, "In the midst of our heartbreak over the sudden passing of our brilliant Game Master, we vow to continue Louis's legacy—by moving forward with the show, the game, the escape."

When asked if Russell's death might have anything to do with the unsolved murder of season four contestant Alicia Angelos, the show's representative declined to comment.

Sierra swiped black lipstick across her lips. She hadn't worn her armor all weekend. Sure, she also hadn't left the villas all weekend, but she had no idea when she'd grown comfortable enough with her teammates to let her guard down around them. She might've wondered if finding a dead body was one of those life-changing experiences that bonded people, but then, it hadn't exactly gone that way with her first team.

She stepped out of the bathroom to find Carter and Beck at the kitchen island, finishing off bowls of cereal. They'd been subdued these last few days. All the contestants had been. Even Jarius hadn't acted half as obnoxious as usual around the complex.

Sierra had done a lot of baking. Chocolate chip cookies, scones, focaccia, a peach pie. Adi had escaped into his books—at least when he wasn't staring at Alicia's note, trying to figure out the secondary code she'd left behind, hoping it might further implicate Ranielle. Carter had been glued to her phone ever since news of Louis's death had gone public, trying to keep up with the outpouring of emotion on the Domain. In the wake of the report, Carter had done her due diligence as a top influencer by releasing a video highlighting some of the greatest moments from *The Escape Game*. Sierra doubted that most viewers would pick up on the fact that she'd only included moments in which Fitzy, with his offbeat energy and goofball charm, made the Game Master look rather dull in comparison.

Of all of them, Beck was the only one who felt compelled to keep rehashing everything that had happened, making it clear to Sierra that he was the sort of person who actually liked to talk about his feelings.

What a foreign concept.

But he didn't want to just talk about Alicia's note and the Game Master. He wanted a plan. What were they going to do? When were they going to go to the police about Ranielle?

Sierra's answer was always the same. She'd go to the police when she had evidence. Solid evidence.

She kept hoping that maybe the police would figure it out on their own. That maybe this time Ranielle had left behind some trace DNA, fingerprints, *something* that would pin Louis's murder on her. Then Sierra could come forward with Alicia's note and explain her theories, and finally, finally her sister would have justice.

But she'd been watching the news, and so far the only sightings of Ranielle had been coverage of the *grieving widow determined to continue her husband's legacy . . . with another season of the blockbuster reality show already in preproduction.*

Gross.

"Are we ready for today?" Sierra said, grabbing the last scone and slathering it with a heavy dose of butter. "Semifinals."

"Do you think we'll still get a clue?" said Carter.

"I'd say everything will be the same, including the dexterity challenge. Speaking of, I've nominated Beck as our competitor."

Beck rubbed his hands together. "I hope it's something epic, like riding one of those bucking bull machines. I've always wanted to do that."

Sierra smiled faintly, pulling the scone apart bite by bite. "Has anyone seen Adi this morning?"

As soon as she asked, Adi emerged from his bedroom, freshly showered and fully dressed.

"Whoa," said Beck. "Someone's getting an early start."

"Got a meeting."

"With who?" asked Sierra.

"Ranielle," Adi said. "That promo thing for Sweetbrier Resort, remember?" He reached for the plate that had once held scones, then made a face. "Who took the last scone?"

Sierra made a big show of cramming it into her mouth.

He rolled his eyes. "I'll grab something from the dining hall."

"Don't forget to get some deets on Sweetbrier!" Beck said.

"You really think Ranielle is going to tell me anything important?"

"She's got to have information on her laptop. If I ever get a chance to search the property, it would be really helpful to know if there are, like, underground tunnels, or what the security system is like. That sort of thing."

Adi stepped into his tennis shoes. "So you want me to log on to Ranielle's laptop, find confidential information, and steal it somehow . . . all while Ranielle's back is turned?"

"I mean. You know. You could. If it works out."

"Right," Adi drawled. "That'll be a no from me."

He opened the front door to reveal Lisa on the other side carrying an enormous package. It was flat, about the same size as the top of the coffee table and covered in brown paper.

"Delivery for Team Helsing," she said.

"Thanks?" said Adi, helping her bring it inside.

They set it on the dining table. "Have y'all been holding up all right?" Lisa asked.

"What's it to you?" said Sierra.

"That's Sierra-speak for *Yes, we're doing okay; thanks for asking,*" said Beck.

Sierra scowled. "Is not."

Lisa gave a wan smile, then waved. "Okay, well, good luck on today's round."

Carter shut the door behind her as Adi inspected the printed sticker on the package. "It's addressed to all of us. *Team Helsing. Villa #1.* Too narrow to be a horse head, at least."

"Horse head?" said Carter.

"*The Godfather*? Mario Puzo?"

She stared blankly.

"Never mind."

Adi tore off the paper, and Sierra's gut lurched.

Maybe not such a terrible joke after all.

It was a painting. It was one of *her* paintings. Or at least, a print of one of her paintings, neatly framed and matted. *Dance Macabre.*

But someone had ruined it.

Her artwork had shown a woman in a black gown waltzing with a hollow-eyed skeleton, while two more skeletons danced across a mirror-image background of roses and thorns. Someone had taken a picture of Sierra's face and glued it over the woman's. The skulls of the three dancers had been replaced with photos of Beck, Carter, and Adi.

Red paint marred them all. *X*s over their eyes. Slashes across their throats.

And written along the bottom in sharp, dripping capitals—

GIVE UP, HELSING
OR YOU'RE NEXT

34
Adi

Adi had offered to stay. He had *wanted* to stay. He certainly didn't want to be sitting here, listening to Ranielle Russell clack away at her laptop, acting as if he didn't exist. He was used to being ignored, but really. She was the one who had dragged him to the studio first thing on a Monday morning, when he could have been back at the villa, figuring out who had sent that vandalized print.

Sierra had logged on to her online store to look up her recent orders. The prints were fulfilled by a third-party printer so she didn't need to be hands-on with shipping and fulfillment. It had taken her all of three minutes to find the details.

That print had been ordered the day after they'd arrived on the show, and it had been sent directly to the studio's address. No name, no specific recipient. The package had been signed for by the receptionist.

It could have been anyone.

Looking visibly shaken, Sierra had told Adi to go, that they were fine. Just another prank. Adi suspected she was more upset at seeing her own artwork defaced than the actual message.

But . . . maybe not. The scrawl bore a striking resemblance to what had been in her sister's coffin.

WE GET WHAT WE DESERVE

What sort of sick asshole . . .

He shuddered every time he thought about it. And when he remembered Sierra's attempts to hide her emotions, and Beck looking so aghast that there were creeps in the world who would do this to fellow humans, and Carter—

Carter, who had broken their horrified silence by saying, of all things, "What a stunning use of planar symmetry in this background, Sierra."

It made Adi want to laugh.

It made Adi want to punch someone.

He was pretty sure, though, that Ranielle Russell had not been the one to send them that painting, no matter how much she enjoyed messing with contestants. No . . . She had to be thinking that she was in the clear over her little murder spree. She wouldn't risk a threat that might turn the attention back on her.

This was the work of a saboteur. Someone trying to get in their heads. Someone who wanted them to screw up during the semi-finals. Someone who had been targeting them from the start.

Jarius? Team Dread? Elijah?

He wished he was back in the villas, puzzling it out with his team-mates. He wished he was anywhere but in this stuffy office, not-so-patiently waiting for Ranielle to take a break from her busy email schedule or whatever she was doing. He knew why she'd summoned him this morning. He knew what she was going to ask.

He still wasn't sure what he was going to say.

He'd almost forgotten about the host offer in the chaos. Despite what Ranielle had said, it was impossible to imagine the show going on without the Game Master. And to boot Fitzy out, too? It would be a whole new show—the Clue Masters would be livid.

Although Ranielle had made it clear that Hitflix wanted to take the show in a new direction.

With Victor Cunningham. Maybe *he* would be the new Game Master.

Adi breathed through a nervous tremor. Hitflix had asked for Adi especially, so he would outlast Ranielle Russell, too, when she was arrested for her husband's murder.

But.

But.

Adi's instincts told him there was something about the suicide note that wasn't adding up.

Tell Rani I love her.

The office door swung open without a knock. Adi glanced over his shoulder—then bolted upright.

"Here I am," sang Symphony, floating into the room. "Traffic was such a bear! I trust you haven't been waiting long."

Ranielle's icy gaze shifted from her computer screen to Symphony and back again. "As it's now nine thirty-seven, and we were to meet at nine o'clock, safe to say we've been waiting for thirty-seven minutes."

"I'm worth every second," Symphony chirruped.

Though there was a chair beside Adi, Symphony sank onto the sofa, and Adi's stomach churned to think how he had done the exact same thing the first time he'd been called to this office.

"Hello, love," his mother said, beaming at him. "You're still looking too skinny. You need definition in those arms. I brought some more shake packets—"

"What are you doing here?" he barked, then turned to Ranielle. "What is she doing here?"

"I've been asking myself that a lot this past year," Ranielle muttered. She finally pushed back from her computer and folded her hands on top of her desk. "Your mother will be coming on as a producer next season and—"

"She *what*?"

"—has therefore taken a vested interest in our search for the next show host," Ranielle continued, ignoring Adi's outburst. "She insisted on being here while we discuss particulars."

Adi's face contorted—first with surprise, then disgust, then anger. He would never escape his mother.

Symphony crossed her legs and leaned forward, elbows propped on her knee. "Actually. Now that you mention it, I have some concerns about Aditya as host." Her voice was all sugar and softness, her face perfectly molded into that of the concerned, doting mother.

"What are you talking about?" Ranielle demanded. "This is what you wanted."

"I can't wait to hear this," Adi drawled.

Symphony's unnaturally plumped lips fluttered into a smile. "It's just . . . Aditya is still so young."

"He's older than Fitzy was when he hosted our first season," Ranielle said, not missing a beat.

Symphony carried on as if she hadn't heard. "And he's quite inexperienced when it comes to show business. Being a contestant is one thing, but to *host*? That's a level of responsibility I'm not sure he's prepared for."

Adi's jaw dropped.

"And of course, he has the rest of school to think about, and college after that. He has his whole future ahead of him. I don't know if this is the best course."

"You may be a producer," said Ranielle, "but Hitflix execs' opinions trump yours. And they want Aditya." Adi was tempted to cheer for her—before he remembered that she was almost certainly a cold-blooded murderer.

Symphony kept talking. "I'm not sure he's *really* what the show needs. I was watching some recent episodes—"

Adi snorted. Yeah, right.

"—and I think you'll agree, Ranielle, this show is ready for an infusion of feminine energy. A softer touch. A more *elegant* flair." She swished her fingers, and suddenly, Adi understood.

"You've got to be kidding me," he said.

Symphony looked at him, all tenderness. "Darling, it's nothing personal. Even you have to admit, you've never taken the slightest interest in acting. Whereas this is my life. My soul. What I could bring to the show is far superior to anything you, or any of those young people, ever could. A sense of presence. Confidence. Experience. And let's not forget"—she looked back at the producer, puckering her lips—"a certain amount of sex appeal."

Adi pressed a hand over his eyes. He didn't know what was worse—that his mom had mentioned her own sex appeal in front of him, or that she had driven here in Monday rush hour traffic to steal his contract.

He knew he shouldn't be surprised. This was painfully on-brand. But while he'd expected his mother to milk his contract for all it was worth, it hadn't crossed his mind that she might try to take it for herself. It was a new low.

"Thank you for that riveting sales pitch," said Ranielle. "But as I've explained numerous times, Hitflix wants a contestant as our next host. A *winning* contestant. And, as our contestants are teenagers, that means, by default, they want a *young* contestant."

Symphony's nostrils flared. Uncrossing her legs, she jabbed a manicured nail toward Adi. "He hasn't agreed yet. So no—*I'm* sorry, Ranielle, but I must implore you to reconsider."

"I am not reconsidering." Ranielle faced Adi, eyes blazing. "But she does make a point. Are you taking the gig or not? I have a lot on my plate right now, and if you're declining the offer, then I need you both out of here so you can stop wasting my time."

Adi's mouth opened, but no words came out.

Defiance roiled inside of him. He was tempted to say yes for no other reason than to see the look on his mother's face. He would meet his dad, and live at Sweetbrier Resort, and be free of her, finally free.

But something held his tongue.

Because at least one thing his mom had said was true. He'd never had any interest in show business. This wasn't the life he wanted, no matter the perks.

He was saved from answering by a knock at the door.

Vera walked in, fuming. "We can't get the"—she cut off abruptly when she noticed Adi, and her nose wrinkled—"*spinny thing* to work."

"What are you talking about?" Ranielle demanded.

"The *spinny thing*," Vera said, more forcefully. "On Soundstage D. They want you to come take a look."

"For god's sake," Ranielle said under her breath. "Do I have to do everything around here?"

Vera snorted. "Tell me about it."

Ranielle stormed around her desk. "Aditya, wait here. Symphony, out."

Symphony jumped to her feet. "We aren't finished."

"Yes, we are."

Ranielle and Vera stalked out of the office. Symphony marched after them. "Ranielle Russell, I will not be dismissed. This discussion is not over—" Her voice faded into the bustle of the studio.

Adi looked from the door to Ranielle's desk, with its open laptop. Back to the door. Back to the desk.

Well, damn. Here was that opportunity Beck had hoped for.

He drummed his fingers on the arm of the chair, considering his options. He could do nothing, and avoid ticking off Ranielle should he get caught. This was clearly the right choice.

Or option B—he could do this one ridiculous favor for Beck, who evidently saw himself as an amateur treasure hunter. Beck, who just might be as delusional as Symphony. Beck, who truly seemed to admire Victor Cunningham, even though most people would have hated him. Beck, who had insisted from the beginning that the Helsings needed to be a team. That they *were* a team.

With a heavy sigh, Adi got up and shut the door before approaching Ranielle's desk. An email was open on the screen, half-finished—a communication between Ranielle and someone at Hitflix.

Adi's own name caught his eye. He skimmed the email in disbelief.

He hadn't even accepted the deal yet, but Ranielle was already promising that he would be the next host—person of color, gorgeous, clever, loved by the audience, witty enough to bounce off his cohost.

How much did Hitflix buying the next season hinge on him saying yes?

And a better question . . . Was that what he wanted?

He didn't know. *He didn't know.*

He scanned to the bottom of the email, where his audition video was embedded, along with brief notes.

Season Five Audition Video: Aditya Parvesh

Producer notes:

Having regrets.

Although the kid seemed witty—loved the phony comment.

And he **is** *gorgeous. The next Alicia?*

The next Alicia? What the hell was that supposed to mean?

Footsteps in the hall made him jump. He looked up, holding his breath until the footsteps hurried away.

No time to waste. He typed *Sweetbrier* into the file search.

The first folder that popped up said *Sweetbrier Resort—Season 6*. It was full of documents, pdfs, photos, even video files. Jackpot.

A cart beside the desk held bins full of *Escape Game*–branded swag and merchandise. Adi grabbed one of the USBs and inserted it into the computer port.

He hesitated. This could have a lot of top-secret information about the resort. What would his dad think? Would he be angry if he found out?

Then again, Victor Cunningham did sort of owe Beck and his family after buying their land so cheaply. He could have chosen to share a portion of the treasure, but he hadn't. If there really was more gold out there, and Beck had any hope of finding it . . . what could be the harm? It wasn't like he was going to use these files to infiltrate the resort and pull off a heist or something.

He began to copy the files over.

"Call the electrician, get them here ASAP. Find whoever the fuck is doing this!"

Ranielle's voice was close. Too close.

Adi drummed his fingers on the desk, watching as the bar showing the download's progress ticked slowly, slowly . . .

"Come on, come on, come on . . ."

The doorknob turned.

The door started to open.

Adi reached for the USB. The download was almost there. Almost—

The door stilled. "Symphony, I swear to god, if you don't leave right now I'm calling security."

"Oh, now who's being melodramatic?" came his mother's saccharine reply.

Download complete.

Adi snatched the USB from the port as Ranielle threw the door open. A lifetime of living with Symphony had Adi's body reacting without conscious thought.

Get rid of the evidence.

He went to slide the USB into his pocket. Only when he heard it drop on the carpet did he remember he wasn't wearing his favorite jeans.

"What the hell are you doing?" Ranielle said.

"Admiring your desk." Adi searched for the USB with his tennis shoe. "Is this mahogany?"

Ranielle's nostrils flared as Symphony walked in behind her. "Is annoying me a hereditary trait?"

Oh *crap*. The folder was still open.

"Uh—not sure that's been scientifically proven," said Adi. "But either way, you're going to have to tolerate me a while longer." He spread his arms. "Congratulations! I've decided to take you up on your offer."

Ranielle's eyebrows flew up.

Symphony planted her hands on her hips. "No, Aditya, you and I must discuss—"

"There's nothing to discuss. I've made up my mind. Ranielle, we have a deal. Adi Parvesh, cohost of *The Escape Game,* starting season six."

Seeing the look on his mother's face made the whole selling-his-soul thing almost worthwhile.

"Well," said Ranielle, her shoulders sinking visibly. "That's excellent to hear. Truly excellent."

He thought he'd overdone it, but clearly Ranielle's mind was buzzing with things like Hitflix deals and annoying celebrities. And murder.

Adi dragged the USB toward him as Ranielle turned to Symphony. "Our business here is concluded. And I wasn't joking about calling security."

Symphony's face reddened. "I will be discussing this with my people. *And* Victor."

Adi's pulse jolted.

He was tempted to call out as Symphony stomped from the room, but instead he used Ranielle's distraction to exit the folder that contained everything she had about Victor's resort.

As the door slammed closed, Adi bent for the USB but had to jump up again as Ranielle turned back to him. "I'm glad you and I could come to an agreement." She moved around the desk, ushering Adi to the other side so she could reclaim her office chair. "I trust you'll take the extra assistance, then."

"I'll—what?" Adi's thoughts shifted away from the USB lying beside Ranielle's fancy pointed heels.

"I told you. I don't have losers on my staff. You'll take the cheats, and your team will win the season."

Adi hesitated.

"What's the matter?" Ranielle said. "You don't think your team deserves a million dollars?" Her face soured. "Or are you still agonizing over your integrity?"

She said the word "integrity" like it was something to be ashamed of. But there was a satisfaction to defeating each room, each challenge, using his own skills. His and his team's.

And if it ever came out that he'd cheated, what would his father think?

"You believe your team can win on their own?" Her lips curved into a tight smile. "You've barely been clinging on each week. And knowing what I do about Team Dread's next move, you don't want to walk out of here without the advantage."

Damn Team Dread. *Another* snag. They were so focused on Helsing when Mind Hack had clearly been the stronger competitor.

Adi flinched when he realized what he'd thought.

Team Dread had won every round. Mind Hack was a stronger competitor.

Ranielle was right.

"Come on, Aditya," Ranielle said. "Do you want to win, or not?"

Adi walked down the corridor, mind spinning.

What had he done?

Panic buzzed in his ears. This wasn't how he wanted things to go. This wasn't—

"Adi?" Adi spun around as Fitzy stuck his head out of an open door. "Aren't you supposed to be in makeup?"

"Aren't *you*?"

Adi hadn't meant to snap, but the last thing he'd wanted was to be caught coming out of Ranielle's office, especially by the guy whose job he was about to take.

"I'm on my way," Fitzy said, stepping from the room. "I just had . . ." He gestured inside. "Packing to do."

Adi caught the name LOUIS AUGUSTUS RUSSELL on the door plaque and piles of boxes on the desk. "Shouldn't that be an intern's job?"

Fitzy's face twisted bitterly. "You'd think so, wouldn't you? But Ranielle doesn't trust anyone else in there. Don't know why. It's not like he kept his puzzles and notes in his dressing room."

"Hey!" They turned as Vera stormed around the corner. "What are you doing?"

"Playing laser tag," Fitzy said. "What does it look like, mate?"

"I am not your *mate*." She eyed the empty bookshelves past the door. "Why were you in Louis's dressing room?"

"Because apparently tedious tasks are in my job description." For the first time, Adi noticed that Fitzy was losing his temper. "What's your problem now, Vera? It's bad enough I lost a guy who was practically a father. I don't need any more hell from you."

Vera leveled him with a look and shut Louis's door. The reptilian tail on her shoulder twitched as she locked it.

"I'm looking forward to the day I no longer have to deal with you," she spat, then turned and stalked back the way she came.

"That day would come sooner if you'd quit," Fitzy said, earning an over-the-shoulder glare.

"Seriously," said Adi. "What's her problem?"

Even he had enough decorum to appreciate when someone was grieving.

"She's bananas, isn't she?" said Fitzy as they headed toward makeup. "You'd think a social media manager would be, you know, social." There was a beat of silence before Fitzy said, "I didn't know she had a key to his dressing room."

Now that Adi thought about it, yeah, that seemed odd.

Fitzy scoffed. "For a second I . . . Nah." He waved his hand as if batting away an idea.

"What?" Adi said.

"Well . . ." Fitzy pursed his lips. "Do you think she's glad those creepy clues will stop now that Louis is gone?" Before Adi could ask exactly what he was implying, Fitzy changed the subject. "Saw your mum raging down the corridor earlier. Sheesh. She makes Vera look like sunshine and rainbows."

Adi stepped aside to let a set designer push a covered trolley past. "Yeah. It's great having a mom who only cares about me when I'm useful."

"Useful?"

"Like giving her a free pass to Ranielle Russell. Beyond that, I could walk off a cliff and she wouldn't bat an eyelid."

"I know what that's like," Fitzy said. "My dad kicked me out when my stepmom had a baby. Who wants a moody teenager when they can have a widdle bubba that's all theirs?"

"Ouch."

"Yeah. Ranielle and Louis took me under their wing after I moved to the States. They liked what I did back home—some soapies and stuff. And my agent is friends with Ranielle. When he introduced me, she was keen to have me as the face of the show. I took the gig and never looked back." Fitzy stopped Adi before the corner that led to the makeup room, his brow drawn. "Can I ask you a question?"

Trepidation crept across Adi. It was bad enough that his mom used him. If Fitzy was about to ask for some sort of Hollywood connection through Symphony . . .

"I was wondering if . . ." Fitzy scratched beneath his shirt collar. "Being Carter's teammate and all, I was curious . . ."

Oh no. This was even worse. Anything but sappy teen romance drama.

Fitzy plowed on. "Has she mentioned me? Or does she, like, have a boyfriend back home, or . . . ?"

"I wouldn't know," said Adi, willfully pretending he hadn't noticed how Carter swooned every time Fitzy entered the soundstage these days. "We're not that close."

"Right. Yeah. Of course." Fitzy looked downcast. "Not like I could do anything about it, anyway. If Ranielle found out, my ass would be gone."

Adi didn't answer. Fitzy was already gone, even if he didn't know it yet. And once Fitzy was fired and the season was wrapped up . . .

"So you're actually serious about her?" Adi regretted it the moment the words were out. This was none of his business. More than that—he didn't care about Fitzy's love life, or Carter's, for that matter. "Never mind."

"Nah, it's cool," said Fitzy. "We're not supposed to get involved with the contestants. Ranielle's real strict about that. I never cared before, but it's different with Carter. *She's* different. You know? Like, she's so *awkward* in person." He chuckled. "I mean that as a compliment, I swear. Not like the fake Hollywood types you usually meet around here. But then you see her videos and she's so smart and confident, and sexy as hell when she's explaining math-y things I don't understand."

Adi stared, wondering if Fitzy was as oblivious as he pretended.

Carter, not one of those fake Hollywood types? Sure, she had turned out to be a competent teammate, and Adi had to admit that she wasn't anything like he'd expected. But she hid behind a cartoon. She wore grungy pajamas at the villas but those ridiculous outfits whenever she was out in public. She was an *influencer*.

"How often do you find a girl who's that smart, and that beautiful?" Fitzy went on. Apparently, yes, he really was that oblivious. "But this gig is everything to me. Not just because it's literally the best job in the world, but also . . ."

"Also what?"

"There's this little green card issue. As long as I'm employed here, it's all golden, but if I lost this gig . . ." He grimaced. "Well. Back to Oz we go."

35
Carter

Carter eyed her reflection in the dressing room mirror, holding still so the costume assistant wouldn't prick her with a safety pin. This week, they'd been stuffed into red-and-white-striped vests and suspenders. Carter wasn't sure what the outfits were supposed to be. A barbershop quartet, maybe? Beck had been given a straw boater hat with a red ribbon, which had made him positively giddy, while Sierra flat-out refused to put on a red bow tie. Adi was late, which was stressing out the costume designers.

Or maybe everyone was stressed-out, period. Carter was certainly on edge. Not only had they already been delayed nearly two hours because of some technical difficulties on set, but also the Game Master was dead, and Ranielle Russell might be a murderer, and the internet was buzzing with conspiracy theories and rehashing the ribbon riddle and wondering if there really was going to be a big "killer reveal" in the finale, and suddenly this family-friendly competition was the scene of murder and drama and revenge, and here she was, normal-awkward-nervous Carter Kelly, caught right smack in the middle of it. People expected her to have answers. She did indeed have answers, about Alicia and Louis and Ranielle, but nothing her fans would want to hear. Hopefully the world would never find out it had been her who had discovered Louis's body, because then she'd have to record a video about it, and she really, really didn't want to.

Then there were her parents, who *did* know she'd found the body. She'd had to talk them into allowing her to audition for the show in the first place after what happened last season, then there was the drink spiking and the freezer incident, and now this. They'd been determined to catch the next flight to LA and drag her home.

It had taken hours of arguing before they finally started to calm down. Another hour before they agreed to let her stay.

But if they ever found out about the painting that had been delivered to their villa that morning, or the knife in the cow's heart, all bets would be off.

She couldn't leave. Not when they were so close to the finale.

"There you are!" said Sierra as Adi hurried into the room.

"Yeah, sorry," he said. "Got held up."

Two assistants dragged him in front of the costume racks and started yelling at him to get changed, fast, fast.

"Well?" said Beck. "How did it go?"

Adi met Beck's gaze in the mirror as he took off his shirt. He gave a quick shake of his head. "Sorry."

One word. Barely any inflection. But they all knew what it meant. No info on Sweetbrier Resort.

Beck looked crestfallen. "Thanks anyway."

"Shake it off," said Sierra. "We need to focus."

Beck physically shook himself. "Aye-aye, Captain. Don't worry about me. I'm focused as a laser."

A line producer entered. "Who's ready to get mic'd up?"

"Sierra and Beck are good to go," said the stylist, putting away the safety pins and adjusting Carter's vest. She swept her gaze from Carter's shoes to her face, then frowned and said, "Can we get makeup in here to do something about these eyebrows?"

Carter raised a hand to her face.

"Yeah, sure, I'll send someone," said the producer. "Sierra, Beck, with me."

"See you on set," Beck said, giving Carter a high five as he passed.

Carter returned her gaze to the mirror, turning her head from side to side. Great. Not only did she have to worry about murderers and saboteurs, but now she had to think about her eyebrows, too.

"Don't forget these," said the costumer, handing Carter her glasses.

Carter groaned. "Could we not for this one? They're uncomfortable."

"Producer's orders," said the assistant.

"The glasses aren't your idea?" Adi asked, doing up the buttons on his white dress shirt.

"Are you kidding? I hate these things. And the itchy designer clothes. If I could do it again, I'd make Kick It Carter a frumpy, legging-loving nerd with perfect vision." She sighed. "Also, what's the point of them fixing my eyebrows if they're going to be hidden behind these ridiculous frames?"

He grunted quietly, still watching her.

"What?"

"Nothing." Adi let an assistant help him into a red jacket with gold buttons. "What are these costumes, anyway?"

She shrugged. "Bellhops? Maybe we have to escape the Ritz-Carlton."

"I'm pretty sure no one ever wants to escape the Ritz-Carlton."

A guy arrived with a makeup kit and pulled out some tweezers and a pencil. Carter tried not to grimace at each pluck.

"How was your meeting?" she asked, glancing sideways at Adi, while another assistant put product in his hair.

"It was . . . fine."

Carter peered at him from the corner of her eye. Clearly it had *not* been fine. "Did something happen?"

Instead of answering, he said, "Do you remember in the limousine, before the kickoff party, when Jarius said you have to want it so bad you'd do anything to win?"

"Sure."

His stare bore into her, so intense it made her shiver. "How bad do you want it?"

It was, perhaps, the most real question he'd ever asked her. Here they were, mere minutes from the semifinals. Two more rooms and they could have it all. No longer would she be Kick It Carter—influencer, Solve Specialist, contestant.

She would be Kick It Carter—winner, champion, maybe even real-world detective. And she would have done it beside three of the coolest people she'd ever known.

Three people she was honored to think of as her friends.

"I want it," she whispered. "I want it really bad."

He held her gaze for one last beat. "That's good to know."

Carter had the strangest sensation that maybe she'd said the wrong thing. "Adi—"

"Done," interrupted one of the assistants. "Go get mic'd up."

She was tempted to argue. But then she remembered where she was. What they were about to do. "Okay. See you out there."

Adi watched her in the mirror as she turned to leave. His lips quirked into an almost-smile, but there was something in the look that worried her.

As the makeup artist and assistant turned their focus to Adi, Carter slipped into the hallway and headed toward the set where Fitzy and Louis usually introduced the upcoming round.

How unsettling this would be without the Game Master and his wry quips. Did Ranielle really think the show could be salvaged without him?

She was nearly there when a hand grabbed her wrist and yanked her to the side. Her breath caught in her throat, and she opened her mouth to scream as she spun to face—

Fitzy.

"Sorry! I'm sorry!" he whispered, throwing his hands up. "I wasn't trying to scare you."

Carter pressed a hand over her rampaging heart. Fitzy dragged her behind one of the movable set pieces—a wall on wheels.

Once she could breathe again, Carter smacked his arm. "You scared the daylights out of me!"

"I'm sorry. Really." But she could tell he was trying to stifle a laugh.

"I guess I could have been more subtle. I wanted to see you before we start filming."

"Is something wrong?"

"No. Nothing. I just . . ." He glanced toward the corridor, then took Carter's hands and pulled her farther behind the set piece. Her stomach swooped at the touch, free-falling when he didn't immediately let go. "I was talking to Adi earlier, and our conversation got me thinking." His blue eyes were intent as he held her gaze, his fingers curling around hers. "Two weeks from now, this season is going to be over. And as far as I know, there aren't any rules in my contract about dating a *former* contestant."

He paused, the words hanging between them. Carter's pulse fluttered. This close, she could smell the clean detergent scent of his shirt, the mint from his mouth. This close, she could see the tiny freckle next to his left eye that the makeup artists always tried to cover up.

"So I was wondering," Fitzy went on, sounding both confident and nervous, "if maybe, two weeks from now, I could ask you out on a date?"

Carter's mouth went dry. She licked her lips. Fitzy's gaze dropped, catching the movement. Her entire body thrummed.

"I . . . I would like that," she said. "Except . . . I'll be going home."

"I know," he said quickly. "But the show will be on break until the next season. Assuming there is a next season. And I don't have anything else going on, so it would be pretty easy to, you know. Come visit? For a bit?"

She laughed. A short hiccup of a sound.

James "Fitzy" Fitzgerald was asking *her* out on a date. Was offering to get on an airplane and fly across the country to see her.

A voice in her head whispered that this was preposterous. A boy like him could never like a girl like her.

She told that voice to shove it.

"I'd like that."

His smile brightened. "Okay, then. In two weeks, expect my call."

"I will."

He beamed at her and she beamed at him, and she was so grateful for that fake wall because if anyone saw them in that moment, holding hands and grinning like dopey cartoon characters, she never could have lived it down. But in that moment, she didn't care.

This boy liked her. Of all the boys, *this* one liked her. More than that, he understood her. He knew what it was like to play a part for the cameras. To hide behind a persona. To feel like you could never show your authentic, ridiculous self to the world.

Somehow, she knew she could show her ridiculous self to him.

"Guess we should probably . . ." Fitzy jerked his head toward the corridor. "You know. Before they send a search party."

"Yeah. Right." Biting her lower lip in an attempt to dampen her smile, Carter pulled her hands from his grip and turned away.

"Carter?"

She eagerly spun back. "Yeah?"

Fitzy's gaze had become a question, and she very much knew the answer.

She took a step closer, reaching for the back of his neck, while an arm pulled her against him.

His lips were soft, slow, undemanding—and Carter's knees were useless as she sank into him. Only then did he deepen the kiss, their bodies molding together.

Her first real kiss, and it was everything. Sweet and sensuous and with James Freaking Fitzgerald.

The moment was brief—too brief—but Carter forced herself to pull away, even as Fitzy's mouth tried to follow her. He groaned, a quiet sound that made her lightheaded. She pressed a hand against his chest, her eyes fluttering open.

"What was that for?" he whispered.

"I'm pretty sure *you* kissed *me*," she whispered back.

"Did I?" His eyes twinkled. "Oh. Then I guess it was for good luck."

Her smile was impossible to tame this time as she untangled herself from his grasp.

They returned to the hallway. Carter paused to fix a lock of Fitzy's hair that had *mysteriously* gotten misplaced, and when she turned back—there was Adi.

She drew up short.

So did he, his gaze jotting from Carter to Fitzy and back again.

Carter blushed, thankful it was only Adi. Her teammates were the only people in the world she trusted about this.

But Adi didn't give her one of those knowing looks like she'd expected. He just inhaled sharply and said, "Come on. We're late."

"Well, Team Helsing," said Fitzy, "here we are again. Round three. How are you feeling?"

He might have been doing a marvelous job of acting like nothing had happened, but Carter was definitely not imagining the way his gaze lingered on her longer than the others when the cameras started rolling.

How was she feeling?

Pretty amazing, actually. She tamped down her grin, though, knowing it would hardly be appropriate so soon after Louis's death.

"Oh, you know," said Sierra. "It's been a week."

"That it has." Sorrow flashed across Fitzy's face, but he gave himself a small shake as he turned to face the cameras. "But the show must go on. And as you know, we have a tradition for our semifinal round. One that goes back to season one's espionage room." Fitzy returned his wicked grin to them. "Helsing, do you know what tradition I'm talking about?"

Beck pumped his fists. "The dexterity challenge!"

"Nailed it! During the semifinal, each team selects one member to attempt a feat of skill and daring, but you won't have any idea what the challenge is until the room begins. So, have you chosen who will compete?"

"Beck," said Sierra. "He has mad skills."

Carter nudged Beck with her elbow. "He's our Beck-of-all-trades."

"All right, Beck, it sounds like—" Fitzy was interrupted by a buzzer.

Sierra let out an animalistic roar.

"Ah, that's not good," said Fitzy. "Team Dread's targeted you again."

Adi huffed a breath through his nose.

"At least this time we've called it tit for tat," said Sierra. "We're using our snag against *them* this round. Jarius and Delphi will be competing in handcuffs." She looked into the camera. "You're welcome."

"Oof, that's gonna be rough. Maybe they deserve it after keeping you *tied up* all season." Fitzy winked at the camera. "But that's how the game is played. Today, Team Dread gets to choose your challenger." An envelope was handed to him by one of the set assistants. He opened it, reading slowly to keep them in suspense. "Unfortunately, they have not gone with Beck." Fitzy gestured at Carter with the corner of the envelope. "Carter Kelly, they've chosen you!"

Horror curled around Carter's spine. She was the girl who was all elbows and knees, who had the upper body strength of a ramen noodle.

She tried to think back to the dexterity challenges from past seasons, but in that moment, all she could remember was Alicia Angelos in a helmet and protective gear racing through an obstacle course.

A hand on her shoulder gently shook her from her trance.

"It's okay," whispered Beck. "You've got this."

She definitely did not have this. This was a disaster.

"Carter," said Sierra. "Relax. We don't even know what the challenge is yet. It could be anything."

Memories of the other seasons trickled through Carter's fog of panic. The episode where competitors had to sneak through a maze of lasers like superspies. The one where they had to mimic breakdance maneuvers. The one where they had to build a tower out of giant wooden blocks.

She wasn't sure about breakdancing or contorting her body around lasers, but she could play Jenga.

Maybe this would be okay.

"Let's find out about the room you're about to enter," said Fitzy. "Years ago, the carnival was a favorite family destination."

Carter glanced down at her striped vest. *Ah*, they were carnies!

Fitzy continued, "But when the town fell on hard times and tourists stopped coming, the carnival had to shut its gates. Decades passed, with the abandoned rides and tents becoming a haven for crime and vandalism. Now rumors have begun to circulate that one member of the carnival family, a mischievous clown, never left at all. In fact, they say the fun house is possessed by the clown's spirit, and while many curious souls have dared to enter the fun house . . . none have ever returned. You, Team Helsing, represent a new carnival empire that wants to take over the old grounds and restore them to their former glory. But before you can do that, you must break the clown's curse by escaping the fun house . . . if you dare."

Fitzy punctuated this last sentence with an over-the-top evil laugh. Despite Carter's mounting anxiety, she found it adorable and hilarious and why couldn't she stop staring at his mouth?

"Carter, as the starting challenger," said Fitzy, "come stand by me for today's clue."

Beck gave her arm a squeeze as she joined Fitzy in front of the cameras.

"Unfortunately, Louis—" said Fitzy, but then he paused, his breath catching. It was like watching the facade ripple away. Gone was the lively, untouchable show host, replaced by . . . a guy. Just a guy. He adjusted his stance, blinking through shining eyes.

"Get it together, Fitzy," the director barked in their earpieces.

"Right. Yep. Hang on." Fitzy cleared his throat, still shuffling.

Carter's hand itched to reach for him. There had been countless interviews in which Fitzy had called Louis a father figure. They'd been so close. Ever since finding Alicia's note and learning that the Game Master wasn't the stand-up guy she'd imagined him to be, Carter had seethed with anger, as though his misdeeds were a personal betrayal. And maybe they were, given her spiked drink. She'd hardly mourned his death at all. But Fitzy didn't know any of that. To him, a dear friend and mentor was gone.

"Let me try that again." Fitzy drew a breath and arranged his features into a sad smile. He turned back to Carter. "Unfortunately, I'll have to be the one giving today's clue, in honor of our genius Game Master. Carter, are you ready?"

"I'm ready, Fitzy."

"Right. Your clue is: It's all fun and games at the carnival, so don't be afraid. This game should be easy as pie." He paused, then laughed. "What does that mean? I have no idea! I'm just the host. Now then, let's put on those blindfolds!"

"Wait . . . that's it?" said Carter, sure she'd missed something. "That was the clue?"

Fun and games. Easy as pie.

Oh god—what if the challenge was a pie-eating contest? She'd become a meme for sure!

Mortified, Carter put on her blindfold and let herself be led into the next studio, taking comfort in the sounds of her teammates' footsteps around her, at least until they vanished into the distance. She'd have to do this part alone.

She tried to shut down her niggling doubts, but they invaded her mind all the same. She was going to fail. They were going to lose in the semifinals and it would be her fault.

Well—hers, and Team *Jerks*. What did they have against her team, anyway?

"When I say the word," came Fitzy's voice, interrupting her internal tirade, "you may remove your blindfold and begin. Three . . . two . . . one . . . *Escape!*"

THE ESCAPE GAME

SEASON FIVE

Round Three: Welcome to the Fun House

THREE TEAMS REMAINING

00:30 s3
Tunnel to Mirror Maze
Ticketing and Balloon Balcony

36

Carter

Carter pulled off her blindfold. She was standing on a small balcony with a narrow staircase curving down to one side. On a ledge in front of her, dozens of darts with brightly colored fletching were arranged into rows. Over the balcony was a drop of maybe twenty feet, and directly across from her, a wall of balloons, each one labeled from one to twenty-five.

Balloons. Darts.

She knew this game. She'd played it countless times at the autumn fair that came through town. So many carnival games were scams, but popping balloons with darts? Now that was something she could do. One year, when she was maybe nine or ten, she'd played the game twelve times in a row until she'd earned enough tickets to get the stuffed snail that still sat prominently on her bookshelves at home.

Carter grinned, lightheaded. She might actually be able to pull this off.

She picked up a dart. Only then did she spot her teammates below, standing in front of a humongous door that was painted to look like a creepy clown. Darkened light bulbs surrounded a FUN HOUSE sign, while a RIDE INOPERABLE—DO NOT ENTER message hung crooked over the door.

Beck cupped his hands around his mouth. "You can do this, Carter!"

She focused on the wall of balloons, lifted the dart, and threw.

Her first dart struck number twenty-two with a satisfying pop. She half expected a bell to go off, but nothing happened. She threw another dart and hit number seventeen. Another pop and nothing else.

Did she have to pop them all?

The third throw—number nine. Number five. Number twenty-four.

With a frustrated grunt, she picked up the next dart.

"Carter!" shouted Sierra. "There's a scanner down here. It says one ticket needed per entry. I think you're looking for four tickets!"

"Tickets," Carter whispered to herself. "Four tickets. Four balloons. Okay. Okay, I can do that." She studied the board of balloons, willing it to give up its secrets.

She zeroed in on lucky number sixteen, because 1.6 kicked off the golden ratio.

She exhaled and threw, hitting number sixteen dead on.

Nothing. No ticket.

Crap, crap, crap.

"What numbers do I hit?" she called down to her teammates, who were busily searching the area in front of the fun-house door.

"We don't know," Sierra called back. "There's nothing down here to indicate any numbers, or a clue . . ."

"Keep popping those damn balloons," said Adi. "As fast as you can!"

Carter grabbed another dart.

Lucky number seven? People liked the number seven . . .

Relax. Breathe out. Throw.

Number seven popped—but no ticket.

She groaned.

"*Easy as pie* my—" Carter caught herself.

And then.

A thought.

Easy as pie?

Or easy as . . . pi?

Her attention zeroed in on balloon number three. She threw the next dart . . . but missed the balloon by millimeters. She grabbed another dart. Aimed. Threw.

Number three burst and . . .

A beautiful paper ticket fluttered down from the board, right into Beck's waiting hand. "You did it!" he cried, waving it at Carter. "We got one!"

One down, three to go.

Carter grabbed another dart. Aimed at number one. *Pop!*

Another ticket!

Number four.

Pop!

"Oh my giddy aunt, Carter!" cried Beck. "How are you doing that?"

A disbelieving laugh escaped Carter's lips as she picked up the next dart. Most people only knew that much of the sequence. 3.14. But she'd memorized pi out to a hundred digits, just for fun. Because, dammit, she was Kick It Carter. Math whiz. Solve Specialist. Total dart-throwing badass.

3.1415 . . .

She couldn't very well pop number one again, so fifteen it was.

Carter grabbed the next dart, weighed it in her hand, took aim, and threw.

Number fifteen burst, and the fourth and final ticket fluttered down to her teammates. The light bulbs around the FUN HOUSE sign flashed and carnival music blared from hidden speakers.

She'd done it. The dexterity challenge was over. The fun house was open for business.

Let the games begin.

37

Beck

Beck held up both hands for high fives as Carter rushed down from the balcony. She smacked his hands then turned to high-five Adi, too, but to Beck's surprise, Adi swooped Carter up and spun her around.

"That was incredible!" Adi yelled.

"I bet that's the fastest anyone has ever gotten through the challenge," said Beck. "How did you—"

"Pi," she said breathlessly, tucking a curl behind her ear as Adi released her. "Easy as *pi*. Get it?"

"Like . . . the number?"

"Enough chitchat!" yelled Sierra. "The clock's ticking." But even she was grinning.

They joined her in front of the clown face.

"There are codes on the tickets," Adi said, flipping them over so they could see the text printed on each side.

VEKQQ
CMH
RKMX
RKWWKX

Adi was quiet for a moment. Then he said, "*K* is almost certainly a vowel, but we're going to need a cipher."

One by one, they each held a ticket beneath the scanner next to the clown's bulging red nose. Once the scanner beeped at the fourth ticket, the doors swung open on loud, squeaky hinges, and cackling laughter filtered out, followed by an eerie voice. *"Welcome to my fun house! Once you're in, you won't want to leave!"*

Beck ran his tongue across the front of his teeth, trying to neutralize the onslaught of textures and flavors this room was conjuring. Bubble gum from the popping balloons, dirty iron from the squeaking hinges, and a medicinal tang from the clown's uncanny laughter.

As soon as they stepped inside, the doors creaked shut behind them.

They were standing in a square room with a checkerboard floor. The walls were painted with disorienting black-and-white swirls covered over in neon graffiti. Three tall mirrors hung on one wall. On another wall stood a giant carnival wheel. The paint was dingy and cracked in places, and trash littered the floor—discarded cups, ticket stubs, even a paper food boat with a few soggy french fries still inside.

The room was so decrepit, so ominous, so authentically disturbing. Beck was smitten. Total Game Master goals.

As one, they moved forward to explore the room. And as one, they yelped and jumped back when the checkerboard floor lit up where they stepped—forest green, vivid orange, sky blue, fluorescent pink.

They glanced at each other, shrugged, and carried on. The floor tiles changed to different colors every time they stepped on them, then returned to black or white as soon as they stepped off.

"Adi, you've got the wheel," said Sierra. "Carter, inspect the mirrors. Beck . . . do you mind sifting through that pile of trash?"

"I don't mind at all," he said, sitting cross-legged on a lit-up purple tile to paw through the junk.

"They're fun-house mirrors," said Carter. "The kind that distort your reflection. This one has a keypad underneath. Uh . . . looks like we need a word, five letters. And this one's got a padlock, so we're looking for a key, too."

"Key, five-letter word," repeated Sierra. "Try the letters on the ticket. *V-E-K-Q-Q?*"

"No go. Maybe something fun-house related," said Carter. "Clown? Music?"

"Creepy as hell," Adi muttered, inspecting the wheel.

Beck smirked. "Not a fan of carnivals?"

"Not a fan of clowns. God, they freak me out." Adi shuddered. "There are three levels to this wheel. Each level is a mix of letters, blank spaces, and the occasional illustrated clown doing, I don't know. Creepy clown things. It's probably the cipher for those tickets if we can line them up right." He started playing with the wheels, frowning as he aligned and realigned them.

"There's something about this graffiti," said Sierra. "Like maybe there's a message hidden in it, but it's . . . an optical illusion?"

Beck reached for the boat of old, soggy fries. Gross. He was about to chuck it into a corner when his eye caught writing under the food. He dumped out the fries to find a code underneath.

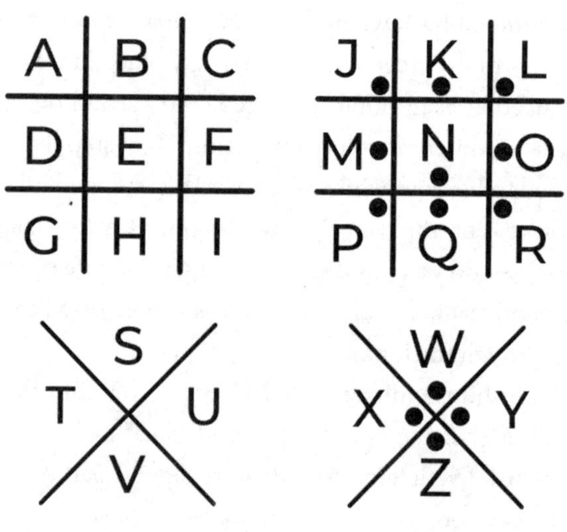

"Adi!" he said, hopping to his feet. "We've got the key to a pigpen cipher."

Adi took one look at the code and . . . scoffed. "Child's play. I've had pigpen cipher memorized since I was twelve."

Beck frowned. "Ooo-kay," he said, returning to his pile of garbage and leaving Adi to his clown wheel.

Suddenly, the room went dark, the bright carnival lights replaced with a haunting purple-black glow. The wheel started spinning. Air blasted from random holes in the ceiling. Mad, clownish laughter echoed off the walls, tasting like gloopy hand sanitizer, followed by that kooky voice again. *"You're not ready to leave yet, are you? We're just getting started!"*

"Did we do something to set that off?" asked Adi.

"The time," said Carter, gesturing at the red clock ticking away above the three mirrors. "It's been exactly ten minutes since we started the round. Maybe it happens in intervals as a distraction."

Not finding anything else of note among the junk, Beck moved beside Carter, eyeing his reflection in the center mirror. He chuckled. "Nice giraffe neck."

"Nice gargantuan chin," she countered.

"A gargantuan chin?" said Adi. "Like this guy?" He pointed at one of the clowns painted on the outer wheel, who did indeed have a long, droopy chin.

"Yeah, sort of," said Beck. "And that one over there looks like . . ."

The two of them gasped.

"That's the clue," said Adi, spinning the wheel so that the long-necked and big-chinned clowns lined up. "What's the third one?"

Beck and Carter crowded together in front of the next mirror. "Short legs and a tall, skinny torso," said Beck.

"Plus a big forehead," Carter added.

Adi found a corresponding clown image on the innermost wheel. Once the wheels were aligned with the three clowns stacked on top of each other, he fished the tickets out from his pocket and started comparing the letters to those on the wheels.

VEKQQ
CMH
RKMX
RKWWKX

"This is it!" said Adi. "The first word is 'floss.'"

Beck made a face. "Seriously?"

Sierra immediately crouched beside the mirror and put *FLOSS* into the word padlock. "Didn't open," she said.

"Next one . . . ARM," said Adi. "Then . . . CORN. And last one . . ." Seconds passed while he scanned the wheel. "*C-O-T* . . . COTTON!"

"Floss, arm, corn, and cotton?" said Sierra. "What—"

"'Candy'!" Carter and Beck shouted at the same time, making Adi jump.

"Oh . . . right," said Sierra. "Candy corn, arm candy . . . I get it." She spun the dials on the padlock, spelling out *CANDY*. The lock popped open. The whole mirror swung out toward her . . . and she was promptly buried beneath an avalanche of rainbow-colored stuffed animals.

"Whoa," said Beck. "That is childhood fantasies right there." As soon as Sierra had extricated herself, Beck held up his arms, hollering, "*Stuffie pile!*" and plunged into the mound of stuffed animals.

"Beck, knock it off," said Adi as the team started to dig through, searching for the next clue.

Beck pretended to do the backstroke. "Let me have this moment."

"Do we have to count them?" asked Carter. "Or sort them somehow?"

Beck grabbed a frog and held it up over his head. "Here's an idea. What if—"

But before he could finish, the lights went out again, plunging them into the same glowing purple. The wheels began to spin. That haunting laughter echoed off the walls.

Beck grimaced, working his tongue in an effort to dispel the thick, medicinal taste from his mouth.

"Adi!" cried Carter. "The graffiti!"

Beck scanned the paint. Not all the graffiti was responsive to the black light, so that the parts that did glow lit up like ancient runes. A pattern of squares and angles and dots.

"Where did that code go?" yelled Sierra.

Tossing aside the frog, Beck started searching for the paper boat with the code on it as the clown cackled. *"Are we having fun yet? I hope you never leave!"*

The voice faded, the lights brightened again, and the glow-in-the-dark paint disappeared.

Sierra cursed.

"Has it been ten minutes already?" said Carter, glancing at the clock. "No, it's only been five. I guess it happens every five minutes. Which means . . . we have to wait another five minutes to know what it said."

"'Watch your step,'" said Adi. "Whatever that means. Now, can we figure out these stuffed animals? God, this room is a literal nightmare."

Beck looked at him, baffled. "Watch your step?"

"That's what it said." Adi took in his teammates' surprised looks. "I told you I memorized pigpen cipher when I was a kid."

"Right," said Beck. "What I was going to say before Bozo started taunting us is that every stuffed animal is a different color. What if we have to put them on the corresponding tiles?" He grabbed the frog and set it on a floor tile by the door, which immediately lit up the same forest green. When Beck moved away, the tile stayed lit.

"Brilliant," whispered Sierra, and Beck preened. "Everyone, let's get these tiles lit up!"

The next few minutes were chaos as they grabbed purple elephants and orange whales and blue koalas, debating if this red chihuahua was more maroon red or brick red, and whether this yellow tile matched the mustard-yellow python or the goldish-yellow hippo.

They soon realized that they only had it right when the square stayed lit once they stepped off.

Beck had just picked up a lime-green chameleon when Carter shouted, "Last one!" and slammed a violet unicorn down on the final square. The second mirror popped open, revealing yet another creepy clown head, its mouth wide open in a fist-sized hole.

"But what about this one?" said Beck, holding up the lizard.

They looked at him, at the chameleon, then at the scattered stuffies.

"Maybe we need it for something later?" suggested Carter.

"Check it for additional clues," said Sierra.

He flipped over the toy and spotted a zipper down its stomach. Sure enough, when he opened it, he found two narrow cylinders inside. He plucked them out. "A mini flashlight," he said, "and a scroll." He unrolled the thick paper, revealing a long message in cursive writing, but written as a mirror image.

Are we feeling nervous yet, O Murderer?

That's right. I'm still here. I bet you regret jumping to conclusions, don't you? I know Louis didn't kill himself.

Because I'm the Game Master. The REAL Game Master. And soon, everyone will know the truth. About me. About you. About Alicia. This is your last chance to end it on your own terms. I dare you to confess before I tell the whole world what you really are.

The finale is coming . . . tick tick.

Beck's nose wrinkled. "That's a headache waiting to happen. But hold on, I can figure it out." He squinted. "'Are we feeling . . . nervous . . . ,' *ugh*, this is going to take forever."

"Hold it up to the mirror," said Adi, but when Beck held it up to the remaining mirror, the distortion from the reflection only made it worse. "Or we can come back to that later," he amended. "There might be normal mirrors in the next room."

"At least we have a black light now," said Carter, flicking on the flashlight and shining it over the graffiti. The message written in runes jumped out at them. "And what about this guy?" She turned to the clown face with the newly opened mouth.

The lights went out again. Beck groaned, holding back the urge to spit out the disgusting chemical flavor as the clown droned on. It really felt like they were doing well this round—if it weren't for these annoying interruptions, they'd probably be finished.

After the clown had made its vaguely threatening statement and its laughter had faded away, the lights returned to reveal Sierra standing in front of the clown head on the wall, eyeing it like she was facing her mortal enemy. "If this thing bites off my hand," she said, "I fully expect you all to chip in part of your prize money to get me a kick-ass prosthetic." Then she took a deep breath and plunged her hand into the clown's mouth.

Beck almost expected Sierra to start screaming, or some awful guillotine blade to come crashing down, or—

"I got something!" Sierra shouted, just as jets of air blew from the clown's eyes into her face and a burst of confetti came shooting out of the clown's nose, swirling around Sierra like a tornado. She screamed—like, an actual *scream*—and jumped back, tripping on a pink fox and falling onto her rear end.

"Are you okay?" Carter asked, crouching beside her.

Sierra looked about ready to murder someone as she held up a key. "Dandy," she growled. "Let's get out of here."

Carter snatched the key out of her hand and slotted it into the padlock under the final mirror. It swung open. Beck perked up, thinking this could be it—the escape! For the semifinals, that had to be a record time.

But . . . no. Beyond the mirror was a circular tunnel at waist height. The carnival music was louder coming through it.

"I'm going in!" said Beck, throwing himself into the tunnel. Sierra followed, but the moment they were both inside, the tunnel began to turn like a corkscrew, sending Sierra crashing.

"Hold on, Sierra!" Beck cried, shimmying through to the end and flopping out the other side. As Sierra tried to regain her balance and crawl forward, Beck reached back into the tunnel, grasped her forearms, and pulled her through with such force they both fell into the next room, Sierra sprawled on top of him.

He flashed her a winning smile. "I love this room."

Sierra rolled off him as Carter and Adi yelped and spat profanities while making their way through the tunnel and tumbling to the floor. The lights went out again, and that awful clown cackled. *"Not so fast! Let's make the fun last!"*

"Oh my god," muttered Adi when the lights came back on. "If I ever meet that guy, I am going to shove that squishy red nose straight up his—"

"Mirrors!" said Carter.

The tunnel had led them into a maze of mirrors, their reflections bouncing back at them and continuing on and on . . . infinite. On the wall, another clock had stalled at 25:06. Twenty-five minutes so far, for the semifinal. That was good, right?

"Beck, where's that note, the backward one?" asked Sierra.

Beck pulled out the note they'd found inside the chameleon and held it up to the nearest mirror, reversing the letters. He started to read out loud. "Are we feeling nervous yet, O . . ." He cut off, tearing his gaze away from the paper to scan the walls around them, landing on one of the small embedded cameras. He swallowed.

"What?" said Carter. "Is it another . . ." She lowered her voice. "Another clue?"

He nodded, and looked at Sierra, whose expression was shadowed. "We're almost out of this room. Let's finish this."

Beck's thoughts were spinning. Another clue. What had the Real Game Master written for them this time?

But then he glanced at the frozen clock, and he knew Sierra was right. They were so close.

He pocketed the letter.

"There's more pigpen," said Adi, shining the black light over the graffiti that was scribbled across the mirrors.

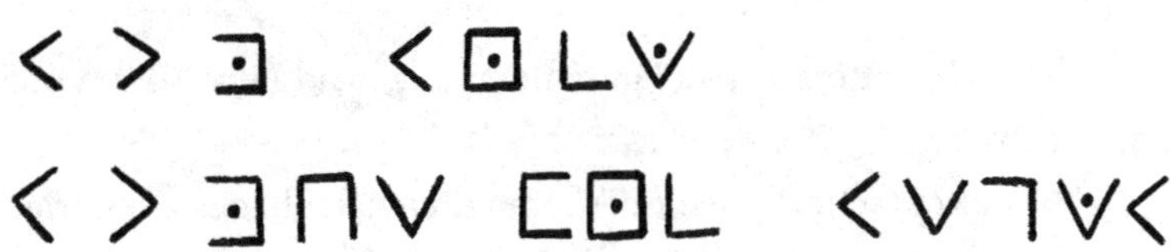

As he examined it, his expression grew increasingly bewildered.

"What?" said Carter. "What does it say?"

"I . . . I don't know," he said, sounding truly concerned. They all faced him.

"You don't *know*?" spat Sierra. "What was all that about having it memorized since you were—"

"It doesn't make any sense, okay?" said Adi.

He pointed the flashlight at the graffiti, revealing a series of runes that definitely made no sense to Beck.

Going symbol by symbol, Adi read out, "*U-T-M-U-N-C-W-U-T-M* . . . It doesn't spell anything. It's nonsense."

"No, that can't be right." Sierra grabbed the flashlight from him. "Maybe we're supposed to start reading over on this side. Or it's an anagram. Or . . ."

"Sierra," said Adi, "I've looked at it from every angle. Nothing works."

Sierra threw her hands in the air. "Why didn't we hold on to that damn food boat? Oh *right,* because Adi had it memorized. Adi is a freaking prodigy. If he says he can read it without a cipher—"

"Reverse it," Carter interrupted.

Adi glanced at her. "What?"

"We're in a hall of mirrors," she said. "What if it's written backward, like . . . like the other message?"

Sierra nodded. "Of course. Adi?" When he glared at her, she added, "I'm sorry for mocking you or whatever, just do it."

"On it, *boss.*"

"Tell me the letters as you figure them out," said Beck. "I've got a good memory."

Beck could practically see Adi's brain doing acrobatics as he tried to figure out what each letter would be in reverse.

"*W-A-N-T-O-U-T* . . ."

"Yes," Carter whispered. "This is it."

"*T-W-I* . . ."

Beck pressed his fingers to his temples, visualizing the letters as Adi read them out.

"*S-T-A-N-D-S* . . ."

Sierra played with her lip piercing.

"*H-O-U-T.*" Adi paused. "That's it. What did that say?"

"Want out? Twist and shout," the rest of them said in unison.

Adi balked. "Literally?"

With a shrug, Beck jumped into the center of the room and belted out a very off-key rendition of "Twist and Shout," a song his parents loved. He sang at the top of his lungs, simultaneously twisting his hips and waving his arms in the air.

The rest of his team . . . did not.

"Oh, come *on,*" he said, holding a hand out to Carter. She spared a self-conscious glance for the cameras, then squeezed her eyes shut and started awkwardly swinging her hips side to side.

"That's the spirit!" cried Beck. "Come on, Sierra!"

With an exaggerated eye roll, Sierra raised her arms into the air and started waving them around. "Something, something, twist and shout," she mumbled.

"You're a star!" shouted Beck. "Now take it away, Adi!"

Adi stood in the corner, watching them with a look of unadulterated horror.

"No," he said.

Until Carter shimmied closer to him and grabbed his hands, pulling him onto their imaginary dance floor. Adi made a face but didn't resist as Carter spun under his arm, and Beck squawked out the lyrics, and Sierra kept her expression completely blank while twisting her body . . .

"Oh god, anything to make it stop," Adi said. Then he took a deep breath and joined Beck for the big finale. "Come on and twist a little closer now, and let me know that you're mine!"

The lights turned off again, plunging them into darkness. The clown's voice came over the speakers, *"Now wasn't this* fun? *Come back and play with me again soon!"*

Then—a square of light as one of the mirrors creaked open, revealing a laughing Fitzy on the other side.

"Team Helsing, you have escaped! And what a truly memorable escape it was."

Interview Room: Alicia Angelos

SEASON FOUR

END OF ROUND THREE: AN A-MAZE-ING CHALLENGE

The camera focuses on Fitzy and Louis Augustus Russell standing outside the door to an escape room, smiling as a sweaty Alicia Angelos joins them, sporting knee and elbow pads. Her crop top is black. Her helmet is pink.

"Did you enjoy that?" Fitzy says as he holds the mic out for her.

She props her hands on her hips, still puffing as she responds. "I regret volunteering for the dexterity challenge."

"You were great," Louis says. "As Game Master, I'm very proud."

Alicia wipes her forehead with the back of her hand. "When that inflatable teddy bear popped up in the middle of the maze, I almost had a heart attack."

"But the trampolines were your true nemeses," Fitzy says.

Alicia groans, shaking her head. "Those trampolines."

"What," Fitzy says, "never played on a trampoline growing up?"

"No, Fitzy, I did not. Thanks." She accepts a bottle of water from someone off-screen and gulps it down.

"I think you did admirably," Louis says. "And between you and me, I have a feeling you're going to make it to the finale. Not that I know the other teams' times," he adds, raising his hands. "I just like your style."

"Well, thanks, Louis." She nudges him with her elbow. "But go on, you can tell me the other teams' times. It'll be our little secret."

Fitzy forces himself between them. "Oi. No conspiring. Some might call that *cheating*. Eh, Game Master?"

Louis's smile falls briefly before his easy confidence returns. "Of course not, Fitzy. Besides, the biggest secret is what I have in store for the finale. And believe me, our viewers won't want to miss it."

38

Sierra

It took all Sierra's willpower to keep up her sour facade rather than join her teammates in the excited chatter as they were led off the stage.

"That has to be one of the fastest times in semifinals history!" Carter said, her eyes bright with exhilaration. "I really think we have a chance this round. I—"

"Let's not get cocky," said Adi. "We have no idea how the other teams are going to do. Maybe it was an easy room."

Carter glared at him, but Sierra could tell her heart wasn't in it. "You're telling *us* not to get cocky? You hypocrite."

"Hey. Team Loud and Obnoxious."

They turned to see Vera standing beside a stack of wooden beams and building supplies. She held up her phone. "You've got twenty minutes before post-round interviews. Stand over by the creepy clown head so I can get some pics."

They posed for a few shots—some with arms around each other, some celebrating with their hands in the air, then some goofy ones.

"Good enough," said Vera. "Adi's up for his interview first. Ranielle wants him on film while he's still got some of that"—Vera swirled a hand in front of Adi's face—"sexy sweat on him."

Carter grimaced. "Ew."

"Don't look at me. I'm not the one issuing orders around here." With that, Vera stormed off, Adi slouching after her.

"Why does she hate us *so much*?" asked Carter.

"Who cares?" Sierra ushered Carter and Beck toward the greenroom. Team Dread was inside, with one notable absence. "Where's Jarius?" Sierra said under her breath.

Delphi, Neil, and Gabriela eyed Team Helsing's carnie costumes dubiously.

"Promising," Neil said with a smirk.

Delphi smacked her bubble gum.

Beck opened his mouth to respond, but Sierra muttered, "Note. Mirror. Now."

"Shouldn't we wait for Adi?" Carter said.

"No."

Beck said in his singsong voice, "We are a team."

"Jesus Christ," Sierra muttered, but let Beck keep the note.

"Whoever this person is, they're brave, planting these messages right under Ranielle's nose," Carter said. "If they're really certain she's the killer, anyway."

"And they're posting them online," Sierra added. "Mind Hack would already have this note, right?"

"Actually," said Beck, "I was thinking—"

"Where the hell have you been?" Gabriela demanded as Jarius swaggered into the room. "We're due in the costume room in, like, two minutes."

Sierra recognized the tone. Her team had used it on each other for the entirety of last season. There was anger under the words. Frustration. Even hatred.

Once again, the producers had found despicable people and put them together to snipe and bicker and invoke audience hostility.

The villains.

Sierra eyed Carter and Beck. While of course Team Helsing had also been subject to the mind games, they hadn't reacted with anywhere near as much ferocity.

But Sierra was this season's villain. So why had she been put with the likable ones? The . . . heroes?

Was Team Helsing being set up to win?

It made no sense.

Jarius shot Sierra, Beck, and Carter a smirk. "Getting a few things organized. Some . . . insurance, you might say."

"Why does that give me an *icy fingers on my spine* feeling?" Beck said.

Jarius cackled. "Spot-on instincts, little worm." He launched himself onto a couch and tucked his hands behind his head, refusing to answer any more of his team's questions.

When Beck and Carter looked at Sierra with wide eyes, she said, "Forget that. What were you saying, Beck?"

"I was wondering if maybe the Real Game Master is a set designer. You know, they have those trolleys full of stuff. One of them could easily slip things into the rooms while they're being reset."

"That's not a bad idea," Sierra said. She tried to think back to last season, if there were any set designers she recognized, but the faces were a blur.

Team Dread was called away for costumes, and after an agonizingly long time, Adi finally returned. "You're up for interviews, boss."

"One sec," Sierra said, gesturing for Beck. "Note, quickly!"

They headed to the giant mirror on the side wall, and Beck unscrolled the note. Sierra leaned forward, frowning at the reflection.

Are we feeling nervous yet, O Murderer?

That's right. I'm still here. I bet you regret jumping to conclusions, don't you? I know Louis didn't kill himself.

Because I'm the Game Master. The REAL Game Master. And soon, everyone will know the truth. About me. About you. About Alicia. This is your last chance to end it on your own terms. I dare you to confess before I tell the whole world what you really are.

The finale is coming . . . tick tick.

39

Adi

The elimination filming was so long that, despite the fact they were supposed to be in suspense, Adi kept tuning out. First, Fitzy had gone on and on about Louis's tragic death. Then they'd watched the in memoriam that had been cobbled together last-minute, showing boring highlights from Louis's life—everything from winning a national spelling bee to marrying Ranielle. Then a bunch of past contestants showed up to talk about their memories of the great Game Master. Last, Ranielle spent a few minutes in front of the cameras, dabbing at the corners of her eyes with a handkerchief while she lied through her teeth about how upset she was.

While Ranielle spoke, Adi's thoughts were on clues and lies, and an imagined vision of Alicia Angelos lying dead and wet in that coffin.

Suffocation. Gloves over the face. Hosed down to remove DNA. Would require immense strength . . .

Do not trust the Russells.

The Game Master on the hotel floor. A fake suicide. A fake confession.

I know Louis didn't kill himself.

Alicia had been seeing Louis. Louis had been feeding her cheats. Ranielle had found out.

Ranielle Russell had killed Alicia Angelos.

They hadn't posted it on the Domain yet. They had to make sure there was no possible way Ranielle could wriggle out of this. They might have their suspicions, but the Real Game Master's promised evidence for the finale would hopefully be enough to see her convicted.

By the time Fitzy started talking about the most recent round,

Adi's legs were aching and he just wanted to get on with it. This was a competition, and Adi wanted to know who had won the damn thing.

The screen played footage from the fun house.

Jarius ripping off his shirt for no apparent reason.

Nadia and Keegan from Mind Hack trying to climb through the spinning tunnel at the same time and ending up in a guffawing heap.

Adi figuring out the runes in the graffiti without having to use the cipher.

All four members of Team Dread doing the twist in the final room and shouting in unison, "Screw you, Pennywise!"

"This round," said Fitzy, "*two* of our teams had a disadvantage! First, Team Helsing used their snag on Team Dread."

The screen showed Jarius and Delphi in handcuffs, kicking stuffed animals across the floor to try to get them onto the right squares. Then it flashed to Neil victoriously pulling three keys out of the clown's maw—and the relief on everyone's faces when they realized two of them were for the handcuffs.

Adi's mouth twisted. It would've served them right to be stuck in handcuffs the whole time. But hopefully the snag had done its job and kept them from being in first place. *Again.*

"While Team Dread opted to use their remaining snag by swapping out Helsing's dexterity challenger!"

The screen flashed to their team talking to Fitzy before the round, Sierra proclaiming confidently about Beck, "He has mad skills."

It cut to Fitzy holding an envelope. "Carter Kelly, they've chosen you!"

The expression on her face for that split second was utter horror, but then the video clip showed her throwing the darts. Popping the four correct balloons. *3-1-4-15.* One. After. Another.

On the risers, Adi offered Carter a fist bump, and she grinned shyly as she returned it.

"Wow," said Fitzy, clapping his hands. "This escape room is going down in history. Teams, how do you feel you did?"

Impatience clawed at Adi's throat. Fitzy talked too much. They needed to get on with the scoring.

He knew that wasn't how reality TV worked. He knew the director and producers had to drag out every little drop of suspense. As stressful as the show was to watch when complete strangers were waiting to find out their fate, it was almost unbearable when it was his own team under the stage lights.

"Carter Kelly!" Fitzy crossed the stage with his microphone. "You dominated this season's dexterity challenge. Once you found the first ticket, it became clockwork. Popping all four balloons in a row, almost like you knew which balloons held the magic tickets. Tell me, was it luck, or did those balloons hold some secret the other teams didn't pick up on?"

"Um. I mean . . . it was . . . easy as pi?" said Carter. Her voice came out wobbly.

Fitzy's lips crooked to one side, amused. "Care to explain?"

"Like . . . the number?"

Fitzy waited a beat, then rolled his hand at her, urging her to go on.

"For real?" Adi said under his breath.

She giggled nervously. "It was your clue, remember? Or, sorry . . . the Game Master's clue. *It's all fun and games at the carnival.*"

Across the stage, Jarius groaned. "*Pi.* Obviously." He reached over and smacked Neil on the shoulder. "Why didn't you get that?"

But Fitzy looked confused, even as he tried to chuckle through it. "And that was . . . helpful?"

Carter stared at him. "Very. He didn't mean pie, the food. He meant pi, the number. You know . . . 3.1415926535897—"

Adi squeezed Carter's arm and she cut herself off.

"That's our Solve Specialist," said Beck, beaming.

Carter continued, "Once I figured out that was what the clue meant, I just had to pop the right balloons. And, thankfully"—her gaze flickered to Team Dread—"I happen to be quite good at darts."

"Well," said Fitzy, "there's no doubt that your quick thinking and skillful dart-throwing gave your team a great start. Are we ready to find out your final times?"

"*Yes,*" said Sierra loudly as some of the other contestants cheered.

"I'm ready, too," said Fitzy. "Team leaders. This way, please."

The scoreboard lit up with the three remaining team names.

Dread
Mind Hack
Helsing

Adi hardly breathed. All he saw was that clock, ticking and flashing.

And then—he heard it.

The cheers from Jarius and his team as their final time flashed.

Dread 36:16

And, what felt like hours later . . . Mind Hack cheering even louder.

Mind Hack 35:42

Adi forced himself to be stoic. *(Let us be in the finals. Let us be in the finals. Let us—)*

Helsing 27:17

Sierra hollered, punching the air. Beck and Carter screamed. In a blur, Carter whirled around and hugged Adi, almost toppling him from the riser.

"We did it!" Carter screamed in Adi's ear.

"*You* did it!" he countered.

She spun away to hug Beck, both of them shrieking that they were going to the finale.

Adi felt off-kilter, as if a support beam had fallen from under him. *First place.*

"Helsing and Mind Hack, congratulations!" yelled Fitzy. "You're going to the finale! Unfortunately, Team Dread, that means that your next escape will be right out of this stu—"

"Hold on, Fitzy," said Jarius, so loud that his voice cut through the speakers like a scythe. "Before we go on, I think there's something everyone needs to know."

Fitzy glanced at Ranielle offstage, who was frowning and speaking into her headset as a buzz of confusion passed around the studio.

Jarius turned toward Adi's team, a smirk on his boyish face.

"Helsing can't be going to the finale," he said, "because I have proof they cheated."

40

Carter

Carter stepped up next to Adi, enraged that Jarius would make such a blatantly false accusation.

"Cut the cameras!" yelled a voice—not the director this time, but Ranielle. The camera lights blinked off. "Jarius, what the hell are you doing?"

"Calling out an injustice," said Jarius, pulling his phone from his pocket. "Isn't it weird, executive producer, that there's been so much scandal associated with this show lately and you're always in the middle of it?"

Carter traded looks with Beck, who seemed as perplexed as she was. Sierra scowled suspiciously.

But Adi's jaw was so tight a muscle was spasming in his cheek. And he wasn't meeting anyone's eyes.

"I'm not in the mood for mind games right now," said Ranielle. "I got enough of that from my late husband. May he rest in peace." She said this with a flippant wave of her hand. "So whatever you've got to say, spit it out."

"I don't have anything to say." Jarius grinned. "You and Adi have already said it for me."

He opened an audio file on his phone. At first there was only silence, and Carter hoped this was some pathetic joke. But then she heard Ranielle's voice.

"Team Dread is planning to use their snag to make Carter do the dexterity challenge, which is popping balloons with darts. I can't help you with that. But the balloons you're looking out for are the first few digits for pi. Three, one, four, and—"

"Pi, sure, I get it."

Everyone turned to Carter, whose face warmed by twenty degrees. She shook her head. "I didn't . . . He didn't . . ."

What was happening?

That was Adi's voice on the recording. Taking answers from the producer.

Cheating.

Fitzy's jaw had dropped. Everyone on Team Mind Hack looked disgusted.

"*There are tickets in the balloons,*" continued Ranielle's voice over the recording. "*You're going to get a code on the tickets—*"

On it went. On and on and on and on, with every clue given in detail. Carter covered her mouth with both hands as Ranielle mentioned the answer to the pigpen cipher. And here she'd thought Adi was a genius.

After an agonizingly long time, Jarius paused the recording.

The air in the studio was too hot, too stifling.

Carter glanced at Sierra. As team leader, she had to do something. But . . . what could she do? What could any of them do? Sierra looked positively livid as she glowered at Adi.

Carter turned to face Adi, too. He could've stabbed her in the chest and she wouldn't have felt so betrayed.

"No," said Adi. His voice was rough. For a split second, he glanced at Carter and said it again, more forcefully this time. Almost . . . pleadingly. "No. I—"

"That was you," said Carter slowly. "Or are you saying it was someone who sounded exactly like you?"

"No. Yes, that was me, but I'm not—" Clenching his fists, he stomped off the risers, approaching Jarius and Ranielle. "Where the hell did you get that recording?"

"From your phone," Jarius said. "Found it while you were in the fun house, sent it to myself. Needed proof, didn't I?"

"This is bullshit. I didn't record anything, and I didn't cheat.

You've seen the footage." Adi raised his voice. "Have the editors check. I didn't use the cheats! I already knew pigpen cipher, and the rest of the team—"

"Ah, so you admit you were offered the cheats," said Jarius.

"I . . ." Adi's eyes flashed, like he wanted nothing more than to haul his fist back and give Jarius a black eye. "My team solved every puzzle without help from Ranielle or anyone else. And Carter?" He thrust an arm in her direction. "She figured out the pi clue on her own. She has the number memorized to a hundred places."

Jarius took a step closer to Adi, putting them toe-to-toe. "You walked right out of that meeting with our esteemed executive producer and told your team everything. And how could you just 'know' the pigpen cipher? It was a cheat. All of it."

"I—"

"Adi, enough." Ranielle's tone was glacial. "The nerve of you to record our private conversation and think it wouldn't come back to bite you in the ass—"

"I *didn't,*" said Adi. "I don't know where the hell that recording came from, but I didn't do any of this."

"Like Kick It Carter pointed out," said Jarius, "that was either you or someone who happens to sound exactly like you."

Adi opened his mouth but slammed it shut again.

Jarius smirked. "That's what I thought. So here we are. The semifinal airs in less than a week, and if this gets out"—he wagged his phone in Ranielle's face—"you're gonna have a lot of disappointed fans demanding a lot of answers."

Ranielle snatched the phone away from him, but Jarius shrugged. "I've got that sound clip saved in a number of places, waiting to be shared with the world." He glanced around the studio. At the other contestants, Fitzy, the crew. Vera leaned against one of the large cameras, practically salivating at the juiciness.

A hot ember of shame burned in Carter's gut. If word about this got out, if people believed she'd cheated, her reputation as a Solve Specialist would be over. The platform she'd built for the past three years would turn on her. She would never be able to show her face on the Domain again—not even her avatar.

And somehow that didn't hurt half as much as the betrayal. Adi hadn't trusted that his team could win. He'd never believed in them.

"Here's what I suggest," said Jarius. "Because ultimately, we all want the same thing. Well . . . most of us do, anyway." He glanced dismissively at Carter and her team before turning his focus back to Ranielle. "A little clever editing, a few clicks of a button, and those times rewrite themselves." He gestured at the scoreboard. "We re-film this elimination, and aww, too bad, so sad, Helsing goes home." He pouted. "But great news! *The Escape Game* gets to continue without anyone knowing how the executive producer tried to cheat on her own show, and in the end . . . may the best team win." He gestured between himself and Mind Hack, who had been watching in deeply uncomfortable silence.

"Yeah, right," said Adi, scoffing. "You're going to throw me under the bus and think I'll keep quiet?"

"Yeah," said Jarius. "I think you will. Unless you want your reputation—and the reputation of your precious teammates—slashed to pieces."

Adi's gaze flickered to Carter and his mouth tightened into a thin line.

Ranielle's nostrils flared.

She had to know her time was limited. She had to know that a secret like this would never stay secret. That even if *The Escape Game* could continue on—past murder, past proof of unfair play—the show was coming to an end.

"All right," she said, barely a whisper in the otherwise silent studio.

"We're going to film the last few minutes again. But . . ." She glanced at the camera. "The times will be different, and Helsing will be in last place."

"No," said Adi, his voice raspy. "Let my team compete in the finale. Disqualify me. They can be a trio. They can—"

"This conversation is over," said Ranielle, spinning on him. "You and your team had better look convincingly disappointed when your revised time is posted, or so help me, I'll make all your lives hell."

Then she marched away.

Carter looked past Ranielle to see Fitzy gaping at her from the other side of the stage. He opened his mouth, and for a second Carter thought he would say something to Ranielle, something to come to Carter's defense. But he hesitated and shut his mouth again. His gaze tightened, apologetic.

Carter nodded tersely. She didn't blame him. This wasn't his battle to fight.

This was on Adi. He had betrayed them.

And now it was over.

41

Beck

"So . . . how are you feeling?"

Beck stared into the barrel of the camera, trying to process Fitzy's question. Trying to process *anything*.

He knew he should be angry. Most people would be angry.

But he felt numb more than anything else, unable to comprehend what had happened. He was supposed to lie. Tell the viewers that his team had come in last place. C'est la vie and whatever.

He didn't think he could do it.

The studio lights were exceptionally bright here, in front of the faux brick wall where contestants filmed their exit interviews. No casual chats about gameplay or rewatching clips. Just raw emotion.

Beyond the stage, Vera snapped a photo of him. She looked cranky, as usual. At least Fitzy, beyond the lens of the camera, had a slightly furrowed brow, as if this fiasco didn't sit right with him.

Beck couldn't get his head around the idea that Adi would cheat. They were supposed to be teammates. They were supposed to trust each other.

It was so aggravating. They should have been celebrating right now. Instead, Beck was going home. No money, and no hope of getting to Sweetbrier any time soon.

"For what it's worth," said Fitzy gently, "I'm really sorry, mate. It's . . ." He glanced at the camera, a flicker of anger passing over his face. "It's a rough go."

Realizing that Fitzy wasn't reading off the script for once shook something loose inside of Beck. He knew, distantly, that anything he said now would be cut apart and pieced back together in some mutation of his true meaning. The only story here was Ranielle's story, and she didn't care about Beck. She never had.

But he wasn't going to be her trained monkey. Not anymore. He would tell the truth.

This entire show was based on lies. There were no geniuses, no teenage savants, no prodigies. There were no villains and certainly no heroes. There were a bunch of actors, saying what they were told to say, and con artist producers pulling every string.

This show was a sham, and Beck was ashamed to have been a part of it.

But no sooner had he opened his mouth than a ruckus broke out beyond the set. People were shouting. Lots of people. Crew members turned to the door. The noise was coming from the greenroom.

Beck ripped off his mic and sprinted toward the hollers and cheers. He barged into the greenroom to find Adi and Jarius wrestling on the floor. Adi was trying to get Jarius's phone.

"Break it up!" one of the film crew yelled.

Sierra waded into the fray and grabbed Adi by his jacket collar. "Pull yourself together!"

"Give me that phone!" Adi practically screamed it. "Give me your goddamn phone, Jarius!"

Jarius got a punch in, clocking Adi in the jaw. Sierra yanked Adi backward. "Stop! Stop it, both of you!"

Adi fought to free himself from her grip. "I never recorded that conversation. He couldn't have gotten it from my phone because *I didn't record it.*"

"It doesn't matter!"

Sierra's shriek rang across the room, silencing Adi. He stilled mid-struggle.

"It doesn't matter," Sierra said again. "You cheated. You ruined our chance to run the finale!"

When her voice cracked, so did Beck's heart. What if they could never prove Ranielle killed Alicia?

Adi met Sierra's gaze. The anger left him in a rush, and he sagged in her grip. She released him, looking disgusted.

Jarius dusted himself off and climbed to his feet. "Whew," he said, grinning at his team. "That was bracing."

Adi stared at the floor. The fight had drained out of him. His jaw was beginning to swell where Jarius's punch had landed.

"*Oh!* Holy shit!" shouted Keegan from Team Mind Hack, staring at his phone, which he'd been using to film the fight a few seconds ago. "You have to see this." He turned the phone screen to his teammates. "The police just released Louis's suicide note. He confessed to killing Alicia Angelos! And Ranielle Russell's being charged for obstructing justice!"

42

Sierra

No one spoke as they were driven out of the complex and to the loser hotel, where eliminated teams stayed until the episode dropped each Sunday.

Sierra's anger had yet to subside. Every time she thought about what Adi had done, it roared up again. He hadn't even tried to apologize. He'd packed his bags without a word while Carter and Beck had hunted through the villa for any stray phone chargers or puzzle books.

When the car pulled up, Sierra grabbed her bags and stormed to the hotel reception to check in.

They were leaving, and she didn't have proof Ranielle killed Alicia. The cops wouldn't keep looking—according to them, they'd closed a murder case. The chief of police had given a press conference that afternoon after releasing Louis's suicide note and confession. To listen to her answering the media's questions, you'd think she'd closed the crime of the century. Alicia Angelos was no longer an unsolved mystery. Why would they want to poke holes?

Sierra wanted to poke holes. Sierra wanted *justice*.

She was given two rooms next to each other.

"You head up," she said, passing around the key cards. "I might stay down here a bit longer." The thought of having to spend a single second more with Adi, especially in an elevator, was making her stomach churn.

Beck and Carter hesitated.

Adi sighed. "It's fine. I'll go up by myself."

Sierra waited until the elevator doors had closed before she said, "What an asshole."

"I don't understand why he did it," Carter said.

"Or why Ranielle offered him cheats in the first place," Beck said.

Sierra shrugged. "People like to look at him. She wanted to keep him on the screen for as long as possible. For *viewership*." She practically spat the word.

"Adi doesn't strike me as the type to take cheats," Carter said. "He likes to show off what he can do."

"Maybe he didn't trust us to pull our weight," Sierra said. "He only cares about himself."

She rolled her battered suitcase to the elevators. The others followed reluctantly.

"Do you think . . . maybe . . . we should talk to him?" Carter said as the doors opened.

"Screw that."

"I'll talk to him," Beck said. When Sierra glared at him, he added, "You're not my boss anymore. I can talk to him if I want."

"I'll talk to him, too," Carter said.

Sierra tightened her grip on her suitcase handle. "Fine, I'll come. At least I'll get to yell at him some more."

When they reached Adi's room, Beck knocked. It took some time for Adi to open the door. When he saw them together, he said, "We'll talk, but I wanted to wait until you'd cooled down first."

"Cooled down?" Sierra pushed past him into the room. "*Cooled down?* There is no cooling down!"

Beck and Carter followed in her wake. Beck closed the door.

"Do you know what you've done?" Sierra demanded. "We have no access to the studio anymore. No access to the complex, no access to Ranielle. We're never going to find proof she killed my sister."

"Look, maybe there is proof. I need to find out where Jarius got that recording—"

"What's the matter with you? Who cares where he got the recording? It's over. You've ruined everything. The only reason you got onto the show in the first place was because your mom bribed the producers, and then you went and accepted cheats, because the only person you care about is yourself!"

"Are you kidding me?"

"Oh right, my mistake. You also care about impressing your greedy-ass father. But news flash. He doesn't want you!"

Adi's face reddened. "You don't get to psychoanalyze me when everything has been about you from day one."

"Wow, good call. I guess I should just *get over* being accused of my sister's murder."

"Of course not! But that's all you are, Sierra! The sister slayer, the bringer of justice, the villain—you let these roles define you. If you didn't need to solve Alicia's murder, you would have nothing."

His words landed with staggering accuracy. This was what happened when people got too close. They saw the raw, vulnerable truth, then they took their shot. She should've learned that lesson by now.

Before the barb could fester, she twisted it into anger.

"Screw you," she spat, wrenching her suitcase around and pushing it toward the door.

"Wait," said Carter. She had her phone out and was staring at it with wide eyes. "The Real Game Master has posted on the Domain again!"

"What now?" Sierra snatched the phone out of Carter's grip to read the post herself.

> **@TheRealGameMaster**
>
> Don't disappoint me, Clue Masters! The police are WRONG.
>
> LAR's "confession" is a FAKE.
>
> Louis Augustus Russell DID NOT KILL ALICIA.
>
> I know the truth, and I can still reveal all in the finale—but you haven't held up your end of the bargain.
>
> Read the clues again. Don't take the easy way out like those

> incompetent detectives.
> SPOT THE LIE.
> Or this murderer will never be brought to justice.

Sierra grunted. "Nothing we didn't already know."

Carter grabbed her phone back and started scrolling through the comments. "Yikes. Some of the replies are harsh. Not everyone's buying the Real Game Master's story anymore."

"People have turned on Louis Augustus Russell," Beck said, settling his chin on Carter's shoulder as they read together. Adi stayed where he was on the other side of the room.

"And so they should," Sierra said. "Even if he didn't kill my sister, he was a predator."

Carter shook her head. "But if they're focused on him, they're not thinking about who the real killer is." She began to type. "Why don't we put Ranielle's name under the Real Game Master's post now?"

"You really want your name attached to that without proof?" Sierra said.

Carter's fingers paused.

"Thought so." Sierra rolled her suitcase past Carter and Beck, through the door. "There's no point. It's over."

Sierra scribbled out another failed sketch and flipped the page to start again. The view of the sunset staining the horizon was supposed to be inspiring.

It wasn't.

She didn't know why she'd come here. She hated the beach. Sand got into her clothes, and she inevitably left with a sunburn. The beach had been Alicia's thing. She'd talked about learning to surf or scuba dive. She'd dreamed of buying a boat and sleeping out in the middle of the ocean. Getting up with the dawn to swim with dolphins.

Things she'd never do. Dreams that had been stolen from her.

The pencil snapped in her hand. She dug another one from the box in her satchel, swiping hair from her face.

She'd been struggling to draw since Alicia's death. Leaving her pen tablet at home was supposed to make her miss it. She'd been hoping to rekindle her creativity while she was here, but buying a new sketchbook and pencil box had proved futile. Her passion was gone. She'd known, ever since the fortune teller's room, when she'd missed the obvious connection that red and blue made purple.

Sierra's time was done. Her creativity had shriveled with her soul.

That's not broken. That's . . . that's incredible.

Her pencil paused on the page as Beck's words drifted through her mind. It had been a total perception shift when he'd said that in the freezer. To see herself as something besides permanently damaged. To dare to believe she could be good, after everything the world had told her.

We'll be your people.

They had been.

And then they'd betrayed her. *Adi* had betrayed her. Betrayed all of them.

Served her right. Sierra had almost allowed herself to be taken in. She'd begun to believe there were decent humans out there, and look where that had gotten her.

There were only monsters in the world. No Helsings.

She got up from the bench, slung her satchel over her shoulder, and dumped her sketchbook in the trash.

Twilight had fallen by the time she reached the lobby. She spotted Carter and Beck sharing french fries at the hotel restaurant. They had their heads together, laughing at something on Carter's phone.

Sierra slowed, waiting for a spark of anger that they could be enjoying themselves at a time like this.

Instead, some of the ice thawed from around her heart. She took a step toward them. Toward Beck, whose smile was still contagious. Toward Carter, who could be so socially awkward yet so eager to let people in.

Her friends.

The thought drummed against her chest like a heartbeat.

But then her gaze found Adi at the bar, holding a book in one hand and eating spring rolls with the other. Sierra recoiled.

People couldn't be trusted.

She hurried to the elevator, leaving the food and laughter behind.

"I am alone," she told herself as she opened her hotel room door.

"I am alone," she chanted as she ran a bath.

"I am alone," she whispered as she scrubbed and scrubbed at her armor until the towel was coated in black and she couldn't tell the bath water from her tears.

Alone alone alone—

There was a knock at the bathroom door. Carter's hesitant voice came through.

"Sierra?"

Sierra shuddered through a sob. "Leave me—"

The door opened. Carter walked in, hands covering her eyes. "We can hear you crying."

Beck walked in behind her, also with a hand over his eyes. His other hand was holding a giant bag of Skittles. "We brought you snacks."

It took Sierra some time to grapple with her voice through her pain. "Go away."

"You're not alone, Sierra," Carter said. "Oof, Beck, you bumped me!"

"Sorry." Beck waved the bag uncertainly. "Where are you, Sierra? I don't want to get the candy wet."

"Jesus Christ," Sierra said. "You can uncover your eyes. I have bubbles."

Both of them lowered their hands. They simultaneously sighed in relief when they realized that yes, the water was appropriately frothed.

"Bubbles are good," Beck said to Carter in a stage whisper. "No one seriously depressed would have bubbles."

Carter sat down next to the bath. "You're not alone, Sierra," she said again.

Maybe she'd been chanting those words louder than she'd thought.

"Carter and I were thinking we should talk to Adi again," Beck said. "If he really does know something—"

"Screw that asshole."

"We still have a few days before we're sent home. And we're completely free. No schedules, no RAs, no rooms to run. Without any distractions, we can put all our focus on proving Ranielle killed Alicia." He pointed at his temple. "Laser."

Carter patted Sierra's arm. "It's not over yet."

"How will we get evidence if we can't get into the studio?"

"We'll find a way," said Beck. "We're still Team Helsing. And hopefully Adi will have something useful to tell us. In the morning," he added, when Sierra opened her mouth to argue. He offered her the bag of Skittles. She eyed it with distrust.

"It's not poisoned," Carter assured her.

Sierra huffed and held out her palm. The rainbow candies stuck to her damp skin, but the sugary crunch was pretty delicious.

Beck offered her another handful and she took the whole bag.

Carter dug out her phone. "We have to show you something."

"What?" Sierra perked up. "Has the Real Game Master posted again?" She hadn't checked the Domain all afternoon.

"Better. Look."

Sierra leaned in and frowned. "It's a cat."

"And a ferret! Look at them! Look— Watch this bit—"

"What does this have to do with anything?"

"It has to do with everything," said Beck, putting the toilet lid down so he could perch on it. "Strap in, Sierra. We've got a million of them, and they will change your life."

43
Adi

Adi sat on his hotel bed the next morning. He'd packed his bag as soon as Beck had gone to meet with Carter and Sierra more than an hour ago. Adi had not been invited to join them.

His phone was open to the bus timetable—only twenty-five minutes and he'd be out of here. He'd make a quick stop at home, pack a bag. Then—

Then an interstate coach out of LA, a couple of hitchhiking expeditions, and he'd be making a real-life escape. There was no way he was going back to his mom's place, and his dad wouldn't help him now. Adi had failed. In every way imaginable.

Someone knocked on the door. He considered ignoring it, but the knock came again, more insistent.

Resigned, he opened up.

Sierra wasn't slathered in her usual makeup, and she wasn't in her boots, which meant she was four inches shorter.

"Hey." She fidgeted with her lip ring. "Can we talk?"

"Are you here to murder me?"

She held out her empty hands. "Weapon-free."

Adi glanced over his shoulder at the bus timetable open on his phone. "I'm sort of busy . . ."

"I'll be quick."

Well. If he was going to disappear, he should probably make amends before he went.

He let Sierra in and snatched his phone from the bed.

Her attention flickered to his packed bag, then back to him. "Why did you take the cheats? We could've gotten through on our own."

"We did. I didn't use the cheats, no matter what Jarius and the others say."

"So why bother?"

Sierra waited, looking vulnerable. There was an openness to her expression. Without the sharp lines on her eyelids and the sneering black lipstick, Adi felt like he could *see* her.

"Ranielle offered me a job as host of the show next season," he said.

She drew back. "What?"

"She brought it up after the first elimination round."

"What about Fitzy? Is she firing him?"

"Hitflix wants him gone. She gave me some spiel about going in a new direction, but I was wondering . . . Maybe she's canning him because he knows something he shouldn't?" He frowned. "You don't think *he* could be the Real Game Master, do you?"

They stared at each other a beat before Sierra's shoulders started shaking. Her fingers touched her lips, as if to belatedly try to stop her growing smile. Then came a sound Adi realized he'd never heard from her before.

She was giggling.

"Fitzy?" she said. "Planting clues? Anagrams?"

"Okay, I see your point."

The giggles were snowballing. "You think he put together that ribbon clue? Using a columnar transposition cipher?"

"Oh god, no."

There were tears in her eyes now. "He didn't even know what pi was!"

A laugh burst from Adi, too. "Fine, fine. I don't know why I said it. God, I hate that guy."

Sierra's good humor faded. She gave Adi a look that made him feel strangely transparent.

"Despite your accusations yesterday," she said, "I don't have nothing."

"Look, I'm really sorry about that—"

"I have Carter. And Beck. And maybe you. That's why I'm here. I wanted to set things straight. Because you were right—I had to cool down. I wasn't ready to listen to you yesterday. I am now. Tell me what you wanted to say about the recording."

"All right," he said. "Ranielle offered me the cheats because she didn't want a loser hosting her show. I told her no at first, but she offered again the morning of the fun-house room, and I had to distract her because she almost caught me stealing the Sweetbrier Resort files for Beck. That was the audio Jarius had. Only, I don't know how he got it. Her office must be bugged."

"Is Jarius even capable of that?"

"He wasn't behind it. I know because Ranielle and I were talking about me being host during that meeting and Jarius didn't say a thing about it. Don't you think that's information he would've loved taunting us with?"

Sierra lifted an eyebrow. "You're saying he didn't know?"

"Exactly. And the only reason he wouldn't have known is because someone else supplied him with an edited version of the recording. Someone has been listening to her. And I was thinking . . . maybe they've inadvertently recorded evidence that could help get her convicted for Alicia's murder, or Louis's."

Sierra leaned against the wall, considering. "The Real Game Master," she whispered. "They know Ranielle killed Alicia, and they're trying to get that missing information they're so desperate for."

"Maybe they're planning to reveal audio proof during the finale."

"This is huge!" Sierra began her signature pace. "We have to get Jarius to tell us who gave him the recording."

"The person behind this is smart. They probably sent it to him anonymously. I think he's a pawn in a larger game."

Sierra stopped pacing. "You're probably right. Argh, I'd give anything to see that final room!"

"I know, Sierra. I'm sorry."

She turned to him. Her expression had him cringing. He owed her an explanation.

"When Ranielle offered that host gig, it felt like my chance to get away. Life at home, it's hell. Maybe not *my sister was murdered* hell, but my mom is . . ." Adi was usually good with words, but he was finding it difficult to articulate what it was like to have a parent who cared so much more about herself than she ever had for her kid.

Sierra's gaze flicked to his duffel bag again. "That's why you're leaving?"

He shifted his weight, unable to look at her.

"Running away won't solve your problems," she said. "Trust me."

Adi had emotionally prepared for his escape. He'd been so sure there were no anchors locking him in place.

But the mystery hadn't been solved. Ranielle was going to get away with murder. If Adi could do one thing before he left, it would be to help Carter, and Beck, and Sierra.

And Alicia.

"We haven't gone home yet," Sierra said. "Last night, Beck reminded me that we're still Team Helsing, and there's still work to be done."

"Like slay the vampire?"

A slow smile crept across Sierra's face. "Precisely."

44

Carter

Carter and Beck had squeezed together on one of the two double beds. Carter was trying to keep her phone screen turned away from him so he wouldn't see the team T-shirts she'd designed. HELSINGS SLAY! THE ESCAPE GAME SEASON FIVE was printed above a glowing chemistry set. Carter had placed the order the day after the funhouse round.

Now she couldn't for the life of her figure out how to cancel the order.

Custom order. Nonrefundable.

Beside her, Beck studied Alicia's cryptic letter about the affair for the thousandth time. They hadn't given it to the detective who questioned them at the villa, knowing he would have used it as further confirmation that Louis was the killer. Now it was their only clue left.

Old episodes of *The Escape Game* played on the TV. Carter should have turned it off. It was torture watching previous contestants puzzling through each round, knowing her time on the show was over.

Sure, there had always been a possibility of elimination, but never had Carter thought it could happen like this. To have victory ripped from their hands when they were so close, when they'd done so well, all because Adi hadn't believed in them.

Beck smoothed the letter across the lampshade on the nightstand. They'd already tried that at the villas. No hidden message had appeared then, and none appeared now. He sighed. Flipped the paper over. Upside down. Back and forth.

"Give it up," said Carter, opening her phone. She had three missed calls from her parents, but she couldn't bring herself to return them, knowing she would burst into tears the moment she heard their voices. Instead, she mindlessly scrolled through her Domain videos. "The key to that would be in Elijah's villa, hidden in a light fixture or something." She stared at her avatar. The bright red hair. The round glasses. A crop top paired with a trendy skirt. In this shot, Carter had the avatar winking and giving a thumbs-up. It was supposed to be encouraging, but now it felt like the character was mocking her. "We're never going to find it now."

Beck's brow was set with determination. He was beginning to act as obsessive as Sierra. "Or maybe it has something to do with episode two's sheet music."

They'd watched that episode a dozen times since finding the note, but they couldn't find anything in it that was relevant to Alicia's letter.

Carter was relieved when she heard footsteps and the telltale click of a key card—anything to keep them from losing their minds.

The door flew open, striking the wall. Sierra burst in, breathless and frazzled.

And behind her, Adi.

Carter tensed. She and Beck might've been the ones to convince Sierra to talk to Adi, but that didn't mean Carter wasn't still mad at him.

"Oh good, you're both here," said Sierra, dropping onto the other queen bed. "We have news."

Carter crossed her arms. "Is it that Adi didn't cheat after all and we're back on the show?"

"Um . . . no."

Carter huffed.

Sierra glanced at Adi, who was standing near the door as though he wanted to leave his escape route open.

"You owe them an apology," Sierra said.

Adi inhaled deeply. "I'm sorry. I really am. I screwed this up for us, and I hate it."

Carter narrowed her eyes. He *sounded* genuine.

"Good enough," said Sierra. "Now listen to this."

She explained how the person who had given Jarius the recording was probably the Real Game Master. The whole time she talked, Adi remained silent, leaning against the wall while his attention darted back and forth from the TV. Like watching old episodes of *The Escape Game* was somehow more interesting than tracking down evidence of Ranielle's crimes.

A silence fell over the group while Carter and Beck digested Sierra's information, until Adi straightened and said, "What season is this?"

Carter glanced at him. "What?"

Striding across the room, Adi grabbed the remote control and turned up the volume. "What season is this from?"

"Um." Carter eyed the contestants on the show, who were scrambling to wrap a strip of mummy bandage around a tall staff covered with painted hieroglyphs. "Season two."

"What episode?"

"Huh?"

"What *episode*?"

She let out a frustrated noise and threw her hands into the air. "I don't know! Second, I think? What does it matter?"

"This is it. What we've been missing." He whipped toward her. "Where's Alicia's letter?"

"Here." Beck picked it up from the side table and handed it to him.

"Does anyone have scissors?"

"Scissors?" Sierra barked. "You can't destroy my sister's letter!"

"We have to." Adi was grinning now. "It's a scytale cipher."

Carter gasped. "A scytale cipher. Oh my gosh. You could be right. Why didn't we think of that?"

"Er. Yeah. Scytale cipher. So obvious," said Beck. Then he looked at Sierra, who shrugged.

"It's when you wrap strips of paper around a cylinder to reveal the message," explained Adi.

A light entered Beck's eyes. "Oh, *that*. Yeah, okay, that could work."

"What if you're wrong?" said Sierra.

"I'm not wrong. But if I am, well . . . take a photo of it first."

After a pause, Carter said, "I think I have nail scissors in my bag . . . ?" She glanced at Sierra, unsure she should be volunteering this information.

A muscle twitched in Sierra's jaw, and she gave a short nod. Carter recognized it for what it was. A vote of confidence. In Adi. In Team Helsing.

Carter climbed off the bed to search through her bag. After she produced the scissors and Sierra snapped a photo, Adi made quick work of Alicia's letter—cutting it into pieces so that each line of text became an individual strip.

Only once he'd completely destroyed the best lead they had did he hesitate. "Crap."

Beck raised an eyebrow. "That's not what we want to hear."

"We need a rod or a cylinder," said Adi.

"I have ChapStick?" said Carter.

He shook his head. "It will only work if we have one that's the exact dimensions of whatever Alicia used to create the cipher. What would she have . . ." With a groan, he slumped against the wall. "The light from the number-four villa. She must have used a lamp base or something."

"Okay," said Sierra. "We need to get back into the villas and figure out which light she was talking about. Do we know anyone on the inside who would be willing to help? Can we trust Lisa?"

"No need," said Beck, crossing his ankles and leaning back into the pillows. "She was probably referring to the flashlight. The one that came with the welcome kit." He reached into the book bag he'd brought in from his own room and produced the flashlight, twirling it between his fingers.

"Nice work, Beck!" Sierra squeezed onto the bed, forcing Beck to be squashed between her and Carter. She took the flashlight and opened her palm to Adi. "Give me those strips."

"This was my idea," he said. "Shouldn't I be the one to do it?"

Sierra shot him a look.

Adi made a face, then gathered up the strips of paper from the letter and handed them to Sierra. She took the first one and, holding one end at the top of the flashlight, wrapped it around so that it spiraled down the cylinder.

She rotated it, scanning the new columns that had been formed from the letters, but Beck spotted it first. He pointed. "Here!"

"*W-I-L-L*," Sierra read. "*G-O-T-O . . .*"

"Go to where?" Beck said eagerly.

Sierra grabbed the next strip of paper and repeated the process, revealing the next words. "*M-E-D-I-A . . .*"

"About the affair?" said Carter. "She was going to go public?"

Sierra already had the third strip of paper wrapped around the flashlight. It only took a minute to go through the entire letter, spelling out Alicia's final message.

Willgoto
*Media_*
about
affair
*black_*
mailing
Rani.
offer4
silence
Iloveyou

"I love you," Sierra whispered as they stared at the final line. The last thing her sister would ever say to her.

Carter reached across Beck to lay a hand on Sierra's leg. "Want to take a minute?"

Sierra swallowed. "No. I want to end this."

"It was blackmail all along," said Adi. "She was blackmailing Ranielle."

Sierra's hands were shaking. "This has to be Ranielle's motive."

Adi dragged a frustrated hand through his hair. "We already had a motive. Alicia was sleeping with her husband."

"Which is bad enough, but this? If Alicia went public about her relationship with Louis, it would destroy the show. Hitflix would drop them instantly. How much money does Ranielle stand to lose if that deal falls apart?"

"That's a good point. But it's still not *proof*."

"Alicia was being reckless," said Sierra, gazing at the translated message. "She knew she was in danger. Whatever Ranielle offered her, Alicia was risking a lot for it."

Suddenly, Beck gasped. "I know what we need to do!" He launched himself from the bed, scattering the strips of paper in his hurry to get up. "We're going to need paper, pencils, and a lot of markers." His face split into a giddy smile. "We're going to make *a murder board*."

45

Beck

Though his teammates hadn't been quite as enthusiastic as he was about making a detective-style murder board, they still chipped in to assemble the information. Carter and Adi headed to the hotel's business center to print the most relevant photos and the Real Game Master's posts, while Sierra made separate cards for every suspect. Beck did his best to compile a workable timeline. He desperately wanted to run to the craft store, as they were missing some key components, like a corkboard, thumbtacks, and colored string. But sometimes one had to make do.

By the time they finished laying everything out on top of the bedspread, it *almost* fulfilled one of Beck's secret dreams. He'd made a real-life murder board. *Cool.*

They stood back to absorb the information.

There was Alicia's letter, in which she confessed her affair with Louis.

Do not trust the Russells.

Multiple (oft dubious) alibis for Alicia's time of death.

Other finalists in bed asleep
Sierra on the streets alone
Ranielle and Louis at home together (lied for each other?)
Fitzy livestreaming from home
Vera posting on social media—at home (??)

The photo Adi had taken of Louis's suicide note.

I killed Alicia. Can't live with the guilt anymore. Please apologise to my fans and everyone I've hurt. Tell Rani I love her.

Details of the two deaths, written out in separate lists.

Alicia: suffocated by hand; death location unknown; time of death between 1–2 a.m.; transported to soundstage via cart; body found wet; missing phone and comforter; no security footage (rolling blackout); strange car at villas close to dawn?

LAR: cyanide poisoning; death location: hotel; time of death around 8 p.m.; two wineglasses (one empty—for Carter?); blond woman on security footage? (Likely Ranielle)

Across the pillows, they'd included details of the various ways in which someone had been trying to sabotage them, or the show. The freezer. Carter's drugged drink at the party. The wrecked painting. The cow heart. And—a sore spot—the recording of Adi taking the cheats.

One full corner of the bed was dedicated to the clues that had been planted in the rooms. The anagram of Alicia's name. *Tenth-Third-F-U (10/3=birthday)*. The alien room video—they'd done their best to remember as many details as they could. The deciphered ribbon code and mirror letter.

"The police think they have their guy," said Adi, pointing at the suicide note. "Ranielle might be charged for lying about his whereabouts and impeding the investigation, but what does it matter? Case closed."

"Besides," said Carter, "we know she can lie through her teeth. She might be able to spin it in a way that makes her seem innocent. Like—she was asleep the whole time, so how could she have known her husband disappeared in the middle of the night?"

Beck frowned. "How wasn't there more DNA left behind?"

"Alicia was a nail-biter," said Sierra. "Even if she fought back, her nails were too short, so there was nothing to find. And the killer was wearing gloves to keep their DNA from getting in her mouth."

"What's this?" said Adi, picking up a photo of a short, handwritten message. "At first I thought we had two different photos of the suicide note."

"Oh, sorry," said Carter. "It's a picture I took in the dressing room before the snag round. That was written on the bottom of a photo. I thought we could use it to compare the handwriting on the suicide note."

"Good idea," said Beck. "Either Ranielle forced Louis to write the note under duress or she forged it. It would be great if we had a way to prove that to the police."

They gathered around the two photos.

This is just the beginning. —Louis

I killed Alicia. Can't live with the guilt anymore. Please apologise to my fans and everyone I've hurt. Tell Rani I love her.

"Does anyone else think something feels off about the suicide note?" asked Adi.

"Like the fact that he didn't commit suicide?" said Sierra. "Or that he confessed to a murder we're pretty sure he didn't commit?"

"I mean, yeah. But there's something . . ." Adi listed his head to the side.

"How about the 'Tell Rani I love her' part?" said Beck. "That feels a bit tongue-in-cheek."

"Yeah, maybe that's it," said Adi, sounding unconvinced.

"His handwriting was very distinct," Beck added, wondering if uniqueness made handwriting easier or more difficult to replicate. "I like how he does his *y*s and *g*s." He pointed to the *g* in "guilt," with its flourishing swirl of a tail.

"Yeah," said Carter. "He replied to one of my fan letters once. I thought his handwriting was so classy I actually tried to make mine more like his—but I was never very good at cursive." A shadow fell over her face. "It was only a postcard, but it meant a lot to me at the time."

Sierra put an arm around Carter, giving her a squeeze.

"Part of me wishes I'd never found out about the affair," Carter said. "That I could still think of him as the Game Master." Her brow furrowed as she stared at the suicide note. "Hold on," she whispered. "Hold *on*."

Sierra's arm fell from her shoulders as Carter picked up the two photos—the bottom of the picture in the dressing room and the suicide note.

"The *g*s," she whispered. "Beck. You're right!"

He blinked. "I am?"

"Give me a second." Grabbing her phone, Carter made a call as she stepped out of the room. "Yeah, Dad? I need you to do me a huge favor. In my bedroom, there's a postcard—"

Barely a minute had passed before Carter burst back into the hotel room. "The *g*s!" she shouted, slamming the phone down on the bed. They were looking at a photo of the back of a postcard, and what was becoming familiar script.

Carter Kelly— Thanks for the fun puzzle.
Keep solving! —Louis

Adi made a face. "That's it? That's all he wrote?"

Carter shoved him on the shoulder. "Shut up. He's a . . . *was* a busy guy. But look. Look at the *g*s!"

The difference was immediately obvious. The *gs* on the postcard curled in a completely different way from the photograph signature.

"Okay?" said Adi, eyeing her warily. "People change their handwriting sometimes, especially people who pride themselves on—"

"Exactly!" interrupted Carter. She pointed to the photograph and then the postcard. "Sometime between season one, when he wrote this, and season three, when he sent me a postcard, he changed his writing style. But the suicide note is using the *old gs*." A grin split her face. "Proof that it was forged. And if it was forged . . ."

"Then the confession is meaningless," said Beck.

"And now," said Adi, "the police know Ranielle was lying about the alibi, which means Louis was lying, too, which would make her the prime suspect in both cases."

"And we've got two motives to boot," said Sierra. "Proof that Alicia and Louis were sleeping together, and that she was blackmailing Ranielle about it."

"We are so good at this!" said Carter. "I knew I took that photo for a reason!"

"What now?" asked Beck. "We go to the police, right?"

"No," said Sierra. "We go to Ranielle."

The ebullient mood of the room fizzled.

"You can't be serious," said Adi. "The last time we went charging off after a potential murderer, we found Louis's body."

"You think the cops are going to listen to a bunch of resentful teenagers? Or *me*? They're sure they've solved a murder case. They're not going to reopen it based on some dodgy handwriting. No. I can't risk letting her get away with it. Not again."

"What do you want to do?" Beck said, eyes wide.

Sierra's expression was grimly determined. "We're going to get a confession."

46

Sierra

Sierra seethed the entire Uber ride to the studio while her team concocted outrageous plans for getting past the reception desk. Adi suggested they sweet-talk their way in. Carter was keen to create a diversion in order to draw out the security personnel. Beck was excited at the possibility of scaling a fire escape and sneaking in through the roof.

Sierra wasn't concerned with how they got inside. She was confronting Ranielle, and she would take down anyone who tried to stop her.

But when they walked into the building, they found the reception desk empty and the lobby quiet. Strange, although Sierra wasn't complaining about the easy access. She deserved something to go right for once.

As they made their way toward Ranielle's office, Sierra heard construction sounds coming from Soundstage A. A sneaky check revealed crews dismantling the set, pulling apart Dr. Theery's laboratory. Soon there'd be nothing but bare walls and concrete floors.

"Don't they usually leave these for the postseason special?" Beck asked.

Sierra picked up her pace.

As they neared Ranielle's office they heard—not drills and sledgehammers—but screaming.

"—can't treat me like this! After everything I did for you and this show!"

"Oh no." Adi groaned. "Tell me it isn't—"

The office door swung open and two security guards emerged, dragging Adi's mom between them. On camera, Symphony always looked immaculate and poised. Now her long hair was a flurry of tangles and her demure smile had been replaced with a snarl.

"Get your hands off me," she snapped. "I'll be talking to my lawyer about this. Don't you know who I am? Don't you—" Her gaze fell on Adi. She gasped. "Aditya! There you are. Tell these men who I am. Get them to release me at once."

The security guards paused to look at Adi, but he stepped aside and held up both hands. "She's all yours."

Symphony shrieked. "Aditya! That is not funny. Aditya!"

Her screams faded as she was manhandled down the corridor.

"That explains why the security guards didn't tackle us when we first came in," Sierra muttered. Squaring her shoulders, she marched through Ranielle's open office door.

The executive producer was standing over a plastic box on her desk, filling it with papers and folders. As they watched, she took an entire drawer and upended the contents into the bin before dropping the drawer to the floor behind her.

"What's going on?" said Sierra.

Ranielle startled, then glowered when she saw them. "Great. More trespassers." She grabbed a pen holder and dropped it into the bin. "Hitflix honestly couldn't go *one more day* without firing ninety percent of the security team?"

"Hitflix is firing people?" asked Adi.

Letting out an exasperated breath, Ranielle shoved the lid onto the box and leaned across it. "They've fired everyone. The show is canceled. Effective immediately."

"What?" said Carter. "They can't do that! The finale is next week!"

Ranielle fixed her with a vicious look. "They're already dismantling the sets, and they'll start tearing that cursed finale room apart first thing tomorrow morning. By this time next week, there'll be nothing here but plywood and rubble. But feel free to send in your complaints." She started pulling books from a nearby shelf. "It's no longer my problem."

"But . . . what about the grand prize?" said Beck. "The money? The invitation to Sweetbrier?"

"Sweetbrier?" shouted Ranielle, throwing the books unceremoniously into another box. "My life is falling apart around me, and all anyone cares about is going to some fucking resort."

Adi winced as she snatched up more books. "And my mother was pissed off because . . . ?"

"How the hell should I know? Some part of her still thought she was a contender for the host position?" She fisted her hands on her hips. "Do I even want to ask what you're doing here? Because if this is about that damn recording, then go ahead. Tell the world the great Ranielle Russell helped a contestant cheat. My reputation is shot at this point, anyway."

"Yeah?" said Sierra, stepping forward. "What's going to happen to your reputation when people find out you killed my sister?"

Ranielle stared at Sierra like she'd started talking in code.

Then she laughed. A shrill, humorless sound. "You teenagers and your goddamn conspiracy theories. I don't have time for this. Get out of my office."

"We know about the blackmail," Sierra continued. "We know Louis didn't write that suicide note. We know everything."

This time, Ranielle looked borderline amused. "Oh, you know *everything*, do you? How quaint."

"Yes, everything." Sierra's anger grew at Ranielle's nonchalance. Didn't she get it? Sierra *knew*. Ranielle would pay for what she'd done. "Alicia left me a note telling me about her relationship with your husband, and how she threatened to go to the media if you didn't give her what she wanted. It's over. My sister will finally have justice."

Slowly, Ranielle's smug expression shifted. A moment of concern, but then . . . regret.

The fire roared in Sierra's chest. Finally. *Finally.*

She had her.

Ranielle's gaze drifted from Sierra to each of her teammates, and back again. Then she walked around the desk and shut her office door.

Instincts had Sierra bracing for an attack. They should have brought weapons.

Carter and Adi both reached for their phones.

But Ranielle paced to the sofa and thumped onto it with a heavy sigh. "All right," she said quietly. "Let's get a few things straight. I didn't kill your sister. I was trying to protect her."

Sierra frowned. "Excuse me?"

"I'm sorry, Sierra. I should've stepped in sooner." She looked at Carter. "I did with you. At least, I tried. When I saw you that first day in Louis's dressing room, I tried to warn you away. I didn't know what else to do without exposing my husband's despicable secret."

Carter shuddered.

"But I didn't do any of that for Alicia," Ranielle continued. "I stood by and let it happen because I didn't have the time or energy for Louis's antics—I had a show to run." She shook her head. "I never expected Alicia to blackmail *me* over it."

"What did you offer her?" asked Adi. "Money?"

Ranielle fixed him with an inscrutable look. "I offered her the world." She left that comment hanging before adding, "In exchange for her discretion, and ending the affair."

"Oh," Adi said, exhaling softly. "You think Louis killed her because she was going to leave him."

"That was my suspicion, yes."

"You told her to break up with him, then provided police with his alibi when he killed her for it," Sierra said. "What . . . the . . . fuck."

She couldn't stop her body from shaking.

"I never knew for certain it was him," Ranielle said, sounding defensive. "And my actions saved the show. That's hundreds of jobs protected, plus the fandom community, plus—"

"Your own bank account, after Hitflix offered to renew the show for season five?" Adi suggested.

Ranielle curled her lip.

"But . . ." Carter said, blinking, "it couldn't have been Louis that killed her. The Real Game Master said it wasn't him."

Sierra massaged her temples. For a moment, she'd lost herself. The whole point of this conversation was that Louis *hadn't* killed Alicia.

Right?

But Ranielle puffed herself up, her fury returning. "The Real Game Master is a delusional hack who I should have fired a long time ago."

"Hold on," Carter said. "You know who the Real Game Master is? Who?"

"You think you need to know every answer to every mystery, but it's none of your goddamn business. This is *not* material for your little social media accounts."

Carter gasped. "I wouldn't post about this!"

"You would," Ranielle argued. "You all would. There isn't one person here who isn't trying to screw me over. Well, congrats—it worked. I'll never get another job in this town after being in charge of this dumpster fire. A murder, a suicide, every asinine fan playing true detective. Give me a break."

"Two murders, no suicides," Beck corrected. "Louis didn't kill himself."

Ranielle glared at him. "Of course he did."

"No—he didn't," said Adi. "The letter was forged. It matched his handwriting from years ago, not recently."

Ranielle scoffed. Then, when she saw he was serious, she spat, "He was in mental distress. Believe me, I know his handwriting. He wrote that letter." Ranielle stood. "For what it's worth, I'm sorry. But the case is closed, Sierra. You have your answers."

Sierra's words vanished. She'd been so sure, *so sure* that Louis hadn't killed Alicia, that he hadn't killed himself. But now she felt like the evidence they'd compiled was as flimsy as a handful of sand sifting through her fingers.

Ranielle made her way back to the door and pulled it open. "I have a lot of packing to do, a lot of paperwork to fill out, and at some point I need to explain to my host why he's getting shipped back to Australia in a few weeks. So if you'll excuse me."

Carter's voice pitched higher. "Australia?"

Adi cursed. "I forgot about that."

Carter looked at him, then Ranielle. "He's getting deported?"

"Wait," said Adi, casting his gaze around the office. "Last time I was here, I . . . dropped something. A USB drive. You didn't find it, did you?"

Ranielle looked ready to strangle him. "I did, actually." She yanked open a drawer and pulled out a small plastic bin. It was filled to the brim with *Escape Game*–branded USBs. "It's one of these. Knock yourself out."

She thrust the bin into Adi's arms, then tried to push them out of her office.

"No," said Sierra, digging in her platform boots. "You can't do this."

"Goodbye, Sierra."

"No!" Sierra wrenched away from Ranielle and bit down the sob that lurched in her throat. "Why did you bring me back? And why put me on the team you were rigging to win? I'm the *villain*."

"Oh, Sierra," said Ranielle. "Do you know what viewers love even more than a great villain? A great redemption arc. Now get out."

She unceremoniously shoved them into the hallway and slammed the door behind them.

Carter spun on Adi. "Fitzy's getting deported? And you knew?"

"I didn't know the show was going to be canceled."

She punched him in the arm. "But you knew he wasn't going to be the host next season, because it was going to be you!"

"He was getting fired either way! This isn't my fault."

"Hey," said Beck, his voice cutting through their argument. "We have other things to be dealing with right now."

They fell quiet, and Sierra could feel them turning to her, staring at her, but her gaze was caught on a distant wall, unseeing.

She'd failed.

Again.

"You okay, Sierra?" asked Beck.

"No, actually."

"It really was him this whole time," muttered Adi. "We were so sure his confession was fake."

"Honestly, I wish he would come back to life so I could kill him again."

As they started down the corridor, Carter took Sierra's elbow. "At least we know why Alicia was willing to give you the prize money. It sounds like she had a pretty powerful hold over Ranielle."

Beck cleared his throat. "Is anyone going to remind her that her office is bugged?"

"I forgot about that," said Carter.

Adi slowed, tucking the bin of USB ports under one arm. "Hang on. We thought the person leaving the clues had bugged her office, but she clearly *knows* who's leaving the clues."

"About that," said Beck. "Who has so much power over Ranielle Russell that she couldn't stop them, even though she tried?"

"And how did they not get fired?" said Carter.

They stared at each other, but no one had any answers.

"Also, Louis *didn't* kill himself," Sierra said, halting abruptly. Their conversation from before was flooding back, bringing fresh conviction. "It isn't just the handwriting. There were also the wineglasses, remember? And I don't buy that he invited Carter over to find his body. He was a narcissist. He wouldn't have wanted Carter, of all people, to find him in that state."

Beck twisted his lips in thought. "But Ranielle seemed really certain he committed suicide. And I know people think I'm naive sometimes, but . . . I think I believe her. I don't think she killed Louis. Or Alicia."

Sierra checked they were alone. So far, the place had been empty. She supposed that when Hitflix fired you, they didn't want you hanging around. "We're no closer than when we started. All that, and we're back at square one."

"And the show's canceled," said Carter, eyes widening. "No finale means . . ."

"The Real Game Master won't be revealing anything," said Beck.

"They're going to dismantle the room tomorrow morning," Adi added.

"Screw that," said Beck, nodding to the door behind Sierra. It was the costume room. "We're not leaving until we have our answer."

47

Adi

"You told me you didn't get anything," said Beck.

"Technically, I didn't," said Adi, hunkering over the costume department's computer, relieved when it didn't require a password to log on. "I dropped the USB in her office and didn't have a chance to grab it again."

He picked a USB out of the bin and stuck it into the port. A folder popped up.

Empty.

He ejected the USB, set it aside, grabbed another.

"How many do you think that is?" asked Beck, eyeing the bin.

"I'd estimate around two hundred," said Carter. "Based on unit size and container volume."

"Great," said Adi, pulling out the second blank drive. "Two down."

"We've got time," said Sierra. "We can't risk breaking into the finale room until we're sure the studio is empty."

While Adi worked, Beck dug through the racks of costumes, which held everything from silver disco jumpsuits to fringed cowboy vests. "I wish we'd taken pictures of our murder board. Now that we know it isn't Ranielle—"

"*Believe* it isn't Ranielle," Sierra corrected. "We have no proof either way."

"Good point. But it would be nice to look at the clues again. I've been thinking maybe the murderer had an accomplice. That would explain some of the alibis. What about your old teammates? Elijah and Cruz?"

Sierra looked up from the costume designer's sketchbook, which she'd found behind the desk. "Maybe. Elijah was quick to point the finger at me."

"Not everyone had solid alibis," Adi said. "Vera could have been responding to social media comments anywhere."

"Right," Sierra drawled. "Suffocate someone, like a photo. Throw the body in a coffin, heart a comment. That sounds like Vera."

"Is it possible the police got the time of death wrong?" Carter asked, trying on a cowboy hat.

Adi plugged in another drive. "Forensics isn't going to screw something like that up."

"But what if they did?" asked Beck. "There could be a laboratory mix-up. A typo in the paperwork. Simple human error. It's not so far-fetched."

"In a high-profile case like this?" said Sierra. "You'd think they'd double-check their work."

"Is there a drug that can slow a body's decay?" Carter asked.

Beck considered. "I don't think she was dead long enough for decomposition. It would more likely have to do with rigor mortis and lividity. Either way, a drug would show up in a toxicology report."

"Ice?" Carter suggested. "It would slow the settling of blood, wouldn't it? Being cold."

"You think someone stuffed the body in a bag of ice?" Adi said.

Carter shot him an annoyed look. "*No*, a freezer. And I don't think anything, we're just throwing out ideas."

"Actually," said Beck, "that might delay rigor mortis and make the time of death appear later than it was."

Adi frowned. "But there'd be signs of . . ."

"Wait," said Sierra. She slammed the sketchbook shut. "Oh my god!"

Everyone gaped at her.

"You, my team, are brilliant. All of you. All of you!"

"Are you having a stroke?" Adi said.

"Alicia was *wet*!" Sierra covered her mouth. "The cops thought she was wet because the killer hosed her down to eliminate any DNA. But what if she was wet because she'd been *defrosting*?"

At first, Adi was skeptical. But gradually, amazement overshadowed his doubt. That made sense. It would explain why the case had been so difficult to solve. *The time of death was wrong.*

"That would eliminate almost every alibi," he said. "It means everyone's a suspect again."

"She couldn't have been killed on the studio premises," Beck said. "The only freezers they have here are small."

"Her phone was found, what, a mile away?" asked Carter. "We could search for restaurants nearby and see if there's a connection to any of the suspects."

But Adi's stomach had begun to churn. "No."

"The missing comforter," Sierra said, not hearing him. "It could have been used to protect her skin inside the freezer. She had it with her that night. The killer could have used it to drag her into any industrial free—"

"Adi?" Carter interrupted. "Are you all right?"

Adi gulped, suddenly nauseated. "What if," he said weakly, "Alicia never left the complex alive?"

"You think the killer used the freezer in our kitchens?" Beck said. "The same freezer we were trapped in?"

The air stilled.

"It's certainly big enough," Carter whispered.

Sierra pressed her hands to the sides of her head. "The food poisoning. If the killer had to move the meat boxes out, like we did—"

"Then Alicia could lie flat on the freezer floor." Carter gripped her stomach. "Yep, Adi, I understand why you're looking like that."

"Wait," Sierra said. "Elijah saw her leave the complex after me."

"Maybe she came back," Beck said softly.

"Speaking of Elijah," said Adi. "That car he heard at four in the morning—if the killer had left Alicia in the complex overnight to freeze, it makes sense they'd be returning before dawn to pick up her body and stage it at the studio."

"What time was her phone turned off?" Carter asked.

"Ten twenty-eight," Beck and Sierra said in unison.

"So they killed her at the villa," said Adi, "then took the phone and drove away before turning it off, to make it look like Alicia was still alive at that time, and that she'd moved to a different location."

"It fits." Sierra's voice sounded far away. "I think you were right, Beck. Alicia must've returned to the complex. Maybe the killer even lured her back. Pretending to be Louis?" She closed her eyes, as if picturing the events as she spoke. "She goes in, only it's not Louis. Or maybe she doesn't see the killer at all. Maybe they attack her from behind. They use a gloved hand to cover her mouth and nose. She struggles . . . clawing, but her nails are too short to catch any DNA, and the killer simply waits until . . . until . . ."

Adi's insides sank. This was nothing like the euphoria of solving puzzles. Alicia's death had been brutal.

And despite how far they'd come, they still didn't know who had done it.

Adi would have felt discouraged, except—

His heart leaped.

"This is it."

His teammates looked at him. Adi turned the computer screen to face them, revealing the open folder. "Sweetbrier Resort—season six."

"Yes!" Beck threw his arms into the air. "Adi, you are like freaking James Bond!"

"But there's no grand prize anymore," Carter pointed out. "No invitation to Sweetbrier."

"Oh, I'll get there someday," said Beck. "And when I do, I'll be ready."

It wasn't long before the sounds of demolition fell quiet and the studio shut down for the night. They used their phone flashlights as they crept down the corridor.

"I can't believe we're going to see the finale room," Carter whispered. "Is it wrong that I'm a *little* excited?"

They came to the doors of Soundstage E, and Adi reached for the handle. "Are we ready?"

Everyone nodded.

After a dramatic pause worthy of a show host, Adi opened up and stepped inside. It took a moment for his brain to interpret the lumps and shapes, and even when he did, he didn't register it right away.

"You're kidding," Sierra breathed.

Adi's phone light landed on a . . . skull? No—a whole skeleton. He swung the beam around. Three skeletons altogether, strings of garlic around their necks. Each hung from hooks in the stone walls.

"Wait," he said. "Isn't this—?"

"The vampire room." Sierra's voice shook, and Adi realized she was lingering in the doorway. Her eyes were glued to the large black box in the center of the floor.

Not a box. A coffin.

"The unaired finale." Carter moved around the space, dust billowing from beneath her boots. "They wouldn't actually reuse the set where they found Alicia's body?"

"It's not exact," Sierra said. "This feels . . . more authentic. The details. The props. But I bet they're using the same puzzles."

Adi flicked a switch on the wall, and electric orange flames sparked to life in ensconced torches around the room.

"Fancy," Beck murmured.

Carter touched a combination lock that sealed the coffin shut. "I can't believe they'd do this."

As one, they turned to Sierra, who stared at the coffin with haunted eyes. Almost as though she expected her sister's corpse to be in there . . . again.

"Sierra—" Beck started.

Abruptly, she snapped to attention. "It isn't like we're going to find *another* body. Start looking for that evidence. Search the skeletons."

They split up, Sierra using a loose stone to prop open the door, keeping it from locking them in.

"This one has a parchment," Carter said. They spoke in hushed whispers, as if they were treading on sacred ground. As if Alicia's spirit might be lingering nearby, waiting for them to find the truth.

Adi pulled a pouch from the bony hand of his skeleton. "I've got a pouch. It's locked. There's a symbol of a fancy cross pressed into the leather."

"Just garlic over here," Beck said. He joined Carter. "What does the parchment say?"

"It's a map with numbers on it. The title reads *The Most Holy of Sites*."

"We need a code to get through to the next room," Sierra said, examining a heavy wooden door with a keypad. "Four digits. I don't remember much from last time."

"You were in shock," Beck said. "Your brain probably blocked out a lot."

Adi headed over to check Carter's parchment map. "This is medieval—or at least, is trying to look medieval. Europe and the Middle East." He touched his finger to the numbers marking different locations. "I wonder—"

"There's something on the back!" Beck said.

Carter flipped the parchment over. "Oh great. A message apparently written in blood. *Our protection is the key for our greatest weapon. Yet it is not enough. We are doomed.*"

Sierra perked up. "The key?"

"What protection?" Beck said, scanning the room. "A shield?"

"Protection from vampires." Sierra slapped her forehead. "The garlic! I knew that."

"The key's in the garlic?" Beck asked.

"For the combination. Count them. The skeletons' fingers indicate the order. This one is holding up the number two, and there are nine garlic bulbs."

They inspected the skeletons, counted the garlic bulbs—

"Seven-nine-five," said Carter, inputting the code.

The coffin swung open so fast Carter jumped back. Sierra looked away.

Maybe, for a second, Adi also imagined finding a body inside.

But all it held was an old book and a sharp wooden stake. Carter plucked the stake from the velvet cushion while Adi picked up the book. The pages had been made to look old, with inked portions of maps inside. "An atlas."

Carter leaned over his shoulder, and he was overly aware of the heat radiating from her body. "Page numbers? A code?"

"It probably has to do with the other map," Sierra said.

Beck suddenly called out, "I found something else on this skeleton!" He dug around the neck bones. "I missed it before because it was under the garlic." He triumphantly pulled out a crucifix necklace.

The moment he did, the skeleton's jaw dropped open and a voice boomed around them. *"Come, we must see and act. Devils or no devils, or all the devils at once, it matters not; we fight him all the same."*

"I recognize that quote," said Adi. "It's from *Dracula*. Actually . . . I think Van Helsing says it."

Sierra grinned. "Nice touch. Any clues on the crucifix?"

Beck didn't answer. Gripping the necklace in one hand, he stared thoughtfully at the skeleton, running his tongue over his front teeth.

"Beck?" said Sierra.

He reached for the skeleton's jaw, closed it, then let it drop open again. The words repeated. *"Come, we must see and act. Devils or no devils . . ."*

When it finished, he squeezed his eyes shut, closed the jaw, then let it play again. His mouth was puckered, like he was biting into something sour.

Adi traded confused looks with Carter and Sierra.

Shrugging, Sierra took the crucifix from Beck's hand. He released it without complaint.

"Doesn't have a symbol or anything," said Sierra, studying the wood.

"Wait . . . a symbol!" Adi grabbed the locked pouch from his jacket pocket. "There's a crucifix symbol on this. It must open it somehow."

Sierra fiddled with the crucifix and it pulled away from the chain, revealing the end whittled into a key. Adi brought her the pouch and they unlocked it.

"Holy water in labeled bottles." Adi tipped the vials into his palm. "And a white rock or crystal or something." It was a strange object, something that sparked an alert in his brain, but the loopy script on the bottles caught his attention first. *River Jordan (I). Our Lady of Lourdes (II). Pool of Siloam (III).* "Holy sites. Where's that map?"

"I've got it!" Beck yelled suddenly. He turned to face them, beaming. "It's the same voice that recorded the message in the alien room video. She used an auto-tuner then, so it was more muddled, but the flavors are the same. Mostly tart, a little fruity." He paused. *"Cranberries."*

Adi frowned. "You said *she*."

"Yes, I did. The Real Game Master." He paused, practically trembling. "It's Vera!"

"*Vera?*" Sierra laughed. "No way."

"And exactly why," came a sardonic voice, "does that surprise you?"

In the set's doorway, a figure loomed, illuminated by the lights of the corridor. The team leaped back. Adi was sure he wasn't the only one picturing axe murderers in that moment—until he saw who it was.

"Speak of the devil," Carter said.

"Took you long enough." Vera crossed her arms. She was in a halter top, showing off her full tattoo, an inked chameleon curled around her shoulder. "I guess you deserve a Scooby Snack. Now, what the hell are you doing in here?"

"What do you think?" said Sierra, storming toward her. "The show is canceled. This room is going to be destroyed tomorrow. We're here to find *your* last clue. But how about you save us the trouble and tell us who murdered my sister?"

"Save you the trouble?" Vera barked. "Why? Because you've made my life so easy? Go to hell, Sierra. I don't owe you anything."

"But you're the Real Game Master," said Beck. "You're dying to tell people the truth."

"Yes, I am!" Vera slammed a hand against one of the stone walls. "But no one ever listens to me. You and the other contestants roll your eyes and make comments behind my back, but you have no idea. You have no idea how integral I am—to everything!"

"That's not true," said Carter. "You're the bridge between the show and the fans. The Domain owes you so much. All the interviews and behind-the-scenes footage and—"

"Screw social media. I'm not some publicity lackey. No one gets it. You Clue Masters think you're so smart, but even with Louis dead, no one *gets it*." She pressed a fist to her chest. "I'm behind everything.

Creating the rooms, planning the puzzles, designing the special effects. It's me. I'm the goddamn Game Master. But does Ranielle ever give me the credit I deserve? Hell no. That would 'mess with the show's image.'"

"You're kidding," said Carter. "I've been following Louis for years. Read every article, every news story . . ."

"Oh yeah?" said Vera with a bitter laugh. "And how well did you know him, reading all those fluff pages? Did they mention his penchant for teenage girls?"

Carter drew back, her expression shuttering in a way that made Adi clench his fist.

"So you're the real Game Master," said Sierra. "And no one knows?"

"Since season two," said Vera, a touch of pride in her voice.

"Right." Carter shut her eyes. "The puzzles in season one were pretty terrible. The show only gained traction because the hosts were so endearing."

Vera scowled. "Louis wasn't the genius everyone thought. He was better as the showman. The face. While I hid in the shadows because I'm not *beautiful* enough or *thin* enough for television."

"I mean," started Adi, "your personality is also a little—"

Vera shot him a look.

"—fantastic," he quickly amended. "Totally made for TV. Can't imagine why they didn't want you."

"That isn't right," said Beck. "You deserve credit—for designing the game but also for catching the killer. The *real* killer. No one believed you, did they?"

"I *found* it. Evidence he was here that night." Angry tears misted in Vera's eyes. "I told the police, but the timing was wrong. They said he had an alibi. They said I was mistaken. *Mistaken!*" Desperation tangled in her voice—a growing need to be heard. "I didn't know what it was at first. But I put it in my pocket when I was doing final checks on the room, no idea that Alicia was lying dead in the coffin. It was only days later that I realized—but it had already been through the wash . . . and then I couldn't fucking *find it*—" She caught herself as her voice lifted into a shriek. After a slow exhalation, she said, "And months later, by the time it finally resurfaced, you know what the police told me? That it wasn't proof. They kept going on about that damn alibi. So I thought, I know who'll help. The people who have always admired my work, even if they didn't realize it was mine."

"The Clue Masters," breathed Beck.

"All I had to do was create a fake account and throw the clues onto the forums. Eventually, someone would have to figure out how he managed to trick everyone. How he'd gotten away with it." Her expression turned angry again. "But you didn't keep up your end of the deal, did you? You want your murderer? Then figure out the damn lie!"

"The time of death is wrong," Sierra shouted back at her.

Vera stepped back, startled. "The time of death?"

"The killer used the freezer in our complex," Adi said. "That's why Alicia was wet—it was melting frost. The real time of death was before one a.m. Maybe as early as ten. We think the murderer came back early the next morning to pick up her body and stage it here in the coffin."

Vera snapped her fingers. "I knew there was something off about the report! I thought maybe he'd paid some corrupt coroner or something . . ."

"*Who?*" said Carter. "Who is it?

Vera looked like she wanted to laugh. "You really haven't figured it out yet?"

Adi growled in his throat. Vera was enjoying this *way* too much.

But Sierra, who seemed less perturbed by Vera's secrecy, said, "I thought you hated my sister."

"Oh, I did. She manipulated people, flirted to get whatever she wanted. Even Ranielle fawned over her. 'Make her look good, Vera! We need the fans to love her!' She couldn't have her precious new host making a fool of herself."

A flood of ice swept through Adi's body. "New host?"

Vera snorted. "Hitflix wanted to make her the host for the next season. That's how her team was doing so well—Ranielle was giving her cheats." Her tone turned sardonic. "Sounds familiar, doesn't it, pretty boy?"

Adi spun to Sierra. "I saw Ranielle's notes on my audition video! She'd written 'the next Alicia.' I thought it was some sick serial killer thing, but what she meant was she'd offered Alicia the hosting gig and was planning to offer it to me, too."

"That's why Alicia said she'd give me her share of the prize money if she won," Sierra whispered. "She was moving on to bigger and better things."

"But wasn't she blackmailing Ranielle about her affair with Louis?" Carter said.

Sierra shook her head. "I see what happened now. She planned to blackmail the Russells and knew it was dangerous, so she left that note for me in the painting. But when she confronted them, Ranielle told her she had something better than a one-off payment. She was going to give her a high-profile job in Hollywood. That's why Alicia's behavior changed from being scared to downright arrogant."

Adi's mind was working overtime. "And the killer didn't want her to take the job. He'd have too much to lose if she did." He looked down at the small white rock still in his hand.

Not a crystal. A shark tooth.

The relic—the evidence—left behind.

He curled his fingers around the pendant. "Did he know?"

"He wasn't supposed to," Vera said. "But I guess he found out. That's what I believe the message on Alicia's coffin was supposed to mean. *We get what we deserve.* It was aimed at Ranielle, because he thought he'd lost his job and wanted to take the show down with him. The guy's unhinged."

He'd killed Louis, assuming Louis had been planting the clues. He'd realized the "relic" from the poem was his missing shark tooth—Adi had even caught him searching the Game Master's dressing room . . .

"Fitzy," Carter said in alarm, the name little more than a disbelieving gasp.

"It was Fitzy," Adi whispered, clenching his fist tighter around the shark tooth. He felt the urgent need to apologize—for what, he wasn't sure.

But Carter was staring beyond him, at the set door. And as he turned, he already half knew what he was going to see.

James "Fitzy" Fitzgerald, the show's beloved Australian nincompoop, was standing there.

And he was holding a gun.

48

Carter

A gun. He had a *gun*. It couldn't be real. Because what would Fitzy, her Fitzy, be doing with a gun?

But the moment passed and her denial dissolved into a chill down her spine.

Fitzy had killed Alicia.

He wasn't going to . . .

He couldn't actually . . .

Cold sweat beaded on the back of her neck as Fitzy strolled toward them.

At least he didn't look maniacal. Actually, he looked mildly irritated.

"Goddamn it," he said. "What are you doing here?"

Carter didn't realize she was retreating until her back collided with the wall, nearly knocking one of the skeletons off its hook. The clack of the bones drew Fitzy's attention to her, and she shivered.

He narrowed his eyes. "You shouldn't be here." He turned his gun to Vera. "Clever influencer wannabe. I thought it was Louis, but you loved taunting me with how wrong that was, didn't you? I had to bug Ranielle's office to figure out what the hell was going on. Wasn't until I heard the two of you discussing the puzzles for the finale that it clicked. The *Real* Game Master. Shit, Vee, have you been behind this show the whole time?"

For a bizarre moment, Carter was put off by the fact that Fitzy, family-friendly game show host, was swearing.

"You bastard," Vera snarled under her breath. "You've made my life a living hell."

"Hey, at least I have some respect for you now. Isn't that worth something?" Fitzy jerked his gun toward the back corner. "All of you, stand there."

The others shuffled, silent, panicked, between the wooden door and a skeleton, but Carter couldn't move. Her entire body was numb.

Fitzy's attention landed on her again. His expression turned sardonic. "Sorry, love, I'm not in the mood for another make-out session right now. So *move*."

His tone was cruel enough to make Carter jump. She edged nearer to the door, clutching the wooden stake. Next to her, Adi was holding the map and the three vials of holy water—maybe they could throw a vial at Fitzy's head. The thought was so ridiculous that Carter almost started to giggle and had to clamp a shaking hand over her mouth.

Fitzy rubbed his jaw. "Think, Fitzy. Think, think, think. *Fuck*." He swung the gun at them again, and they flinched. "What are you even doing here? You were eliminated!"

Carter could hear the others' breaths around her. Could feel each subtle shift and shudder.

"I need to know why," Sierra said. Voice steady. Cold.

Fitzy shook his hands in the action of strangling air, the gun waving with the movement. "She was going to take my job! I've been here from the start, since we were a tiny production on YouTube. She couldn't just swoop in and take it from me. I would've been deported! Back to my dad and my stepmom, who hated me so much because of a few inconvenient bruises on their precious little baby—"

A horrified breath whooshed from Carter's lungs. She couldn't be hearing this.

"And Louis?" Adi said.

"I thought he was the one leaving the clues. So when he bragged about his new conquest"—he scowled at Carter—"I thought I'd meet him at the hotel first, for a friendly chat."

"In a blond wig?" Adi said.

"I couldn't be recognized by the hotel staff, obviously."

Obviously.

Carter's brain moved through sludge. This Fitzy was not the host who had made her laugh with his silly antics and terrible puns. Surely not the boy who had looked at her like she was smart and special and beautiful. Surely not the boy who had kissed her like . . . like he *wanted* her.

"I asked him to stop leaving the clues," Fitzy continued. "He told me it wasn't him, but I thought he was lying. Lying to *me*! After years of tolerating his arrogance, his smug looks. *God*, that pissed me off."

Adi groaned softly. "The note! The *s*. That's what it was!"

Carter shook her head, unable to tear her gaze from the gun. "It was the *g*s that were—"

"No, the *s*. In 'apologise.' *Please apologise to my fans.* It's been nagging at me all this time."

Carter frowned.

"It's the British spelling. The *Australian* spelling."

"Dammit," Fitzy said. "I always forget that one."

"How about," Beck said, "you let us go and we promise not to tell a single person?"

"Yeah, right. Uh-uh." He swung the gun toward Vera, who had been trying to subtly slip her phone out of her pocket. "Away."

Vera scowled and left her phone where it was.

"You've been trying to sabotage us," Adi said. "All those threats . . ."

"I figured the easiest way to keep my job safe for another year was to make sure you didn't make it to the finale. Ranielle only likes winners, and there was no way she'd hire Jarius or one of his cronies. The fans *hate* them."

"The cow's heart?" said Beck. "Locking us in the freezer?"

"Spiking Carter's drink," Sierra added with a growl. "And defiling my painting."

"Nailed it," said Fitzy. "Though the freezer was pure serendipity. I saw you sneak into the kitchens and used the circumstances to my advantage."

Beck's voice shook. "What were you doing in the complex in the middle of the night in a balaclava?"

Fitzy pressed the barrel of the gun to his lips in a shushing motion, looking almost boyish. "Meeting with Team Dread. We may have been conspiring to take you down. Nothing personal."

Carter gaped. "You're the reason they've been targeting our team with all the snags!"

"It wasn't hard. Jarius is easy to manipulate, and he liked the idea of being the one to take down the *great* Kick It Carter."

Carter's insides churned. The way he said it, with such outright disgust.

The reality of the situation crystallized. Any lingering denial disappeared.

Fitzy had never meant a single word he'd said. All the smiles, the little flirtations . . . He'd been using her.

"I'm beginning to see why Ranielle wanted to replace you," Adi said.

"Shut your hole," said Fitzy, aiming the gun at Adi's head. "Or I'll do it for you."

Carter didn't know what possessed her. One moment she was cowering against the wall. The next, she was shoving her way in front of Adi, staring down the barrel of the gun.

"Why?" she demanded. "Why did you pretend . . . Why *me*?"

Fitzy rocked back on his heels and, to Carter's surprise, seemed to actually be considering the question. He slowly lifted the gun, pointing it at the ceiling instead.

Carter drew an unsteady breath. Behind her, Adi pressed a hand to her arm, like he meant to shove her away, but she held her ground.

"I mean, I did always think that cartoon of yours was pretty hot,"

Fitzy said at last, "even if the real you leaves something to be desired."

Humiliation burned across her cheeks.

"Or maybe it's because I knew you were Louis's type, and it's fun to play. I was surprised when he told me about your hotel date. Didn't expect that from you, Carter." He clicked his tongue. "Too bad I had to kill him before things got interesting."

"You asshole," Adi growled. "You sick, disgusting—"

Before he could finish, Sierra let out a growl and snatched the stake from Carter. "You killed my sister!"

She crouched like she was preparing to lunge at him—until Fitzy calmly replied, "I never said *that*."

It stopped her in her tracks. Sierra's face twisted, livid but confused. "You . . . But you just—"

"I wanted to keep my job. But transporting Alicia to the studio, hiding her in the coffin—that was me cleaning up someone else's mess."

"What?" Sierra whispered, at the same time Vera snapped, "Bull!"

"Honestly, James," purred a distantly familiar voice. "I thought we were here to find some silly clue. I didn't realize we'd have so much company."

Heels clacked on the stone floor. A figure appeared, haloed by the corridor lights. There was a *bang* as the door closed behind her, locking them inside. Carter stepped back, pressing against Adi's chest.

"What the hell?" he whispered.

It took Carter a long moment to realize who she was looking at, and when she did, her heart sank to the bottom of her stomach.

Symphony Parvesh. Adi's mother.

THE ESCAPE GAME

SEASON FIVE

Round Four: The Stakes Just Got Raised

49
Beck

Beck was beginning to feel like he was in a soap opera.

Symphony's dark eyes narrowed as she scanned the room. "This is problematic, isn't it?" she said, her attention landing on her son. Her lip curled, but Beck couldn't tell if the look was anger or disgust or merely annoyance at the complication. "Why are you here?"

Adi tried to speak, but no words came out.

"It was *you*?" said Sierra. "You killed my sister? But— You didn't even know her!"

"Of course I knew her," Symphony snapped. "I met her on set that first week of filming. I took her under my wing. Taught her how to make the camera love her. I mentored that bitch!"

Bewildered, Beck met Carter's gaze.

But then—he realized. All those times Alicia had disappeared when Louis had been on set. She had been meeting with *Symphony*.

"She had potential. We could have done great things together," Symphony growled. "And then she stabbed me in the back. It was bad enough when Ranielle told me they'd decided to give the host gig to Alicia instead—that's Hollywood for you, isn't it? Always passing over the talented, experienced actress for the flavor of the week. But when I saw Alicia getting out of Louis's car that night, I understood what was really going on. She slept her way into *my* job! I was supposed to be host! *Me!*"

Fitzy faced her. "You said they were bringing you on as producer!"

"Details," said Symphony, flicking a hand. "Ranielle promised the host position to me first, before Hitflix started getting hot and bothered over my little protégé. I knew that once Alicia was out of the picture, they'd see reason. I'm the star here. I deserve this."

"Oh my god, that's why she tried to steal my contract," Adi said, so quietly, Beck suspected he was talking to himself. "She didn't want to be producer. She's been gunning for host since season four."

Fitzy's expression twisted with fury. "You told me that once you were co-producer, you'd make sure my job was safe."

"Yes, well. I lied," Symphony said, so flippant it was like she didn't even realize Fitzy was holding a gun. "Besides, you were getting fired one way or another. That's on Ranielle, not me."

"I helped you!" said Fitzy. "I did everything you asked. Who had to get her frozen-ass carcass from the villas? Drive her halfway across town? Do you think it was easy loading her up on that cart, arranging her in that coffin—"

"I didn't tell you to take her to the studio," snapped Symphony. "I said to *dispose* of the body, not make a spectacle of it."

"I had to send a message! No one screws me over and gets away with it. Not Ranielle, and sure as hell not you. You swore I'd keep my job if I took care of that *catastrophic* mess you made for us."

"It wasn't like I planned to kill her." Her eyes flashed. "But she'd been plotting against me. When I realized how she'd betrayed me . . . Well. Things escalated quickly." Her anger faded and she shrugged, like the difference between talking to Alicia and murdering her was no big deal.

Fitzy's nostrils flared. The gun wavered, and for a moment it seemed he might shoot *her,* but then he swung it around toward Beck and the others. "If I'm screwed, I'm taking you with me. So how do you propose we deal with this?"

Beck pressed back against the wall, tugging Carter closer to him.

"You killed her," whispered Sierra. Beck wondered if she had heard anything else of the conversation. "Over a . . . a job. A pathetic hosting job on a reality competition. That was worth her life?"

Symphony rounded on her. "This *is* my life! My career! Do you know what I had to endure to get my ex involved with this show? The hoops I had to jump through to get that offer from Ranielle?"

Beck could see Sierra's fury burbling up, reaching the surface—

"She! Was! My! *Sister!*"

Sierra raised the wooden stake. Fitzy lifted the gun. But then Vera was screaming, a guttural warrior's cry, as she shoved Sierra out of the way and grabbed the stake from her hand.

Vera rushed—not at Symphony but at Fitzy.

Surprised, he jerked the gun out of her reach and sidestepped. Vera crashed into the stone wall. If she was hurt, she showed no sign of it, immediately spinning around and stabbing the stake into the back of his shoulder.

He let out a roar of pain. The gun went off, the sound deafening in the small room. Carter screamed and ducked. Beck crouched beside her, his arms around her shoulders. Symphony was yelling and Fitzy was shouting and the gun fired again—

Someone yanked on his arm. Beck dared to look up.

"Come on!" Adi shouted, shoving him toward the wall.

No—not the wall. The door. The big wooden door. That was . . . *open*? Adi had figured out the code to the keypad while Fitzy and Symphony were talking.

"Go!" Adi cried, pushing Beck and Carter through. "Hurry! *Sierra!*"

Beck stumbled through to the other side and barely had time to register his surroundings—more stone walls and vaulted ceilings and an entire wall of books—before he spun back around to see Adi with his hand on Sierra's wrist, yanking her through the doorway.

"Vera!" Carter screamed.

Vera was on the ground. There was blood. A lot of blood.

Fitzy was distracted by the wound in his shoulder, but when he saw the others were escaping he swung the gun, aiming for them—right as the door slammed shut.

Beck stood panting, hands on his knees as he struggled to drag in stilted breaths. He braced himself for another gunshot, but it didn't come. Instead, Fitzy started pounding at the door, trying to force it open.

"H-how?" Carter gasped. "How did you open it?"

"The place names on the holy water coincided with the numbers on the map," said Adi, breathlessly falling against the wall.

"But you didn't have the atlas," said Carter. Sweat matted her curls to her temples, and her eyes had a dazed, horrified look in them. Beck suspected they all had that look.

"I know where Jordan is," said Adi. "And Lourdes. It wasn't that hard to figure out. Holy *shit,* that was my mother."

"Vera . . ." said Carter. "We left her there. She could be . . ."

"I'm calling the cops." Sierra whipped out her phone. She covered her opposite ear as she turned away from the sounds of Fitzy repeatedly ramming something into the door.

"They won't get here in time," said Adi.

"In time to save Vera?" asked Carter weakly. "Or . . ."

She didn't have to finish.

Adi looked alarmingly ill. "She was in one of her moods the night Alicia died. I remember her throwing shit around, screaming at me. She'd come home late. Late—because she'd been out *committing murder.*"

Beck squeezed his shoulder. "I'm sorry."

Every thump on the door made him flinch. How long could it hold?

"We have to play the game," he whispered.

Realization dawned on Carter's face. "Every room ends with an escape."

"Yeah," said Adi with a humorless laugh. "Where Fitzy and my *mother* are on the other side."

"Not this time," said Carter. "They're trapped in the first room, at least for now."

"Right," said Beck. "We need to stay a step ahead of them. Solve the puzzles, get out. Once we're in the studio, and they're still locked in here . . ." He swallowed hard, knowing that he was grasping at tenuous hope. They were stuck with a murderer and a maniac with a gun. But the police would be on their way. They just had to play through the game. That was it. They could do that.

"What are we waiting for?" said Adi. "Let's get the hell out of here."

Beck forced himself to focus. To ignore the pounding on the door, each thump like a splinter in his tongue, and take in the space around him.

It was *glorious*, actually. The stuff of escape room dreams. They were in what appeared to be the dining hall of a Gothic castle, with hand-sawn wooden beams, enormous iron chandeliers, a wall of dusty books complete with a rolling library ladder, and a series of medieval tapestries on one wall. A table in the center was set for several guests, with fine china and silverware.

Carter made her way to the other side of the massive hall, where a gate stood blocking their exit, held in place by a rope-and-pulley system fastened with an iron padlock in need of a key. "This isn't the last room. Look."

Beck joined her. Beyond the gate was a cemetery, boxed in by more towering stone walls. In the corner stood a marble mausoleum. Grayish-blue lighting gave the effect that the cemetery was cast in silver moonlight, and the limbs of a scraggly tree held animatronic bats, blinking at them with red eyes.

Vera had outdone herself.

But thinking of Vera made Beck think of her body crumpled on the ground, and the blood and—

He spun around, trying to focus on the task before them. His eyes fell on a large fireplace. "A sword!" he cried, rushing to grab it off hooks above the mantel. Not sharp, but the blade was heavy enough that it could do damage.

"Good idea," said Adi. "We should arm ourselves."

"I thought we were trying to solve the puzzles?" said Carter, who had started inspecting a locked curio cabinet with leaded glass doors.

"Arm ourselves while solving puzzles," he clarified.

Carter took in a shuddering breath. "Okay. We need a key for the gate, and this cabinet has a four-letter alphabet code. There are goblets and wine casks inside."

"There are spaces for the goblets on these place settings, once we can access them," said Beck, approaching the table with its long black cloth and high-backed chairs. "And there's a box here. Locked." He inspected the place settings, checking each platter.

"These books are real," said Adi, his voice laced with awe as he pulled a leather-bound tome off one of the shelves. "My god, I think they're actually *old*, too. Hold on, this one is by itself. Could be important?" He reached for a book on an otherwise-empty shelf. As soon as he grabbed it, a piece of paper slipped from the pages and fell to the floor. He held it up to the light. "It has some numbers written in the top corner and tiny holes poked in random places. I think I need to overlay it on a page."

"Or *pages*," Carter suggested. "Try putting it over the pages in that book that correspond to those numbers. Maybe it'll reveal a message."

"Right. Yeah. Obviously. Sorry, my mind isn't running on full power right now."

While Adi flipped through the book, Beck lifted the final plate on the dining table. "Aha!" he said, scooping up a piece of yellowed parchment. "I found something!" He scanned the paper. "It looks like a guest list."

Nikolai Drakon	*A-*
Morgana Drăculești	*O+*
Vali Voyvoda	*AB+*
Desdemona Țepeș	*A+*

Kristoph Draconem *B-*
Constantin Dragulya *O-*
Beneath the moonlight, we shall dine.

"Yum," he muttered to himself. Then to the others, "Looks like we're hosting a dinner party for the Dracula family, and they're expecting a wide selection of blood types."

"What are you all *doing*?" shouted Sierra. She had lowered the phone and put her hand over the speaker. "The police are on the way and I'm trying to tell the operator everything that's happened, and you're talking about having a dinner party and serving *blood*?"

"Not me," said Beck defensively, gesturing at the paper. "It's a clue."

"Why are you wasting time with—" Sierra cut off suddenly, her eyes focusing on the heavy wooden door. Only then did Beck realize what she was hearing, or . . . not hearing.

Fitzy had gone silent.

"They're trapped in there," said Adi. "If they can't force one of the doors open, then they'll have to solve the holy water puzzle."

"The map," said Carter. "Do we—"

"I dropped it." A shadow fell over Adi's face. "Trying to get everyone out. They have everything they need to unlock the keypad."

"How long before the police get here?" asked Beck, who could hear the muffled voice of the operator on the phone.

"Ten minutes," said Sierra faintly, her gaze darting around the room as if seeing the elaborate set for the first time. "Okay. Okay, we can do this. You're right. We have to stay ahead of them for ten minutes." She lifted the phone to her ear again, and her voice took on new conviction. "We're going to try to solve this room and get back to the studio. Ranielle Russell will know where the entrances to the room are."

She didn't wait to hear the operator's response, just set the phone face up on the table. "What's our status?"

Beck went down the list of what they'd found so far, and what they were looking for. A four-letter word for the curio cabinet, a way to open the box on the table, a key to raise the gate. The code in Adi's book.

But then Adi groaned and straightened from what he was reading. "No good. It's the last clue." He read:

By the coffin I did find
A relic that was left behind.
If you recognize this tooth,
Then surely you will know the truth.
Seek justice for Alicia's ghost
And condemn our once-beloved host.

"Familiar tooth?" asked Beck.

Adi held up a small white fang. "It was in the pouch with the holy water. Vera's evidence. She must've seen him wearing it during the livestream, then found it that morning before everyone had come into the studio. It was her proof that Fitzy had been here to plant Alicia's body."

"Vera risked a lot to expose him," Beck said. "Let's make sure we get that evidence to the cops."

Adi nodded grimly and pocketed the shark tooth.

"Oh!" Sierra bellowed. "I found an alcove behind this tapestry! There are a bunch of engraved metal plates with names on them. Desdemona, Nikolai . . ."

"Here!" Beck and Carter called at once. Sierra dumped the nameplates onto the table. Each one had a colorful gem embedded beside the name . . . but nothing about blood types.

"How do we know which nameplate goes where?" Beck said.

"Found a diary!" Adi shouted. He'd given up inspecting the

crowded bookshelves and was pulling the diary out from beneath a log in the fireplace. The pages were burned around the edges. He turned to the first page and groaned. "There's a lot of text here. This might take a minute."

"Do your thing," said Sierra. "What's up with that?"

Beck followed her pointing finger. High in the vaulted ceiling, above the iron gate, one portion of the wall was draped with heavy black cloth. Beck hadn't even noticed it. His thoughts went to the words at the bottom of the guest list. *Beneath the moonlight, we shall dine.*

"If there's a window behind that, it would let in the moonlight," he said. "Or the fake moonlight, anyway."

"But it's so high up," said Carter. "How are we supposed to . . ."

Before she could finish, Beck rushed to the library ladder and wheeled it along the shelves. He pushed it as far as it would go, then bounded to the top. But even standing precariously on the uppermost rung, he knew he wouldn't be able to reach. "There's a rope looped on this end," he called down to the others. "Do we have anything that can reach it? Like a broom handle or—"

"A sword?" said Sierra. "Like the one you tucked into your belt loop?"

"Oh yeah!"

Gripping the bookshelves with one hand, he leaned out toward the cloth, sword outstretched. The blade slipped into the loop of rope and he pulled.

The rope came loose. The swath of fabric fell, drifting dramatically to the floor and revealing a stunning stained-glass window.

Far below, Carter cried, "The table!"

Beck glanced down. From his vantage point near the rafters, he had a perfect view of the dining table and the beams of colorful light hitting each plate.

"The gems!" said Carter, unnecessarily, as Sierra had already started sorting the nameplates according to their colorful jewels and the beams of light. When she'd finished, they held their breaths, waiting for something to happen. But nothing did.

Nothing, except for a thump at the door that sent Beck's heart into his throat. They waited, listening for the telltale sound of a keypad beeping.

But Fitzy and Symphony fell silent again.

Exhaling, Beck had started down the ladder when Adi called up to him, "Hold on! There's a book mentioned in this diary. The writer says it's hidden on the top shelf, behind 'the dragon.' It has to mean that!" He pointed.

Beck spied the dragon-shaped crystal bookend two shelves over. Normally he would have climbed down and pushed the ladder into place, but never had he felt so intensely the ticking of a clock. He gripped the edge of the bookshelves and sidestepped, Spider-Man–style, across them.

"Beck!" Carter cried. "What are you doing?"

"Not looking down," he said, toeing some books out of the way. They fell to the floor, and he tried not to think about how their loud thuds would mimic the sound of his own body if he fell.

His palms were sweating. His arms shook. But adrenaline was flooding his veins and he barely had time to think before he had reached the shelf and shoved the dragon bookend out of the way. There, behind it—a book. "Here!" he cried, tossing it down to Carter. She screamed and fumbled with it a few times—sending a loose sheaf of paper flying out from between the pages and across the stone floor.

Not bothering to return to the ladder, Beck scrambled down the shelves.

"Symbol cipher!" yelled Sierra, studying the paper. "Bats, crowns, crosses . . . Anyone know what this connects to?"

Carter pointed. "The tapestries!"

Beck hadn't given the tapestries much thought yet. The first showed a stag lying amid a bed of flowers. The second—a dog hunt with a castle in the background. The third depicted two people stomping grapes in a barrel. The fourth, a band of musicians.

"Yes . . ." said Sierra, then more forcefully, "Yes! The dogs in that second one look like this symbol, the one for *L*. And the musician playing . . . What is that? A lute? That's the letter *D*."

"The stag antler, *V*," said Adi, pointing. "And the third one . . ."

"*A*," said Carter, who had run to the curio cabinet to input the four-letter code. "It has to be 'Vlad.'"

Adi and Sierra looked from the tapestry to the cipher. "A bunch of grapes," said Adi. "Of course."

The lock clicked and Carter threw open the glass doors. She pulled out the first goblet. "This one is labeled 'O-negative'!"

"On it," said Beck, snatching up the guest list again while the others carried the goblets to the table, matching them to the bejeweled nameplates. As soon as the last goblet was set into place, the box in the center of the table popped open.

"The key!" they shouted in unison. Sierra grabbed it first and ran for the device holding the gate's pulley. She twisted it into the keyhole and yanked off the padlock. Adi grabbed the crank and began to turn. The iron gate rose upward.

Sierra and Carter both ducked beneath the gate when it was barely more than a couple of feet off the ground. Adi stopped cranking and dived after them. Beck was right behind him, until he remembered Sierra's phone still sitting on the table. He turned to run back for it, grabbed the phone off the table—and heard a noise that made his blood run cold.

A keypad beeping.

He froze.

The door swung open. Fitzy stood there, his face twisted with frustration, still clutching the gun. Blood had soaked through his shirt over his shoulder.

Beside him, Symphony had her arms crossed, drumming her fingers against her forearms. "These puzzles," she said, "are a pain in the ass." She looked at Fitzy. "Don't just stand there. Do something!"

He raised the gun.

Beck ran. There was a shot as he slid beneath the gate like a baseball player coming into home base. He barely registered the others screaming, or that Adi had the sword extended through the gate, swinging hard for the rope. But the blade was too dull. Adi let out a roar as he swung, cut, sawed—while Fitzy and Symphony rushed toward them.

The rope frayed. One strand. Two—

The weight of the iron bars snapped the final strand. The gate plummeted to the ground, separating them from the castle room.

Symphony reached through the gate, clawing at Adi. He jumped back, plastering himself against the stone wall.

"Oh, come *here*, Adi. Why must you always make everything so difficult?"

Fitzy stuck the gun through the bars and fired again—once, twice—but must have realized his aim was too limited from this angle and stopped firing, leaving Adi to sink down against the wall, shaking.

Holy hell. Symphony was really going to stand there and watch Fitzy kill her own child.

Fitzy refocused on Beck as he scrambled across the spongy ground. Beck dived behind the nearest gravestone as the gun fired again. The bullet pinged off the marble, sending bits of stone and dust flying over Beck's shoulder. He covered his head and curled into a tight ball, pressing against the stone.

Then— *Click. Click.*

Fitzy swore loudly, the sound salty and metallic in Beck's mouth. "It's out of ammo!"

"You'd better have more, Fitzgerald."

"Beck," whispered Sierra.

He peeked over his knees. Sierra and Carter were crouched beside the wall of the mausoleum, staring at him with horrified eyes.

"You're hurt," Sierra said.

He stared at her, not comprehending. He wasn't hurt. His heart was pounding so hard he thought it might do permanent damage to his rib cage, but he wasn't *hurt.*

Then he noticed the wetness on his skin. He looked down. Saw the deep crimson spreading across the side of his shirt. Realized that it wasn't Fitzy's voice making him taste blood.

Which was so . . . so *weird.* He knew about people going into shock. But still . . . shouldn't he have felt something?

The iron gate clanked as Symphony rattled it.

"Mom, what the hell?" Adi cried. "Why are you doing this?"

"You wouldn't understand, you selfish brat," Symphony snapped.

Fitzy laughed. "Guess the apple really doesn't fall far from the tree."

"Shut up, Fitzy! I've heard enough out of you tonight."

"I've heard enough out of you to last a lifetime," he retorted.

While they argued, Beck listened to the sounds of metal and mechanics, of a handgun being reloaded bullet by bullet.

Fitzy had indeed brought extra ammunition.

"How do you two even know each other?" Adi yelled, sounding like he'd finally snapped.

"Oh, darling, we met plenty of times at the studio last season while Ranielle and I were discussing the terms of our agreement."

"Did you just call me 'darling'? *You're trying to kill me!*"

"You aren't exactly giving me a choice, are you?"

"Yeah!" said Adi, exasperated. "The choice is to *not kill me*."

Symphony made a sound in her throat like he was being unreasonable. "I am not going to prison because you and your geeky little friends couldn't mind your own business. Fitzy, what's taking so long with those bullets?"

"I've been stabbed in the shoulder, bitch!"

Beck looked around, frantic for a weapon, or an escape, or hope, any sort of hope, really.

What he saw were two dozen creepy statues staring down at him, and the names of a bunch of dead people, and a mausoleum that might have offered shelter if it wasn't for the keypad promising that he wouldn't be getting in without a code.

He read the words on the door, chiseled into the marble:

THE FAMIL DRACULA
FROM D ATH WE H VE RISEN
IMMO TAL WE STAND
TRONGER IN NITY
UNDIVIDED BY U BRAGE
OR DEATH

He stared, the words blurring together as sweat dripped into his eyes. It took a long time to notice the missing letters, but once he did, the clue was obvious. "Year sum," he said to himself. Then, to the others, "We need to add the years together. That's the code."

"What?" snapped Sierra. "All of them? There are more than twenty gravestones here! We don't have time . . . *Crap, crap, crap.* Where are the police?"

Beck looked at the nearest gravestone.

ABIGAIL COVALI
B. 1766—D. 1792

And the stone beside it, with a name he recognized.

MORGANA DRĂCULEŞTI

B. 1449—

No death date because, of course, she hadn't died. She was a member of the Dracula family. She was immortal.

"Not all of them," he said. "Just the ones without death dates, I think. This one is 1449."

Sierra and Carter exchanged looks. To see all the stones, at least one of them would have to leave the cover of the mausoleum.

"I can see two from here," said Adi. "1517 and 1580."

"Hold on," said Sierra. "I need something to write this down. What can we—"

"No, I've got it," said Carter. She closed her eyes, face scrunched in concentration. "We're at 4,546 so far."

Sierra shot her an impressed look, then glanced at Beck. "How many Draculas do we think there are?"

"There were six dinner guests," he answered. Three more.

"I see another one," said Sierra. "1702."

"6,248," Carter murmured.

Beck scanned what he could see of the cemetery, not knowing if the two remaining gravestones were to his left or right. Closer to the mausoleum . . . or closer to the gate.

He dared to lean forward enough to spy Adi against the stone wall. Adi met his gaze. His brow creased—Beck must've been looking pretty awful, if the worry in Adi's expression was anything to go by.

Then Adi set his jaw with a look of grim determination. Beck had a flash of understanding seconds before it happened. "Adi, wait—"

Adi raised the sword and hollered, shoving the blade through the bars, straight into Fitzy's gut. The gun dropped, skittering back toward the table.

Fighting his instinct to stay hidden, Beck grabbed the gravestone and used it to propel himself to his feet.

While Symphony howled a string of insults, Beck darted down the row of headstones, ignoring the first stab of pain in his side. Searching, searching . . . there! *Vali Voyvoda.*

"1537!" he shouted, skidding around one marker, ignoring the gargoyles leering down at him.

"Get the gun!" Fitzy grunted. "We'll tell the police it was . . . self-defense." His voice was garbled with pain. "Sierra attacked us. You were trying to protect your son."

"You better not be dying, Fitzgerald," growled Symphony. "I'll need your testimony."

"Just finish this!"

A gunshot made Beck jump. Adi was yelling and Carter was screaming and—there! *Kristoph Draconem.* "And 1655! That should be all of them!"

"9,440!" said Carter.

Sierra darted around the corner of the mausoleum. Beck met her at the door, but she was already inputting the code. *9-4-4-0.*

The door unlocked, the most glorious sound Beck had ever heard.

"Adi, come on!" Sierra shouted.

Beck stumbled inside. Sierra and Carter followed. More gunfire. Beck lost count of how many bullets had been shot. He pressed his hands to his side and looked back, afraid he would see Adi lying face down in the graveyard, swathed in moonlight and mist.

But no—Adi was running, gripping the handle of the sword as he hurled himself over the nearest gravestone, charging into the mausoleum. Behind him, still trapped beyond the gate, Fitzy was on the ground, covered in blood where Adi had stabbed him. Symphony had the gun now, her face set with determination.

Another bullet pinged off the heavy marble door as Carter shoved it closed.

Beck followed the others down a set of stone steps, expecting to be free. But when he reached the foot of the stairs he found exactly what was advertised—the inside of a mausoleum.

And no apparent means of escape.

50

Sierra

They were trapped. Nowhere to go. Vera was in desperate need of medical attention, and—

"Beck!"

Carter rushed to hold Beck as he sank to the floor. His face was pastier than normal, beads of sweat forming on his skin. Carter helped prop him against the wall. His weak smile turned into a grimace. "It's starting to hurt, actually."

Sierra looked to Adi, the hopelessness of their situation overwhelming. "Did you just kill Fitzy?"

"I don't know. The sword is pretty dull, but he was bleeding a lot." His grip tightened on the handle. "We can still finish the game. Get to safety."

It was his determination that pulled her back. They had a goal. Beck being hurt didn't change that. As long as Symphony and Fitzy were stuck behind the iron gate, they had a chance.

"Put pressure on Beck's wound," she said to Carter.

"Oh. Right. I knew that. Sorry." Carter looked almost as pale as Beck as she pulled off her Mathletes sweatshirt, revealing a camisole underneath.

"We've got time," said Sierra. "I bet that gate weighs a ton."

"My mom can be freakishly strong when she wants to be," Adi said. "All those protein shakes, I guess." Then his face crumpled. "I had no idea. I didn't . . . I still can't believe . . ." He slid to the ground, dropping the sword. "In some ways, this doesn't feel real. And in other ways, it kind of makes some bizarre sense. Like, maybe I should have figured it out?"

"How could you possibly have figured it out?" Carter asked, pressing her sweatshirt to Beck's wound.

"The gloves. The killer wore gloves, right? My mom's always wearing driving gloves. Paranoia about UV rays and age spots."

"It's . . . true," Beck stammered softly. "UV rays can kill you." He snickered softly, before adding, "Sorry. That's not funny at all. I don't know why I'm laughing."

Adi covered his eyes. "And her obsession with getting back in the business. Trying to convince Ranielle to give her the host job. I should have suspected something."

"Come on, Adi," said Sierra. "Be fair to yourself. It isn't like you saw a bloody comforter lying around your house, or a phone with a sparkly dolphin case or something."

Adi went still. After a beat, he took his hands away and gave her an incredulous look. "Sparkly *dolphin* case?" He groaned. "Yeah, I've seen it."

"You're kidding," said Sierra.

"You never told us what her phone looked like! And Symphony has a whole pile of phones— She's totally materialistic, hoards all this stuff—"

Sierra started to pace. "Fine. It doesn't matter. We need to focus."

She took stock of the room. A large marble coffin leaned against one wall, Dracula's crest engraved on the lid. Another four-digit alphabet lock kept it shut. Each of the walls had a Renaissance-style painting. She tapped the coffin. "We're going to have to slay Dracula."

"We don't have the wooden stake," said Carter.

Adi hefted the sword up. "This will have to do."

Beck pumped an arm into the air and wheezed, "Team Helsing for the win."

"Stop moving around so much," Carter said. "I think your binder is slowing the bleeding."

He dropped his arm. "Awesome."

Sierra glanced up the steps. "Was anybody counting how many bullets were fired that second round?"

"Five," Adi said without hesitation. "They've got one more."

Sierra returned her attention to the paintings. "Let's not give them a chance to use it. Are there letters hidden inside the art?"

Adi pulled himself to his feet and moved closer to a painting of several children playing in a vineyard. Sierra stood back, hoping a shape would reveal itself from a distant perspective.

The other paintings showed a naked baby Cupid firing an arrow into the heart of a lady, a hunter aiming a gun at a deer, and a king lounging on a throne.

"I don't see anything," Adi said.

From the door at the top of the stairs came a rattling noise.

Sierra tensed.

"Do we think the mausoleum door auto-locked?" Carter said.

Beck murmured something, and Carter leaned closer to hear.

Sierra tugged at the ring in her lip, holding her breath. "Come on, we can do this—"

Carter gasped, pulling away from Beck. "You're a genius! The grapes. The vineyard. Like the grapes from before."

"It's the same picture code as for the curio cabinet," Adi said. "The grapes were—?"

"*A*!" Carter cried. "And the stag with the antlers was *V*."

Sierra's heart leaped to her throat. Of course! The hunter was aiming his gun at a stag, not a deer. They were going to do this. They were actually going to get out—

"So we have *A* and *V*?" Adi said, searching the other paintings. "What could the word be? It's only four letters."

"'Vlad' again?" asked Carter.

Adi dropped his sword to try, but it didn't work. "Lava?" he suggested. "No, there's only one grape painting."

"There was a heart in the code." Sierra pointed to the painting of the Cupid. "What letter did it represent?"

Adi shook his head. "I don't remember."

Beck and Carter stared at Sierra, wide-eyed.

She turned desperately to the other picture. "The king—a crown? There was a crown somewhere near the start of the alphabet."

"Maybe *B*?" Carter said. "*B-A-V*? No."

Adi paced in front of the upright coffin. "It's no good. We don't have the code. We need to think of words that have *A-V* in them."

"*Save*!" Carter said. "I bet the crown stood for the *E*!"

Adi tried *S-A-V-E* for the code. No good. Neither was *HAVE* or *GAVE*.

"It has to be something to do with vampires," he said, frustrated. He tried *V-A-M-P*.

Sierra shut her eyes, pleading with her brain to put the pieces together. "We have to think how Louis thought."

Beck coughed, then groaned. "Vera."

"Vera. Right." It had been Vera all along, that obnoxious but brilliant girl who never got the credit and always lived in the shadows, risking her life to expose the killer—

"*Vera*," Beck said again.

Carter squealed, lifting the hand that wasn't holding Beck's wound. "Adi! The code! It's—"

"VERA!"

Suddenly, Sierra could see it all. The silver earring in the chem lab jar, a perfect match to the one so often dangling from Vera's ear. The palette of vivid eyeshadows tucked in with the clutter in the alien bunker. The chameleon stuffie that matched her tattoo.

Her final message in the fun house: *And soon, everyone will know the truth. About me.*

She'd been planning to reveal herself as the real Game Master in the finale!

Before Adi could input the code, the door above them wrenched open. Sierra launched herself to the side, out of view of the narrow steps. But Adi stayed right where he was, his fingers fumbling with the lock as he input Vera's name.

"Adi!" Carter yelled.

He was either incredibly brave or—

Or nothing. He was just incredibly brave. He was putting his life on the line to get them out of there.

Heels clacked on the steps. Carter positioned her body to shield Beck. Sierra watched the doorway. The gun appeared first. A lacquered fingernail twitched on the trigger—Sierra moved too late—the gun went off, but so did the coffin lid. Adi leaped out of the way as a mannequin body of Dracula sprang out, immediately jerking back as the bullet struck it. Sierra's momentum took her forward anyway, and she shoved Symphony's arm sideways, making her stumble. Carter bounced up from her place and charged low, aiming for Symphony's legs. Her tackle was enough to slam the woman to the ground. Carter ran to pin her, but Symphony squirmed free from Carter's grip, kicking her in the face. Carter rolled back, clutching her bleeding nose.

Sierra slowed to a stop as Symphony staggered to her feet. She was still holding the gun, aiming it for Sierra. Her beautiful face was blotchy with anger, her mouth twisted into a sneer.

Slowly, Sierra raised her hands in surrender.

"It's empty," said Adi. "You're out of bullets."

Symphony snarled. "Am I now?"

Sierra's breath caught. Symphony seemed sure of herself. Too sure. Her gaze darted to Adi, who'd picked up the sword and was standing at Dracula's open coffin. The mannequin's eyes glowed red like the bats outside, his fangs bared.

" 'Massacre in the Mausoleum,' " Symphony croaked. "That's what the headline will be. My career might be over, but I'll go down in a blaze of glory. No one will ever forget the name 'Symphony Parvesh.'" She curled her lip. "And my name will never again by overshadowed by your damn father's."

Adi held the sword like a baseball bat, ready to swing. "You sure about that?"

She laughed. "You're so ready to defend Victor Cunningham? You don't even know him."

"He's better than you. He has to be."

Symphony turned the gun on him. "'Violence with Vampires!'" There was a deranged edge to her voice now. She arced the gun toward Carter, still on the floor. "'A Dance with the Devil!'"

Adi looked at Sierra, jaw set, eyes blazing. *One,* he mouthed.

One? One what?

Symphony pointed the gun at Beck. "Does it hurt?" she cooed—a fake imitation of maternal concern.

"I'm . . . totally . . . fine," Beck wheezed.

"Not for long," said Symphony.

Two, Adi mouthed.

Sweet Jesus. What was happening?

Symphony turned the gun back to Adi's head.

"Three!"

"No!" Sierra yelled, flinging herself in the barrel's path, right as Adi spun around and slammed the sword through Dracula's chest. The mannequin fell forward. A secret door at the back of the coffin sprang open, revealing a bunch of cops and Ranielle Russell—

There was a deafening *bang*. Carter screamed.

Sierra jerked backward in horror. Colors flared in the corners of her vision. There had been a final bullet after all.

Adi had been wrong.

She'd trusted him with her life. She'd actually *trusted* him, and this . . . this was what she got for trusting anyone. Never again. Never—

A blur as people rushed past her. Someone was taking Symphony down, wrenching the gun away. Others were swarming around Beck. The gunshot resounded in Sierra's ears. She heard it over and over.

It took a long time for the pain to come. Or any sign of blood.

There was color everywhere. And gunshots. More bullets, more explosions—

"Sierra. Sierra!" Adi was by her side.

"I— She— She shot me—"

"She didn't shoot you," said Adi. "It's fireworks. You're not hurt."

Sierra dragged her gaze away from her torso and watched as mini flares went off from hidden pockets in each corner of the room.

"Fireworks," she said weakly.

Adi grinned. "Fireworks. For the finale."

Sierra patted herself down. No pain, no blood, no bullet holes. "Christ." Regaining her senses, she whacked him in the chest. "I can't believe you did that!"

"Did what?" he said, rubbing where she'd hit him.

"Started counting and expected me to figure out what the hell you were doing. Are you out of your mind?"

"What was I supposed to do? Mime it?"

"I trusted you!"

"Yeah, and it turned out fine, didn't it?" His expression softened. "But hey. Thanks for jumping in front of an imaginary bullet for me."

"Never. Again."

"You have the right to remain silent—"

They looked over to see a cop wrenching Symphony Parvesh's arms behind her back. She was almost beautiful in the colorful lights. Blue flares glinted on the steel of her handcuffs; red illuminated across her cheeks. The image had Sierra's fingers itching for a paintbrush.

She waved as Symphony was dragged from the room.

The nightmare was over. The killer was caught. Alicia would have justice.

And they had escaped.

THE HOLLYWOOD HERALD

Alicia Angelos's Killer Is Behind Bars . . . and You'll NEVER Believe Who It Is!

Police flooded the *Escape Game* studios last night after a showdown between a number of contestants; the show's host, James "Fitzy" Fitzgerald; and Symphony Parvesh, star of the blockbuster film *The Cursed Tomb* and current spokesperson for Best Life Nutrition. Parvesh has allegedly been arrested for the murder of Alicia Angelos. Fitzgerald remains in critical condition with a stab wound to the abdomen. Eyewitnesses claim that during the altercation he confessed to assisting Parvesh with covering up Angelos's death. Fitzgerald has also become the prime suspect in the death of "Game Master" Louis Augustus Russell, which police are now investigating as a potential homicide.

The Escape Game has been under fire since its previous season, when eighteen-year-old finalist Alicia Angelos was found dead inside one of the set props. The show has been battling rumors and accusations surrounding Angelos's death for as long as the case has been open.

Executive producer Ranielle Russell, wife of the late Louis Augustus Russell, stated that Hitflix had already decided not to continue their partnership with the show into a sixth season. When asked about the one-million-dollar grand prize, she declined to comment.

Want More?

Louis Augustus Russell Found DEAD

The Escape Game *Season Three Breakdown—the REAL Winners and Losers*

Victor Cunningham's Dark Secret?

Nine Things You Need to Know about Alicia Angelos's Unsolved Murder

51

Carter

"And that's it," said Kick It Carter while clips from the show played in the background. "The sordid tale of *The Escape Game,* season five. Now, Clue Masters, I have a big request to ask of you."

The avatar swiped her hand, changing the screen to a picture of Beck in his blue lab coat. "We at the Domain have started a fundraiser for Beck Matheson, who remains in critical condition. The medical bills are piling up, and any help you can give would be beyond appreciated. Thanks for sending your love and support. I'm Kick It Carter—still alive, still kicking, still solving!" She threw a peace sign at the camera and the video ended.

Carter let out a long breath. That had taken *forever* to edit.

As she started to upload the video, there was a knock at the door. Her parents stood on the threshold, continuing to pretend they weren't completely freaked out by the fact their daughter had nearly died last week. They'd been overbearing since she came home, but after watching Adi get shot at by his own mother, Carter wasn't going to complain about a little overprotectiveness.

"I'm heading to the store," her dad said. He was dressed to the nines in a checkered blazer and cashmere scarf, the cream a contrast against his dark brown skin. It was overkill for a trip to the store, but that was her dad. "Thought I'd pick up some pie for later."

"Is there anything else you need?" her mom added, her tone thick with worry. She, on the other hand, was in a fluffy robe and slippers, her Irish orange curls a flurry.

Carter thought of the poem Adi had quoted for her at the villa, which she'd been compelled to look up later. Lord Byron.

And all that's best of dark and bright

Meet in her aspect and her eyes

Adi hadn't met her parents, but boy, was he astute when he wanted to be.

Carter shook her head. "I'm good. Thanks." She proved it with a thumbs-up that was as fake as her avatar.

Having completed their hourly check-in, they left, though reluctantly. Carter grabbed her phone again. Over the last few days, she'd been inundated with messages on the Domain. She'd even received a thank-you from Vera, of all people, who'd been released from the hospital after being treated for a dislocated shoulder and nonfatal bullet wound.

There'd been a lot of activity on the site in general, including a post from Elijah. He'd written an anguished poem about lost love and saying goodbye. At the end, he'd mentioned taking some time to find a new purpose in life, then promptly shut down his Domain account.

Sierra and Adi had been quiet, though. Carter tried not to let it bother her. They'd been through a lot, and she understood if they needed time to recalibrate. She trusted they would reach out to her when the time was right.

But that confidence didn't protect her from the swell of loneliness that got bigger each day. She'd finally found her people, and yet she felt more alone than ever.

Still scrolling through the Domain, a stream of comments caught her eye.

> Fitzy4Ever818299: Fitzy x Carter was my OTP! The way he looked at her during the studio tour?! YOU GUYZ, my heart is breaking!! 💔💔💔
>
> OmegaPuzzler: I didn't get the Fitzy/Carter thing. He could have any girl he wants, and he picked her? Ummm no. But now I know he was just messing with her? OK that tracks

KaPowPow: What is wrong with you? Carter is a hero

OmegaPuzzler: Hero, yes. Awkward loser with an annoying laugh? Also yes. Just saying—not Fitzy's type

KaPowPow: She's not his type bc HE IS A PSYCHOPATH

OmegaPuzzler: to each their own

Insides roiling, Carter tossed the phone aside. Beck would have told her to ignore the haters, but that was hard to do. Especially when they were right.

I did always think that cartoon of yours was pretty hot, even if the real you leaves something to be desired.

Shuddering, Carter glanced in the mirror. The red had started to grow out of her curls, leaving a strip of natural black roots. Her nose was still slightly swollen from when Symphony had kicked her. She was wearing frumpy pajama pants and her brand-new HELSINGS SLAY! T-shirt, already christened with a spaghetti sauce stain.

There had been a time on the show when she'd thought maybe she could become as sophisticated as her alter ego. With her friends behind her, she'd begun to feel invincible.

But that girl in the mirror wasn't Kick It Carter.

Kick It Carter wouldn't have been taken in by Fitzy's lies. Kick It Carter would never have fallen for such a scumbag.

And if she had to become Kick It Carter to ensure no one ever treated her like that again, that's exactly what she would do.

First—she was going to need more hair dye.

She picked up her phone to place an order just as a new notification came in.

Carter frowned. That couldn't be right.

She opened the fundraising app. Checked and triple-checked the alert.

Status: Fully Funded!

Most recent donation: $915,866.21

Donor name: Victory Escapades, Inc.™

52

Sierra

Though the painting was small, Sierra felt it could be her best work. It depicted a woman kneeling and handcuffed amid a landscape of moss-covered headstones, while fireworks exploded overhead. The vibrant colors bled into a starry sky, where the skeleton of a girl watched from the heavens. Her skull and clavicle were adorned with red roses and black lilies. She was dead, but she was smiling.

Sierra gripped the canvas in both hands as she stared down at her sister's headstone.

"I love you," she whispered to the empty cemetery. Strange how awkward the words felt on her tongue. It had been a long, long time since she'd said them. She and Alicia had fought so much. Had disagreed on everything. They had resented each other, screamed at each other—

But in Alicia's final note, the coded message she'd left for Sierra to find, she'd written those words. *I love you.*

Sometimes the simplest things were the hardest to say.

Beck would have laughed at her for thinking that. He would have kept pestering, with his incessant optimism, until she was forced to admit that telling people you care about them isn't hard after all. At least, it shouldn't be.

But Beck was still in an induced coma. No indication from the doctors when he would wake up.

Jesus, she missed her team. Carter's nervous giggle and fierce loyalty. Adi's sharp wit and the way he was always hiding behind a book. Beck's infallible smile, his boundless enthusiasm.

It had been a week since she'd given both her statement and the shark tooth to the police. With nowhere else to go, she'd come back home—an apartment filled with half-finished sketches and drying tubes of paint. She needed to start figuring things out. Putting her life back together. Stop living in the past.

She needed to move on. From her sister's death. From *The Escape Game*.

She had fought the monster and won.

What was she supposed to do now?

As she propped the canvas against the stone, she felt eyes on her. She glanced around. It was only her and a flock of crows in the cemetery, but there was a vehicle outside the far gate. Some fancy black town car with deeply tinted windows.

The engine started, breaking through the silence, and the car slowly pulled away.

A chill ran down Sierra's spine.

It wasn't until she was leaving the cemetery that she saw the black envelope hanging from the gate's iron bars, swinging from a gold velvet ribbon.

53

Beck

For the rest of his life, Beck would credit Sierra's chocolate chip cookies for bringing him back.

Her gift, freshly baked, had been delivered the morning he came out of the coma. It had been like crawling out of a dark hole, guided only by his watering mouth. It was the orange zest. It had to be.

There had been a stream of gifts ever since. A T-shirt from Carter and a stack of classic fantasy novels from Adi. Countless bouquets of flowers from his aunts and uncles and cousins. He'd even received gifts from the Clue Master community—alien stuffies and lollipops shaped like chemistry beakers.

But it was one card in particular that held Beck's interest the most. The only card in all the bunch that did not tell him to *get well soon.*

The moment Beck's parents went to grab a snack from the cafeteria, he reached for the black envelope on his nightstand. The card inside was linen cardstock. The words printed in shimmering gold.

Team Helsing,
Though it may not have been easy to find you,
the search has been well worth the effort.
It seems we all lost a great deal in the aftermath
of the Escape Game *fiasco, but the keys to*
success lie in our persistence and courage.
Therefore, as the founder of Victory Escapades,
it is my pleasure to extend this invitation.

Yours,
Victor Cunningham

Behind the note was a postcard depicting a glossy image of Sweetbrier Resort. On the back, handwritten in thick marker, were the words

Are you ready to play?

Beck leaned against the hospital bed and twirled the *Escape Game*–branded USB in his fingers.

He grinned.

"Game on."

54
Adi

Adi's life was in shambles. He had spent the morning walking aimlessly around his house, feeling the velvet drapes, lounging in the Qing dynasty armchair, picking the Chihuly sculptures up from their pedestals. He was surrounded by millions of dollars' worth of stuff, and all he saw was junk.

His mother was in prison. It would be months until her trial, and afterward, Adi expected her to be handed a life sentence.

The state had assigned him a social worker, who was dutifully trying to get ahold of his father, but so far, Victor Cunningham had been impossible to reach. Somehow, this stung a thousand times worse than his own mother trying to kill him. Surely his dad would come for Adi now that his mom was no longer in the picture.

And yet, nothing.

Adi had no interest in being shipped off to live with some distant relative, which left only a few options, as far as the social worker was concerned. He could be set up with a foster family. He could go to a home with other boys his age. Or they could petition the court for a declaration of emancipation so that he would no longer be under the custody of either parent, which sounded a little bit like freedom. It would take time, and there were a lot of legal matters to untangle. Symphony's home, her bank accounts, her belongings.

He didn't want any of it. Not the stuff. Not the money. Not the baggage. He was tired of being trapped in this house, stifled, unable to breathe.

He needed to get out of here. Away from his mother and her narcissism. Her delusions. Her selfishness. Her inability to love anything but herself.

He was in the foyer, his hand on the doorknob, when he heard a *crash* from the kitchen.

Adi whirled around. The house had been silent as a grave all day.

Slamming cabinet doors. Shattering glass. The unmistakable rumble of the trash compactor.

Heart racing, Adi grabbed a nude marble statuette and held it aloft as he crept toward the kitchen. He nudged the door open with his toe, preparing to bash the intruder over the head.

A man stood with his back to Adi, pulling boxes out of a cupboard. He wore a perfectly tailored plaid suit—amethyst and gold.

The man turned, revealing a matching vest and bow tie, his black goatee peppered with silver.

Victor Cunningham tossed one of Symphony's protein shake mixes into the garbage bin and smiled.

"Hello, son," he said, pressing a finger onto a black envelope on the counter and pushing it in Adi's direction. "I've brought you a gift."

To be continued . . .

ACKNOWLEDGMENTS

We are beyond grateful to everyone who helped bring this book into the world.

To our agent, Jill Grinberg, who believed in this book from day one, and helped shape and mold it with such invaluable insights and feedback. Many thanks also to the team at Jill Grinberg Literary Management—Lisa Barelli, Katelyn Detweiler, Sam Farkas, and Denise Page. You are rock stars.

We are thrilled to have worked with such an exceptional team at Penguin Young Readers. Rūta Rimas, Gretchen Durning, Jen Klonsky, Jocelyn Schmidt, Jen Loja, Shanta Newlin, Emily Romero, Christina Colangelo, Bri Lockhart, Alex Garber, Felicity Vallence, Shannon Spann, Becky Green, Debra Polansky, Natalie Vielkind, Madison Penico, Alex Campbell, Rebecca Aidlin, and so many others have worked behind the scenes to make this book the best it could be and to get it into the hands of readers—we commend, celebrate, and appreciate you!

We owe so much gratitude to George Diamond, forensic investigator, for the detailed and brilliant input on forensic processes, murder, death, and decay.

Many thanks are also owed to our copyeditors and proofreaders—Sola Akinlana, Delia Davis, Esther Reisberg, and Kellie M. Hultgren—for the keen eye and attention to detail; to illustrator Jeremy Enecio and designer Theresa Evangelista for the stunning cover; and to artist Owen Pomery for the incredible maps.

Endless gratitude to our assistants, Joanne Levy and Annie Bucknall, for everything from web development to giveaway management and a million things besides.

Special thanks to Marissa's mom for letting us use her real-world story about a co-worker getting trapped in an industrial freezer (she's okay), and to Marissa's dad for his hands-on laser-tag research (even though that scene got cut from the final manuscript . . . It could still become bonus content!).

And of course—to our families: Chris and Scout; Jesse, Sloane, and Delaney; our loved ones; our BFFs; our support posts, counselors, and cheerleaders. This is a dream come true for both of us, and we are so grateful to have you with us, every step of the way.